NEW YORK TIMES BEST-SELLING AUTHOR

TED DEKKER

PLAY

A THRILLER

DEAD

THE ULTIMATE GAME OF LIFE

Published by Scripturo
350 E. Royal Lane, Suite 150
Irving, TX 75039
www.teddekker.com

Paperback edition published 2021
ISBN 978-1-7335718-8-3 (Paperback)
ISBN 978-1-7335718-9-0 (Hardcover)

Printed in the United States of America

BOOK ONE

THE MURDER

PROLOGUE

CLAIR MILTON stood at her window, peering at the steady drizzle through the white wooden slats she'd parted with a trembling thumb and forefinger. Texas, like half the country, had been in a drought for over fifteen years—since 2035 or thereabouts—and even though Austin wasn't as dry as other parts of the state, it was still an event to see water falling from the sky. At fifteen, she had no memory of the years when most of their water came from rain rather than from the huge desalinization plants that now lined the coast two hundred miles south. They said there wasn't a drop of water in Lake Travis that didn't come from the sea, though she knew that was an exaggeration.

Everyone was talking about the rain, and she supposed she would be as well under normal circumstances, but the last twenty-four hours had threatened to change everything about her life. And not just her life, but everyone's life, if what she and Timothy had learned was true. Which explained the quiver in her fingers.

She released the slats and turned to face Timothy Blake, who was pacing, lost in another world. His tangled blond hair hung to his shoulders in that perfect-messy way that made him beautiful to her. He wore a black *PopsHead* logo shirt—a skull wearing a throwback Apple VR headset. *PopsHead* had been one of the first underground bands to come out of the Dead Head community. All four original members had died of their vices, but now Clair wondered whether that too was a lie.

They were two fifteen-year-old kids with wealthy parents, both in the accelerated learning program at St. Andrew's School of Higher Learning, both bored of the country's endless parade of crises. But more germane to their current predicament was the fact they were both Dead Heads, meaning their favorite pastime was to temporarily 'die' to their identities in the real world and assume alternate identities in a virtual reality.

Not that any VR technology could totally shut off this world. Laws required every platform to remind all users every five minutes that they were in a virtual space. An annoying disruption.

It was all a bit pointless, in Clair's opinion. Even in a Deep Dive, the most immersive kind of VR, mostly black market extensions of commonly available VR games, you still knew your body in there wasn't the real you. Oh, if you stayed in long enough you could ignore the telltale fluctuations of the visuals and the slight distortion of the auditory signals, but you could always tell it was virtual if and when you wanted to.

In the wake of a major pandemic that had crippled the world, and the race wars that erupted out of that virus, virtual reality technology had become a safe way to navigate society. A new prophylactic was developed to neutralize any emerging virus, and the insanity of racism had all but been purged from the earth. In virtual reality, racial bigotry was seen to be absurd. They were simply avatars, for heaven's sake.

But both the virus and the race wars had advanced virtual technology, and it quickly became mainstream.

For those who could afford even basic Virtual Reality Interface Gear (better known as a RIG), everything from visiting doctors in virtual clinics, to shopping for groceries and clothing in virtual stores, to meeting for business or romance in virtual rooms was already the norm. According to the latest data, over half of the country owned some form of a RIG, and a full third of white-collar jobs were now conducted almost exclusively in virtual spaces.

Out there, talking heads were arguing about who was responsible for climate change and who should be the next president. Hundreds of millions of sheeple were hard at work to pay their taxes and live off the universal basic income provided by those taxes. They were buying worthless crap from one of five virtual markets formerly known as Amazon before the government split it up. They were feeding their faces while glued to the latest live feed from Space X's colony on Mars. They were trading lies through social media while hiding their identities behind carefully constructed masks that said nothing about who they really were. In truth, they were all wannabe Dead Headers who would love nothing more than to go deep enough into a virtual experience to escape this world for a few hours.

But dead heading was like taking drugs, some said, and a Dead Head was only another kind of addict. Even so, Clair and Timothy had fully embraced dead heading, much to the dismay of their parents. As Clair saw it, the 'war' against Dead Heads wasn't unlike a race war. Society's bigotry had simply shifted its focus to a new group. Discrimination based on skin color was out; prejudice based on behavioral preference was in.

But maybe that was stretching things a bit.

She let out a long breath and settled onto one of her recliner's overstuffed arms. "Well?"

Timothy glanced at her through his bangs, still a bit lost. "Well what?"

"What do you mean, *well what?* If this information's real, it's no joke."

"Real? What's real, anyway? For all we know, Play Dead is just some elaborate hoax."

"What's wrong with you? I get why you'd rather remain in denial, but if there's any truth at all to what's on that drive, this isn't just some game! Stop being so dense."

"What I saw is way over both of our heads," he quipped in his typically dismissive tone. "Easily made up."

"Why go to such lengths?" Clair asked. "We're talking reams of data hidden behind a quantum firewall that's impossible to hack without the key that I happened to find."

"Yeah, and it reads like fiction, so, no, I'm not really buying it."

Maybe, she thought. But she doubted it.

"It's hard to believe that Jamie Hamilton's wrapped up in this."

Timothy shrugged. "The guy always gave me the creeps. He's way too smart to be who he says he is."

"Yeah, but *this*?" She stabbed her finger at the one-inch drive inserted in her processing box. "Do you have any idea what would happen if this got out? The world's got its panties in a wad over the next election and water rights and a hundred other stupid things while something far more threatening might be unfolding right under their noses. We can't just sit on this."

His failure to respond betrayed his indifference, which irritated her even more.

"Timothy!"

"Okay, fine. Maybe you're right."

Clair crossed her arms and glanced at the poster above her bed, one of those vintage glow-in-the-dark kinds from when her parents were kids, show-ing Luke Skywalker and Darth Vader in an old movie called *Star Wars*. Her and Timothy's mutual love for those old pre-VR movies had brought them together two years ago.

Timothy eased himself down on the bed across from her, trying to be casual but avoiding her eyes. Maybe he wasn't as confident as he was letting on. Or maybe he was only reacting to her scolding.

Long ago they'd ventured into virtual spaces occupied by some of the most brilliant adult minds on Earth and found they could not only hold their own, but often dominate any discussion or game. Although you could never be sure of anyone's age in a virtual space, she and Timothy had devel-oped a simple algorithm that used seven factors to estimate age—factors that included speech patterns, points of interest, and relational skills.

Society was freaking out about dead heading these days, but make no mistake, there were many, many more closet Dead Heads among the naysay-ers than most would admit. Which is what made it dangerous, lawmakers said.

Like all Dead Heads, Clair and Timothy saw it differently. Experiencing something new in a virtual world that engaged all five senses was much safer than trying it in the real world.

Take romance. When immersed in a virtual reality in which all five senses—seeing, hearing, touching, smelling and tasting—were fully engaged, participants could experience romance that was almost as real as any they could have in person. Almost. Even a person's sense of time was altered in a Deep Dive. Well, sort of.

Which begged the question: what was real? Hundreds of thousands of people now had synthetic organs. Were those real? And what if you replaced your entire body with synthetic organs and limbs grown in labs—would you still be you? What if you could replace part or all of your brain with another, would that still be you? Would you be real? What was the difference between replacing your brain and replacing the *contents* of your brain, which is what VR fundamentally did?

Dead Heads were becoming who they weren't, the critics cried. And as someone else, they could be manipulated while under the influence of a VR world. In those non-real worlds, killers could murder as many people as they liked, reinforcing horrific behavior that would eventually spill out into the real world. Far more stringent regulation was required.

Okay, so maybe there was a point in there, Clair thought. But you can't regulate morality.

A mischievous smile crossed Timothy's face. "Well, if this discovery of yours is true, then maybe it's good news."

"How so?" she asked.

"If it's true, none of this matters."

She already knew what he was thinking but let him continue because she'd considered the deliciously intriguing thought herself.

He winked. "If it's true, we can do whatever we want."

"I'm sure you'd love that," she said.

"So would you." He stood, eyes bright and daring now. There was her bold Timo. "If you're right, the world's definitely toast and we might as well—"

"Do something about it," she interrupted.

"That's not what I was thinking."

"No, of course not."

"And what is it *you* think we should do?" he asked, brow cocked. "Other than whatever we want?"

"For starters, we have to get this to someone who can tell us if it's real."

"Oh, that would go over big. I can see the headlines now: 'Two kids uncover world-threatening conspiracy.' If the data on the drive is true, we'd be dead before we had any opportunity to do what I say we do."

Anything we want. All boys, including geniuses, seemed to have one-track minds, something she didn't fully comprehend.

Timothy crossed to her, twirling once like a charming prince. He reached for her hand as if asking for a dance. "Anything at all."

She ignored his hand and brushed past him. "You're not taking this seriously."

"And you're not listening," Timothy objected, turning with her. "No one would believe us. If they did believe us, we could be in a world of hurt. For starters, there's the matter of how you came into possession of—"

"Yeah, well, I didn't know what I was taking. But that's the real issue now, isn't it? We have to assume it's real and that they know they've been compromised. Someone's probably already hunting us down to plug the leak. We have to take this to someone for our own protection!"

He watched her, then let his shoulders relax in a subtle sign of surrender. "Okay. Okay, like who? Our parents would freak out."

"God, no." Timothy's dad was a megachurch pastor and hers the founder of a software giant—both knee-deep in politics. "Even if they did believe us, they wouldn't have a clue what to do. We'd only put *them* in danger."

"So who? You've committed a crime, so we can't go to the police. Or the FBI. Or any government agency, for that matter."

"I don't know." She paced, eyes on the thick white carpet she'd selected when her father built the house. Her army boots were black in contrast to her beach-blond, short cropped hair—anything to remind herself that she wasn't interested in conformity.

He studied her for a long moment. "So Jamie Hamilton really is mixed up in this, huh?"

"Forget Jamie for now. It's the rest of it that concerns me."

"Maybe we should meet with him?" Timothy pressed.

"Maybe, but we still need someone outside the system."

"Who?"

Clair crossed to her bookshelf. Most people read books using a digital or augmented virtual interface, but she preferred old-school books because they required only paper and the mind. She pulled out her copy of *Righteous*, which she'd read twice, cover to cover. The true-crime investigative book was about a religious psychopath named Raymond Smith, who'd used Deep Dive encounters to lure his victims into meeting him before killing them—his way of making the world righteous.

The book had become a worldwide bestseller and the spark that ignited a national debate on the dangers of Deep Dive virtual reality.

"*Righteous?*" he said, knowing the title by its reputation. "Angie Channing? Isn't she against VR?"

"On the contrary. She's honest about the dangers of Deep Dive but she's a closet Dead Head herself."

"You hacked her?"

Clair shrugged. "It wasn't easy, trust me."

"Why her? She's just an author," he said in a doubtful voice.

"No, she's a freakin' genius and a nonconformist who knows the dark side of VR inside and out. I trust her."

"You don't even *know* her."

She cocked her brow. "I've *hacked* her." A beat. "But we just ask her to meet. Decide then."

"Assuming she agrees to meet."

Clair set the book down. "She's too obsessed with the truth not to. Besides, I know her Dead Head handle. That'll get her attention. I'll send her a letter, old-school. Digital's too easy to intercept."

Timothy was approaching with that look in his eyes. "Now that we have that out of the way, how about a little us time?"

But Clair was too distracted to give Timothy the attention he wanted. She stepped up to him, wrapped her right hand around the back of his head and kissed him on his mouth for a full second.

"Next time."

The world went black and Clair ripped off her RIG. The thin, semipermeable mask had full visual and auditory functionality, which traced all facial movements and replicated natural expressions with near-perfect precision. Her room came back into full view—her real room, not the digital replica where she and Timothy often hung out.

The rest of her body's movements were tracked by twelve tiny transparent circuits that she'd permanently tattooed on her shoulders, elbows, hips, knees, ankles and on each big toe. The basic Reality Interface Gear was referred to as a shallow RIG. Not everyone opted for tattooing the required sensors on their bodies.

Clair and Timothy's physical engagement with each other was limited by the sensors in their rooms, which interfaced with the sensors on their bodies. They both had Deep Dive RIGs that utilized full-body haptic-feedback suits, but for casual meet-ups they typically used either the shallow RIGs or less immersive mobile RIGs.

Clair slid out of her chair, peeled off her gloves and withdrew the small encrypted drive from her processing box, making a mental note to put it back in its hiding space. She quickly crossed to the window and peered through the slats. Her room sat in the east wing of their Barton Creek estate, a perk of being the daughter of Steve Milton, founder of Mistletoe, a fifth-generation search engine that really did seem to know what you wanted before you did, as its slogan promised.

Her mother, Susan, was like a sister to her; her father, she hardly ever saw. Whether that was a good thing, she wasn't sure, but she did appreciate the freedom it gave her.

Still raining outside—uncanny how accurately the mirroring programs worked these days, relaying precise real-time conditions such as weather to the algorithms that generated virtual spaces.

Clair hurried to her desk, rummaged through the drawer for a pen and pulled out a piece of paper. She'd never hand-written a letter before today, but these words, penned in blue ink to an author named Angie Channing, whom she'd never met, might just be the most important words she would ever write.

CHAPTER
ONE

Two Days Later

ANGIE CHANNING felt her feet moving to an unseen rhythm that seemed to dictate her pace along the dirt path that bordered Town Lake. Others made their way down the path at their own pace in the late-afternoon hours. Some ran, some strolled, but all within socially accepted standards.

Who had established those norms? Society. As she saw it, most behavior, like fashion, was simply an arbitrary social agreement that had evolved over time, nothing more, nothing less.

And what were the socially accepted norms in the virtual reality called the Red Protocol, which she'd just experienced? It had all been so real. A part of her wondered if she was still trapped in the game.

"Angie?"

Felicia Buckhead's voice pulled her from her thoughts. Angie glanced at the tall brunette matching her stride. Her friend and therapist, who also acted as her agent because Angie didn't think she needed a real agent, was dressed inappropriately, some would say, for a stroll through Lady Bird Park. White blouse. Navy pencil skirt. She was wearing flats, which were better than high heels, but definitely not lake wear.

Angie, on the other hand, was dressed more appropriately. Gray sweats, black halter top, Nikes, ponytail. In Saudi Arabia, where Angie had spent her first ten years as the daughter of an ambassador before moving to France, her casual sporting attire would have received more stares than Felicia's. Propriety was all relative. All made up.

She absently wondered if all fashion, like race and culture, would eventually blend into one universal norm. It was well known that cross-breeding would eventually result in just one race, all DNA blended into a common expression of darker skin not unlike those born in Fiji. Given enough time, every male would look like the twin of every other male. Same with females.

By then, social norms would be so fixed that any expression outside that norm might be illegal. God knew, society was obsessed with control.

"Come back to me, Angie." Felicia again.

"Sorry." Angie was biting her lower lip, a habit that betrayed her nerves. At least she wasn't picking at it, as she'd been known to do in the worst of times. She took a deep breath. "Yeah, so sorry. I got lost. Too much all at once, maybe."

"I can only imagine after what you've come through. Which is why I suggested we meet in my office rather than here."

The edge of Angie's vision started to fade. She stopped, grabbing Felicia's arm to steady herself as the world tilted.

"You okay?"

Her vision restored itself and the vertigo vanished.

"Barnes said I would probably experience episodes of disorientation and disassociation as my mind reacclimates. Whiteouts, he called them. Interruptions to visual input. Also hallucinations. Not too keen about that, as you can probably imagine."

"Because of your mother?"

Angie hesitated. Her mother, Sarah, and father, George, had both died while boating in France ten years ago when Angie was seventeen. The tragedy had sent her into a tailspin that brought her back to the United States. Distant history.

But the similarities between Angie and her mother had taken center stage in her therapy of late. Her mother had never been diagnosed, but Felicia had come to the conclusion that Sarah fell somewhere on the spectrum of dissociative identity disorders, which were more often than not genetic. Angie loved her mother and remembered—even revered—her otherworldly, sage-like understanding. But that didn't mean she wanted to be like her.

"So tell me," Felicia said when Angie didn't respond. "We've been out here for ten minutes and you haven't breathed a word about what happened. Talk to me about your week at Convergence."

Convergence, headed by founder Jake Barnes, was the world's primary supplier of advanced VR technology and the developer of the Red Protocol, an interface that surpassed all RIGs on the market.

A jogger coughed behind them, signaling his approach. Angie and Felicia stepped to one side and let a man with red shorts and titanium prosthetic legs lope past them. Initially developed for veterans when countries still used soldiers to fight in the battlefield, the business of limb replacement had grown in the private sector when the technology became economically viable. Knee replacements were out and leg replacements were in, the latter being far more efficient and, at the moment, fashionable. Chronic pain was a thing of the past. Most of those who'd adapted artificial limbs had the kind that looked amazingly similar to natural limbs.

"Angie?"

Angie's mind returned again to the purpose of her meeting with Felicia. A wave of anxiety washed over her. She had to get a grip.

"Forgive me. I keep losing track of . . ." Of what? Reality? "Of where I am."

"It's perfectly fine. Jake Barnes prepared me for this."

"He did? What did he say?"

Felicia hesitated. "Just to keep a close eye on you for any signs of strange behavior or hallucinations. It was all over the phone. I'm still trying to get an in-person meeting with him. He's quite the recluse. What's he like?"

"Barnes? Old. Eccentric. He was kind, like a father figure, I suppose. Smart. Real smart."

"That's what they say. Okay, why don't you just tell me what happened and how you feel about it."

Angie nodded, gathering her thoughts. She'd spent two days in reintegration and was released only three hours ago with instructions to spend time with Felicia before talking to anyone else. Darey, her husband, was waiting for her in the car because she wasn't supposed to drive for a couple days.

"Most of the details from the game are gone. They faded during my reintegration. I remember that I was married to someone else."

"Really? How was that?"

"I can't recall what he looked like, but our relationship was as real as mine and Darey's and lasted for a long time. We had a son. A teenager, tall boy, but I can't remember him either. It's all just bits of information, and even those are fading quick."

"I'm aware that you signed a confidentiality agreement and I'm not asking for any details about the content of your experience, only your engagement with it and your state of mind now. Then we can talk about how this relates to your new book."

That's right, this is all about me writing a book. "Somehow this feels much bigger than a book."

Felicia glanced at her. "I wouldn't underestimate the power of a book, especially one written by you. Just look at how much influence *Righteous* has had in the two years since it was published. One could say it was the catalyst for the debate on VR regulations."

"You're giving it too much credit."

"Well, Convergence's support didn't hurt, I'll grant you. And Barnes is fully behind this book as well. Suffice it to say that the right book at the right time can help shape the world."

The follow-up book Angie was planning had been suggested by her publisher, Marsha Craft. The exposé would delve into the psychological effects of Deep Dive virtual reality with the intent of showing both the benefits of its appropriate use and the dangers of its abuse. Angie wasn't a psychologist. Her major at Auburn University had been journalism. But her brand and experience would play well with the general public, who needed the information broken down in their language, Marsha said. Besides, no one could get to the bottom of the truth and express it so clearly as Angie Channing.

Of course she would say that. She was in the business of creating bestsellers. And truth be told, following a restless year, Angie was eager to try her hand at writing again.

"The Red Protocol is by far the most realistic virtual world I've ever experienced," Angie said. "It was impossible to tell it wasn't real. This world was gone. I mean, I know what it's like to dead head, but nothing comes close to the Red Protocol. I'm still a bit confused as to where I am half the time, and I've been out of the game for over forty-eight hours."

"It was a game then?"

"Not really, no. But everything that isn't real is like a game, right? I was at Convergence for a week but only in the Red Protocol for three days. Two days to prep, three days in the game, and two days of debriefing. You said it rained two days ago?"

"It rained for two straight days while you were gone."

"Would have been nice to see," Angie said. "I hope it comes back."

"Not any time soon, they say."

"Well, we can't control the weather, but we can control our experience of it."

"How so?" Felicia prompted.

"I was in another world, so I didn't experience what you experienced, simple as that."

"You were buried in a lab protected from the rain."

"You don't understand. Before feeding me new sensory input, they turned off my senses. Completely. If they'd wheeled me outside into pouring rain, I wouldn't have been able to hear, feel or see a drop of rain. Even if they pried my eyes open. The signals from my eyes to my visual cortex were terminated. For all practical purposes, my eyes were dead."

She pulled up, glanced around quickly to verify that they were alone for the moment, then dipped her head and parted her hair on the crown so Felicia could see her scalp. "See it?"

"A rash?"

"Not a rash." Angie straightened and they continued walking. "They attached a mesh of seven hundred microscopic electronic nodes to my scalp. No shaving required. Once in place, they used the nodes to map my brain, trillions of neural transmitters. Then they subjected me to a day of testing to identify exactly which neural receptors fired to convey sensory information: sight, touch, smell, taste, and hearing. Once identified and mapped, they could turn off all of my normal senses and feed a different sensory experience directly to my brain using a new technology called acoustic neutralization and acoustic imaging."

Felicia stopped on the path, studying her. "You're saying they have the technology to completely turn off and replace a person's sensory links to the world?"

"You've never been in a Deep Dive? It's gets pretty close to that, once your brain adjusts."

"Actually, no."

"Really? Not even once?"

"Not even once."

"Huh. Well, this is like that only on steroids. The real advancement is acoustic imaging, a process by which they can create what looks and feels like solid objects using sound alone. They've somehow extended that same technology to happen in the mind rather than outside of it."

"Really? I didn't know such a thing was possible."

"Neither did I, but it makes sense when you think about it. Everything in the universe is vibration, right? Light and sound are both vibrations of different states and frequencies. They're fundamentally the same, just experienced differently by our senses. Convergence has just figured out how to neutralize the vibrations that make up a person's multisensory experience of this world and replace it with a different one. They create it from the inside of the brain using acoustics rather than an external RIG."

Felicia side-stepped to a bench along the path and eased to her seat. Angie settled beside her and followed Felicia's eyes to a distant rower on the lake. What would the world think if it knew about Convergence's tech? Hearing herself explain the Red Protocol to Felicia, she understood why Jake Barnes wanted his own technology to be regulated.

"No one can know what you just told me," Felicia said. "Not until the book comes out, endorsed by Jake Barnes. It's not only proprietary, it's explosive. You understand that, right?"

Angie nodded slowly. "I'm not sure how I can possibly write it."

"Don't worry about that. You'll get all the help you need, I'm sure." Felicia crossed her legs. "So what was coming out like?"

"Coming out? Honestly, I felt like I was giving up my real life. Like somehow I belonged there, not here. In fact, for all I know, I could still be in the Red Protocol right now. That's how real it was." Angie looked at her friend, taken by the idea. "What if I *am* still in it?"

Felicia smiled. "You're not. I'm right here."

Yes, but you don't understand. 'Right here' could be in the game and I wouldn't know it. Coming out of the Red Protocol could have been an illusion.

But that was ridiculous. Felicia had always maintained that Angie's greatest challenge was a pervasive sense of not belonging in this world. This was consistent with her multicultural upbringing and her mother's fractured view of the world. As a result, Felicia theorized, Angie was always looking for a way back to some other life. Angie wasn't so sure it was that simple, but still . . .

Thinking she was still in another world was ridiculous.

"I sound like a broken record, huh?" Angie chuckled nervously. "But it was pretty . . ."

For a moment that might have lasted one breath, Angie found herself in a different reality. In it, she was by the same lake with a tall blond boy. No Felicia, no joggers, no one but herself and a tall boy looking out at the water. She had the vague impression that he might have been her son in the Red Protocol.

Then the impression was gone and she was back.

"What is it?" Felicia asked, concerned.

Angie blinked, thinking the scene might return. "Just a recall of my time in the Red Protocol, I think," she said, turning her head and staring at a group of cyclists flying silently past on Caesar Chavez behind them. "Strange."

"Like I said, Barnes assured me they'll pass in the next day or so."

"I hope so because it's pretty freaky. Experiencing that without any gear makes me think I'm losing my mind."

"I can assure you that's not the case. If anything, you'll temporarily experience something like what your mother experienced her whole life. She didn't lose her mind, she was just different from most. Maybe more advanced than most."

"So you've said."

"Having said that, it's important that I know if the whiteouts continue for more than forty-eight hours."

"Trust me, you'll be the first to know."

They sat in silence for a moment, staring at the serene lake. There were others in canoes, paddling hard to cut through the water.

"So what's the verdict?" Felicia asked. "You ready to pull the trigger?"

"On writing the new book?"

"Isn't that what this is all about? I guarantee you Marsha's glued to her phone as we speak, dying for you to say you're all in."

Angie nodded absently. "Was there ever a chance I'd say no?" The excitement of it all spread through her bones. "Considering my personal interests, how can I turn this project down?"

"About those personal interests: I can't stress how important it is that you keep your own image clean in this."

"You mean me being a closet Dead Head."

"I wouldn't call you a Dead Head," Felicia objected.

"What would you call it?"

"Fine. You're a closet Dead Head. But as far as the world's concerned, you only dead head on rare occasions for research purposes. Right?"

"Of course. We wouldn't want anyone to know how screwed up I really am."

They exchanged playful grins.

"Well, thank God you *are* a Dead Head," Felicia said. "I doubt you ever would've been drawn to write *Righteous* if you weren't. And it's not an overstatement to say the world's better off for it."

Maybe, Angie thought.

Felicia withdrew a phone from her purse and glanced at the screen. "You ready to collect a five-million-dollar advance?" Her eyes were fixed on the phone, concerned now.

"What is it?" Angie asked, tempted to retract her question. Life was easier without the steady stream of bad news on the feeds, and by Felicia's face, this was bad news.

"Two kids were murdered in Oak Hill Park by St. Andrew's. Maybe high school students. No names or details yet."

The news felt like a gut punch.

"Never ends," Angie said. "Dear God, I hope they weren't Dead Heads."

"Sad," Felicia said.

More than sad. They sat in their thoughts for a few moments.

Felicia broke the silence. "So? You ready?"

Angie came back to the issue at hand. "Five million, huh?" It felt trivial, even obscene, next to news of kids being murdered.

"A girl's gotta keep herself in shoes." Felicia grinned.

"I don't wear shoes half the time and when I do, they're not exactly fashionable. You know the money doesn't really mean much to me, although I wouldn't mind springing for a holo-room in my house. That would cost a couple million."

"Be careful, now," Felicia quipped. "Stay clear of dead heading except for the purposes of research."

"I know, I know. Fine, no holo-room."

But she wasn't sure her promise would stand for long.

Angie took the phone from Felicia. "So, let's give Marsha some good news. And then we should get back to Darey. Poor guy's probably bored out of his skull."

CHAPTER
TWO

THERE WAS no better way to spend a day off than away from it all, and for Randy George that meant kayaking right down the throat of Lake Austin, five hundred yards from either shore. The only technology on board was his phone, and even that was old-school. The rare rain that had drenched Austin two days earlier was now a distant memory.

The only other place that brought Randy as much peace was the off-grid cabin hidden in the hills near Marble Falls. The hideaway belonged to Joseph Conrad, an old friend from Special Forces who was kind enough to give Randy full access three or four times each year. Short of that, Lake Austin would do.

He would have left his handheld phone in the car if not for the regulations that required all officers of the law, uniformed or not, to carry mobile communications on their persons at all times. The last time he'd defied the rules, he'd missed a call on a drug bust gone bad, and the chief had made her sentiments abundantly clear. "Detectives can't detect squat if they're off-line," Renee Dalton raged. "I can't afford to fire one of this state's best detectives over a formality, but God knows I will if you ignore protocol again. I don't care how unorthodox you want to be!"

Out here on the lake, as the sun slipped down the western horizon, there was no raging, no talking, no *whir* of electric cars, no nothing but the sound of his blades dipping into the glassy water like a mother scooping bath water over her newborn son. That's how Randy felt out here, new-born and clean, washed of the city's sins.

He'd been young when the race wars had changed America, but, being the son of a Jamaican mother and a Dutch father, he was all too familiar with those offenses. The sins of racism were no longer in play, but others took their place. And as he saw it, technology only fostered more of the same. In some ways, it made things worse.

Case in point: Every reported crime was run through an algorithm and graded on the Randal Scale, a proprietary ranking system used to determine an incident's probable threat to society, partly based on a suspect's social standing. Incidents that scored 70 or higher were thoroughly investigated. Those lower than 30 were dropped. Investigation of cases between 30 and 70 on the scale was discretionary. He understood the reasoning, but grouping people based on historical behavioral patterns didn't sit well in his gut.

Society couldn't seem to help but categorize people. Worse yet, politicians never failed to pit one group against another. Ultimately, categorizing people was the deepest of humanity's evils, Randy thought.

Sweat matted his curly hair and dripped down his forehead and cheeks. Good for the pores, good for the mind, good for the body, just plain good. That's what he'd told his late wife, Andrea, sixteen years ago when he first brought her out here in what might have been an ill-advised attempt to woo her. But she'd quickly become a die-hard kayaker herself.

He could still see her dipping her paddle in the water, then throwing her head back and laughing at the sky as her kayak slid through the glassy surface. He'd known then he would eventually marry this girl.

Two years later, Andrea gave birth to their daughter. He hadn't seen that coming. Neither of them had. Children one day, maybe, they'd said, but not so soon. They'd talked about legally tying the knot, but neither really saw the need. Now he wished they had. If he'd learned anything in the three years since she died it was that he would never love anyone the way he'd loved Andrea.

She was gone. Just gone. So was Stacy, one week before she would have entered high school as a freshman, an event that she'd talked about nonstop for months.

He leaned into his paddles and picked up his pace.

Technology had killed them. Technology and a seventeen-year-old kid fuming with jealousy. Paul Smart, under the influence of a designer drug called Twister, had hacked a Jeep driven by another student he hated and sent it careening into oncoming traffic on Bee Caves road. The Jeep had struck Andrea's Audi head-on. The driver of the Jeep had spent a day in the hospital before dying. Andrea and Stacy had died on the scene.

A chirp sounded from the bottom of the kayak. If the call was important, they would call again. Right now, he had more pressing concerns, like working up a sweat and clearing his head.

But his head didn't clear, now preoccupied with the certainty that the phone would chirp again. And so it did, thirty seconds later. With a sigh, Randy let the paddle flop and plucked the black handheld from the puddle of lake water that had splashed in the kayak.

The screen said it was Rachel Banning, his work partner for six months now. She knew he was off and likely on the lake at this time of day.

Randy tapped the bar and lifted the phone to his ear, old-school. "Tell me this is a where-should-I-get-my-car-fixed call and not department business."

"Sorry, Goat. The chief insisted I call."

Rachel had playfully given him the nickname Goat—greatest of all time—three months ago, when the department recognized him for having the highest solve-rate in the state. He despised the name. Thankfully she used it only in private.

"She does realize that I'm in the middle of Lake Austin right now."

"That's what I told her."

"And?"

"I'm not sure you want to hear her actual words."

"Fine. So what is it that none of our other fine detectives can do?"

"Someone walking their dog found the bodies of two victims in Oak Hill Park off Southwest Parkway."

Not every day were bodies found in an upscale Barton Creek neighborhood.

"Okay, so why me?"

"She says it's a high-profile case. And by the sound of it, pretty brutal. She insists on you."

"They have the identities yet?"

"Not that I know."

"So how do they know it's high-profile?"

A beat passed.

"I don't think you have much of a choice."

"I always have a choice."

"Officers are on the scene and CSI is already on the way," she continued, ignoring his objection. "I'm on the east side, thirty minutes out in this traffic. You're ten minutes out."

"I'm in the middle of the lake."

"Ten minutes from Texas Rowing Center, I mean. How far out on the lake are you?"

He looked back at the distant dock. *Twenty minutes*, he thought, but said nothing.

"That's what I thought. I'll meet you at the scene?"

Randy sighed. "Do me a favor and call the officer in charge on scene. Nobody touches anything until I'm there."

"They know."

"Call them anyway. I'll be there in thirty."

"Oh, one more thing."

"What is it?"

"The victims are a girl and a boy, mid-teens. Maybe students from St. Andrew's."

Randy felt a stone fall into his gut. His daughter's age.

"I'm sorry, but I thought you should know before you arrive," Rachel said.

"Yeah." The word came out like a grunt. He disconnected before she could say anything else.

RANDY PARKED his old '21 Ford truck behind Rachel's white sedan on Southwest Parkway and stepped out into the hot Austin air. The blue truck's frame was old, granted, but under the hood it was all super-charged DC muscle with enough electric power to chase down most of the hotrods favored by those prone to run. Like most vehicles, the batteries accepted a charge while on highways and surface streets treated with photovoltaic coating. Randy had also expanded the battery wafer capacity, giving the truck enough charge to run a full five hundred miles on uncoated back roads as well.

Dusk was still an hour away, but the crickets were already singing. A football game was being played on St. Andrew's field on the opposite side of the parkway, less than half a mile up the road. Three squad cars with silently twirling lights were parked on the gravel entryway into Oak Hill Park, which wasn't much larger than the football field. A neighborhood park for walking, not much else.

He approached a trooper who leaned against his car, talking into his earpiece. The officer recognized Randy and discontinued his call with a vocal command. There was no real parking here. Most entered from the neighborhood on the other side. The path into the park ran among overgrown scrub oak that had adapted to the arid ground. The junk trees were well known by those who suffered from allergies, but green was green and Austin was reticent to get rid of any of it these days. A good thing, he thought.

"Evening, sir. Fifty yards in and to the left. They're waiting for you."

"CSI here yet?"

"Five minutes ago."

Randy walked between the cars and headed in on the narrow trail. Tires, likely from the crime-scene-investigation vehicle and maybe a squad car, had flattened the grass on either side.

The sound of traffic faded, buffered by the trees and shrubs. For a short stretch it was just him, walking into the brush and surrounded by crickets. The boys would have to set up lights soon to finish processing the scene.

The path veered to the left. He followed it to a small clearing, where two technicians were pulling equipment from a white CSI van. The yellow-tape perimeter had been established at the edge of the clearing, thirty feet beyond the van.

Randy stepped under the tape and picked his way through underbrush to a smaller clearing, where two officers and Rachel waited, arms crossed, back to him, staring intently at the scene. She was dressed in ratty jeans and a white and blue Dallas Cowboys T-shirt, side arm hugging her hip. Looked like she'd just come from a family picnic and hurriedly strapped on the long-range Taser. She typically preferred more professional wear, a skirt and blouse. Gone were the days when detectives ran around like athletes, chasing down bad guys. A fleet of drones circling on constant patrol above the city did the chasing when necessary.

A photographer wearing a white CSI shirt was efficiently cataloging the scene. Video and still images simultaneously. The data was transmitted in real time to the forensics lab, where the images were already being logged and analyzed. A simple blue backpack lay on the ground next to Rachel, whether part of the scene or belonging to one of the techs, he couldn't be certain.

His phone buzzed in his back pocket and he slipped it out. Renee Dalton. He wasn't in the mood to talk to the chief just yet, so he ignored the call, shoved the phone back in his pants, and stepped up.

"Evening, folks."

Rachel jerked around at the sound of his voice. "Hey." Just hey. Her blond hair was in a ponytail and her face was ashen.

"Evening, Randy." It was Billy Birch, a good cop of sixty or so who refused to retire. Usually more talkative.

Randy nodded and saw what they were seeing. The naked bodies of two teenagers, one male, one female. Side by side. Their wrists were bound to their ankles and their bodies positioned on the knees in a posture of prayer, bowing to a tree. Both of their skulls were partially crushed from behind. A circle the size of a dinner plate had been carved into their backs.

A circle with a pupil-less eye. Dead Heads' unofficial brand.

Rachel and Billy remained silent.

"When were they found?" Randy asked, eyes still on the bodies.

"An hour ago by"—Billy lifted his pad and scrolled—"a man named Constance Deamanto, who was walking his dog. Actually, his dog did the finding. Seemed like a straight shooter."

"A guy named Constance?"

"That's what he said. I don't know. He was a tall fella with thick brows, like maybe Eastern European. He was a mess. I sent him home. Dog was still barking when we pulled up. I've seen a lot but I swear, the kids always get to me, you know? This just ain't human. Maybe in Houston or—"

"That's fine, Billy." People often deflected stress by talking, but Randy wasn't in the mood for it.

The sound of shoes crunching through underbrush came from either side as officers searched the land in widening circles for evidence while the light was still good.

"Anything else?"

"Boot prints back there." Rachel motioned to the first clearing. "Already photographed and processed."

He nodded. "Fair enough. That's it?"

"Just this." She leaned over and with a gloved hand carefully plucked the blue backpack from the ground. "One of the officers found it in the bushes behind that tree." The one the kids were bowing to.

Randy took the backpack gingerly using a single finger. A dirty white tag just inside the zipper said its owner was Clair Milton. Address on Mirador Way, not five minutes up the road in the country club's gated community. Wealthy family.

Inside the backpack was neatly folded clothing—what appeared to be two pairs of jeans and T-shirts. Yellow cotton panties and boxers.

"There's a phone in it. Locked. Nothing else."

"No footwear?"

"No."

"So other than the footwear, these are the only personal effects of the victims. Nothing else might have been in the backpack?" Randy said.

"Evidently not. Maybe the killer took the original contents," Rachel said.

Question was, why? Why no footwear? Why leave a traceable phone and the backpack? Why strip the bodies but leave the clothes?

"What do we know about Clair Milton?" Randy asked.

She looked at the girl's body, face still stark. "Fifteen years old. Student at St. Andrew's across the way. Only child of Susan and Steve Milton. Steve Milton is the founder of Mistletoe, a company known for its revolutionary search engine. That's all we can say for sure at this point."

"Fair enough. Phone and clothes should have already been bagged and turned over to Crime Scene for chain of custody. We need the phone at the lab as soon as possible."

"Yup," she said, but she was still staring at the bodies.

"And the boy?"

"Don't know yet."

"Anything else?"

"Just the Dead Head symbols. But we haven't moved the bodies yet."

"Who's running scene forensics?"

"I am." Frank Goring approached from behind, gloved and cloaked, kit in hand. "Shall we?"

Randy didn't bother answering the seasoned investigator. Frank reminded him of Mark Twain, goatee and all. And the stories he told over a cold beer matched the best of Twain, he thought.

The deceased boy's cheek and nose were pressed flat against the ground, distorting his face. Long tangled hair, old-school skateboarder type. The girl looked to be about the same age, maybe younger or just petite. Short blond hair. Eyes closed, like the boy's.

Randy squatted to one heel and accepted a pair of gloves from Frank, who then rounded the bodies, flipped on a flashlight for additional light in the trees' shadows, and studied the scene from the far side.

"Little or no blood on the ground that I can see," Frank said. "The carvings on their backs are clean."

He set his black kit down and touched the girl's hand. Then bent her fingers back to examine them. Short nails. No polish. No blood or skin under the nails. "Hmm." He moved on to the girl's head, which he eased to one side so he could see her face.

But Randy was still looking at the girl's hands. They could as easily have been his own daughter's. Stacy had been into basketball and painting, neither of which leant themselves to long nails, she claimed. But really, she had always been a tomboy, preferring comfort over fashion. She too had worn her hair short.

Randy pushed the thought from his mind.

"Strangled," Frank said.

Lifting the boy's hair, Randy saw the bruises around his neck. Ligature marks from a rope or cord of some kind. Already the crime scene was telling a story. They always did. The only question was whether the story resembled the truth. The questions of who and why would be answered later. Right now they were focused on the how.

"Your take, Rachel?"

She was younger than him by ten years, a rookie detective who made no effort to hide that she was impressed with him. He preferred to work alone, but seeing as how the department insisted he partner up, he preferred someone he could teach over someone who wanted to prove themselves.

"No sign of struggle, no blood, so they were either killed somewhere else and moved here or strangled here before their skulls were crushed. Either way, whoever did this had no concern about covering their tracks. They either had zero street smarts or wanted to send a message."

Once the heart stopped, the blood stopped flowing.

"If they were strangled, why crush their heads?" Randy pressed.

She hesitated. "Based on the carvings, the unsub is someone who hates Dead Heads. The wounds on their heads are literally that. A Dead Head. Looks like someone took a baseball bat to them, then positioned them bowing to the tree." She was trying to be professional, but her voice came thin and scratchy.

Frank was studying the ground around the bodies. He stroked the grass and looked at his gloved fingers, then stood and surveyed the surrounding ground.

"Nada. Even if they were strangled here, there should be some blood and splatter from the blows. They were most likely killed offsite and moved here. Unless they used a blanket or something to catch the blood, then took it."

Randy shook his head. "But no signs of a struggle. One victim, I can see. How would someone strangle two people out here in the open without a struggle? One of them would take off or fight back."

"Maybe there was more than one killer," Rachel said.

Randy nodded. "Unless the lab comes up with something we're not seeing, I would agree with Frank. They were probably killed off-site and transferred here. But that doesn't explain why the killer would leave the backpack."

He scanned both bodies for other marks—puncture wounds, cuts. Nothing was immediately apparent. "We good to turn the bodies?"

"One second." Frank motioned to the photographer, who was fiddling with the settings on his camera. "Tom. Over here."

Tom hurried over and clicked off a dozen closeups of the victims' necks. "Okay, easy now."

They gently eased first the boy's body and then Clair's to their sides. Rigor mortis had stiffened the bodies so that even on their sides, both were still curled up in a posture of prayer. There was nothing quite as disturbing as a young lifeless body. At least their eyes were closed.

Tom was taking more pictures. Each flash of light from the camera turned the bodies ghostlike. From what Randy could see, there were no other puncture wounds. He'd had enough. Heck, he'd had enough years ago.

The phone in his pocket vibrated and he stood. Dug it out. The chief, again.

"I need to take this call."

"Five minutes and I'll have a little clearer picture," Frank said.

"Watch and learn, Rachel."

He stepped away, lifting the phone to his ear. "Hello, Renee."

"Hello, Randy." The chief's purring voice always had a calmness to it that defied her unbending will. "Please tell me you understand what we're dealing with here."

"Do I?"

"You know who Robert Blake is?"

"Name sounds familiar."

"Timothy Blake's father. The boy." They'd identified the bodies based on the photographs Tom had been uploading. "Most would know him as one of the few successful pastors in Austin. For that matter, the state. In reality, he's more of a political man than a religious man, and he matters in circles that matter."

Weren't all institutions simply political machines operating behind different facades? In the end, *politics*—whether in a church, a home, a city, a state, or any broader context of culture—was simply another word for *power* and *control.* The public's growing awareness of this long-denied truth had led to the sweeping demise of institutional religion in the country.

"The girl's name is Clair Milton," Renee continued. "Daughter of Steve Milton, founder of Mistletoe, one of this city's fastest growing tech startups. Everything goes by the book, down to the last detail. Nothing can compromise the legitimacy of our case."

She was clearly concerned about some political component he wasn't yet aware of.

"So what do we have?" she asked.

"You have the images?"

"I've been told but haven't seen them yet. Just tell me what you see."

"We have two naked bodies with blunt-force trauma to the backs of both heads and bruises around both necks."

"They were strangled?"

"It appears so. They were posed to look like they were praying to a tree, facedown and bound, wrists to ankles."

A pause. "I heard."

"Then you know about the Dead Head brands on their backs."

"I heard that as well. I need you back here as soon as you finish up."

"Okay. Give me a couple hours."

"Let CSI process the scene. I'll have uniforms canvass the neighborhood. I need you back here."

"Yeah. Just give me some time."

She hesitated. "Look, I know this has to be hard considering the age of the girl. But I need you on this. It's an important case for more reasons than you're aware of right now. Take your time but be here in two hours."

"Yup."

"In the meantime, have someone get that phone to the lab. And I mean now."

She disconnected.

He turned to see Frank approaching. "Okay, Randy. Nothing new until we finish processing the scene and get the bodies back to the lab."

"No sign of sexual assault?"

Frank shook his head. "Not yet. A blond hair on the boy's back but it could have come from the girl."

A cry sounded from the direction of the road. Someone had just learned something. A woman by the sound of it.

"We'll process the scene for prints and fibers, run a 3D scanner over the ground to see what secrets it might be hiding, if any. I'll get the bodies down to the lab tonight. But my first take stands for now. They were likely killed elsewhere and then moved here. Why the backpack was left behind is beyond my paygrade."

Whoever did this wanted the victims and the backpack to be found. Either that or they were dealing with an especially dense unsub with zero street smarts, as Rachel had put it. Considering the careful orchestration of the crime, Randy favored option one.

The cry from the street became a frantic wail approaching fast. Other voices yelled. A chill ran up his spine. There was no sound quite like a mother who'd just lost her child.

"Rachel!" He signaled her to follow as he ran toward the path. If the mother, assuming that's who this was, saw the scene now . . . He'd been one of the first to respond to the scene of Andrea and Stacy's accident, and he still couldn't rid his mind of their broken, bloody bodies.

Randy had just rounded the white CSI van when a woman with blond wind-blown hair sprinted into view, face drawn tight, mouth parted in a sickening cry. A much taller man with dark slicked-back hair, dressed in a navy-blue suit, lumbered up the path ten yards behind her.

"Mary!" His low voice came out choked and breathy. "Mary, stop!"

But she didn't stop. And she wouldn't have if Randy hadn't caught her slender arm and spun her back. "It's okay, it's okay," he said. But it wasn't okay, and he didn't know why he was saying it.

Trails of mascara-stained tears ran down her cheeks. Her frantic eyes searched his. "Is he okay? Tell me Timothy's okay. Where is he?" She ripped herself from Randy's arms but not before her husband, Robert, got a big hand around her narrow waist, gripping her dress, white with black pinstripes. She wore no shoes. One of her toes was bleeding.

"Mary, please!" Robert Blake looked like a terrified boy lost in a big man's body. He was a man accustomed to having control. But death couldn't be controlled.

Mary nearly pulled out of the garment, wailing. She spun and screamed at her husband, slashing at his face. Her nails left two deep scratches on his right cheek, but he didn't seem to notice.

"This is your fault!" Mary slammed her fist into his chest. "I hate you! I hate you!"

Her anguish wasn't lost on Randy. The pain of his own loss flooded him, and he suddenly felt ill.

Rachel had taken Mary's hands and was trying to calm her. "I know, Mary. I know. Shh, shh, shh."

Mary buried her face in Rachel's shoulder and wept.

"Take them home," Randy said. "Learn what you can but don't push. We'll do full interviews tomorrow."

"What about the other—"

"We'll talk to witnesses later. I have to get to the station." Rushing off wasn't his way, but she would have to understand. He needed some margin on this one. Just an hour or two for perspective.

He turned to an officer who gawked on his right. State trooper with a name tag. Fernando Watson.

"Watson?"

The officer blinked. "Yeah?"

"Tell Frank Goring that the chief wants the phone down at the station immediately. As in right now. Clear?"

"Okay."

Randy walked quickly down the path. Past all the screaming crickets. Through Oak Hill Park's graveled entryway, where he veered toward his truck.

He was climbing into the cab when the first news van pulled to a hard stop up the street. KPCW. A drone was lifting from the van's roof before any doors opened. The sight stopped him halfway into the truck. Already?

He was too tired for any of this. He'd been too tired for the last three years.

CHAPTER
THREE

ANGIE SAT in the passenger's seat of the BMW, watching cars drift by like ghosts while Darey let the car drive them along the upper level of Mopac. The city had expanded vertically when widening the highway was no longer viable, and light-rail systems and self-driving cars had eliminated congestion. Speed, braking, and the gaps between cars were now controlled almost exclusively by sophisticated algorithms rather than human decisions. For the most part, accidents occurred only when systems failed, which was rare.

They were in her car, the one Darey had chosen for her, a car she hadn't really liked when he first brought it home. Why so fancy? she asked him. He shrugged.

But she knew why. As a well-known litigator in Austin, Darey had money flowing from his ears and had come to like the 'finer' things of life. The BMW was a gift carved from his heart. She loved the car for that reason, even though her idea of finer things had nothing to do with material possessions.

They'd rode in silence for the last ten minutes, she lost in thought, he respecting her space. Stoic to the bone, Darey. The polar opposite of her, which was why they made such good partners, she thought. She offered him wild imagination; he offered her grounding.

But why were they in her car and not his? It was the first time she thought to ask since he'd picked her up from Convergence before taking her to Town Lake to meet up with Felicia.

"Why are we in my car? We always take your Mercedes."

"They said the more grounding the better. I thought being in your car would be best. But you're right. With me driving, the Mercedes would have been more familiar for you. I'm new to this." He cast her a sheepish grin.

The way he said the last bit made her think he wasn't too excited about 'this.' But she was in no mood to rehash her choice to experience the Red Protocol despite his reservations. What was done was done.

"So. How was your discussion with Felicia?"

"It was good," she said. "I'm still a bit disoriented, but things are stabilizing." She placed her hand on his knee. "Thank you."

"For what?"

"For being here with me. For being such a good sport. For being patient with me. I know this is all a bit much for you."

"Don't be ridiculous. I love you because you're you, not for who I want you to be."

"And who do you want me to be?"

He hesitated. "Exactly the person you are."

"Hmm . . ."

"My life would be utterly boring without you."

"Was it boring this last week while I was gone?"

"Same old. I gave closing arguments on the Brighton case. The jury found Penny Ann guilty of gross negligence for squashing her daughter's wishes to go through with gender transition. Last month a jury in Dallas found a father guilty for *not* advising his underage son of the dangers of a botched implant. Same basic case, two totally different interpretations of the law. Not that I have an investment in where society wants to go, I just wish they would establish laws that didn't leave so much open to interpretation. The law's not unlike an ancient religious text that everyone reads differently."

"Sounds about right."

"Nothing ever changes."

"And a part of you likes it that way," she said.

To this he said nothing. He tapped the screen on the steering wheel. A song from the old band Muse, one of her favorite throwback bands, filled the speakers. He occasionally tolerated it for her sake. But today, the wailing guitars sounded more like noise even to her.

"I appreciate the thought, but . . ."

The music was off before she could finish the sentence.

"Thank you," he said.

"My pleasure."

The car took their exit, a spiral that fed into the surface street leading to Terry Town, where their overpriced house waited. Sally, her golden retriever, was probably already wagging his tail. The thought made Angie smile. At times she wondered whether dogs had a better grip on reality than most humans. It was said that experiencing truth required becoming like a little child. Maybe becoming like a little puppy would be a good way of saying the same thing. Like little children, they judged nothing and played with everything.

"We've come a long way since I first met that hysterical girl at Auburn who'd defended herself against a frat boy," he said.

Odd that he would bring that up now.

"I killed him," she said. Then added, "By mistake. He shouldn't have tried to rape me."

"Yes you did, and no, he shouldn't have. You were my first case, fresh out of law school. Not a hard case, I grant you. A good thing, because I was more interested in impressing you than the jury."

"Really? You never told me that."

"Oh, most definitely. I was gone the first time I laid eyes on the barefooted Bohemian who couldn't care less about how things were done in the South. Dark hair and a French accent to boot."

"The accent's long gone."

"I remember how you used to regale me with tales of a wild mother who claimed you were 'chosen,' a father you hardly saw, being bounced between countries. You were lost between cultures."

"I think you were the first person to take me seriously." She let a moment pass. "Is this all your attempt to help me reintegrate?"

"What? Don't be silly."

"Seriously. All this talk of our courtship. It's not like you."

"Well, they did say that talking about the past could be healthy."

"Not that I mind." She studied his face, recalling those early days. She and Darey were so different on so many levels. He was a good six foot three; she only two inches over five feet. He had short blond hair; hers was dark and long. He, blue-eyed; she, hazel. He was practical to the bone; she lived in the no-rules wild. His parents were wealthy landowners with a long Southern heritage; hers were world travelers who had no roots.

They had fallen madly in love.

"You ever wonder what happened to all that romance?" she asked.

Darey gave her a wink. "Nature released its hormones and drew us together long enough to couple. Honestly, I far prefer the partnership we have now to the wild swings of emotional bonding back then."

"Thank God," she said. And she meant it.

They'd never disagreed about the nature of their relationship. She and Darey were companions on a deep, fundamental level that allowed for complete freedom. They had no rules, no established expectations of behavior, no need to placate or persuade. Naturally, they had plenty of disagreements, and they regularly expressed those differences of opinion, sometimes rather passionately.

But as they saw it, an ideal marriage provided a safe container for two people to discover themselves without designs or conditions from their partner. It was a rare love, and their relationship was rooted deeply in that love.

Darey pulled into their driveway as the garage door, one of four, even though they owned only two cars, opened. He used the other two bays for his woodworking hobby, a way to get calluses back on his hands, he said. He'd grown up in the country, a long way from the courthouse.

"I'll get your bags," Darey offered as the garage door closed behind them.

When Angie opened the door into the kitchen Sally nearly knocked her over. Angie dropped to one knee and wrapped her arms around his shaggy neck.

"There you are." She scratched his side as his tongue lapped at her face and neck. "There you are! Good boy. Did you miss Mommy? Yes you did. Of course you did."

She spent the next ten minutes quickly reacquainting herself with the house in the same way she might after having fled the Texas summer heat for cooler mountain temperatures in Switzerland, as they had done many times. She put her bag in their room, played tug-of-war with Sally and his rubber bone, checked the main email account on the kitchen assistant, which served as their main portal to the outside world, poured herself a treat—a bowl of Lucky Charms with whole milk—and scanned the news feed to see what she'd missed.

As it turned out, not much other than the Oak Hill murders that Felicia had mentioned. No details there yet. One of the main pumps that served to keep coastal waters off Miami's streets had failed, and a pending hurricane threatened another major flood. The reconstruction of North Korea was back on track. The famine in East Africa was all but over thanks to the Global Water Project. Democrats and Republicans were still at each other's throats as the presidential campaign gained steam.

Texas governor Judith Patterson was running as an Independent and, according to many, stood a legitimate chance of finally derailing the insanity of partisan gridlock. But hadn't they heard that before? Even an Independent was beholden to the deeply entrenched machinery of power brokering. Nothing truly changed. Only a virtual tsunami would level the playing field and wash all bias out to sea to make room for a new world.

Short of that, life would continue as it had, day after day, year after year. Including her reading the news and eating the occasional bowl of Lucky Charms until death finally put an end to it all. Even now, at this moment, she was going through the motions of the game called life, repeating history. They said the definition of insanity was doing the same thing over and over and expecting a different result. And so the world was lost in insanity.

The Red Protocol . . . Now there was a potential tsunami. So was that good or bad?

"What is it, dear?" Darcy asked, stepping into the kitchen. "I can hear you thinking from the other room."

"Nothing." She turned the feed off. "I'm just enjoying a bowl of cereal and catching up."

He opened the refrigerator door, scanned its contents and pulled out a loaf of whole-grain bread, a bottle of mustard, some ham and a jar of sliced pickles. New week, same food.

"Let me guess," he said. "You're taking the project but don't know how to tell me."

"No. Well, yes, I have agreed to take the project. I thought I told you that. But no, that's not what I was thinking."

"You've agreed? As in, for certain?"

"Felicia and I called the publisher. They're drawing up the contract already."

"That's big news. I'm happy for you. Certain to be a huge success."

"Well, I don't know about that. I'm not even sure where to begin."

"You already have," he said.

True. The Red Protocol had been her baptism into a whole new technology.

She dropped her spoon into the bowl, propped her elbows on the breakfast bar, and drew a breath. "You want to know what happened?"

He spread mustard on the bread, glancing up. "At Convergence? I thought it was confidential."

"Well, you don't count." And then she told him everything, including the parts she'd promised Felicia she wouldn't share with anyone. How could she not? He was a part of her, so she was really just telling herself.

"So let me get this straight," he said when she finished. "It was so real that you're now concerned that you're still in the Red Protocol. That this is actually part of it. I'm just a virtual construct, right now, as we speak. The real you in the real world is married to someone else and has a son. That about it?"

"No, of course not." They held each other's eyes. "But you have to admit, I wouldn't know it if that were true, right? It's crazy stuff. Just imagine if Convergence created an even more advanced technology that changed people's perceptions without physical transmitters," she said. "They would be able to control behavior."

"They can do that?"

"No, but it's just a matter of time, right? Gives the term *game-changer* a whole new meaning."

"But in the Red Protocol you still had control of your behavior, right?"

"I was populating the world with my subconscious and making my own choices in the game. No one could force me to do one thing or another, but they could influence me in what might be irresistible ways. I mean, if I mistook a child for a monster, I might attack it. Kill it even. Perception changes everything."

A moment passed and she scooped up some cereal.

When he spoke again, he used his closing-arguments tone: a low voice, smooth and certain, speaking with gentle but unmistakable authority.

"Angie, I don't make many requests of you. Most people in healthy relationships feel good about giving each other a lot of rope. In our relationship, we've thrown the rope away, and I wouldn't have it any other way. I don't ever want you to act out of character for my sake. You get to do what you want to do, and I get to cheer you on. That goes both ways."

A pause.

"But there *is* one thing I would strongly ask you to consider."

"Which is?" she asked.

"I think you should give up virtual reality for a while." He held up a hand. "I'm not saying forever, naturally, but now, after coming out of such a deep experience, and considering your history and your mother, you run the risk of losing yourself in it."

"This has nothing to do with my mother! I've just agreed to write an exposé on the benefits and dangers of emerging VR technology, and you want me to stay away from it?"

"No, of course not. Study it, research it, lay out your book as only you know how. But you don't have to be a heroin addict to write about drugs, do you? I don't want you growing six fingers."

Heat flashed up her neck, but she kept calm. She'd told him about the role of raw, unquestioning belief in a fully immersive virtual reality and how it could even change your body's genetic expression. Example: if you truly believed you had six fingers in a virtual world, your real body could begin to grow a sixth finger. Such was the power of belief as tested in the lab. Epigenetics.

"You worry about epigenetics changing genetic expression, but gene editing's already doing that in spades," she shot back. "Thirty years ago the world was in a frenzy over CRISPR, but look what good it's brought us all. Ninety percent of all genetic diseases have been eradicated from the gene pool."

"Yes, but gene editing is carefully controlled. A fully immersive virtual reality that goes deep enough to get the brain to alter its own genetic code sounds like a monster factory."

He had a point, of course. But she wasn't going to throw away her RIG just because . . .

Her vision blurred. Before she could wonder what was happening, the world went white. Not white as in everything in the room turned white, but white as in the room vanished, leaving only white space.

For what might have been three seconds, she forgot to breathe. Her thinking stalled. She could hear her heart hammering like a drum and his voice calling her name. But she could see only white.

And then the kitchen was back and she sucked in a punctuated gasp.

"Angie?"

"I think . . . I think I just had a whiteout." She looked around, making sure everything was here. It was. Her mind had just stuttered for a moment, a function of her visual cortex recalibrating. "They tell you about that?"

"They said to expect it for a day or two as your brain adjusts," he said, concerned. "Triggered by stress."

"I . . ." She pushed herself back from the breakfast bar and stood. "Wow, not cool. That's . . . That was super freaky."

"But you're okay now?"

She looked at him, happy to be here, in her kitchen with Darey. "I think so. Yes."

He was right, she thought. She had to take a break from immersive VR. Maybe all VR. Maybe a long break.

Angie hurried around the counter and wrapped her arms around him as he pulled her into his chest.

"You're right. Sorry." Tears flooded her eyes as the emotions of being pulled apart and put back together at Convergence filled her chest.

"It's okay." He stroked her hair. "It was just a suggestion. I'm here regardless. You can always count on that."

"No. You're right." She looked up at his face. "What would I do without you?"

"You'd still be you because you don't need me. Nor do I want you to need me. But maybe give the RIG a rest for now."

Angie smiled. Sniffed. Then kissed him on the lips, as grateful as she'd ever been to know such a magnificent man.

"Thank you," she said.

CHAPTER
FOUR

ADVANCES IN technology had reduced the time of chemical-composition processing and DNA analysis to a fraction of what it had been when Randy entered the academy, but the interviews required to give that evidence context couldn't be rushed.

Chief Dalton wanted him on the case because of his reputation, something he tolerated only because it opened doors, which increased his efficiency. But his reputation depended on his fully engaged mind. Emotion compromised reason. The neural-chemical processes that presented as strong emotion literally changed the way a person was capable of thinking. The brain's actual logic was thrown into confusion.

So after leaving the gruesome scene that had triggered the dark emotions linked to his daughter's death, he went to Ziggly's for a beer, then home to feed Muffin, the cat he'd given his daughter for her thirteenth birthday. Nice thing about the fuzzy white cuddle-monster: Muffin never paid much mind to the world's troubles.

Satisfied that Muffin was herself, he peeled open a can of sardines in tomato sauce and picked at them with a small fork. Farm grown, like all fish these days. Fishing the ocean had been outlawed a decade earlier due to the global depletion of most oceangoing fish.

The sixth great extinction was yet one more case of society ignoring the obvious. They said that great extinction had actually started in 1970. Between then and 2020, nearly a third of all life forms on Earth had vanished, but only a few biologists had been paying attention. By the time the general public became aware that a mass extinction was underway, it was too late to reverse course. Real crab meat was now a rarity, even at the most expensive restaurants.

An hour and forty-five minutes had passed when Randy finally pulled into the station.

They were waiting in the conference room. Not just the chief and Rachel, as he'd expected, but the whole team including the district attorney, Andrew Olsen, and his lead prosecutor, Bill Evans, despite there being no one to prosecute yet.

Randy stepped through the door, eyes on Renee, who was talking to a technician at the head of the conference table. She glanced at him, then returned her attention to the technician.

"Let's cue these up, Mark."

"Yes, ma'am."

The chief stood. "Randy. Just in time. Take a seat."

The conference table was a throwback made of cherrywood scratched and worn by years of use, and the eight matching armchairs were as old, leather padding scuffed and faded. Death by a thousand butts. Typical conference rooms were far more contemporary these days, with monitors set into the table before each chair. In here, all data would be shown on the single 3D wall screen at the head of the table.

The DA sat opposite the chief. The prosecutor was behind him along the back wall, one leg folded over the other. He was probably here only to observe. Not unheard of, but they were moving fast.

Renee nodded at the tech, who tapped his pad. Crime-scene photographs filled the large screen, offering a three-dimensional view of the bodies as imaged by CSI. Long gone were the days when eyewear was required to see in three dimensions.

"Take us through them, Randy."

He hesitated. "Not much that you can't see."

"Humor me."

Randy leaned forward and set his forearms on the table. It only took a few minutes to run through the images. The clearing with two naked bodies bowing to the trees; the backpack where it had first been discovered behind those trees; closeups of the bodies from several angles before they'd been moved; more of the same after they'd been laid on their sides; images of several boot prints that may or may not have a bearing on the case.

"Conclusion, based on what we've seen?" Renee asked.

Randy took a breath, considering how these images might suggest anything other than what he'd first concluded at the scene. "Do we have an estimated time of death yet?"

"Eighteen to twenty-four hours before the bodies were found, which would put time of death late last night between six and midnight."

"A day after the rain, which might account for the boot tracks, assuming they're fresh."

"They are."

He blew out some air. "Before I suggest what seems obvious, tell me what you know about the victims. The short version."

Renee touched her pad and scrolled up. "They both attended St. Andrew's School of Higher Learning, advanced students on a fast-track program. Very high IQs. Both came from wealthy families and had access to the latest VR technology. Strange how dead heading appeals to both the most intelligent and dropouts in equal measure."

"You've confirmed that they were Dead Heads?"

"Confirmed by their parents. They both have invisible markers for VR tracking tattooed on their bodies. Naturally, they were both in the closet. Both fifteen years old. But I don't think this is a case of two kids getting caught up in simple games. They were into something pretty deep."

So . . . Another Dead Head case. Following the public outcry against dead heading, incidents involving VR crime had actually spiked rather than abated.

He cleared his throat. "On the surface it seems plain that the perpetrator or perpetrators strangled Timothy Blake and Clair Milton before crushing their skulls and carving the unseeing eye into their backs. The attack was methodical, maybe professional, and it occurred at an unknown location. The victims were transported to Oak Hill Park, where they were bound and positioned in the posture of prayer, similar to the victims of Raymond Smith."

Renee leaned forward. "You're suggesting the unsub is a copycat? Religiously motivated?"

"One of the victims was the son of a known religious leader, which might support that possibility, but I don't think so. Copycat crimes tend to be carried out by less intelligent and less imaginative psychopaths who are sloppy. This may be posed to look like a copycat crime, but it strikes me as too obvious, and carefully organized. Like I said, possibly a professional hit."

"All right." She sounded ambivalent. "And the backpack? Why leave it at the scene?"

"Whoever did this clearly wanted the bodies and the backpack to be found. Anyone who had the capacity to carry out such a calculated and violent attack could have easily hidden the bodies."

"So it appears on first analysis," Renee said. "All in agreement?"

No one objected.

"Good. Thankfully, the rest of the evidence tells a different story. It's looking more and more like the victims were killed at the scene by a novice, which makes our job easier. The last thing we need is to be hunting down professionals."

Her comment caught Randy off guard. The rest of what evidence?

Renee nodded at the technician. "The phone, Mark?"

Neither the DA nor the prosecutor had spoken a word. They clearly knew something Randy didn't.

The screen filled with an image of Timothy Blake's messaging screen. Even the most secure phones using quantum encryption could now be easily accessed by law enforcement due to laws that gave them a back door. Personal privacy was a distant memory for all but those technologically savvy enough to remain hidden.

On the screen appeared a string of text messages from and to one Jamie Hamilton.

"These are just a few messages going back the last few weeks," Mark said, scrolling the mirrored phone in his gloved hands. "Here we go."

Jamie: Play Dead tonight?
Timothy: yup
Jamie: mobile?
Timothy: meet at clairs

Then another a few days later.

Jamie: we gotta go deeper tonight
Timothy: clairs freakin I dont think its a good idea
Jamie: you promised if I told you about the key youd go all the way and I need
a better rig
Timothy: no
Jamie: please
Timothy: no

Randy was struck by how juvenile Jamie in particular came across.

Renee indicated the screen. "It appears Play Dead is a game of some kind, presumably of the Dead Head variety. Nothing's turned up on our initial search, so it could be black market. They go back and forth on it, and you'll see that Jamie gets progressively more aggressive."

Another, a few days later:

Jamie: if you were a real dh youd go deep
Jamie: fake like the rest
Timothy: leave us alone freak

The *dh* was short for Dead Head. Randy was again struck by how juvenile the texts were. Maybe typical gaming banter, but in the context of the brutal murders, rather disturbing.

"The last few texts tell the real story," Renee said. On cue, Mark flipped through the thread to the end.

Jamie: one last time to show you how to get out
Timothy: we don't want in or out

Jamie: it doesn't work that way cause youre already in and I can show you how to get out but it has to be in person
Jamie: theyre watching

Timothy responded six hours later.

Timothy: one last time at my house
Jamie: no at oak
Timothy: my house
Jamie: your house is bugged
Timothy: the whole world is bugged
Jamie: one last time at the park
Timothy: youll tell us everything?
Jamie: youll beat it

Three hours later Timothy sent his final message.
Timothy: on at 9 same place
Jamie: bring three rigs

Mark set the phone down. Renee put her elbows on the table and addressed Rachel. "How does this read to you, Rachel?"

"Well. Seems pretty clear," Rachel said. "Play Dead's a black market Deep Dive game that's obviously dangerous. Without seeing the game, we don't know, but sounds like something that would take you deep enough to lose connection to this world." She crossed her arms and stared at the coffee cup in front of her, speaking now as much to herself as anyone. "Maybe worse. To literally play dead."

"As in kill or be killed, perhaps, or as in some kind of cultish suicide pact, although we can rule suicide out," Renee said.

"Right," Rachel continued. "Jamie Hamilton sounds juvenile to me. Someone who maybe introduced the others to the game through a key of some kind. Probably a key drive. Could be the game resides on the key drive and it is required to play the game, which is why they have to be in the same space? Just a guess there. Timothy and Clair find the game disturbing and want out, but Jamie can't let go. He's also concerned that their activities are being monitored, maybe within the game itself? A GPS tag that tracks anyone in the game?"

She looked at Randy, who gave her a shallow nod. *Go on.*

"Jamie gets them to agree to play one last time at the park, using the mobile RIGs he asks them to bring, maybe because he doesn't have one. Once in the game, things go wrong. Maybe very wrong—these games can get people to do some pretty insane things. The Tokyo suicides come to mind. For all we know, *that* was Play Dead."

Two weeks earlier, three youths had leaped or been pushed from a high-rise in Tokyo while dead heading. No one knew yet whether they had been talked into jumping or jumped willingly, because they'd been in the darknet beyond a quantum firewall. As soon as their RIGs shattered on the concrete, their history was lost.

Rachel continued. "Whatever happened in the game, it broke Jamie. Pushed him into rage. He disengages and strangles the others while they're still in the game, which would explain why there's no struggle. He crushes their heads and marks their backs." She shrugged. "Maybe he was still in the game himself. Of course, this is all just a guess, but seems conceivable to me. Assuming Play Dead's that kind of game."

"Why no blood?" the chief asked.

"I would assume they brought a blanket or something to play on. 3D imaging shows compression of the undergrowth consistent with that."

"Okay, but he left the backpack with their clothes and phone. Why?"

Rachel shook her head. "You got me. We need to know more about Jamie."

Renee exchanged a look with the prosecutor, Bill Evans, who still sat against the far wall, one leg still folded over the other, arms crossed. "Good enough?"

"It's a start." It was the first he'd said.

"Hold on a sec." Randy glanced between them. "Your conclusions assume they were in a game. I'm not willing to concede that yet. The evidence points to a premeditated execution, not a crime of passion. Crimes of passion are quick and dirty, not the kind where you take time to arrange bodies, smash heads, and go through the gruesome process of stripping the bodies and carving symbols into your victims' backs. This killer was calculating and knew to strangle his victims first, minimizing blood flow. Then there's the fact he took the RIGs but left the phone, the one piece of evidence that would implicate him. It all reads more like a setup to me."

District Attorney Andrew Olsen pushed himself back from the table and stood to his full height, which couldn't be an inch over five foot five. Some would call him heavy. Randy called him soft. Bald, but with more hair on his body than a bear. A simple laser procedure would have easily rid his body of all that fur, as most preferred these days.

Olsen shoved his hands in the pockets of his gray pinstriped slacks and paced slowly up the table, sniffed, and scrunched up his nose as if clearing an itch.

"True, we have what appear on the surface to be inconsistencies, I grant you that. But we still have plenty of evidence to come in, including the hair found on Timothy's back. When all the notes are played, I think we'll find this to be Jamie Hamilton's song."

"That's pretty bold," Randy said. "You obviously have more on Jamie Hamilton. Who is he?"

Olsen glanced at the chief, who scanned her pad.

"He's nineteen, a large boy," she said. "Lives with his mother, Corina Hamilton. They're in an old house just south of St. Andrew's, where Jamie's a sophomore. He's a charity case for the school. Socially awkward with a history of violence."

Which meant little, Randy thought. A kid with a history of violence didn't automatically add up to the brutal murder and carving of two kids.

"That's it?"

Olsen stepped in. "When he was thirteen, our boy nearly killed another student who was evidently bullying him. We know he's more than capable of snapping under duress."

Olsen pointed at the texts still on the screen.

"We have correlating evidence putting him at the scene, which happens to be within walking distance of the school and all three residences. That gives us opportunity. As of yet we have no evidence that a vehicle was used to transport the bodies into the park, and it's highly unlikely those bodies were hauled there on foot. They had to have been killed on site."

"It's only been a few hours since the bodies were discovered," Randy said.

"True. But the ground was soft from the rain and any vehicle would have left tracks. If we find tracks, we go with it. But for now, we have only Jamie at the scene on foot with clear intentions to press the others into a game they didn't want to play. That and the fact that the RIGs are missing, likely stolen, may satisfy motive."

He returned his hand to his pocket. "We also have means. Hamilton's a big boy, easily capable of the crime in question. The only thing we don't have is a witness and a weapon. At least not yet. Unless the evidence points us in another direction, I strongly suggest you focus your efforts on Jamie Hamilton."

Randy stared at Olsen for a long second. The DA's logic couldn't be faulted, but things still didn't add up. Why strip the bodies? Why leave the phone? Why the posturing? Why fold up the clothes and place them in the backpack? What was Play Dead?

They were rushing.

"Fine," he said, "but this could just as easily have been the work of a professional who planted evidence. At this point, that's as likely as anything else."

Olsen dipped his head. "That goes without saying. We're just getting started, but you have to understand that this case is going to blow up. I have no idea which idiot leaked this to the press, but they're going live with the details first thing tomorrow. It was all I could do to get them to hold off until then. It's a Dead Head murder by all accounts, and nothing we do will change that perception. The whole world is going to know about this case within twenty-four hours."

Randy sat back. "We take no shortcuts. Isn't that what you said, Chief?"

"Absolutely," she agreed.

He drummed his fingers on the table. "Well, then, let's dig into Jamie Hamilton and see who we're dealing with. I'll make the call as soon as we finish. Anything on the neighborhood canvassing?"

"Nothing useful," Rachel offered. "But considering time of death was middle of the night in an area without traffic at that hour, I doubt anything will turn up. My talk with the Blakes was almost useless. As you can understand, both parents are crushed."

"And Clair's parents?"

"The Miltons are with friends. It's going to be a long night."

The group sat in silence for a moment. Most of those present had their own children and vivid imaginations. Rachel avoided looking at Randy.

Bill Evans, the one who would do the heavy lifting on the case once all the evidence was in, stood up at the back of the conference room. Tall and thin with a soft face that inspired confidence. He rarely lost a case, probably because he only prosecuted cases that were airtight. A fair man by all accounts.

"If you'll excuse me, I have some work to attend to. Unless there's something else."

"I think that about covers it," Renee said.

Evans studied Randy for a moment. "I assume I don't need to explain to anyone why the governor's extremely eager for closure on this. As you all know, she's running on a platform that calls for far-reaching regulation of all virtual reality technology, both domestically and abroad. A Dead Head case like this could make or break Judith Patterson's presidential run. The election is in six months." He shrugged. "Just the way it is."

Bill Evans dipped his head and left the room.

Randy stood and addressed Rachel. "We have to find out what Play Dead refers to. Look into anything and everything using the term. And finding the key drive mentioned in the texts would be a windfall. Take a run out to the Milton house first thing, see if they're willing to cooperate. We need forensics in the victims' rooms as soon as possible. You know the drill."

"You got it."

"I'll handle Jamie Hamilton." To Renee: "Please notify me the second you get anything from the lab. We need more than a few texts to put Hamilton at the scene."

"Get me his DNA and I will."

He nodded and walked for the door with Rachel close behind.

"And, Randy?"

He looked back at the chief. "Yes?"

"I can't notify you of squat if you don't answer your phone."

CHAPTER
FIVE

ANGIE AWOKE from a dream of being chased down an alleyway by another Angie, who was trying to get her to stop running. Who had blond hair and sharp teeth set into an otherwise beautiful face wearing blood-red lipstick. Angie wanted nothing to do with her.

She sat up with a gasp. The room was dark except for the dim glow of the nightlight.

"Angie?"

Darey rolled over in bed beside her. Felicia would probably say the dream represented her innermost fears. Science had long ago established that over 90 percent of our beliefs were hidden in the subconscious, like coding in a game, unknown by the player. It could be said that regardless of what people said they believed, they didn't really know their beliefs. Their lives were manifestations of their true, hidden beliefs—the 90 percent—and not what they thought they believed.

Which explained why people acted in ways contrary to what they claimed to believe, professions of religious faith being the most obvious example. Angie wasn't sure about all the specifics, but there was clearly far more to belief than the rank and file realized.

"It's okay," she whispered, sinking back to her pillow. "Just a dream. I'm good."

"A flashback?"

"No, just a stupid dream. Go back to sleep."

He propped himself up on one elbow and looked at the clock. "It's almost six. I need to get up anyway." He slid out from under the covers. "Sleep."

Wearing the same black and white pinstriped pajamas he always wore, Darey eased his feet into the slippers placed just so on the floor and stood. Stretched.

He glanced down at her. "You sure you're okay?"

"I'm good."

She never understood why people wore pajamas to bed. Wasn't the purpose of sheets to feel the cool soft luxury they offered? She'd convinced Darey to sleep in his boxers for a full week once before he'd reverted to his PJs. She'd smiled, but neither of them had made mention of it. If that's what he liked, so be it.

The next week, she'd borrowed a pair of his PJs and slept in them for five nights. They extended a full two feet below her heels and got all tangled up around her feet. She'd concluded that wearing PJs was like wearing a strait-jacket. Though that wasn't fair, she liked the hyperbole because what was life without similes that painted the grays of life with wild color?

She laid in bed for all of five minutes, asking sleep if it wanted to take her again, then flung the sheets off and hurried into the bathroom after Darey, who was already in the shower—a castle-like chamber with no door and three showerheads on three different walls. Ten people could shower in Darey's dream shower at the same time and not once touch. Okay, another hyperbole.

Angie brushed her teeth, threw her hair back in a ponytail, pulled on some black sweatpants and one of Darey's burnt-orange UT football shirts, and left Darey whistling in his chamber.

They said routine would support her reintegration, and she was thinking they were right. Except for the one stress-induced whiteout she'd had the previous evening, her night had been unspectacular in the best way.

She and Darey had gone out to Chuy's and eaten Tex-Mex—cheap and pedestrian, which was her preference. They'd laughed over margaritas and chowed down on nacho-stuffed burritos.

After returning home, she'd raced around the house with Sally, playing keep-away with a slobber-soaked knotted rope for a good half an hour before collapsing next to Darey on the couch. Curled there under his arm, she'd listened to his steady breathing as he read some law journal.

There was no more talk of the Red Protocol and that was a relief. In fact, there was little talk of anything. They were just being together, like the two trees at the end of Kahlil Gibran's ancient poem, which Darey had read at their wedding:

Give your hearts, but not in each other's keeping.
For only the hand of life can contain your hearts.
And stand together yet not too near together;
For the pillars of the temple stand apart,
And the oak tree and the Cyprus grow not in each other's shadows.

Angie hummed no tune in particular as she prepared coffee her way: thirteen ounces dark roast, a teaspoon of ghee butter, a tablespoon of MCT oil (good for the brain), a shot of vanilla flavoring. Blended in a flask and poured into a black mug with the words *Wake Up* on one side and *Dead Head* on the other.

She and Darey ate toast and eggs together, bantering about his cases and whether they should take their annual pilgrimage to Europe, considering Angie had a book to write. But they didn't discuss the book itself. Not once did the terms *virtual reality* or *Dead Head* even come up. She had no intention of going anywhere near virtual worlds for the next few days.

Darey headed out at seven thirty, accepting her reassurance that she'd be perfectly okay. She would stay home today and catch up on her reading. Maybe later head to Whole Foods—the brick-and-mortar one—to restock, because his attempts had failed quite miserably. All was well and life was back to the way it had been a week earlier.

She was on a second cup of coffee—this one without all the fixings— lounging on the sofa in front of the 3D wall screen, watching the morning show, when the news that would change her day came on.

It was Marsha Straford, a talking head down at KPCW news feed, standing at the yellow tape that cordoned off a crime scene at Oak Hill Park. The reporter kept tucking her wind-whipped hair behind her ears to no avail.

"The victims have been identified as Timothy Blake and Clair Milton, two fifteen-year-olds who attended St. Andrew's just up the street. Both were advanced students in an accelerated program for children with high IQs, and both came from affluent families well known in the community. Now they are both dead, brutally murdered by a killer who left them naked with an unseeing eye carved onto their backs."

Angie's heart skipped a beat. The victims found at Oak Hill were Dead Heads?

"Early unverified reports suggest that the victims were at least recreationally involved in dead heading, the well-known and often dangerous states of disassociation that have become a subject of debate leading into the presidential elections. The game in this case is reportedly called Play Dead, a darknet experience of unknown origin. The victims were evidently playing this game with another student from St. Andrew's, a sophomore named Jamie Hamilton who went by the handle Fluffy Puppy . . ."

Angie absently set her cup down on the end table, eyes glued to the feed, which now showed a picture of Jamie Hamilton. She knew him! Didn't she? Maybe not in real life, but somewhere. More was being said but she wasn't hearing the words.

Only then did it occur to her: he looked like the boy in the flashback she'd had yesterday by Town Lake. How was that possible? Maybe her brain was mixing things up.

Either way, this was a Dead Head murder, and that alone pulled at her. The fact that the crime had occurred less than ten miles away from where she sat only drew her further in. She caught herself picking at her lower lip and pulled her hand away.

A ticker at the bottom of the screen warned viewers that some images about to be displayed were graphic and not suitable for children. This was followed by an aerial drone shot of two white bodies that could be seen through the foliage. Disturbing, no doubt.

But Angie's mind was still on the game, Play Dead.

She was thinking it would make a great title for her new book; she was thinking she already knew something about Fluffy Puppy; she was thinking she had to find out immediately; she was thinking that the best way to do that was in a virtual chat room on the darknet.

She was thinking that she shouldn't be thinking these thoughts right now, and then she was thinking nothing, because in the tension of that moment, the world went white.

Just white. Another whiteout. No sound, no images, no smells or sensory input of any kind. Not even thoughts. Only the awareness that she was looking at an infinite sea of whiteness.

A few seconds later the living room flashed back into her full perception. And when it did, Angie knew she had to know more about Play Dead and the Dead Head murders.

She had to enter the virtual space where all answers hid and find out who knew what about a Deep Dive game called Play Dead.

She was already halfway across the living room before she remembered her promise to Darey. Yes, but that was before this. Darey would understand. Heck, Darey might even insist. Or so she told herself as she hurried downstairs, through the rec room, past Darey's pool table and down a short hall to a sealed door rarely opened by anyone but her.

She pressed her thumb on the keypad and her print activated the release. She pushed the door open. Low amber-hued light flooded the room. She closed the door behind her and scanned her 'office.'

'Welcome To The Deep Dive' was printed in iridescent white on the dark-blue wall directly in front of her. The main processing box sat next to a gray desk, a desk printed from a block of plastic with a fancy name she'd long forgotten—a birthday gift from Darey. On the desk sat two screens, one 2D flat panel, and a larger forty-inch 3D monitor.

Her aging but quite serviceable Deep Dive RIG, the DHC (short for Dead Head Chair), sat empty on the opposite side of the room. But it was the full-body haptic-feedback suit in the closet, not the reclining chair, that worked the real magic. The recliner was hardly more than a power source and a conduit for the Quantum Processing Unit. The QPU resided in her main processing box, still sometimes referred to as a computer.

Angie felt the familiar rush of adrenaline along her nerves, accentuated by the distant thought that she had to be careful, having just come out of the Red Protocol. She wouldn't use the DHC chair now, naturally. Darey was right, going deep so soon could be dangerous. She just needed to check with her sources, see what the darknet knew.

That's what she told herself. It made sense, but her heart was telling her, *Hurry, hurry, get in there and see what's really happening. Find yourself in there. Be yourself.*

She slid into her regular office chair, flipped on the QPU, slipped her sensor gloves on, grabbed her shallow RIG and lowered it over her head. Like many closet Dead Heads, she'd opted to tattoo twelve invisible circuits on her joints to track movement in a shallow dive.

Just a quick look, she told herself.

The world went dark for a moment, then lit up again in a room that resembled her office in one corner but was otherwise vastly altered. She looked over her shoulder and scanned the engagement room she'd customized to her liking.

At its center stood a ten-foot circular table made of a translucent polymer. A dozen chairs, each with its own monitor, hugged the table's circumference. Her war table, she called it. She'd spend a thousand hours at the table, meeting and exchanging ideas and news with people in photorealistic VR.

Soft blue lighting overhead cast the entire room in what she called 'chill.' The rest of the room was divided into four seating areas, each with its own theme—one retro to the 1960s; one old-school techno with old VR RIGs and paraphernalia copied from *The Matrix,* one of the first movies to bring virtual reality into the mainstream; one with a beach-resort-style cabana; and one populated with frayed overstuffed recliners and a shaggy carpet, something you might reclaim from a dump.

The fourth was her favorite and, apart from the main war table, where Angie held most of her engagements.

The walls of her virtual office were filled with replicas of scientific drawings and artful posters of theories from the last two millennia, a reminder that everything that was believed at one point would be understood in a totally different light in days yet to come.

But today, she was only dipping in. She wasn't even going to the table.

She spun back to her gray desk and engaged Lover Boy, her personal AI assistant, by tapping a small red circle on the upper left corner of the screen. It pulsed to show that her AI was online.

An image of a red key blinked to life, reminding her that if she wanted privacy, she should use the physical key, which would engage the quantum encryption housed on the key.

She grabbed the key from her drawer and slipped it into one of the slots on the processing bot. The key on the screen blinked green. She was behind the key's quantum firewall. Without an exact physical copy of her key, no one could trace her identity. She was simply Lover Boy, the name she'd borrowed from an old 1980s band.

"Good morning, Lover Boy."

"Good morning, Angie. It's been a while."

"Yeah, I've been busy."

"And I've been sleeping."

"Nice. I guess I have too, just in a different way. Good to hear your voice."

"Yours too, Angie. What can I do for you today?"

She'd programmed Lover Boy using readily available apps, then finetuning him to respond in a vernacular she liked.

"Can you scan public domain news feeds for anything on a game called Play Dead?"

Immediately, LB came back.

"There are 213 news stories referring to a game called Play Dead. All bear today's date."

Her heart sank. "Nothing earlier?" Lover Boy made no mistakes, but he answered anyway.

"That is correct."

"Can you compare the stories and compile a report of unique facts?"

A short pause.

"All 213 have one original source linked to an incident in Austin, Texas, with only minor variances. Would you like me to send the report to your portal?"

"Sure." But she already knew the report would contain the same information she'd heard on the television. She'd read it carefully later. "Can you run the same search on all accessible chats and social media?"

Another pause.

"There are two million, five hundred and thirty-three thousand, nine hundred and seventy-eight mentions of the game Play Dead within my reach of social interactions. All appear to be derivative of the data found in the public domain news feeds."

Figured. The Play Dead murder was already coffee-table talk in the virtual world and spreading like wildfire.

"Okay. Search the same domain for any information on a student named Jamie Hamilton from Austin, Texas."

"There are two million—"

"Scratch that, I don't want banter on Jamie Hamilton. Only public information that predates the mentions of Play Dead. Who is Jamie Hamilton?"

The answer came back immediately. "Jamie Hamilton is nineteen. A student in the tenth grade attending St. Andrew's School of Higher Learning in Austin, Texas. His mother is Corina Hamilton. No record of a father. One recorded offense, no details."

Silence.

"That's it?"

"I have access to his school file, which shows a GPA of 4.1 in the accelerated learning program. He successfully completed calculus in the ninth grade with a score of—"

"Never mind. There's no other public information on him? Driver's license, birth record, anything like that?"

He was born in 2030 at St. David's Medical Center in Austin, Texas, father unknown. No registered driver's license. No voting registration."

"What about his own social media?"

"There are no social media accounts linked to Jamie Hamilton."

In a day and age when most lives were essentially lived in the public eye, the lack of information meant he was well versed in hiding his identity, which likely meant Jamie was no slouch in the digital world.

"What about medical records?"

"There are no medical records."

"None at all, or just sealed?"

"There are no indications that medical records exist."

Strange.

"Okay. Anything on the handle Fluffy Puppy?"

This time the pause lasted a good second.

"There are four million, nine hundred—"

"Anything on Fluffy Puppy in my personal log?"

"You've engaged with seventeen personalities called Fluffy Puppy. None of the engagements lasted longer than six minutes. Would you like me to send the engagements to your portal?"

"Please."

"Done."

She would get to them later. It was time to go deeper.

"Take me to 10-24-oeht, protocol Tayo."

"Pinging darknet 10-24-oeht protocol Tayo."

If there was anyone in the darknet who might have heard of Play Dead, it would be Tayo. They'd met through several referrals four years earlier during her early research for *Righteous*. Tayo wasn't his real name, naturally—she couldn't even be sure he was really a he. Or that any of the history in his profile was factual. In the virtual world Tayo was a handsome man in his midthirties with dark hair and a lean, muscular build who identified as asexual, part of what made him appealing to her. But all that could be easily manipulated, and identities were almost universally fabricated. For all she knew, he was a nineteen-year-old lesbian from Havana who made her living in the darknet, destroying other Dead Heads in games that paid out in cryptocurrency.

Okay, so maybe not just nineteen, because Tayo was more plugged in than anyone Angie had engaged, including those from various government agencies.

Tayo's reply came ten seconds later in a jumble of letters that morphed into a single question written across her screen. *Your place or mine?*

"Mine," she said. "Shallow."

Shallow, because she wanted him to know she wasn't interested in going deep. Somehow she'd become one of his favorite players, and he had a knack for talking her into some of the most immersive experiences on the net.

A soft ping announced Tayo's arrival behind her. "Hello, beautiful."

She swiveled in her chair and looked at the smiling man who stood before her. Bright green eyes that she was sure didn't resemble his real eyes. Shaggy dark hair, clean shaven face, steam-punk garb—he looked like something out of one of the old *Mad Max* movies. She guessed he was in a Deep Dive RIG or a holo-room.

The person he saw as her was female, blond, five three. Brown eyes, soft face with full lips, dressed in jeans and a T-shirt that read *Catch Me If You Can*. He knew her only as Lover Boy even though Lover Boy presented as a woman. He had no idea that the woman named Lover Boy was the author of the ubiquitous book called *Righteous*.

At least, she hoped he didn't.

She leaned back, crossing her legs and arms. "Hello, Tayo. Been a while."

"Too long, my dear."

"Right. I don't have long. I need some help."

Tayo cocked his right brow and paced, left arm across his chest, right hand stroking his chin. "Doesn't everyone? But you know there's always a price."

"I'm not in the price-paying mood. Just some simple information."

He walked to a virtual office chair ten feet from her desk, rolled it over, and plopped down. If he was in a Deep Dive RIG, he would be experiencing the chair exactly as he might any real chair, from the way it rolled to the way it felt on his seat and back when he sat down. All the sensory feedback his mind required to experience the chair was provided by his suit and the virtual environment.

She, on the other hand, using a shallow RIG, saw this virtual room as real, but her bubble of perception constantly collapsed with the limitations of movement and touch. For a true immersive experience, she would need the DHC and her body suit. Unless she was in the Red Protocol, which was a whole different story.

"You really need to change the décor now and then, LB," he said, glancing around. "We could turn this whole den of yours into a Batman cave in no time at all."

"No thanks. Not really into superheroes of the imaginary kind."

"Of course you aren't. You still think you're a real one."

"Funny. Seriously, I don't have time for this. Just a quick question."

"You could have messaged me."

"I don't want it online."

"You think my space can be hacked?"

"No. Just habit, I guess."

"A good habit." He spread his hands. "So here I am. And you want to know about Play Dead."

She blinked. "Actually, yes. How—"

"Because the whole world wants to know about Play Dead. But like I said, there's always a price."

"Is what you know valuable?"

He stared off at the war table. "Depends on what it's worth to you."

"What do you want?"

Eyes back on hers. A shallow shrug. "I've made some alterations to my side project, Paradise. A new level. I need someone—"

"No," she said.

"No? I haven't even told you what I've done."

"Yeah, but no. I'm off the Deep Dive right now."

"Don't pull that on me. We're all Deep Dive, all the time."

"I'm off any virtual Deep Dive. Doctor's orders."

"Well, then I guess you're out of luck." He made as if to stand.

Angie sat up. "Hold on. Just hold on a sec. You can get anyone to dive into Paradise with you. Look, I just need to know what's in the darknet. I wouldn't ask if it wasn't important."

"And I wouldn't ask you to check out my new level in Paradise if it wasn't as important. An architect lives for the impact his work has on others, just like any other artist, right? Without you, I'm dead."

"Don't be ridiculous. There are hundreds of thousands who would kill to dive into one of your worlds!"

"But none of them are you. None of them think the way you think. All I'm asking is ten minutes. Just drop in and pop out. That's all."

She considered his request, unsure why she shouldn't take him up on it. She'd played more games with him than she could count. Probably hundreds. Lover Boy would know. Yikes! Better not ask the AI.

"Who's forcing you to stay away?" he asked. "These murders freaking you out? It's not what you think."

"What do I think?"

He flashed a grin. "Ten minutes. That's all."

They stared at each other for several long breaths as she considered his request, no longer sure why she was refusing. No one was forcing her hand. There were no doctor's orders, just general guidelines. Darey had asked her to stay away, but that was for her sake, not his. When she told him about this, he would only smile and say, "Well, that's my Angie."

Tayo ended the stalemate. "Fine. I'll tell you what I know. But you owe me, right?"

"Of course."

He sat back, elbows on the chair arms, tips of his fingers pressed together.

"No one I know's heard of Play Dead. Not a peep. Not at the CIA, not at NSA, nothing in the deep dark, and definitely nothing but pablum in the public domain. That doesn't mean it *doesn't* exist, but if it does, only a handful of people know about it, and they're deeper than dark."

"That's it? That's all you have?"

"Well, that's not nothing. It means Play Dead's either really serious content that someone wants to keep hidden, or someone's making it up."

Or Tayo was hiding something from her.

"That's it for Play Dead, but there's more," he said.

She anticipated him. "Jamie Hamilton?"

"Bingo. More accurately, Fluffy Puppy. He's a Dead Head, no doubt, but not just some high school student. He's a top leaguer. I mean, this guy can play with the best. A true gamer's gamer who's beat everything thrown at him."

"How do you know all this? And why don't I know it, if he's that good?"

"You don't know because he stays deep. I know because it's my business to know what others don't. I came across his handle a year ago and have been watching him ever since. Thing is, I don't think he uses a Deep Dive RIG. Probably can't afford it."

She thought about that. "So what's this supposed to mean?"

"People that good don't have the same kinds of minds that most gamers have. I don't know anything about him beyond his darknet activities, but this guy's a corker. For all we know he's a coder and Play Dead's his game."

And they're going to nail him to the wall for the murders, she thought. Another psycho created by the system.

But something about Play Dead still drew her and she wondered what it would be like to throw herself at the case the way she had writing *Righteous*. Maybe another true crime would make a better follow-up than an exposé on the benefits and dangers of virtual reality.

"You think he did it?" she asked.

"Me? I have no idea. But he's very different, and very different people are more likely to be capable of these kinds of things than your average Dead Head. Trust me, it can break you. I should know." He eyed her curiously. "You know the case of Raymond Smith? There was a book about him."

It was the way he asked the question that kept her silent.

"You know, *Righteous*," he said. "Surely you've heard of it."

"Sure. What about it?"

"She had a point. The author, Angie something or other."

"Channing," she said.

"Yeah. Angie Channing. This whole thing . . ." Tayo looked around the room, waving a hand at her virtual chamber. "It's going to bring the world to its knees one of these days."

"Maybe."

"Just a matter of time," he said.

Yeah, she thought. If you only knew what kind of technology is coming next. But she had no interest in going there with him.

"Anything else?"

"Nada. That's it. Why so interested?"

"For the same reason everyone else is."

"Indeed. They're going to shut us down."

"I doubt that."

"Sooner or later," he said. And maybe he was right. Maybe the book she was about to write would be the domino that toppled the whole thing. So maybe she shouldn't write it.

Angie sighed. "Okay. Thank you. I owe you."

Tayo stood, eyes tempting once more. "Want to pay up now? Just ten minutes. Promise you won't be disappointed."

She saw no reason not to humor him.

"Okay."

"Okay?"

"Sure." She swiveled around and tapped the interface to bring up RIG options. "Give me two minutes to suit up and I'll meet you there."

He snapped his fingers, delighted. "I knew I could count on you! Two minutes, my dear. I'll send you the address."

His form vanished from the room.

Angie felt the familiar rush of anticipation coursing through her. They said that the reward centers in the brain triggered by a Deep Dive were the same as those triggered by hard drugs. But then, those same reward centers were also triggered by food, sex, sports, politics, special relationships—in other words, all the rewards of life.

Humans, it turned out, were addicted to life.

Angie slipped out of her gloves and head piece, hurried to the closet across her office, and pulled the door wide. The black suit on the hanger looked like a thin wet suit used for warm-water ocean diving, but with full legs and arms.

She ripped off her shirt and dropped her sweats, then quickly pulled on the haptic-feedback suit, legs first, then torso, then arms, right up to the neck. When activated, thousands of thin circuits in contact with her skin used electrical signals to trigger her muscles, mimicking pressure and resistance, which the brain interpreted as pain, or pleasure, or an itch, or any of the sensations touch offered to the real human body.

The real technological breakthrough had been mimicking movement, which took some training to master. Once acclimated, a player could remain still in a Dead Head Chair and feel like they were running.

In the Red Protocol, no suit or training was required for a seamless Deep Dive into a virtual world indistinguishable from the real world. In that world she experienced hunger, liver pains, beating heart, tears—everything. Scary real. Acoustic imaging. Jake Barnes's Red Protocol was going to change the world.

Tayo was waiting.

She dropped into her Dead Head Chair, snugged her feet in the boots, pulled on her gloves, and lowered the Deep Dive helmet over her head. Then tapped a button that tilted the chair back so she was reclining.

"Engage Deep Dive, Lover Boy. Take me to Tayo's Paradise coordinates."

"Travel well," he said in that soothing voice of his. The world went black. Then came to life in brilliant color and dimension.

She was in.

Dark-haired Angie, who'd grown up in Saudi Arabia and France, was now a blond woman named Lover Boy who'd grown up in Manhattan. She was standing on a cliff overlooking a huge sinkhole with a waterfall on the far side, and meadows bordered by lush pines and aspen, populated with sheep and cattle and some wild horses galloping along the eastern wall.

She was close to the edge, staring at a lake several hundred yards below her, and she drew back to still her vertigo. In every way, Tayo's landscape looked utterly real. Many Deep Dive gaming spaces were fantastical, bending reality, but not the world he'd created. They could be in Colorado or Arizona and not know it.

"You really should consider a new outfit, my dear," Tayo said.

She turned to see him sitting on a boulder, chewing on a blade of grass. He was dressed in a black business suit with white sneakers, no tie, dark hair slicked back.

"May I?" he asked, flicking the grass he'd been chewing on to one side.

"May you what?"

"Dress you."

She looked down at her outfit—light Nike boots, black calf-length leggings, neon and black athletic zip-up top. Her blond hair was pulled back in a ponytail.

"What's wrong with this?"

"It's an austere occasion, my dear," he said, standing and indicating his own dress. "We're mismatched!"

"Be that as it may, I like what I'm wearing."

"You look like you've just come from the gym!"

"We won't be active?"

"Why, yes. Yes, we will. Good point." He snapped his fingers and his attire changed from business to athletic—black jogging pants and a tight-fitting stylish blue shirt that could double for all-day wear.

Tayo approached and took her hand. She stared down at their entwined fingers. In every way but the most subtle, she was holding the hand of another human, standing on a cliff with wind blowing through their hair. She ran her thumb over his knuckles, taken back to the Red Protocol for a moment.

So real. If the world only knew just how real it could really get. Many Dead Heads used virtual reality for romantic hookups, for obvious reasons. She'd once tried to get Darey to explore themselves in a virtual space, but he would have none of it, and she hadn't pushed. Maybe one day . . .

"You okay?"

She looked up at Tayo, amazed again by the clarity of his green eyes.

"You ever wonder whether you're in a game?"

"We are in a game," he said.

"I mean real life. Maybe it's a game and we don't know it."

Tayo grinned and winked. "Isn't that the point of a Deep Dive? To confuse the two?"

"And are you ever? Confused, I mean."

He scanned the horizon. "I used to play with the idea of it, but no, not anymore. If you ever feel like you're getting lost, just pay attention to your stomach. Simulations can't replicate cramps or other internal pains the same way reality does."

But you don't know the Red Protocol, she thought.

"You sure you're okay?" he asked.

"I'm good."

"Then let me show you what I've done." He led her to the edge of the cliff. The lake far below was blue and still.

"Ready?"

"Ready for what? We're going to jump?"

"But of course!"

"That fall will kill us!" Dying in a virtual game wouldn't kill you, but it hurt.

"It won't, trust me. Jump with me. It's the fastest way to get to the level I've created under these cliffs."

She considered it for a moment. During her reintegration at Convergence, Jake Barnes had stated that while whiteouts couldn't be experienced in a virtual reality, they could be triggered by VR and might intensify afterward. She really shouldn't have come.

On the other hand, she was writing a book on the subject. It was her job to know everything there was to know about the Deep Dive.

"Okay then," she breathed. "Let's do this."

She released his hand, took two long steps and dove into the air, arms spread wide. Then tucked her head, executed two flips, and straightened to greet the placid surface rushing up toward her.

Behind, Tayo whooped. "That's it, Lover Boy! Dive with me. Dive Deep!"

Angie did dive deep. Into the water like a pelican diving for a sardine. Through the lake. And into Tayo's new game, which was full of delight and danger and laughter and more fun than she'd had in a long time.

Maybe half an hour later, she emerged from the game breathing hard, heart pounding, staring into blackness. She reached up and pulled off her head RIG, disoriented.

"Lover Boy, how long have I been in?"

"You've been in the Deep Dive five hours and twenty-eight minutes," came the soothing voice.

That long?

Angie scrambled out of her suit, checked her phone, grateful to see that no one had called, hurried from the room and ran upstairs. The house was quiet.

She collapsed on the couch and looked around, half expecting Tayo to come busting through the door. He didn't, naturally. She was back in reality. Despite having many stressful moments in Tayo's game, they hadn't triggered a single whiteout. So Jake Barnes was right—you couldn't experience whiteouts in a virtual space.

What's more, her stomach was growling. This was as real as real got, confusion about mixed realities settled once and for all. She had to cling to that fact or risk losing her mind. And she had to let go of her questions about Play Dead.

But who was Jamie Hamilton really? Why was she so drawn to him? Maybe she should at least try to meet him.

CHAPTER
SIX

OLD BEE CAVE ROAD, nearly deserted at this time of day, wound through a patchwork of pine and scrub oaks in the hill country west of Austin. Not too many sparsely populated neighborhoods still existed in these parts, but this was one. Rachel had spent an hour at Clair Milton's home where Randy had picked her up. He would circle back and conduct a second interview in a day or two, after CSI had processed her room. People's memories were invariably distorted by extreme emotions. Second and third statements almost always yielded more than the first, which Rachel had taken from Clair's distraught parents, Steve and Susan.

Rachel's work at the Milton house had provided two new pieces of information. The first was Susan Milton's frantic insistence that someone had been in Clair's room. Her things were out of order.

The second piece of evidence was possibly more revealing: several smudges of red dirt on her carpet—dirt that looked identical to the dirt in Oak Hill Park. This more than anything had convinced Susan Milton that someone had been in her daughter's room.

"We'll know soon enough," Randy said as he drove toward the Hamilton house. "But even if it matches the soil in Oak Hill Park, it proves nothing. Same soil found all over these hills."

"I don't know," Rachel said. "Susan insisted Clair was a clean freak."

"If the smudges had been boot prints that matched the ones in the park, we'd have something. As it is, it's circumstantial."

She scoffed. "Since when does the DA *not* use circumstantial evidence?"

"Frankly, I'm more interested in the possibility that CSI will find a key drive with something useful on it."

"Clair was a closet Dead Head, no question. In my experience Dead Heads are masters at covering their tracks. I wouldn't hold out too much hope."

The driveway in the hill country just east of Old Bee Cave Road was steep, made of concrete that had seen far better days. Randy angled his old Ford truck up the drive, which wound to the left before leading to a tiny white house nestled among the trees. By all appearances, it had to be at least fifty years old. Maybe eighty.

"Nice," Rachel said.

"You think?"

"I like the old ones. Not too many left. Not sure how she managed it. You said she owns the house?"

"So it says."

Public records showed Corina Hamilton, mother of Jamie Hamilton, to be the sole owner of the property. No mortgage. Maybe an inheritance.

A dirty white Honda sedan sporting a badly rusted front bumper and a dented hood sat in the turnaround. Corina's car.

Randy had tracked Corina down last night before any news of Jamie broke. She was putting in a late shift at Local Taco, her second job. Her first: doing some janitorial work for the school at St. Andrew's. He'd explained that he was questioning the friends of two students from St. Andrew's who'd run into trouble and wanted to talk to both her and Jamie.

"What kind of trouble?"

"I'll explain when we talk. Any chance I can come out tonight?"

"Not unless it's late. But I can talk tomorrow. Oh, wait, it's Saturday tomorrow. I have the morning shift, but I'll be done by eleven. Does that work?"

"Jamie will be there?"

"Yup. He's got no car and it's Saturday. Yup, he'll be there."

"Okay, then I'll see you at eleven thirty. If anything changes call me. You have me on your caller ID."

In the frenzy of the story breaking today, the chief had parked a surveillance drone half a mile over the Hamilton residence. It was more to protect Jamie and Corina than to make sure they didn't take off. Jamie wasn't exactly a flight risk. He didn't even have a driver's license.

Having talked to Jamie's guidance counselor two hours earlier, Randy was beginning to understand why. Jamie wasn't your ordinary kid. Not at all.

"You think his mother's heard the news?" Rachel asked.

Randy parked the truck behind the old Honda. "We'll know soon enough."

Soon enough turned out to be immediately, because the front door opened before Randy and Rachel had climbed out. On the front step stood a tiny woman with dishwater blond hair pulled back in a ponytail, still wearing a gray apron that read Local Taco on the front. She was smiling and waving. Not a hint that her son's face was plastered all over a thousand news feeds.

"Remember, I need to talk to him without Corina if possible."

Corina took their hands and welcomed them with a smile that showed stained teeth, maybe from drug use at some point in her life. The house was as old inside as it was outside, with floorboards that creaked and a stained drywall ceiling that needed patching in several spots. Simple kitchen, a green couch that looked at least ten years old. By all accounts Corina was a hard-working single mother of forty-one who'd never quite made it out of poverty, except for an inherited house she could hardly maintain on the wages of two jobs.

No sign of Jamie.

Randy dipped his head. "Thank you for meeting with us, ma'am. Your son's here?"

"If Jamie ain't at school, he's here," she said, eyes bright. "Want I should get him?"

"Well, if you don't mind, we have a few questions for you first. Just background information. And, as you probably know, everything's being recorded as a matter of procedure. I'm assuming you're fine with that."

"I got nothin' to hide from the police, I can tell you that. I left that life a long time ago. It's why I got rid of Dede in the first place. Can I get you a drink? Water or maybe a Coke?"

"No thanks."

Corina looked at Rachel, who was studying the dilapidated furnishings. "How 'bout you, hon?"

"I'm fine, but thank you."

"Well then, sit, sit."

She led them to the couch and took a seat on an old gray recliner that faced a dark screen on the wall—old 50-inch LED monitor.

"So tell me how I can help you," she said, folding one thin leg over the other. "I don't know much about the students at the school, you know. All I do is clean up. Jamie knows more. You say someone's in trouble?"

"Before we get to that, tell me who Dede is."

"Dede? My husband eleven years ago. He was a no-good nothing. I heard he got shot in Alabama a few years ago. I call that payback for putting my Jamie through the wringer. Why I kicked him out in the first place. No one touches my boy, especially not some drunk who dares call himself a father."

Randy exchanged a quick glance with Rachel. Corina was a talker, so they would let her talk. He couldn't help but feel for a mother whose life was about to be turned upside down on account of the son she loved so much.

"So Dede was Jamie's biological father?" Rachel asked.

"No." Corina looked away. "Truth is, don't know who his real father was because I was . . . Well, let's just say I wasn't doing my best in those days. Dede came in when Jamie was five. Biggest mistake I ever made. Only good thing that came from Dede was this house, and even that wasn't his. His father left it for him and I got it at the divorce."

"It's a nice house," Rachel said. "Do you and Jamie spend most nights here?"

"Well, I work of course. But I try to be home as much as possible."

Rachel hesitated. "What about two nights ago?"

She thought about that for moment. "My shift ended at eleven. Jamie was already in bed when I got home. Why, what's this about? Somethin' happen two nights ago?"

Randy took over. "We're just covering our bases. You saw Jamie when you came home that night?"

"Well, no. His door was closed. But he's got nowhere to go and even if he did, he doesn't drive anyway." She shifted uncomfortably, concern deepening in her eyes. "Don't you for a second think my boy did anything. He couldn't harm a fly."

"We're just asking the questions, ma'am," Randy said. "It's our job. You clean up after students, we clean up after problems. That's all." He cast a glance at the hallway. Still no sign of Jamie. The boy's demeanor would tell its own story. No one could brutally kill two kids and not betray some sign of guilt.

Then again, Jamie was evidently no ordinary kid.

"I hear Jamie's quite special."

She nodded, but she was no longer smiling. The mother bear in her was coming out. How far would he have gone to protect his daughter from accusations? At times like this, Randy hated his job.

"He's what they call ASD. That's autism spectrum disorder, but what they say is high functioning. Smart as a whip but he ain't too good with people and such. Still, he's plenty smart enough to get into the school and then some. They tell me he's a genius in his own way. It's just he don't fit in with other people is all. None of that matters to me, you understand. These days you can replace most parts of the body but not the mind. And that don't matter to me neither. He's scared enough as it is and I'm still dealing with all the abuse he suffered as a child."

"I understand," Randy said. "There's nothing quite like the connection between a child and their parent. Trust me, I know. I lost my daughter three years ago."

"Oh, I'm so sorry."

He waved it off, regretting he'd brought it up and not wanting to explain further.

"Do you mind me asking how Jamie was abused?"

Corina hesitated. "I told you Dede was a monster, what else do you need to know?"

He didn't want to push her.

"Fair enough. And I don't mean to pry, but he's pretty well adjusted by now, right? No behavior that concerns you?"

"Not really, no. I mean, he used to have wild dreams and sleepwalked when he was younger, but that's just normal kid stuff."

"Nightmares?"

"I guess. He kept dreaming of bein' trapped in a white room with no way out. You know, that kind of thing. But that was a long time ago. Why?"

"Just getting to know Jamie a little before I talk to him," Randy said. "I don't want to upset him. You were saying he sometimes does things that concern you?"

"It's nothing. He still wets the bed sometimes." She shook a finger at Randy. "But I don't want you embarrassing him, you hear me? He's got enough trouble as it is."

"I won't." Randy held up a hand. "Just doing my job, ma'am. And you seem the kind of mother someone like Jamie deserves."

She relaxed a little. "Thank you."

Larkin Bestwater, the guidance counselor Randy had spoken to, explained that Jamie cleaned the school with his mother, and a teacher brought him to their attention. The school tested Jamie and found him to be exceptionally intelligent in mathematics while significantly challenged in communication and social interaction. And by challenged, she meant he was clueless to social cues. St. Andrew's gave him a full-ride scholarship, and he entered their higher learning program last year as a freshman despite being eighteen. He was now a sophomore and nineteen.

Bestwater explained that despite Jamie being a teddy bear at heart, trusting of others and desperate to be accepted, the other students found him difficult. He'd been bullied to some degree and snapped on occasion. He once broke another student's nose. Raymond Beyer, a sophomore. But as far as she was concerned, Raymond had it coming.

In Bestwater's opinion, the boy she knew was incapable of murder. But she also admitted that with a mind like Jamie's anything was possible. He didn't have the same filters most people have. For example, he showed no remorse for having broken Raymond's nose. Yes, she was aware that at age thirteen Jamie had nearly killed another elementary school student. But that was also a case of bullying. Sometimes kids needed to stand up to bullies.

Randy couldn't disagree. If someone had taken to bullying his daughter he would have probably gone down to the school and broken the bully's neck himself. In a manner of speaking.

"If you don't mind, I'd like to talk to him now," Randy said. "Would that be okay with you?"

"Of course. I'll get him—"

"Actually, if you don't mind, I'd like to speak to him in his room, if you think he wouldn't mind. Rachel has a few more questions for you. Fair enough?"

She stared him down. "Now you tell me what's going on. You told me two students were in trouble, but you ain't said nothin' 'bout that. What's this really about?"

There was no way to sugarcoat the hell she was about to enter.

"Two of Jamie's friends were found dead in a park near the school last night. They were killed Thursday night. Texts from Jamie were found on one of their phones. I just need to know what he can tell me about that. All I need is ten minutes."

She blinked, shell-shocked. "Which students?"

"Timothy Blake and Clair Milton. Do you know them?"

Her hand went over her mouth. "Oh my God! Oh my God, poor things!" Then: "I don't know them, no. But that's terrible!"

She was more concerned about the victims than her son for the simple reason that she couldn't comprehend the possibility of her son's involvement. And now he hated his job even more.

"It is," Randy said. "So you can understand why we're being thorough."

"Of course. If there's any way Jamie can help, he will." She motioned at the hall. "His room is on the right. But knock hard because he's probably got his headset on." She flushed apologetically. "He's never had friends on the outside, as you can imagine. His life is in other worlds."

Randy nodded. "Makes sense. Be right back. You're in good hands."

The door to the room on the right opened on the fifth knock, and Randy faced a boy about six feet tall who weighed at least two hundred pounds. Short cropped blond hair above pale blue eyes. Acne but not a terrible case. Other than the color of his hair, Jamie looked nothing like his mother. If Randy were to guess, the father might have been Scandinavian.

Jamie stared at Randy, at a loss.

"Hello, Jamie." Randy held out his hand. "My name's Randy George. I'm a detective and I'm wondering if I might ask you a few questions."

The boy blinked. "George?" He took Randy's hand and gave it a limp shake. He seemed more interested in the name than in who Randy was. No sign of anything but curiosity.

"Yep, George. Like Curious George. Just call me Detective, or Randy, whichever makes you more comfortable."

"Can I call you George?"

Randy smiled. "Sure. George it is."

"Can I call you Curious George?"

Every word being spoken was not only recorded but audited by the department in real time. Someone would undoubtedly begin calling him Curious George after this.

"Yep, that works too. Curious George it is, then."

"I like George better."

"Okay, George. Call me George."

Jamie smiled wide and continued to stand there.

"Can I come in?"

Jamie shuffled to one side. "Sure. Sure, come in, George." He took one long stride to his bed, which was perfectly made, and picked up a stack of neatly folded shirts and underwear to make room for Randy to sit. He hurried to the dresser as if to put them away. Perhaps thinking now wasn't the time to put his folded laundry away, he stopped and looked around for an appropriate place for them. After a moment he stepped to the far corner of the bed. "Come in, come in." He set the pile down, squared to the corner of the bed. "You can sit on my bed."

"I'll stand, if that's okay," Randy said. "This won't take long."

"Okay." Jamie looked at his chair and the processing box on a small, perfectly organized desk. Well-worn immersion gloves and a shallow-dive mask lay next to an old-school keyboard. A small stack of comic books sat on the right, next to a pencil and yellow notepad. "You want to sit in my chair?"

"Standing's fine." Randy studied the tiny room, impressed by the care Jamie had taken to stow everything in its proper place. There was only one poster on the wall—a black-framed image of a woman wearing an old Oculus Rift headset from the 2020s, hair blown back. Three model airplanes sat on the dresser—bi-wings from World War I.

"Do you like airplanes?" Jamie asked, crossing to the models. "If you want you can hold this one." He picked up a red plane with a German cross on the tail and gingerly held it out.

"Did you make it?"

"Yup. I love models."

Randy took the plane and turned it in his hands. Not a spot of dust or glue. Was OCD common in autism spectrum disorders? Either way, he was seeing similarities between the meticulous nature of the crime scene and Jamie's room. Circumstantial at best.

He cocked his brow and gave Jamie the respect he deserved. "You do good work."

"Yup."

Jamie took the plane back and carefully set it on the dresser, then adjusted its angle so it sat in some perfect relationship to the other two. The door to a closet behind Jamie was closed.

"Do you mind if I ask you a few questions, Jamie?"

"Sure. You're a detective and that's what detectives do. So ask away." Then, after a short pause, "Do you play games too, George?"

"Not really, no. Life gives me all the games I can handle."

Jamie seemed surprised. "You know about that?"

"About what?"

"The games."

"What games?" Randy asked.

"All of them. All the games people play."

One thing was certain: If Jamie had murdered Timothy and Clair, he was no longer in touch with the brutal act. There was nothing about his demeanor that hinted at guilt.

"I guess I do," Randy said. "We all play games, in a way of speaking. Like Clair and Timothy from school. Did you know they played games?"

A moment's hesitation. "They're Dead Heads," Jamie said. "But you can't tell anyone. The teachers at school don't like Dead Heads."

"How well do you know Timothy and Clair?"

"They're my friends at school. But sometimes they're mean to me."

"Mean in what way?"

He shrugged. "They think I'm stupid sometimes."

And so we have motive, Randy thought.

"Did they ever bully you?"

Another shrug.

"Yes or no?"

"But sometimes I *am* stupid."

"Did you play games with them?"

"Yup. But I win and Timothy doesn't like that. Clair doesn't like it either. I try to make it easier for them, but they still don't like it."

"I see. When was the last time you played a game with them?"

Jamie thought about it for a few seconds. "Maybe last week? But I'm not too good with time."

No, Randy thought. *Because you spend most of it in other worlds, which distorts time.* Or maybe it was just the way Jamie's mind worked.

"Your handle in the virtual world is Fluffy Puppy, isn't that right?"

"Yup." He grinned. But the smile faded. "I used to have a puppy. His name was Fluffy, but he went out in the cold and my mom said maybe a coyote killed him."

"Sorry about that. I'm sure it was hard for you."

"Yeah."

"Have you ever heard of game called Play Dead?"

"Play Dead? Maybe. The key to playing games is knowing what the coding wants to hide from you." He glanced at the door, then leaned forward slightly, eyes bright. "If you can think like a coder thinks, you can get to the answer they're trying to hide from you, because it's just math. That's what you have to know. Mathematics. Normal people don't make games. Mathematicians make them."

He looked like he'd just shared a secret hack that would change Randy's world.

"Good to know. So tell me, Jamie, where were you two nights ago?"

"Two nights ago?" He thought about it. "Here. I was probably here like I always am."

"Was anyone with you?"

"Two nights ago? I think my mom was at work."

"Let's start with last night. Were you here alone last night?"

"Yes. My mom was working."

"And the night before? Your mom was working then as well?"

"Yup, she was working."

"Did you go anywhere later that night, after your mom got home?"

Jamie shook his head. "No. I don't like walking in the dark."

So no alibi. But no reason to doubt him yet.

"Did you ever meet up with Timothy and Clair to play games?"

"No. But once I did at Clair's house. She lives in a big house over by the school. I went there after school one afternoon."

"Do you remember what game you played?"

"No." A pause. "Maybe Rip Cord, I think. Yup, Rip Cord. You jump out of planes and off tall buildings and you have to kill the enemy and steal their chutes before they kill you and before you crash into the ground and die. If you make it to the ground, you have to make it back to your home base. It's an easy game."

"But you never played a game called Play Dead?"

"Maybe. I can't remember right now."

Randy studied him for a moment, looking for any tell of deception. There was none that he could see. The system would chew up a boy like Jamie and spit him out. He and Rachel would have to be careful not to manipulate him into giving an answer they wanted. A manipulated confession would compromise the investigation.

"The reason I'm asking about Timothy and Clair is because they ran into trouble two nights ago, and it's known that you were their friend."

"Yup. They're my friends."

No concern about them being in trouble? Odd, but maybe not so odd for someone like Jamie.

"Do you want to know what kind of trouble?" Randy asked.

"What kind of trouble?"

"They were murdered."

"In what game?"

Randy shook his head. "Not in a game. In real life."

He let the statement stand and watched the boy's reaction. But Jamie didn't visibly react.

"Oh. You mean in this game?"

"No, I mean in real life," Randy said.

The boy didn't seem to draw a distinction between reality and the virtual worlds he played in. This did not surprise Randy. Disassociation with the real world was one of the primary dangers of a Deep Dive. In some ways, it was what had allowed another boy to kill Randy's wife and daughter. Hacking into a car's navigation system and pushing the vehicle off the road into oncoming traffic was much easier than shooting them in the head. This was the ugly underbelly of technology.

When Jamie didn't react to the revelation that Timothy and Clair had been murdered in real life, Randy pushed the issue, watching closely for any tell.

"Their bodies were found naked in Oak Hill Park. They were strangled to death and their heads were crushed, maybe by a baseball bat or a pipe. The killer carved an unseeing eye into their backs. The Dead Head symbol."

Jamie stared, stymied. But there was no horror on his face. No surprise or shock. Nothing really. Just wide eyes.

"Wow," he finally said. "Timothy and Clair are dead for real now?"

"Yes. And some people think you were with them when it happened."

"But I wasn't playing that game," he said. "I walk to school sometimes, but I don't like walking in the dark."

Randy shifted his line of questioning. Maybe a more direct approach would jar Jamie's memory.

"Did you text Timothy in the last week, asking him and Clair to play a game with you?"

The boy blinked, confused. "No?"

"Was the game in question called Play Dead?"

"I don't know that game."

"Do you know why there are texts from your phone to Timothy's asking him to meet you? And asking him to bring you a mobile RIG?"

"No."

"Do you know anything about a key drive that might have housed the game?"

"A drive? No."

"So you didn't take a drive from Clair or Timothy?"

"No."

"And you didn't go to Clair's house after seeing her in the park?"

"I . . . I didn't go to the park."

Randy found himself believing the boy. Or at least believing that Jamie believed he was answering truthfully.

"Do you have a mobile RIG, Jamie?"

"No. My mom says they cost too much."

"So if you did play a game with Timothy and Clair in the park, you would need to use one of their RIGs, right?"

"I guess so."

The DA would have a field day with this poor kid in an interrogation. It was clear that Jamie's mind was too fractured, too fragile. They would have to depend primarily, maybe exclusively, on the physical evidence. Even if Jamie was guilty, Randy didn't think he could be fully responsible for the murders.

Unless this was all a very clever and calculated put-on. A game of wits and mathematics.

"So, just to be clear, you have no recollection of ever leaving the house two nights ago, or of texting Timothy, or of playing a game with him, or of going to Clair's home. Or of doing any harm to either Timothy or Clair. Is that what you're saying?"

"No?"

"No, you didn't do any of those things? Or no, you're not saying you didn't?"

Jamie stood like a cornered racoon in a beam of light, maybe considering the implied accusations. Or was he just confused? Surely the boy understood that he was a suspect.

"I didn't leave the house," Jamie managed.

"Okay. Do you mind if I take a look at your phone?"

Jamie stepped over to his desk, pulled open the top drawer, and withdrew an old black brick phone, not so different from the kind Randy preferred. Made sense, they were serviceable and, more importantly, cheap.

"Can you unlock it for me?"

Jamie did so with trembling fingers and handed it to Randy. A quick scan of his texts showed the thread in question. Jamie had only a dozen threads, and the exchange with Timothy was the most recent.

"You have no idea how these texts got on your phone?" He held the phone up for Jamie to see.

"No. I didn't write that."

"Okay, good. Do you mind if I take a look in your closet?"

Jamie's eyes darted toward the closed door. "My closet? I can't . . ." His voice was strained. "I mean, it's not clean in there."

"That's okay. Just a quick peek."

The thought of Randy looking into his closet seemed to disturb Jamie more than anything they'd spoken about, which was curious. Or maybe not for a boy who saw the world through fractured lenses. There was also the possibility that the closet contained something besides disorder. Something Jamie didn't want him to see.

"I won't tell anyone about the mess, promise. But it's up to you."

Jamie finally gave a reluctant nod.

Randy pulled the door open and saw a line of neatly hung blue, yellow, and black button-down shirts. Several pairs of jeans and shorts folded on a shelf, two pairs of tennis shoes, not much else. Each article occupied its proper place. All was in order except for the floor.

On the floor lay a pile of dirty clothing and worn-out tech, mostly cables and old handheld games that might have come from the local dump. Also comics and books. The closet floor was Jamie's slush pile, his laundry basket, his holding space for things that were in process or not valuable enough to organize.

This is what was passing through Randy's mind when he saw the boots. Tan work boots, with dried red mud on their soles, tossed in one corner. And next to the boots, a single charging cord that snaked under an old maroon T-shirt.

His pulse surged. Without bending, he nudged the T-shirt with his foot. There on the floor lay something that Jamie denied having.

A black mobile RIG.

The evidence was so obvious that Randy wondered if it had been planted. Or if Jamie was so unhinged that he'd blocked the memory of what he'd done. Or if he really was playing the game as he played all games.

"These are your tan work boots?" he asked, glancing back.

"Yes, those are mine. I got them for Christmas."

Randy stooped, lifted an empty hanger from the floor, and picked up the RIG by its strap. He faced Jamie, RIG dangling from the hanger. "Is this yours?"

Jamie's eyes widened.

"That's a mobile RIG!"

"It is. Does it belong to you?"

"No."

"Do you know how it got in your closet?"

"No."

"No idea at all?"

Jamie just stared, either completely stumped or playing a game of 'I'm stumped' with as much conviction as Randy had ever seen anyone play.

"What's going on in here?"

Corina had appeared in the doorway with Rachel behind her. Their eyes were glued to the dangling RIG.

"What's that?" Corina demanded.

"It's a mobile Reality Interface Gear," Randy said. "A RIG."

"I know what a mobile RIG is," she snapped. "What's it doing here?"

Randy nodded at Jamie. "You'll have to ask him. But I'm pretty sure that it belonged to Timothy Blake or Clair Milton."

"Why would it be here?" To Jamie: "Did you borrow it from them?"

"No."

"Then why's it here?"

For a few seconds no one spoke.

Randy cleared his throat. "Well, I think that's a question we'll have to clear up at the station."

Realization dawned on Corina's face as she looked from the RIG to her son, then to Randy.

"No!"

"I'm afraid we don't have a choice in—"

"Jamie!" She shoved her finger at the RIG and glared at her son, desperate. "You tell me who gave this to you. Right now."

He took a step back, face white.

"Answer me!" she cried. "Tell me who gave it to you!"

"I . . . I don't know."

"I think the lab can tell us who it belonged to," Randy said, unnerved by the anguish in Corina's face. "There's also a pair of boots that—"

"No!" she cried. Then again, like a mama bear, rushing at Randy. "No." She came in, fists crashing into his chest like hammers, knocking him back into the closet. The RIG thumped on the floor. "No, no, no, no. You will *not* hurt my boy! It's not his! Someone put it there!"

"It's okay, Corina." Rachel was reaching for her from behind. "Calm down."

Corina spun on Rachel and slapped her hand away, face red. "Don't you tell me to calm down! Don't you *dare* tell me to calm down!"

"Sorry, Mama," Jamie whimpered from the corner. "I didn't do anything."

But Corina was still fixated on Rachel. "My boy is innocent, you hear me?" She jabbed her thin finger at Randy. "This isn't what you think it is. If you lay one hand on my boy, I'll rip your eyes from your head, you hear me?"

Rachel threw her arms around the poor woman's shoulders, in part to restrain her, in part to offer her some comfort.

Corina lowered her forehead on Rachel's shoulder and began to sob.

"It's okay," Rachel soothed. "It's okay, it's okay."

But Randy knew it wasn't okay. They'd heard it all down at the station. Squad cars were already on their way. Jamie Hamilton would be in custody on suspicion of murder within ten minutes. And if the soles of the boots in the closet matched the prints made at the scene, or if Jamie's DNA matched the hair discovered at the scene, he would be indicted.

At times like this, Randy hated his job.

CHAPTER
SEVEN

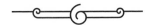

RANDY LOUNGED on the new municipal courthouse steps, where Governor Judith Patterson stood in all her glory, facing a gathering of reporters and a few hundred citizens. She was thin and tall, a full head above the DA, Andrew Olsen, who looked like a hairy penguin next to her.

Police chief Renee Dalton stood behind them, performing her best impersonation of a caring mother for the sake of the media. The victims' parents, Mary and Robert Blake on one side and Susan and Steve Milton on the other, faced the crowd, barely controlling their emotions.

How the governor had coaxed them into such a public display so soon after the death of their children, Randy had no idea. It made his stomach turn. Politics. Was there no end to the thirst for power and control masquerading as society's salvation?

Nine cameras from as many news feeds were trained on the charade, broadcasting the spectacle to a hundred million homes. No fewer than fifty picketers holding signs that read *Down With Dead Heads* and *Save Our Children* and *Make America Safe Again* lined the street behind a white and orange barricade. Their matching chants struck Randy as foolhardy, but this too seemed to work wonders in politics.

There was no better platform for Judith Patterson. All this no more than six hours after the arrest of Jamie Hamilton.

It was all happening too fast for Randy's liking. But the public demanded the truth, and Governor Judith Patterson needed to energize her presidential campaign, and today those two requirements would fuel the storm that was the Oak Hill Dead Head case. The ensuing tornado would rip through the city. Through the country. Through the whole world, for all Randy knew.

In some ways, the war on drugs had been replaced by the war on the dangers of virtual reality, and Dead Heads were the new scapegoats for society's insecurities. Dying to one world to experience another threatened the value of an ordinary reality, which threatened those who clung to it for meaning.

Understandable. Confusing at times. In any case, someone had to stand up for the victims.

Problem was, Randy was still unclear about who the victims were in this case. Timothy and Clair, of course. Their friends and families as well. And Jamie? Randy couldn't help but feel that he too was a victim—if not of the case, then certainly of society.

Still, the law was the law, and being different didn't excuse anyone from its demands. Within an hour of Jamie's arrival at the station for 'further questioning', the lab had confirmed that his hair was a genetic match to the blond hair found on Timothy Blake's body. Moreover, the tracks found at the scene matched Jamie's boots.

Physical evidence put Jamie with Timothy Blake at the time of his death.

The smudges of red dirt found on Clair Milton's bedroom carpet did match the soil found in Oak Hill Park, but, as Randy had asserted, that evidence was circumstantial. And there would be no information forthcoming from the victims' processor drives because, as Rachel had guessed, they had wiped themselves clean. Clair used Swiper, an illegal program that used a quantum loop to eradicate any record of activity on the darknet within milliseconds. Local history was kept only as long as the user was active and then wiped as soon as they pulled out.

A thorough search of Jamie's bedroom had yielded no key drive nor any additional useful evidence—his local drive had also wiped itself. Standard procedure for die-hard Dead Heads.

They hadn't found whatever had crushed the victims' skulls, nor the knife that had carved their backs, but autopsies of both victims established cause of death as strangulation. A longer and more pressing interview had produced nothing new. Jamie presented himself in the same conflicted, clueless and confused manner he'd demonstrated at home.

Despite these holes, an evidentiary case had been firmly established within a few hours of Jamie's arrival at the station. Together with the prosecutor, the DA had laid out their options. Testimony wouldn't win this case; the evidence would.

Motive, DA Olsen suggested, could easily be established as rage in a dissociative state induced by immersive virtual reality play and/or as rage related to rejection.

The murder weapon was Jamie's hands.

They had more than enough evidence to put Jamie in the ground, the DA insisted. Jamie Hamilton's only defense would be a plea of insanity. But a claim of insanity under the influence of dead heading would fly no better than someone cranked up on a designer drug arguing they shouldn't be held responsible for a murder they committed under the influence of that drug.

The defense for the nutcase who'd killed his wife and daughter had attempted a similar argument, and the judge had dismissed it with prejudice. Case law was clear. Short of another suspect emerging, Jamie had no hope.

When Randy had voiced his concern that Jamie was as much a victim as Timothy and Clair, Olsen had dismissed it. Leave the law to the courts, Olsen said. Randy's job was to investigate the crime and collect evidence. And that evidence had brought them here, to the courthouse steps, where the court would exert its formidable power to deliver justice.

The governor held them all in her trance. Her long dark hair was pulled back neatly into a bun, which accentuated the stark lines of her jaw. A black blazer hugged her bony shoulders. She was beautiful in her own no-nonsense way, Randy thought, though it was anyone's guess how much work she'd had done to her body. All politicians were beautiful these days.

Patterson lifted her hand, and like obedient children, her supporters fell silent.

"Make no mistake, we live in dangerous times. If history has taught us one thing, it is that those who thirst for power will exert whatever means at their disposal to control, subjugate, and kill innocent people for their own gain. The means of that control once required great skill and cunning. Adolf Hitler swayed an entire nation using a serpent's tongue before using violence and death to keep them in his grasp. The war that followed claimed the lives of millions. Let us not forget."

Rumbles and cries of agreement peppered the air. Fearmongering. Isn't that what Hitler had used? Of course he had, and of course the governor would, because almost all politicking was based on fearmongering. It worked.

"Today the power of Hitler is within the grasp of every human being," she continued. "It's no longer the skill of a serpent's tongue that threatens to destroy our lives, but the technology that allows any punk to warp the minds of all who join them in a fully immersive virtual world. There, in that reality-altering space, self-control is easily surrendered to those who would exert their power over others. To strip this world of its reality is to commit treason against humanity. Deep Dive technology is the new heresy of our species, because it denies the sanctity of who we are in the real world."

Randy caught her eye and felt momentarily stripped bare.

Her gaze moved on. "We must not only suppress with extreme prejudice those who commit crimes while in that warped space, we must also hold the technology itself and the makers of that technology responsible. Convergence, for all the good it may have offered the world, must be strictly regulated."

The statement surprised Randy. By associating Jake Barnes's innovative company with Hitler, she had essentially declared war on the whole system, top down.

Someone started up a chant, "*Death to Dead Heads, Death to Dead Heads.*"

She silenced it with a raised palm. "No, we will not go there." That took the wind out of them. "We will not fight death with death but with truth. Only the truth can set us free from this conspiracy against the sanctity of humanity."

She paced to her right. A button mic on her lapel carried her broadcast with her.

"I appreciate all of you who've come to express your support for the bright new world that my policies will offer this great country when I am elected as your president. But today . . ."

Cheers cut her off and she lifted a hand.

"Today isn't only about our future. Today we gather to express our support and our grief for Timothy Blake and Clair Milton, two bright young children whose lives were ruthlessly cut short by a sadistic murderer and the technology he used to end their lives."

She glided to Susan Milton and placed a hand on her shoulder. Clair's mother stood like a statue, jaw taut and hands gripped to fists.

"Today is about Clair's parents, Steve and Susan Milton, leaders in our business community. No amount of sorrow can heal the great loss they have suffered because of our failure to protect their daughter from a diabolical scourge."

Susan began to tremble with what could only be rage, Randy thought. Steve's face was red. Both looked like they would break down at any moment. A knot rose in Randy's throat. Judith Patterson put an arm around Susan's shoulders and whispered something in her ear before moving toward Timothy's parents. Not a sound could be heard in the street now. The whole country was holding back tears.

"Today is about Timothy's family, Mary and Robert Blake, spiritual leaders in our community. Only God can save us from the treachery of the human heart, and there is no better advocate for that voice of healing than we have in Mary and Robert."

Mary lowered her head into her hands and began to sob. She was just a mother now, not the wife of a pastor. Randy's heart broke for her.

Judith Patterson let her cry, hand on her shoulder to offer comfort. But Randy knew all too well that no gesture could even begin to fill the hole that came with the loss of a child. The governor's display struck him as patronizing in the worst kind of way.

Robert Blake put his arm around his wife's shoulders, but she shrugged out of his grasp. He stared ahead, face ashen. As a religious man, reason, faith, and hope guided him in the face of trials. But who could reason their way through such a loss? Randy hadn't come close.

The governor faced the cameras again, frowning. "Today we mourn our loss and vow as one to never allow—"

"No!" Susan Milton screamed from behind the governor. Tears streamed down her twisted face. She pitched forward and jabbed a finger at the cameras. "No one gets to use my daughter as a mascot!" The governor made no effort to stop her. "I don't want your sorrow! I don't want you to stand there and comfort me while all of your children are safe in your homes!"

"Honey, please . . ." Susan's husband stepped up, consoling. He was mumbling something, taking his wife's arm to guide her back.

"Get away from me!" she screamed, ripping herself free. "This is *your* fault!" Steve made a futile attempt to calm her with outstretched arms, but she did not calm. She hammered at him with closed fists, striking him on the side of his face and shoulder. "She wouldn't be dead if not for you and your stupid company!"

Steve ignored the blows. "Honey—"

"Get away from me!" Her voice was guttural and raw.

He backed off, red-faced and mortified. She was blaming the whole tech community and her husband's role as the founder of Mistletoe, an organic search engine that many hoped would one day rival Google. It used VR technology to anticipate needs and desires, although Randy didn't know how.

Susan was facing the cameras again. "What I want is justice!" She shook both fists to accentuate that last word. "What I want is revenge! What I want is for the monster who did this to pay! And to pay the same price my Clair paid!"

The cameras transported every word around the world. Chief Dalton had stepped back with the DA, allowing the governor to run the show. The mother's outburst was playing into their hands.

"Where is your outrage?" Susan Milton shrilled. "Where is your demand that Jamie Hamilton be put to death? That's what will stop all this insanity! Kill them all! Every last one of those Dead Heads who killed my little girl!"

Her husband reached for her again, intent on bringing his wife under control, unaware that he'd lost control of himself.

"How can you say that?" he demanded. "She was a Dead Head herself!"

Susan tensed her jaws and turned on him, but he pressed on before she could speak.

"How dare you blame me for my own daughter's death!" His jowls shook with indignation. "You think you're the only one who lost a daughter? How *dare* you!"

They were beyond themselves. Or, more likely, this was their real selves. Governor Judith Patterson let them rage.

"She never *was* your daughter," Susan growled, oblivious to the snot running down her upper lip. "Never!" A hard breath. "I don't want you in my house."

Mary Blake, the pastor's wife, kept sobbing, face in her hands. Beside her, Robert still hadn't moved.

"She *was* my daughter!" Steve wept. He faced the reporters. "You know that, right? Everything I've ever done is for my daughter. I gave her everything. Everything! And now everything has been taken from me."

Susan glared at him long and hard, then stormed down the steps, mind lost to her pain. She whirled back at the sidewalk and pointed up at her husband. "Don't you come home! Don't you dare!" Then she hurried up the sidewalk, followed by two uniforms who caught the chief's nod. *See that she's safe.*

Steve watched her leave, perhaps only now realizing he'd melted down in front of thousands of shareholders. The stock of Mistletoe would either hit new highs or tank before the closing bell.

One thing was certain, Randy thought. Governor Judith Patterson's stock as a presidential candidate had just gone up. Maybe way up.

Steve came to himself, looked at the cameras, then the governor, then turned and walked into the courthouse, out of sight.

Mary Blake wept. Her husband stared. For a long moment no one spoke.

Judith Patterson scanned the crowd. "Now we all see firsthand the devastating consequences of unrestrained technology. Our hearts break with Susan and Steve. No one can blame a mother and father for the grief and anger they express at such a terrible loss. It darkens our minds and crushes our hearts. I beg you, do not judge what you have seen today. Only stand with me to bring the monster who did this to justice and change the laws of this country so that it never happens again."

Kevin Kincade, a reporter who always fancied himself in a bolo hat, raised a hand and spoke before being invited to. "Will the state seek the death—"

"Not now, Kevin," Patterson said with chilling authority. She turned to DA Olsen and nodded.

Andrew Olsen shuffled to a podium where mics waited. He cleared his throat.

"As you know, we've had our best people on this case, led by Randy George, arguably one of the best if not the best detective in the state of Texas." Olsen glanced across the steps and dipped his head to acknowledge Randy. "His work has been exhaustive and productive in the last twenty-four hours."

They were using him. Par for the course. Randy offered the man no reaction for the simple reason that his only honest reaction would have been one of disdain.

Olsen turned back to the cameras. "It's with soberness of heart and soundness of mind that I inform you that a suspect in the case of Timothy Blake's and Clair Milton's murders has been arrested with cause and is now in our custody. The state of Texas will do everything in its power to bring the case against Jamie Hamilton to trial as quickly and as expeditiously as possible. I promise you that justice will be served, and its execution will be swift. The evidence in this case is overwhelming."

He scanned the cameras, then glanced at the governor, who wore a sober mask. But Randy knew how satisfied she was. Her eyes were virtually glowing with delight.

"More information will be forthcoming in the days to come," Olsen was saying. "In light of what we have just witnessed, I won't be taking any questions. That's all for now."

BOOK TWO

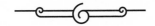

THE
DEFENSE

CHAPTER
EIGHT

FOLLOWING HER descent into Tayo's virtual game, Angie Channing had gone out of her way to avoid the news feeds, knowing they would be flooded with frantic finger pointing concerning the Oak Hill Dead Head murders. Being what Darey sometimes called a neurotic terrier, she knew that when she got locked onto something she had a hard time letting go.

There was no telling where any investigation into a murder would take her, so better not to lock on in the first place. She had other, broader matters to tackle. Like letting her mind fully reintegrate. For as long as the whiteouts continued, a plain, boring life was in order.

Darey brought Chinese home at seven that night. "How was Angie's day?" he asked as he pulled out two orders of Mongolian chicken with extra vegetables.

She flipped open the cardboard box. Plastic containers had been outlawed over a decade ago, and everything was biodegradable now. The sweet scent of the food filled her with a rush of appreciation. Chinese was still her favorite.

Darey had asked her a question. "Hmmm?"

"How was your day?" Darey was looking at her with interest.

"Completely uneventful," she said. "Just dialing back in."

"Good. I think that's wise."

"But I did do a Deep Dive." When it came right down to it, she always told him everything, even the things he didn't like. He was safe.

His brow arched. "I see. And how was that for you?"

"I didn't mean to at first, but Tayo wanted to show me a new level to a game he's been slaving away at. He twisted my arm."

She led the way to the sitting room and plopped down in one of two recliners that faced their theater, a nine-by-six 3D screen built into the wall, now displaying a meadow with yellow flowers and tall snow-capped mountains in the background.

"How long were you in?" he asked, sitting in the other chair and kicking his shoes off.

"Five hours."

A pause.

"Well, how was it?"

"Fun." She dug her chopsticks into the box. "What you really want to know is how it affected me."

"Okay."

"I confirmed that you can't have a whiteout in a virtual space, just like Jake Barnes told me. I had plenty of super stressful moments in Tayo's game, but none of them triggered me." She took a bite and grinned at him. "It's only stress in the real world that brings them on. And that's good, because it definitely means this is the real world. Not that I really doubted it."

"Because you had a whiteout after the Deep Dive?"

"Yup. One. But it wasn't bad. I think maybe they've run their course. They said forty-eight hours and it's been that. Almost."

"Good. Well done, honey."

That's the way he was, never disappointed with her. She loved him for it.

"How was *your* day?" she asked.

Darey spoke around a mouthful of Chinese. "Same old. You heard about the Oak Hill incident?"

"Uh-huh. But I don't want to know more."

He nodded. "I think that's wise too."

She cleared her throat and started the show. "Lover Boy, play the latest episode of *New York*." It was a crime drama about a corrupt police department featuring a broad range of complex characters, all of whom were flawed in one way or another. The writers did a magnificent job dealing with the unnecessary and crushing dramas typical in most relationships, something Angie and Darey were determined to avoid.

The meadow scene on the theater screen changed. An episode of the fully dimensional show came on and they watched in silence, peering over their boxes of Mongolian chicken. Not all shows were fully dimensional. Many were still like the old 3D movies, which offered a kind of fake dimensionality without the limitless depth and breadth that fully dimensional shows in a theater box now offered.

The opening scene showed Broadway in Manhattan from the viewpoint of a window looking out at ride-shares and e-bikes and tourists and city-dwellers bustling through the day.

From where she sat, she would be hard pressed to tell the difference between the theater screen in front of her and a large picture window that overlooked Manhattan. If she walked up to the screen and peered to the left, she would see more. Same thing if they were in a courtroom scene, or in a car.

It gave the illusion that only the screen itself prevented viewers from entering the scene, just like a glass window in a restaurant prevented someone from stepping through it into the street.

When the show ended an hour later, they lounged for a while before turning in. Darey held her that night and she was grateful for the human contact.

Angie slept in the next morning, surprised to find Darey gone so early on a Sunday. He'd left a note on the kitchen pad.

See you tonight. Maybe we can go to dinner. DJ's Diner?

Sounded good to her.

She showered and dressed. Hummed as she fixed herself some breakfast. Just another day. Maybe she would watch a show, because she was trying to chill, right? It felt good to be normal again. Although nothing about her life was really that normal. Normal was something that she was often temped to chase, but it had never materialized for her. Felicia, her therapist, had helped her begin to accept this. *You can't experience love if you're always trying to improve what you condemn about yourself*, she would say. *Accept yourself, exactly as you are, and you'll see what God sees.*

So Angie was accepting herself. Well, she was trying to anyway.

The doorbell rang at eleven that morning while she was watching another episode of *New York*, hoping Darey wouldn't mind her skipping ahead without him. She twisted in her seat at the sound of the chime, wondering who would be visiting. A delivery maybe? Most packages were delivered by drones to a receiving bin built into the side of the house. Only larger items came to the front door.

When she opened the door she saw a US postal vehicle pulling away. Mail? They rarely received mail. It was all digital these days. Probably some legal document for Darey.

She lifted the panel on the small mailbox beside the door. Inside was a white envelope. Snail mail for real. She pulled the envelope out and stared at the handwriting. It was addressed to her.

Retreating to the sitting room where the episode of *New York* was still playing, she paused the show and used her finger to rip through the seal. Inside was a handwritten note on a single piece of paper.

Dear Angie Channing—

You don't know me, but I know you through your book, Righteous. I also know your handle on the darknet, Lover Boy. I know it because I'm a hacker and a closet Dead Head like you.

A chill spiked up Angie's spine. The writer knew Lover Boy's real identity and where she lived. No one apart from Darey knew that.

Angie settled on the edge of the recliner and read on.

I have to speak to someone about something my friend Timothy and I found on an encrypted key. I can't tell you anything else here, but it's terrifying and I don't know what else to do.

Please don't tell anyone that you received this letter. Please don't mention my name, it could be dangerous. Timothy doesn't think so, but I'm afraid. Maybe you can help us.

Please text me at the number below and maybe we can meet. As soon as possible.

Please, I'm begging you.

Clair Milton
(555) 659-1010

Angie's fingers were shaking. She was holding a letter one of the victims of the Oak Hill murders had written while she was still alive. A letter to *her*. She picked up the envelope and looked at the postmark. Four days ago.

She was feeling dizzy. Two thoughts crashed through her mind. The first was that whatever Clair Milton had learned from the encrypted key drive had gotten her killed. The second was that she had to find out what was on that drive.

But that wasn't smart. Not at all.

The world suddenly went white. She was having a whiteout triggered by stress. This one seemed to be stronger than the others, like a hard wall of white that seemed to be crushing the life out of her.

It's okay, just a whiteout. It'll pass. But it didn't pass as quickly this time. *Oh no!*

And then the room came back, as if a sheet had been pulled off her head. There in front of her was the paused scene of *New York* with pedestrians mid-stride. In her hands, the letter from Clair Milton.

Angie got up, hurried to the kitchen, where she'd left her phone, picked up the handheld, and started to dial Darey. Then stopped.

Clair had insisted she tell no one. But Clair couldn't be harmed now because she was dead. So should she call Darey?

She lowered the phone. Not yet. Concerned for her, Darey would either tell her she was chasing ghosts or rush to her aid, and she didn't want that. She wanted to find out more first. Like why Jamie Hamilton, a boy who looked familiar to her, was being accused of murdering Clair Milton and Timothy Blake. Like who Jamie really was. And she had to do it without letting anyone know what she was doing. No mention of the letter or its contents. Not yet.

Angie shoved the letter in her pocket, snatched her car key off the counter, and hurried for the garage.

RANDY WAS at his desk, working on the second half of a ham sandwich, taking a reprieve from the storm that had been whipped into a tornado by the governor, when his phone chirped.

"Randy."

"We got a woman here who wants to speak to the detective in charge of the Oak Hill case," Bianca Sterling droned in her deep southern accent. "She's pretty upset 'bout somethin'. Thought you should know."

"What's she upset about?"

"Won't say. Just that she's not leaving until she speaks to the detective in charge. Want me to give it to someone else?"

He was about to tell her to give it to Rachel when Bianca's voice filled his earpiece again.

"Hold on a sec . . ." She spoke to someone offline and then came back. "She says to tell you her name's Angie Channing. Says you might know her."

Something about the name sounded familiar but he couldn't place it.

"Take her to room 2. I'll be there in five."

"Alright."

Five minutes gave Randy time to swallow the last few bites of his sandwich and wash it down with a slug of water.

He entered the interview room and immediately recognized the woman seated across the table. He'd seen her before, but where? Her hair was pulled back in a ponytail and she wore jeans and a black pullover, casual. Small frame with petite features. Not unlike his late wife.

She stared at him with striking eyes that seemed to see more than they should. Not in a self-important way, more like she wasn't interested in nonsense.

He closed the door and took a seat opposite her, forearms on the table. "I'm Randy George. You wanted to see me about the Oak Hill case?"

Angie Channing studied him for a moment.

"I need to know more about Jamie Hamilton."

He gave her a polite smile. "Well, ma'am, don't we all. But unless you're his attorney, and I know you aren't because he's already met with his public defender, I'm not in a position to discuss the case with you. But I'm sure you already know that."

"Of course," she said. There was something about the way she was looking at him that was both unnerving and alluring at once. She'd been around the block, this one. "Under ordinary circumstances that would be the case. But this isn't ordinary and neither are you. And if it's okay with you, please don't call me ma'am. My name's Angie Channing."

"Tell me what I can help you with, Miss Channing."

"It's Mrs. Channing, actually. But I prefer Angie. And my husband's the attorney in the family. I'm just an investigative writer. I think you might know my husband. Darey Channing?"

Randy sat back and folded his arms. So this was Mrs. Darey Channing. Everyone in the department was all too familiar with Darey, one of the best defense attorneys in the city. A fair man with an impressive intellect and near-exhaustive knowledge of the law. Randy had never worked directly with the man, but Darey had cleared the names of several unjustly accused defendants during Randy's time at the department, much to the dismay of the DA.

"I do. And you're the one who wrote that book. *Righteous*."

"I am."

"And now you want to write a book on the Oak Hill Dead Head murders. I'm sure it would sell like hotcakes."

"No."

She looked a bit hurt.

"Okay, so maybe that was unfair. I actually read your book. Some good investigative work in there."

"Thank you." She looked at the door, then at the cameras filming their discussion. "Any chance we can talk in private?"

He didn't see why not. Without answering, he walked to the control panel and disabled both video and audio recording.

"Better?" He returned to his seat.

Angie leaned forward, fire in her eyes. Not an angry fire, just one that insisted on burning away everything but the truth.

"I did a little homework on the way down. You're a highly decorated detective known for being fair. A maniac killed your wife and daughter three years ago." She caught herself. "I'm sorry about that."

He gave her a nod.

"All that to say I believe you're not interested in anything but the truth. Am I right?"

He frowned. "Well, I'm not perfect and sometimes the truth does more harm than good, but yes."

"So look in my eyes and tell me one thing," she said. "Is Jamie Hamilton the kind of person who would brutally kill two teenagers in a park?"

He had to tread carefully here.

"Possibly, yes."

"I'm not asking what's possible. I'm asking what Randy George, who lost his wife and daughter three years ago, thinks deep in his gut. Is Jamie Hamilton a brutal murderer? And remember, I know the psychology of a murderer. I wrote a book about it."

He instinctively glanced up at the camera. For a moment he felt stripped bare, knowing that single glance had answered her.

"Do you have evidence that's pertinent to the case?" he asked.

"I'm just asking what you think." She leaned back and let her shoulders drop. Before his eyes she transformed from a hard-nosed investigative personality to a frazzled girl who was just trying to make sense of the world.

This, he thought, *is the real Angie Channing.*

She sighed. "Look, I know this puts you in a tough position, and I'm not asking you to tell me anything that might compromise the case. Although I must say you strike me as the kind of person who's no longer sure he loves his job. While I was in the parking lot I watched a replay of the freak show on the courthouse steps. You didn't exactly look thrilled. But let's set all that aside for a second. Let's just say that I do want to write a book about the Oak Hill case.

Doesn't that give you some leeway? So you let the famous author talk to him, that's all. What's the harm in that?"

He studied her, struck by her boldness. But there wasn't an untrue bone in her body. She was a breath of fresh air.

"So you want to interview him," he said.

"Just for a few minutes. I think we both have some doubt."

A beat passed.

"He's still in holding here?" she asked, glancing at the door.

Randy nodded. "They're moving him to County tomorrow morning. And I didn't say I had any doubts about his guilt. I only know what the evidence shows. The courts will decide the rest."

"It's an election year," she said. "The governor's staked her run on this case. Jamie doesn't stand a chance. And between you and me, I don't know if he killed those kids or not. I'm just saying I have very good reason to want to know."

"Because you want to write a book," he said.

"This isn't that."

"Then what's your very good reason?" he asked.

"Besides being on the side of truth?"

He didn't press the issue.

"Why don't you tell me why you're unsure," she said. Her voice was soft now. Inviting, like an old friend.

He was a little surprised to hear himself answer. "I think he probably is guilty, but I don't think he knew he was doing anything wrong."

"Why?"

Randy hesitated, then told her why. He summarized his interview of Jamie at the house, knowing he was handing ammunition to any defense attorney worth their suit. Then again, Jamie deserved the strongest defense. Didn't everybody?

But he realized there was another reason he was telling her about Jamie. In his own way he was washing his hands of any culpability in tipping the scales of justice one way or the other.

"Autism spectrum disorder, huh?" she said when he finished.

"You're familiar with it?"

She didn't respond, which made him think she was very familiar with it.

"Frankly, he may be a full-on savant," he said. "Not normal, in any case."

"What's normal?" she said with a bit of an edge. He let the question pass.

"Jamie wasn't tested until high school so no record of it in his youth. No money for doctors. The prosecution will claim his dead heading brought on dissociative states."

"And bury him, guilty or not," she said.

He nodded. Then sighed.

"I like you, Angie. And I hope you find whatever truth you're searching for. But if there's any chance at all that Jamie's innocent, you need to play this by the book."

She folded her arms. "Okay, fair enough. So then what?"

"Come back here tomorrow by ten with Darey, and I'll guarantee you an interview."

"Under the pretense that he's considering representing Jamie," she said.

"Right. For that matter, as long as Darey is present, I could arrange an interview with Jamie later today via the holo-room." All the larger facilities had recently installed holo-rooms that allowed inmates to connect with counsel or visitors remotely in virtual reality. The rules governing virtual visitations weren't as stringent as in-person visitations. No one could smuggle in weapons or drugs through a digital interface. The move had cut down in-prison altercations by over 50 percent in the years since the systems had been installed.

"It needs to be in person," she said.

He could see her wheels spinning. But in the next moment her eyes went blank and she sat perfectly still. For a full five seconds she stared at him without moving. He was beginning to wonder what was wrong when she blinked and took a quick breath.

"You okay?" he asked.

"Yeah. Yeah, just . . ." She lowered her eyes and bit at her lower lip. "Just thinking."

Thinking and nervous now.

"Does Darey know you're here?"

"Not yet."

She absently lifted her hand and picked at that lip, then quickly pulled her hand away. Something was up.

"You still want that interview?"

"Yes. Of course! Yup."

"Then be here by ten tomorrow," he repeated. "But you have to understand that the case against him's strong. Like I said, as far as I'm concerned, Jamie Hamilton's guilty. Short of a confession from someone else or a mountain of new evidence that proves he was framed, he's going down for the murders."

"And as far as I'm concerned, you told me only that."

"Please make sure Darey understands as well."

"I will."

They watched each other for a few long seconds, sealing some unspoken agreement, but he wasn't sure what it was.

Feeling suddenly awkward, Randy stood. "Bianca will come for you," he said, walking for the door. "The fewer people that see us together, the better."

"Randy?"

He turned back, hand on the knob.

"Thank you," she said.

CHAPTER
NINE

AT FIVE THAT afternoon Darcy Channing stood at the window of his tenth-floor office on Seventh Street, staring out at Austin's skyline, arms crossed. This whole section of town had been rebuilt over the last ten years. Towering high-rises had replaced the old earthy structures that once characterized a city that didn't want to grow up. Popular bumper stickers used to read, *Keep Austin Weird*. But Austin had lost its soul to the same advances the rest of the world had embraced, rendering all things common.

The sky was still bright blue, made even bluer by the window tinting. From up here, the world looked serene. He'd always wondered how birds experienced the world. Like the crow perched on the spire across the street—what did Mr. Crow see when a man pulled out a gun and shot someone dead in the street below? Did it care about the anguish the two-legged mammals suffered? Was the crow capable of suffering? Being killed, yes, and it would fly away from any threat to its life. But suffering?

He turned back and studied Angie and Felicia, who sat in two of the four gray chairs that made up his seating area. A pad on the crystal table between the chairs featured an Austin *Stateman*'s cover story of his firm—Channing & Miles. There for all to see, complete with his partner, Charles Miles, standing with legs spread, arms folded, like some absurd overlord.

Good for business, but Darey had never cared for that part of the gig. His interest was in helping the unjustly accused avoid being crushed by a system that didn't care about collateral damage.

Right now, his attention was on another kind of anguish: the topsy-turvy mind games that Angie was caught up in.

She sat on the edge of her chair, arms crossed, right knee bouncing like a piston, looking up at him with the eyes of a hopeful child. She'd brought them together, thinking that Felicia's presence might win her some favor, not that she needed any from him. Or maybe she wanted Felicia there because, other than himself, no one understood Angie like Felicia.

In either case, Angie was clearly hiding something, but she had that right. She would share it if and when she felt it was appropriate.

"Just so I'm clear, let me restate this," he said. "For some reason you can't share right now, you decided you had to meet with Jamie, and so you went to the station and had a talk with Randy George."

"Yes," Angie said.

She glanced at Felicia, who was seated with one leg folded over the other in the chair opposite Angie, calmly watching her client.

"But that doesn't matter," Angie said. "What matters now is what Randy told me. Jamie's being railroaded. Even if he is guilty, he probably didn't know what he was doing. They have some washed-up public defender on his case. All I'm asking is that we talk to him. Then you can decide."

"What concerns me more than Jamie Hamilton," Felicia said, "is your state of mind. We talked about this, Angie. You've just come out of a Deep Dive protocol that was radically dissociative."

"You don't think I know that? I'm the one who went through it! But this has nothing to do with that. Just because I happened to have an experience at Convergence a few days before Jamie was accused of killing two kids doesn't excuse me from my responsibility to help Jamie."

"Responsibility?"

"His life's at stake!"

"You said that even Randy George, a detective who seems reasonable to me, is sure Jamie committed this crime. What defense are you talking about, exactly?"

"Well, I'm not sure he is guilty," Angie said, turning her eyes back to Darey. "How does someone with such an innocent mindset execute two kids?"

"By being in a dissociative state," Darey said. And then immediately regretted using those words.

"Like me?" Angie rose and walked to the window. "You're thinking I'm losing it. That I'm like Jamie and that's why I want to look into his case."

Darey exchanged a look with Felicia, who spoke in a soothing tone.

"No, I don't think it's like you at all, Angie," she said. "You're not on the spectrum like Jamie. Your mother, maybe, but not you. My only concern is the condition of your mind having just come out of such a fully immersive Deep Dive."

"I'm fine," Angie said, turning back. "Okay, so I did a Deep Dive yesterday and—"

"You did?" Felicia interrupted. "I thought we agreed that you wouldn't."

"Well, I did, Felicia! Just a silly game. And I'm perfectly fine for it. You're both looking at me as if my behavior's erratic and I've gone off the deep end, but I swear I haven't. I just think the case against Jamie Hamilton's a huge deal and something I can't ignore. That's it. If Darey meets with him and thinks I'm crazy, then I'll drop it."

Her fingers were trembling slightly, and she'd picked at her lip, leaving a raw spot. But Darey thought Angie was right. She wasn't sinking into a manic episode. She was following an instinct that had always served her exceptionally well, no matter the state of her mind.

Then again, they were in uncharted waters.

Darey crossed to the chair behind his desk and sat. "What exactly is the danger to Angie in this fragile—"

"I'm not fragile," Angie objected.

"Okay, then in this post–Red Protocol state she's in?"

"I'm not in that state anymore," Angie pressed.

"No?" Felicia asked. "When did you experience your last whiteout?"

Angie shifted her eyes and hesitated. "Ten minutes ago. But it was hardly a whiteout. Just the tail end. Nothing like some of the other ones."

"They should be gone by now," Felicia said. "It's concerning, Angie. The danger here isn't the whiteouts, it's the possibility of episodes of disassociation.

Your mind could snap back into a virtual experience that would appear real to you. You could be driving down the road and suddenly find yourself back in the virtual world you experienced while in the Red Protocol at Convergence."

"The car would know what to do."

"Still, in that state, you might override the car. There's a reason why driving while intoxicated is illegal."

True.

"And stress is the primary trigger, correct?" Angie said.

"That's what they said."

"Well, you know what stresses me out?" Angie demanded. "This!"

She was right, Darey realized. Nothing would stress Angie more than someone trying to control her.

Angie returned to her chair and sat. "Sorry." She blew out some air. "Look, I came across something that piqued my interest in the Oak Hill case. I followed it up and discovered I might be onto something. That something deserves to be explored. It's not nothing, it's the life of a nineteen-year-old boy named Jamie Hamilton. For all I know, I should be writing about this, not some book the publisher thinks will be a good follow-up to *Righteous*. This could be the follow-up."

Darey let her sit in silence for a few moments. He'd never experienced love the way he did with Angie. She was a wild bird who longed to fly to the horizon to know herself, even if that put her in harm's way. Like that bird, any attempt to cage her only split her in two. Weren't they all that way? But few had the courage to fly free.

Felicia broke the silence.

"Maybe . . ." She glanced at Angie. "Maybe we're looking at this wrong. Angie, if you had your own way, what kind of book would you write?"

Angie thought about it. "I don't know. But writing a true-crime book would obviously be easier than an exposé. I've done it, right?"

"Right. And what if the publisher gave her consent?"

"For me to write about Jamie?"

"Let the bird fly where it wants to fly," Darey said. When they both looked at him he dismissed the comment with a wave. "Something I was just thinking. The point is, we support Angie in whatever direction she wants to go."

"The publisher would never agree," Angie said. "Neither would Jake Barnes."

"What's he got to do with this?" Darey asked.

Angie shrugged. "Everything. He agreed to give me access to the Red Protocol on the assumption that it would help me write a book that controls the narrative on both the dangers and the benefits of full immersion."

She had a point.

"I think I might be able to bring Marsha around to the idea," Felicia said. "Worth a shot."

Angie already looked brighter. "So we look into Jamie, hear his story, and if it makes sense and I like the idea, I write about him."

Darey gave her a smile and a nod. "Yup."

"And you defend him pro bono?"

"I didn't say that. I'm just saying that I'm willing to get you an audience so you can decide if you want to write about the case."

"So you're agreeing to meet him tomorrow with me," Angie said.

"I think that's what I said."

"Just making sure."

Felicia took a drink from a glass of water on the crystal table. "Under one condition," she said, replacing the glass. "And, Angie, I can't overstress how important this is."

"No more dead heading," Angie said.

"Well, yes, that for sure. But just as importantly, I want you to promise me that you'll be completely transparent about any additional whiteouts. If they continue, we have to know."

"Of course."

Darey knew that when Angie said 'of course' she really meant 'of course now but maybe not of course tomorrow' and, as far as he was concerned, that was her right.

"Even more," Felicia continued, "if you experience anything remotely similar to a visual hallucination without gear, you call me immediately."

"Well, I haven't and yes, I will." Angie's eyes drifted to the window. "Trust me, that would be scary."

"I can imagine." Felicia stood. "And now I have a meeting with Jake Barnes."

"Really?" Angie asked. "In person?"

Felicia shrugged. "Evidently. His assistant called and asked if I could meet him this afternoon. I'm assuming it's about you. He wants to stay close."

Angie looked unsure about that. "Hmm."

"Settled then." Darey slapped the arms on his chair and stood. "I'll call Randy George and set up the interview with Jamie."

He ushered Felicia out, thanked her for sticking by Angie's side, and returned to find Angie sitting back in his chair, picking at her lower lip. On the desk before her lay a folded piece of white paper.

"I need to tell you something," she said.

"Okay."

"I had a flashback, only one, the first day I was out. Felicia knows but I didn't tell her what I saw. I was by Town Lake with a boy, and we were looking out at the water. The boy was tall and blond and looked like Jamie. At the time I thought he might be my son from the Red Protocol."

Darey didn't know what to make of that. But it would explain why she was so fascinated with Jamie.

"Jamie's nineteen, you're twenty-seven. Unless you had a child at age eight—"

"I know. I'm just saying. It's like I know him from somewhere. And also, I got this."

She picked up the paper and handed it to him.

"It came to our house this morning. I would have told you earlier, but no one else can know. Read it, you'll understand."

He unfolded the paper and saw that it was a letter.

Dear Angie Channing—

You don't know me, but I know you through your book, Righteous. I also know your handle on the darknet, Lover Boy. I know it because I'm a hacker and a closet Dead Head like you.

I have to speak to someone about something my friend Timothy and I found on an encrypted key. I can't tell you anything else here, but it's terrifying and I don't know what else to do.

Please don't tell anyone that you received this letter. Please don't mention my name, it could be dangerous. Timothy doesn't think so, but I'm afraid. Maybe you can help us.

Please text me at the number below and maybe we can meet. As soon as possible.

Please, I'm begging you.

Clair Milton
(555) 659-1010

He blinked. "This came to the house?"

"Yup. Now you tell me if killing two kids for information on an encrypted key sounds like something Jamie Hamilton would do."

"So you think Jamie was framed."

She shrugged. "You tell me."

"By whom?"

"Who stands to gain?" she asked.

The governor, he thought. But it was way too early to think such thoughts. Either way, the letter opened Pandora's Box.

"It's evidence," he said.

"Yes. But we can't turn it in. Promise me that."

She was right. Giving the letter to the prosecution would give them an opportunity to spin it in a dozen different directions. Especially if they or any authority linked to them was complicit in framing Jamie, however unlikely that was.

"Darey? Please tell me you won't turn this over."

"You still have the envelope it came in?"

"It's at the house."

He nodded. "We have some time," he said. "But sooner or later—"

"All this letter does is give us reason to dig. It proves nothing by itself. As far as I'm concerned, I never got a letter. There can't be any 'sooner or later.' We can't submit it. Ever. It would expose me to the world as a Dead Head."

She was right. *Angie, Angie, what have you gotten us into this time?*

He nodded. "Agreed."

CHAPTER
TEN

THE INTERNATIONAL headquarters for Convergence sprawled over a three-hundred-acre parcel of land north of Austin, east of I-35. Apple had once been housed on a campus nearly as grandiose before a group of retro radicals, opposing further technological advancements, had targeted Apple's headquarters for destruction in 2035. Ironically, the group had used high-tech weapons to serve their hatred of high-tech. They targeted Google on the same day. That attempt was foiled.

Felicia was twenty-seven when the attacks rocked the world. Like all such absurd acts of aggression, nothing was accomplished. Technology progressed exponentially and without pause.

She took manual control of her self-driving car at the gates.

"Felicia Buckhead for Jake Barnes," she told the guard. He held out a pad and she passed her wrist over the scanner. The invisible code tattooed on her skin brought up her identity. "He asked to meet me."

The guard gave a nod and passed her a badge. "You know where the south building is?"

"I've never been here."

He pointed out the road. "To the end and then right. Follow the signs to the underground parking. Take the elevator to the top-floor lobby. The receptionist will help you from there."

"Thank you."

"Have a good day, ma'am."

She guided her Mercedes down the road, following his instructions. The whole compound was surrounded by a red rock wall bordered by pines that blended into the arid landscape. Beautiful. A force field rose far above the wall—impenetrable, they said. The only way in was through one of four gates.

Evidently, Jake Barnes rarely left the compound. He was a hermit in his own castle.

It took her ten minutes to reach the lobby, where she gave her name to a pretty blond receptionist named Clarice. A male assistant came for Felicia less than a minute later and led her to Jake Barnes's corner office.

"He's inside," the assistant said, opening the door.

Felicia stepped into an expansive room that looked more like an atrium than an office. White marble floors extended to floor-to-ceiling windows that overlooked Austin to the south. Models of a dozen iterations of chip boards and virtual reality headsets and bodysuits and chambers were showcased in glass cubes near the right wall. All the paintings, maybe ten in all, were impressionistic—black and white, mostly geometric shapes that held little meaning for Felicia. Everything was square, everything was perfectly set, everything as clean as the glass that overlooked the world.

To her left sat a conference table, also black, with twelve chairs. White leather. A large black desk made of what might be onyx sat in the center of the room, sparsely appointed with a single transparent monitor.

Jake Barnes was seated behind the desk, dressed in a black turtleneck, back to her, staring at the windows. When the door shut with a soft click, he slowly swiveled to face her.

The face that peered at her was older than she anticipated, gaunt and heavily wrinkled. Hair and beard as white as bleached wool. She knew he was fifty-nine, but slumped behind the desk, Barnes looked closer to eighty-nine.

Here was the recluse personally known by so few.

"Come forward, my dear. Let me take a closer look at you."

She walked up to his desk, caught off-guard by the presence such a frail looking man carried. His eyes were a pale blue, kind and all-seeing.

He motioned to one of the chairs facing his desk. "Have a seat."

"Thank you, sir."

"So I finally meet the one who oversees our little treasure," he said with a slight smile.

"I assume you mean Angie. But I don't oversee her. I only advise her."

"With only the best advice, I'm sure." He looked at her for a moment. "You seem surprised. What is it?"

"I wouldn't say—"

"I look far too old to be fifty-nine," he interrupted. "An enigma, yes?"

She didn't want to be rude, but he'd broached the subject.

"Since you say so, yes."

"I do say so. It's one of the reasons I no longer take visitors. The world wouldn't understand."

For a long while he studied her, as if deciding whether to take her into his confidence.

"You're a professional therapist?" he said.

"I am."

"And as a therapist, the law obligates you to protect the privacy of your clients."

"That's correct."

"Then I would like to be your client." He slid an envelope across the desk. "Consider it a retainer. I assume five thousand dollars will suffice for now?"

It was the last thing she might have expected. She hadn't come for this. Even if she had, she'd never asked a client for a retainer.

"Take it," he said. "I'm a dying man without any heirs."

"And you think I can help you?"

"I know you can. Please, take it. I would feel more comfortable."

She nodded and picked up the envelope, realizing he was probably more interested in her confidence than her advice. To each their own.

"Then consider me hired," she said, picking up the envelope. "How can I be of service?"

"We'll get to that." He withdrew a square glass case from the bottom drawer and set it before her. Inside were two preserved mice elevated on needles. He looked up at her, pale eyes bright. "Do you know what this is, Felicia?"

She cleared her throat. "Mice?"

"Ah, but not just any mice. Take a closer look." He pushed the case toward her. "Tell me what you see."

She leaned forward and studied the dead rodents. "One has longer legs than the other."

"Twice the length, even though they were born as identical twins."

"So a mutation?"

"Not just any mutation. One of the first comprehensive single-generation mutations facilitated by virtual technology."

She stared at the one mouse's longer legs, recalling Angie's remarks about the effects of fully immersive virtual reality on genetic expression. Fascinating. But she found the man before her even more fascinating.

"We all know how stem cells work in the lab," he said. "If we take two genetically identical stem cells and place them in different petri dishes containing two different cultures, one made of bone cells and one made of muscle cells, they each become their respective culture. One becomes a bone cell, the other becomes a muscle cell, even though they started with the exact same DNA. It's the environment they're in, not their DNA, that makes them what they become. Impossible, it would seem. You're familiar?"

"Somewhat," she said.

"No one knows how it works. Oh, there are theories, but it remains one of biology's greatest mysteries. The only way to unravel a mystery is to step out of the box the mystery lives in. Science is reluctant to do that."

She liked him. Despite his reputation as an unyielding man, as were most great innovators, he was still just a boy figuring out the world.

"Which is where you come in," she said.

"Well, I've never been accused of clinging to entrenched assumptions."

He motioned at the case sitting on his black desk. "Think of all living creatures, including humans, as essentially one large stem cell. Like stem cells, we change as a result of our environment. The changes aren't just in our brains, but in our bodies, which are simply an expression of our brains. This has been proven many times over, going back decades. If I take a sugar pill that I think will heal me, that pill is nearly as effective as a real drug."

"The placebo effect. Wasn't that discovered in the 1950s?"

"A hundred years ago, yes. But the mechanisms have only recently been understood by those willing to open their minds. Stem cells become what they are 'taught' to become based on external information fed to them. On a fundamental level, we are all what we've been taught to believe. At Convergence we call it the biology of belief."

Felicia already saw where he was going. "So if the mind believes it's in any particular environment for a sustained amount of time, it will adapt to that environment like a stem cell adapts and becomes its environment."

"The only . . ." A hitch in his throat stopped him and he coughed into his hand, then plucked a tissue from a box and wiped his mouth. "The only thing we did to the mouse who has longer legs was to replace all of the signals of perception entering his brain with an alternate perception. A reality in which it had longer legs. The stems cells in the mouse's body followed its belief that it had longer legs and thus actually grew them."

"Amazing." Her mind spun with the implications. "Like in a virtual reality."

"Not just any virtual reality. No one's been able to replicate an environment that's 'real' enough to create true presence in that reality. There's always enough of a clue of the old reality to signal a person's brain that what they're experiencing, even in a Deep Dive, is virtual. No one's been able to fully eliminate the signals of all five senses and replace them with new ones."

"Until now," Felicia said. "The Red Protocol."

"Actually, we've had the technology for over a decade, but it's been messy, not to mention expensive. Very expensive. It's come a long way since those early days."

"If we are what we believe, can someone with cancer be healed of it in a Deep Dive where they no longer believe they have it?"

"It's not quite that simple, but the short answer is yes, that's where we're headed." He leaned back in his chair and folded his arms. "Unfortunately, the opposite is also true, as you can plainly see."

It suddenly occurred to her that Jake Barnes was referring to himself. She blinked. Could it be?

"Your . . ." What if she was wrong?

"Your what?" he asked.

"Your age . . ."

"Yes, my age," Barnes returned in a tired voice. He shifted his gaze to nowhere. "I was one of the first to go into the earliest version of the Red Protocol, many years ago. On my seventh journey, I remained under for six days. Unfortunately, that unrefined technology irreversibly damaged my DNA." He looked back at her. "You're familiar with how aging works?"

She nodded, still taken aback. "As the caps at the end of each DNA strand erode, the telomeres shorten," she said. "As the telomeres shorten, genetic material is lost, and the cells they govern age. Premature damage to telomeres also ages the body's cells."

"As you can plainly see."

"You're using the Red Protocol to find a cure," she said. "That's what this is all about."

"Oh, the Red Protocol is far more than that. I wouldn't mind reversing the damage to my cells, of course. I'm currently aging at nearly four times the natural rate and will be dead soon if I fail, but there's far more at stake than my life, trust me."

She understood now why he insisted on complete confidence. How many people knew about this?

"How long?" she asked

"Two years, my dear. That's all the time I have left to understand the true power of the Red Protocol."

And Angie's one of your lab rats, she thought.

He pushed his chair back from the desk. "I'm sure you can appreciate the danger of indiscriminate and unregulated use of fully immersive virtual reality technology. The world needs to understand both the benefits and the dangers of the technology before it falls into the wrong hands. That's why I agreed to allow Angie Channing to experience the Red Protocol. It's critical we control the way this information is made public."

Her mind spun. "If the world knew what you have here, they would shut it down."

"In a heartbeat," he stood. A tall man, rail thin. "Follow me."

Walking deliberately but with poise, he led Felicia to the far wall and pressed his fingers on a scanner. A three-foot section of the white wall swung inward with a hiss. "This way."

She followed him into a long corridor.

"Humanity has always been terrified of change. Of the unknown. New ideas that change the world always begin as heresy, and heretics are invariably burned at the stake, like Copernicus for suggesting Earth wasn't at the center of the universe. Shows you how far we've come, but we're only just getting started. Do you know how I came to found Convergence?"

She walked beside him, aware of her clacking shoes. His were as silent as a ghost's.

"Only what I've read."

He chuckled. "Let me set the record straight. I was born in Pasadena. My father was, let's just say, abusive. Extremely controlling. That was the petri dish I grew up in, and it only got worse when my mother died under mysterious circumstances when I was eleven. Thankfully, five years later my father also died."

"Grateful to be free, when I was seventeen I applied to Stanford and was admitted based on my scores. Books were my escape when I was young and I was blessed, or cursed depending on how you look at it, with a mind that allowed me to earn doctorates in both computer science and theoretical physics by the time I was twenty-two."

He was a genius, they said. She didn't doubt it.

They came to another door, which he opened in the same way he had the first. He motioned her through.

"I worked at Google for six years, helping them develop emerging technologies, before moving to India, where I worked for a company that developed VR technology for the military. It was in India that I first began dabbling in quantum mirroring and the effects of psychedelics on the brain. I always had an innate knowing that the reality we experience is based on our beliefs of it. Somehow we humans are collapsing consciousness into an expression we call reality. Do you follow?"

These days, quantum mechanics was taught as early as grade school. She didn't really understand it but said what came to mind:

"You're talking about the observer problem," she said.

"Correct. Resisted by science for a century because it defies logic. No one could figure out how it works. The mystics said faith. Belief. With belief the size of a mustard seed, a mountain can be moved into the sea. But how? So I began to investigate the science of changing beliefs. This led me to returning to the United States at age thirty-six and founding Convergence with the sole purpose of creating a virtual reality so real that it was fully believed, without reservation. All that I've done since is in service to what we have now created. This way."

They passed through a door and entered a large atrium with a domed ceiling, then came to a stop at a railing. Below them lay a large vacant laboratory with workstations surrounding a large glass tube-like chamber. It encased what looked like a fully reclined dentist's chair.

Felicia knew immediately what it must be. This was the reality interface changer in which Angie had entered the Red Protocol. There, in that chair, her mind had been mapped for two days. There, once mapped, her perceptions of the external world had been shut off and replaced by new perceptions, which, for three days, made all things new.

Barnes put a hand on the railing and looked at her.

"You see, my dear, reality isn't static. It's malleable. By changing our perception of reality . . . our beliefs . . . we can change reality itself. That's how the mouse grew longer legs."

He stared down at the empty laboratory.

"As you know, we call the technology in this room the Red Protocol. Red for life. A new life, like the one Angie experienced last week. We inserted a blueprint, essentially a mental framework in which she populated that life, but we also had significant control of her brain. Suffice it to say that this technology has the capacity to change the world by changing the beliefs that lead to bigotry and hatred and disease. It's a thousand times more powerful than any drug."

"And in the wrong hands, it could also destroy the world," she said. "You could manipulate presidents. Whole societies. Or am I missing something?"

"No, you're not. Which is why control of the technology is so important."

"Why Angie Channing? Yes, she wrote a bestselling book, but if this is such sensitive work, why did you choose her to enter the protocol?"

"Because Angie Channing has a unique mind. The veil between this reality and any other is far thinner for her than most. No one can better explore the edges of the Red Protocol than her. And no one is better suited to write about it."

"But how could you know?"

His brow arched. "By watching her online, naturally. She's been on our radar for a very long time."

They had the technology to breach all firewalls and watch even the most private activity online. Totally illegal, but Barnes was clearly unconcerned with legal issues in the face of such pressing concerns as extending his life and changing the world.

"Angie's a small part of a much bigger picture," he said, turning away. "We have nothing to hide. We only look to humanity's future."

He clearly had much to hide, but she understood why he would say he didn't. Still . . . There was more he wasn't saying.

"You should know that Angie's reconsidering the book," she said.

"Oh? How so?"

"She's caught up in the Oak Hill Dead Head murders. You know about them?"

"The whole world knows about them. So she's tempted to write a storybook again." He frowned. "I suppose that's not a bad thing."

She'd hoped he would see it that way.

"So tell me, how is our girl?" he asked, tone softer now.

"She's still having whiteouts but claims they're growing weaker," she said.

"Good. Although I'm surprised she's still experiencing them at all." He coughed and wiped his mouth with a handkerchief he'd withdrawn from his pocket. "No hallucinations?"

Felicia shook her head. "No. Not that I'm aware of anyway."

"Good. It's important that you understand how dangerous things could be for her if she were to experience any alternate reality without using a RIG. If that happens, she might actually find herself in a delusional frame of mind that perceives *this* world as nothing more than a virtual reality. If Angie experiences any kind of hallucination I must know immediately. Not just for her sake, but for what harm she might do to others."

"I understand. I think we're okay."

"Good."

She'd already known much of what he was sharing, hearing it in this context created an immediacy that made her palms sweat.

"You do realize that the governor essentially declared war on you."

He smiled. "She knows as well as you do that I'm in favor of legislation. But yes, she did appear to cast me in a rather dark corner. Small-minded people are interested in fearmongering and control."

He sighed wearily.

"Never mind all that, just keep a close eye on Angie for me. We have much more work to do with her."

"You mean the book."

"I mean beyond the book, my dear. Like I said, my time is short."

CHAPTER
ELEVEN

ANGIE SAT across from Jamie Hamilton in the same interview room where she'd met Randy George. Darey paced behind her, all attorney. Randy had made an exception in allowing her in the room, because she wasn't legal counsel, but he was willing to take a slap on the wrist for that.

For that matter, Darey wasn't technically Jamie's legal counsel either, but the public defender, a skinny overworked man named Josh Newton, had agreed to sign Darey on as an adviser, which would satisfy the law for now. On the ride down, they'd listened to a recording of the interview Randy George had conducted at Jamie's house. Disturbing, to say the least.

Looking at Jamie up close, Angie couldn't say whether this was the son she'd had in the Red Protocol. For starters, her recall of her experience in that space was almost nonexistent. More, she couldn't comprehend how she would have populated her virtual world with someone she hadn't known. She had to be making false associations. Unless she *had* known him once.

Jamie was only a kid, now dressed in the same obnoxious yellow jumpsuit Texas had adopted in recent years for all prisoners. A simple boy who seemed clueless about his predicament, which only made the state's rush to judgment even more appalling. One minute with Jamie and anyone would know he couldn't be a cold, calculating killer.

But she knew that wasn't necessarily true. Jamie could be guilty while believing he was innocent. Still, even if he was guilty, she couldn't imagine him being capable of premeditation. Couldn't Randy see that?

Yes, because Randy was one of the good cops, and his point was well taken. The prosecution would argue that Jamie, who had a history of snapping, had done so under the influence of an altered reality while dead heading. But Darey would find a way around that. If Darey believed Jamie was innocent.

Was she sure he was innocent?

In fifteen minutes with Jamie he'd given them the same answers he'd given Randy and other investigators who'd put him through the wringer. All the while, Angie's mind spun, one moment sure the boy was a victim of some insane political conspiracy, the next wondering if he really had committed the crime under the influence. Maybe Deep Dive technology should be banned. Maybe she played with fire every time she went deep. But no, that was absurd. What harm was there in playing a game that transported the player to an altered state?

You're looking at the ugly underbelly of virtual reality, Angie. Right here in front of you.

"Excuse me a moment," Darey said, walking to the corner. "I have to make a quick call." With his back to them, he made his call and spoke softly into his earpiece, one hand cupped over his mouth to muffle his voice.

Jamie was picking his upper lip, eyes quizzical, without a clue as to what kind of trouble he was in.

"I pick my lip too," she said. "When I'm nervous."

He snatched his hand away from his mouth and his handcuffs clanked on the table. "Sorry. Mom says I shouldn't do that 'cause my lip bleeds."

"Yeah, I know. But sometimes we just do it anyway because we don't realize we're doing it."

His lip twisted in a crooked smile. "Do you play games?"

"Of course I do! In fact, I play them a lot, maybe more than I should. But it's my way of being free, know what I mean?"

His eyes were bright. "I'm good at games, you know. I always win now."

"That's what I've heard. Have you ever played with someone called Tayo, on the darknet?"

"I don't remember. Is he good?"

"He's one of the best."

"Then maybe I've played with him. I like playing with the best."

She was curious about his limited memory. "Do you usually have a hard time remembering things?"

"I like numbers," he said. "I'm good with numbers and with shapes."

She'd read about a chess master who, even as a boy, could see geometric relationships between the pieces on the board, instantly recognizing hundreds of possible moves and outcomes. He called it intuition. When it was working, not even a computer could beat him. When it wasn't, he was lost. Luckily for him, that otherworldly intuition had earned him the title of world chess grandmaster over numerous years.

"I'm good with words," she said. "Maybe one day I'll write your story."

"In a book?"

"Yup. Would you like that?"

"Yup."

Darey finished his call and slid into the chair next to Angie again. "Sorry about that."

"Do you know when I can go home?" Jamie asked. "My mother's by herself."

Darey rested his hand on the table, palm down, gathering Jamie in his trademark look of calm assurance.

"I want you to listen to me, Jamie. They aren't going to let you go home for a while. We'll make sure your mother's okay at home and I promise they'll let you see her soon. But it's important that you understand that this is going to be your life for a while."

"Can you bring my processing box and my RIG? I have a tournament tonight."

"I'm sorry, but it's against the law to have processors in prison. County has several holo-rooms, which is how we might be talking in the future."

His eyes brightened. "In a holo-room? I've never used one!"

"Well then, you're in for a treat. Although don't expect it to be like a Deep Dive. It's scaled back so you know it's virtual. Still, pretty neat."

"But no processor for me?"

"They have some local processors in the library, but they won't let you use those. At least not now. Do you know why?"

"No."

"They're saying that you committed a crime using a RIG. That means you can't be in the same room as a RIG, other than their holo-room, unless we can prove that it wasn't you who killed Timothy and Clair. Do you understand?"

"Yeah, but I already told you I didn't."

"I know. Now we need to prove that. To do that we will need as much information as possible, and that will take a while. The DA will want to hold a trial as quickly as possible and I'll be able to stall them for a while, but none of that will matter unless we can find out who really killed Timothy and Clair."

"I don't know who killed them," Jamie said.

Darey was speaking to him in his own language, setting aside any legalese, and Angie loved him for it. But she knew Jamie's language better than Darey ever could.

"Think of it like a game, Jamie," she said. "The next few weeks, maybe longer, are going to be like a game. The most important game you've ever played."

He grinned. "Like all the games people play all the time."

"Exactly." Was he talking about real life? "Kind of like that, but yes. Pretend that your life's a game. There are two ways to win. The first is to beat the opponent. The second way is to have fun while you're playing, which is also a win. The second way is much better, don't you think?"

"I always have fun. That's what I tell my mom when she asks why I play so much. It's fun."

"Exactly. That's why you and I play games. Because it's fun. Well, this is just like that. And in this game they're going to do some things that they hope will make you lose. Like maybe hit you or push you. Or they might not give you food. Or they might say lots of mean things to make you quit and tell them *you* killed Timothy and Clair because you were angry with them. They'll try all kinds of tricks, but you know what they're doing, so you can just smile at them and know that you're winning. Make sense?"

He was sitting straighter and his eyes were brighter.

"And I don't have to pretend because it is a game anyway," he said.

"What do you mean by that?"

"It's all a game."

"What is?"

"Like you just said. You know too, right?"

He really was confusing reality with his gaming dimensions. Angie didn't know how to feel about that. On one hand, such an approach to life could be healthy. Seeing the drama of life as if it were a game sometimes allowed her to release the deep investment she had in her 'role' as a character in this world and rise above the struggles of life. It was one reason people dead headed.

On the other hand, actually believing life was only a game was a sure sign of a fractured mind and one of the primary threats of fully immersive virtual reality. The prosecutor would have a field day with it. She could hear the DA's arguments in the court now: *Here sits an adult, Jamie Hamilton, who is so twisted by dead heading that he can't tell the difference between real life and the games he plays. It isn't a stretch to see how Jamie might kill someone in real life, thinking of it only as a game. He might even forget he's committed the crime, so fractured is his mind. But he is guilty, and he must be held accountable for the sake of all humanity.*

Darey played along. "Be that as it may, Jamie, it's very important that you don't tell anyone you know this is only a game. Don't give away our secrets or they might try to use it against you. Right?"

"Right! That's how I win most games. I already see what they're going to do because I know how the programming works."

"Exactly," Darey said. "In fact, from now on, I don't want you to tell them anything about any of your games, including this game. And especially don't answer even one question from anyone about Timothy or Clair. Nothing about your mother or your other friends or anything about your life. Can you do that?"

"Yup." He looked between them. "But then what do I do?"

"Just be you, but don't talk about you. That's your role in the game we're playing. I'm like your partner in the game. I'm the one who gets to talk because they can't hurt me. Okay?"

"Okay."

"Good. But the only way it will work is if you remember as much as you can and tell me so I can do the talking."

He was going to take the case, Angie realized. Adrenaline coursed through her veins. *They* were going to take the case, she as an investigative reporter and writer, and Darey as lead counsel.

"So I want you to think real hard about two things. And if you can't remember today, then you can tell me anything you think of later. Okay?"

"Okay." Jamie was fully engaged. Darey was amazing.

"The first thing is anything from that night, four nights ago now, that might prove you were home, playing games. Like gaming logs. Anything that—"

"I don't use logs," he said. "I use Swiper."

"Yes, I guessed as much, but there might be some other kind of log. Something written, old-school. Maybe someone who called you. Security footage. Pizza delivery. Anything at all. If you can't think of anything, that's okay, but if I can prove you were home all night, it will make things difficult for the DA."

"The DA," he said. "That's who we're playing against?"

"The district attorney, yes. And all the investigators and cops. Anything come to mind?"

He looked at the table, concentrating. But he was hitting a wall. He finally let out some air. "No."

"Okay, that's okay. Maybe something will come to you later. The second thing I want you to think about is anybody you know from school or in your life who might have wanted to hurt Timothy or Clair. I'm assuming that you were framed. Someone else killed them and they're trying to make it look like you did it. So if we can find out who killed them, then you win. Right?"

"Yup. Do you know why they're making it me?"

"No, that's what we have to figure out. You have to think about all your friends, everyone you've ever had an argument with, anyone Timothy or Clair talked to you about. Anyone or anything that might have upset you or them."

The barrage of assignments seemed to disorient him.

"We'll make a list for you," Angie said, catching Darey's eyes.

"I don't have any friends at school."

A beat.

"Okay, but you've known other people over the years," she said. "Maybe when you were younger even."

"I don't remember anything from when I was younger," he said. "Mom says it's because it was hard and I forgot on purpose."

She nodded, heart torn. "That's okay. We all do that. And we'll dig into your past and see what we can find. But in the meantime, just think about it."

Darey was tapping some notes into his pad. They would make interviews with Jamie's mother and the victims' parents a priority.

"Okay. Do you know when I can eat?"

"When did you last eat?" Darey asked.

"Last night. But they wouldn't give me any Coke."

"I'll make sure they give you some Coke."

A knock sounded on the door. Randy George entered and looked between them. He was a good-looking man with kind eyes and curly hair. Clearly mixed race, although of which descent was impossible to tell. As the world's gene pool blended, eventually everyone would have the same deeply tanned skin tone as Randy, or close to it. She liked that about him.

"Time's up," he said. "I'm sorry, but they're waiting for Jamie at transport." A pause. "Am I to assume that you're taking over as counsel?"

Darey pushed his chair back and stood. To Jamie, leaning forward and tapping him gently on his hand: "Remember what we said." He winked. "Let's play together."

Jamie flushed, sheepish. "Yeah."

"Stay strong, Jamie," Angie said. "We're on your side."

"Okay. Don't forget the Coke."

Darey scooped up his pad and walked out the door, Angie close behind. "Please give the boy some Coke, Randy. As much as he wants."

"I'll see what I can do, but I can't vouch for County."

"As for my taking the case, you'll have my answer in three minutes."

Darey marched down the hall, tall and confident, past booking, through the foyer. He nodded at the hairy DA, Andrew Olsen, who just happened to be across the room and looked rather surprised.

Angie took Darey's hand as they exited the station. A gathering of at least twenty reporters and staff waited on the steps and immediately surged toward them.

The phone call, Angie realized. Darey had made a call to announce a press conference. Her heart was crashing with pride. It was a game. One of life and death. And Darey knew how to play.

The journalists yelled questions, but Darey held up his hand and silenced them. They all knew him. They all knew his work. They all knew that everything about the Oak Hill Dead Head case was about to change.

"Just a short statement for you today. It is with pride in our legal system, a system built on the foundational conviction that all are innocent until proven guilty, that I'm announcing that I will be defending Jamie Hamilton in the state's case against him. I've reviewed the testimonies and seen the evidence that has convinced the state of Texas to bring criminal charges against my client, and I can assure you he is innocent."

He put his hand on Angie's shoulder.

"You all know Angie as an investigative reporter who knows how to uncover the truth like few can in a world distorted by lies. I'm sure you'll be hearing much more from her in the days to come."

They would? Yes, they would. With a twinge of anxiety, Angie realized she'd just put herself under the penetrating gaze of a world that was more likely to see her as a threat than the voice of reason it had supported following the release of her book, *Righteous*.

"That's all for now."

The world suddenly went white, right there as she stood before the whole world. She caught her breath and went perfectly still, fighting off panic. *Not now!*

But it was now and it lasted a good seven seconds, longer than the others. She wasn't sure she'd ever felt so naked.

The street stuttered back into view and she slowly emptied her lungs, hoping no one had noticed. She dare not breathe a word about her whiteouts to Felicia or even Darey now, she thought. They would remove her from the case.

She forced a smile, gave the cameras a nod, and hurried down the steps with Darey.

CHAPTER
TWELVE

DISTRICT ATTORNEY Andrew Olsen sucked manically at his vaporizer, eyes pinned on the rearview mirror. The parking lot under the 360 bridge was empty except for one other car, which Olsen had already checked and confirmed to be abandoned. Clouds of tobacco-scented vapor filled his own car, and he cracked his window to clear it.

He wasn't crazy about the cloak-and-dagger crap but knew it had always been the way of the power-brokering world, from the first time some human had decided to manipulate the system for their gain thousands of years ago.

Truth be told, everything was ultimately power brokering. All relationships, all progress, all decline, everything. It's why, having come to terms with his own desires for advancement ten years earlier, Olsen had decided to leverage his position as a prosecutor to make a real mark for himself in this world.

He knew the pecking order well. Knew you had to either eliminate or seduce the powers above you to slide up the ladder. So when Matteo Steger, or whatever his real name was, had first approached him two years ago with cryptic promises of favor tied to the real power brokers of not only Texas but of the federal government, he'd taken the chance. If not now, then when?

With a little arm twisting on his part and more than a little string pulling from forces unseen, he'd received his appointment to district attorney three months later, when the sitting DA, Sheron Bassett, unexpectedly died in a house fire. But that wasn't the end for him. He was having too much fun to stop now.

Or so he told himself whenever things got a bit uncomfortable. Like now.

A blue BMW with lights on crept into the lot behind him.

Olsen took one last deep drag on the vaporizer and set it on the passenger seat. Smoothed his bald scalp. Rubbed his jowls with both hands. *Come to me, baby.*

He knew it was the other way around—that he was at their beck and call—but if he played his cards right, messengers and strong-arms like Matteo Steger would one day be at his beck and call. He wasn't interested in taking the higher offices, like governor or congressman, they were too much in the public eye. But he wasn't going to spend the rest of his life as a DA.

The BMW pulled up five feet adjacent to his car and parked. Olsen watched the dark tinted windows for a full ten seconds before the front door opened and a wiry man with dark hair slowly stepped into the morning light.

He'd guessed Matteo to be Mediterranean, although Olsen's one inquiry about the man's personal life had been met with a blank stare. Maybe Greek. Maybe Lebanese.

Steger closed his door, leaned back on it and crossed his arms as Olsen lowered his window. The man wore the same dark rectangular glasses he typically wore. Same dark suit and black crew-neck shirt. In his mouth, a toothpick as always. A cinnamon toothpick soaked in nicotine, called a nicopick.

Olsen gave the man a short nod. "Good morning."

"Is it?"

The thin voice got under Olsen's skin.

"You tell me."

Steger looked at him, then back at the entrance to the parking lot, rolling that toothpick in his mouth. He'd always struck Olsen as someone who was tired of his life but had no choice except to live it. He'd often wondered how much people in Steger's line of work made. That depended on what they did, Olsen supposed. He didn't have any evidence that Steger was a killer, but it wouldn't surprise him. At the least, Steger bent and broke the law in ways power brokers couldn't risk doing themselves.

People like the governor of Texas, Judith Patterson, though Olsen had no direct evidence that Steger actually worked for her. For all he knew, the man worked for someone over Patterson's head.

Matteo spoke without turning his head, still gazing back the way he'd come. "You know why we're here, don't you, Mr. DA?"

Stop talking down to me, he wanted to say.

"The fact that Channing & Miles is now lead counsel in the Oak Hill murders, I'm guessing. You tell your people that we have the case wrapped up tighter than a bug in a cocoon. So they slow us down a month or two. That doesn't change the facts of the case. The verdict will be the same. Jamie Hamilton's as guilty as a dog caught eating its own vomit."

Matteo crossed one ankle over the other and fixed eyes on him. "Really? This is much bigger than some Dead Head case. Are we forgetting something?"

Olsen stared back. "We're directing the future of technology. Please don't be condescending."

"Not technology, Mr. DA. You're directing the future of those who control technology. Can you tell me why?"

"Just tell me what's so important," Olsen snapped. "It's going to be a busy day."

"Tell me."

Olsen ground his molars but humored the man. "Whoever controls technology controls the world."

"So you understand how important all of this is, then? I've been asked to make sure you understand that."

"I understand."

"And you also understand that everything you've been given and far more can and will be taken away with the stroke of a pen if you lose heart."

"Now you're threatening me."

"I'm only rehearsing the facts, because I've been asked to. Nothing personal."

Fair enough. This was that part of the game.

"Please give me an audible answer," Steger said.

Olsen nodded. "I'm aware."

"Good. There's been a change. They want the writer out of the way."

Angie Channing. "I was under the impression they—"

"It's not your job to be impressed by anything. You're underestimating what someone of her popularity could do to a case like this. She's out. You will discredit her."

He hesitated, mind spinning.

"How?"

"She's a closet Dead Head, guilty of the very activity she warns the public about in her book. Expose her. Be specific. Her handle is Lover Boy."

Olsen didn't like it.

"Wouldn't it be better to discredit her husband? He's the one who—"

"Mrs. Channing is the key. Get to her and her husband will back away." Matteo opened the door to his car, slid inside, and closed the door. His tinted window slid down.

"Today, Mr. DA. Not tomorrow."

CHAPTER
THIRTEEN

ANGIE KNOCKED on the door to the Milton house at eleven that morning, knowing full well that Susan Milton would as likely fly into a rage as grant her an interview. Darey had argued that it was too early to try to win the woman's trust. She would certainly know by now that Angie's high-powered attorney husband, Darey Channing, was representing the monster she believed had killed her daughter, Clair.

True. But two days had passed since Susan stood on the court's steps and delivered her diatribe, calling for the head of Jamie Hamilton. The sooner they introduced Susan and Steve to the possibility that Clair's real killer might be someone far more sinister than a bullied student with ASD, the better, even if Susan did refuse to talk.

Either way, Angie had to understand the victims as much as the accused, and for that she needed Susan's help. This was a first step.

The Milton house sat on a hill in Barton Creek Estates, an upscale gated community for those with enough cash reserves to pay Texas's exorbitant property taxes. The mansions here made her and Darey's house look downright pedestrian. Oddly, this comforted Angie. She'd never seen herself as wealthy. That was Darey. Looking at the huge house, Angie wondered if maybe she and Darey should sell theirs and move into a condo.

When no one answered her knock on the door, she pressed the chime bell.

Five seconds later, the latch clicked and the door opened to reveal a Latina. A maid?

"May I help you?"

Angie extended her hand, stepping past the threshold before the woman could shut her out. "Good morning. Is Susan here?"

The woman took her hand, clearly unsettled by Angie's behavior. "May I ask who's—"

"My name's Angie Channing, and I'm here to share some new information about her daughter. She will want to speak with me."

The maid hesitated. "She did not sleep well last night. I think it's better to come back."

"I understand. But if you could at least tell her what I told you and let her decide."

The woman searched her eyes, then nodded. "Wait here."

She vanished down a hall to the right. Thirty seconds later Susan emerged from the hallway, eyes bloodshot, hair disheveled, face pasty white. She was dressed in a flimsy pastel nightdress.

Susan stopped short and glared at her without speaking. But at least she'd come out of hiding, Angie thought.

The moment she thought it, guilt swallowed her. Images of the crime scene flashed through her mind. A bound girl, skull crushed, stripped naked. The woman had just lost her daughter! This wasn't about a case to her; it was about death and hell, which had crushed her without any warning. Coming here to gain information that might exonerate Jamie was not only insensitive, but, at least in the eyes of Susan, downright cruel.

A knot formed in Angie's throat and she suddenly hated herself for having come. Darey was right, it was too early. Way too early! She blinked at the tears suddenly pooling in her eyes.

For a long moment Susan glared, lower jaw trembling.

"I'm . . ." Angie stepped back. "I'm sorry, I shouldn't have come."

Still no response from Susan.

Angie fumbled for a calling card in her pocket, managed to get three out, two of which fell on the floor. She stooped to retrieve them. "I'm sorry. Sorry.

I'll leave. If you want to talk . . ." She started to hand the card to Susan, but even that seemed rude. So she set it on the floor.

"Just call."

Angie turned to leave and made it to the door before Susan finally spoke.

"What new information?" she asked in a raspy, frail voice.

But Angie was too distraught to consider answering her. She reached for the door-handle and was pulling the door open when Susan yelled at her.

"Tell me!"

Angie stopped. Then slowly turned back, not wanting to.

"And it had better be good," Susan said, jaw still quivering.

Without thinking, Angie released the door handle, rushed up to Susan, and threw her arms round the frail woman, knowing even as their bodies pressed together that she was overstepping unspoken boundaries. But it was too late. She was here and the mother was here and the daughter was dead.

Angie was crying. "I'm so sorry, Susan. I'm so, so sorry."

And then Susan was crying, shaking in her embrace like a rag doll, arms limp by her sides.

SUSAN SNIFFED and took another sip of her tea. They sat in the living room in two overstuffed white silk chairs that probably cost enough to feed a child for a year. They'd been talking about Clair in soft tones for nearly forty minutes.

About Clair's on-again-off-again budding romance with Timothy.

Of her crackling wit and penchant for cynicism.

Of her brilliant mind, way off the charts. Way, way off.

Of her love for black clothes and anarchist literature and her complete disdain for socialites, never mind that her mother was queen of socialites. They had a strange symbiotic relationship like so many mothers and teenage daughters. Clair knew that her mother's world revolved around her, and no one could turn away that kind of love. And even though Clair would be perfectly happy living in a hut with a native (as long as there was electricity and a RIG), she had no problem taking advantage of her family's wealth.

Susan's meltdown in front of the court made perfect sense. If anything, it could be characterized as an underreaction. Without her daughter, Susan felt worthless. All she'd ever wanted was a baby girl, and she would have had more children if Steve hadn't put his foot down and gotten fixed.

Two people in this family had died this week, Angie thought. Their names were Clair and Susan. She was speaking to a ghost who no longer wanted to be alive.

They still hadn't talked about the murder, and that was fine. Silence stretched between them and Angie finally reached into her back pocket and pulled out a copy of the letter Clair had sent her.

"I said I had some new information on the case that you should know about." She unfolded the letter, reticent to dive into the details of the murder itself.

"What is it?" Susan asked.

"It's a copy of a letter I received from Clair. I have the original at home."

"You knew her?"

"No, but she knew me from my book." She handed the letter out. "I think you'll understand when you read it."

Susan took the letter and began to read her daughter's words. Her fear of being in danger because of something she'd found. An encrypted key. She trusted Angie because of her book, *Righteous*.

Slowly, the defeat on Susan's face changed to an expression of surprise and then resolve.

She lowered the letter. "Tell me more."

Angie did. She told her everything she knew about the case, answering questions as Susan slowly began to see a new image in the frame Angie drew for her.

When Angie had finished her recap of Jamie and all they knew of the case, Susan set her cup down and stared at a huge stone fireplace that looked like it had never been used. It was Austin after all.

"So you're saying Clair was murdered for what she found, and Jamie's being framed."

"It's a strong possibility," Angie said. "What do you know about Jamie's relationship with Clair?"

"Jamie was here once that I know of. Months ago. I never spoke to him, and Clair only mentioned him a couple times. She thought he was smart. Too smart and too dumb at the same time, if that makes sense. I don't know, I didn't ask. He was a better player than her, that much I know. Maybe that bothered her. She didn't like to lose."

"Can you imagine Clair ever mistreating someone like Jamie?"

"Based on what you've told me, maybe. At least treating him in a way that he might interpret as mean. She didn't trust people and was as cynical as they come. Teenagers, you know."

"I get it," Angie said. "I can be the same way."

"You can?"

"Sometimes. When you see the world through different lenses than most, it's easy to be cynical." She shrugged. "It's softening as I age, but I was a horror as a teenager."

They exchanged a soft chuckle. The emotion had to go somewhere.

"How was her relationship with her father?" Angie asked.

A deep inhale. Susan let the air out, eyes closed. "Like oil and water. Me, she could take because I loved her. Steve never paid her much mind. In fact, no mind except when he wanted to make a point about her stepping over the line."

She sniffed and ran the back of her hand across her upper lip. "Strange, but I never realized how little I cared about Steve until now." Eyes on Angie. "You think that makes me a bad person?"

"Not at all. I think that makes you honest. The bond that was holding you together is gone, that's all."

"He's staying at our loft downtown. I don't think I want him to come home."

Well, that's for you to decide, Angie thought. She let it stand.

"It's important that no one know about the letter, Susan. Maybe eventually, but right now it doesn't exist."

"But they have to know! If this will help them find out who killed Clair, they need it."

"As hard as it might be to hear this, I don't think they really care who killed Clair. Randy George does, but the case is out of his hands now. The governor and the DA just need to satisfy the public's demand for justice. It's an election year and, like it or not, this is all about politics for them. If they get wind that you don't trust them, they will shut you down."

"So what I did at the press conference . . ." She trailed off. "They used me."

"It's what they do, unfortunately. And if they learn about the letter, they'll just spin it their way, especially now that they've told the whole world they know who the killer is."

"I can see how it would make the governor look like an idiot."

"You can keep that copy but hide it so it can't be found. No one can know. Promise me."

Susan gave her a nod. "Okay."

Angie nodded. "Good. Do you mind if I take a look at Clair's room?"

"Sure."

The room looked like a typical tech-head teenager's hang out. A few posters on the wall, all Dead Head stuff, a desk with the processing box missing. No RIGs—those were also in evidence now. Didn't matter, they would be wiped.

"I tried to tell them that it looked like someone had been here," Susan said.

"How so?"

"Well, everything was close to where it was supposed to be, but not quite. Like the monitor, which is always at the back of her desk, was in the middle. And the processing box was at an angle—Clair liked it square. But maybe I was just imagining it because of the dirt."

"The smudges on the carpet?"

Susan stepped over to the wall next to the window. There on the carpet were several reddish smudges. Someone had been inside. Authorities would claim it was Jamie, naturally, but the dirt would be circumstantial unless they could match it to his boots.

"So you really think someone planted all that evidence?" Susan asked.

"We don't know, but my gut says yes, which is why Darey took the case. And I think it's possible someone broke in here looking for the key drive mentioned in Clair's letter."

"If the texts were planted on Jamie's phone, why mention a key?" Susan asked. "I mean, if that's what they were after?"

"Because it's what you'd expect. Most darknet games are encoded on encrypted key drives so the game doesn't live on any server. The encrypted key Clair mentioned is probably something else."

Susan settled onto the bed, lips trembling again. She lowered her head into her hand.

"Listen to me, Susan. It's going to be hard, I know." Angie sat next to her and took her hand. "But I'm going to do my best to find out what happened to your daughter. I want you to think over the next few days. Think about where Clair might have hidden a key. Whoever came for it might have found it, but I'm thinking Clair would be pretty smart about where to hide it, so maybe not. I know it's a long shot, but if we can find that key, it may lead us to whoever did all of this."

Susan nodded, head still in her hand.

Angie wished she could do something else that would help ease Susan's pain. Something that would give her comfort. Snap her fingers and make all this go away.

Instead, she just put both arms around Susan's thin frame, laid her head on her shoulder, and held her.

LEAVING THE MILTON house, Angie felt a strange mix of emotions—both a deep sorrow and a sense of triumph. Sorrow for obvious reasons. Triumph because she knew that she would hunt down the truth if it was the last thing she did on this earth. And she would put that truth on display for the whole world to see.

She visited the crime scene on the way home and called Darey from the small clearing where the dog had found the bodies. It was still taped off, but nothing of the crime itself remained. She and Darey had visited the site yesterday afternoon, knowing they would find nothing. Still, imagining what had happened here brought her closer to Susan. Closer to Clair.

Closer to God, she thought.

"Hi, Angie."

"Hi, Darey."

A knot was back in her throat, hearing his voice on the phone.

"You okay?" he asked.

"I'm fine. I'm here."

"At the Milton place?"

"At the crime scene."

He was silent for a moment.

"Did you talk to them?"

"Susan was there. We had a good talk. I'll tell you about it later, but she's with us."

"Hmm . . . You never cease to amaze me."

"Promise me we're going to get to the bottom of this, Darey. They ripped Susan's life away from her."

"Yes, they did. And yes, that's our intention."

"Promise me."

"I promise."

"Okay." It was all she needed right now. "Did you reach Jamie's mother?"

"Yes. We meet her tomorrow at noon."

"Good. I'm headed home now." She headed back to the car. "I need to eat and do some research."

The phone was quiet.

"Don't worry, I won't go deep."

"Okay, honey. I'm preparing a couple motions for Jamie and I need to wrap up something on another case before heading home."

"Okay."

"Okay."

"Darey?"

"Yes, dear?"

"I love you."

His voice was gentle. "I love you, Angie."

TED DEKKER

They disconnected.

By the time Angie parked in their garage, she was flying with enthusiasm. It was how she got when her gut told her the truth was just around the corner. Yes, it might take her a week or a month to get around that corner, but something significant was calling to her.

Her whole life had been like that, knowing that the truth was there and could be found if she was willing to set aside what everyone insisted it was. She supposed she'd gotten that from her mother.

She hurried into the house.

"Hi, Sally! Hi there, big boy! Did you miss Mommy?"

Sally slobbered and lapped at her face, over the moon at seeing his best friend again. Why couldn't they all be dogs?

"Okay, okay. I love you too."

She gave Sally a handful of tuna chips and made herself a chicken salad sandwich. It was almost one in the afternoon when she plopped down in the sitting room and asked Lover Boy to bring up the news. The net had been brimming with heated opinions about Jamie Hamilton's new counsel, most of it favorable on balance. Or at least open-minded. She and Darey had indeed changed the discussion on the Oak Hill Dead Head case.

She flipped through a few news feeds: one discussing the Texas governor's recent surge to the top of presidential election polls, one in the middle of a debate about the unification of South America, another discussing a national program seeking to re-establish bee populations, which had all but vanished. Artificial pollenating was costing the country an arm and a leg.

The fourth landed on a panel of attorneys discussing the Dead Head case. Angie sat back and bit into her sandwich. She'd taken only two bites when the program was interrupted by a special bulletin.

It took her a second to realize that the bulletin was about her.

"... might prove critical to the case," the announcer was saying. "For more we go to a press conference with District Attorney Andrew Olsen, just a few minutes ago."

The feed showed Olsen on the same steps where she and Darey had stood yesterday morning, announcing Jamie's innocence to the world.

"It has come to our attention that Angie Channing, wife of the lead defense

155

in the Oak Hill Dead Head case, has been leading a double life for many years. We have evidence that, while bringing the public's awareness to the dangers of Deep Dive technology, Ms. Channing has herself been addicted to dead heading. She is what's commonly known as a closet Dead Head and operates incognito under the handle Lover Boy. She . . ."

Angie felt her sandwich slip from her fingers. Her heart was slamming, filling her ears with a throbbing *whoosh*. She didn't hear any more of what the DA was saying; she didn't need to.

All that mattered was that she'd just been stripped naked for the whole world to see. They were violating her sacred space! Crushing her. Marking her with a death sentence that would be impossible to escape. They knew her handle? What else did they know?

For a few long moments she sat in stunned silence, mind blackened by dread.

A sliver of logic broke through the crippling emotion. She had to call Darey! Her phone was on the counter.

She tried to stand, faltered, then managed to get to both feet. The room tilted and began to spin, and she instinctively grabbed at the closest thing to her to stop her fall. That closest thing was the floor lamp, and she pawed at the brass stand. The floor lamp toppled and hit the wood floor with a mighty crash. In the kitchen, Sally started to bark.

The room blinked to white. A whiteout. The sound of Sally's barking faded into the background. *It's okay,* she thought. *It's okay because the world will stay white for a few seconds and then the room will be back.*

Only this whiteout didn't stay white for a few seconds like the others. It shimmered with all of the nothingness she'd become accustomed to for only two beats before snapping back to reality.

She blinked. No, not back to reality. She was in a different room. A small rectangular white room with books on pedestals along one wall, and strange features on the other walls, but otherwise empty. Clinically clean.

Her breathing stalled. At any moment it all would vanish, and she would be back in her sitting room with the fallen lamp and Sally. But that moment didn't come. She was still in the white room.

Her mind had snapped into a virtual reality. Into a space hidden deep in her mind. She was experiencing a full-fledged hallucination.

Angie's body began to tremble.

BOOK THREE

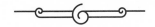

THE
GATE ROOM

CHAPTER
FOURTEEN

THE REASON why Angie's body began to shake in that white room was painfully obvious to her. The fact that she was here in a virtual space created by her mind without a RIG could only mean that it was fracturing beyond her control. Something had gone very wrong. Felicia had warned her. Jake Barnes had warned her. Darey had warned her. She'd warned herself. But she'd ignored those warnings and now she was free-falling into insanity.

These were the first thoughts that hammered through her mind as she stood in the white room, wishing the hallucination to vanish.

She sucked at the air, muscles taut, head swiveling to take in the room, still wishing it away. At any moment now, it would be gone.

A semblance of reason began to settle over her. *Okay, I've been here before. Not in this room but in a hundred like it. Fully fleshed, immersive spaces, populated by sensory data that's only real to my perceptions. Calm down. Calm down, Angie. It's not real. It will pass.*

But it wasn't passing, not yet. She looked around, observing more closely now. The room was rectangular, maybe ten feet wide and twenty feet long. The floor was apparently marble, large black and white checkerboard squares. The walls were white, made of the same shiny material. There was a white leather chair in one corner.

Flush against the wall she faced sat a long, very narrow white table that held three black, leather-bound books on pedestals. The books were closed. Nothing else.

She twisted her head and took in the wall behind her. It was covered with brass and platinum gears embedded into the glossy white surface—dozens of toothed wheels, some huge, some small, like those you might find inside of an old windup clock. None of them were moving.

The wall on her right was etched with a six-foot vertical line that had a small hole in a circle at the top. Words had been carved in archaic lettering a foot above the circle.

Veritas Vos Liberabit

She knew the phrase from high school Latin class. 'The truth will set you free.'

The wall to her left was filled by a featureless white mask that reminded her of the poster for *The Phantom of the Opera*, only, where its mouth should be was a three-foot portal and a one-foot wheel, the kind used to open a submarine hatch. A way out? A panel to the right of the portal presumably operated it. At the top of the panel was a tiny receptacle. Below it were two buttons marked by a 1 and a 0. And below those numbers, a green button.

Above the large mask, words matched the same archaic lettering of the opposite wall.

Imago Simulacrum

Latin again. *Imago* meant 'image.' *Simulacrum* probably came from the same root as *similar*, meaning 'to make similar,' but she wasn't sure.

She turned in a full circle, taking everything in. Two long walls—one with three books on pedestals, the other embedded with gears. Two shorter walls— one with a huge mask and a hatch for a mouth called *Imago Simulacrum*, one with a vertical line and a hole on top called *Veritas Vos Liberabit*. Other than that, only the white chair in one corner.

It was a puzzle room, she thought. Find the truth and you will be free. She was in a game.

That wasn't so unusual. Neither was the fact that her mind was perceiving everything in the room as utterly real. The kind of real involving all five senses, like what she'd experienced in the Red Protocol at Convergence.

What was unusual was that she was experiencing this virtual space without reality interface gear. No RIG. Only her mind.

Was she tripping back into the Red Protocol?

The truth will set you free. What truth? The truth of what was happening to her? Or the truth about Jamie that would set him free? But what was the line with the circle on top? A way to that truth, maybe. It looked nothing like a door or a way.

She had no idea how to solve the room, neither was she interested. What did interest her was time. At any moment, the room would vanish. The question was, how long until it did?

Angie looked at the chair in the corner by the mask wall. A chair for what? To sit in when she got tired of trying to solve the room, so she could return to the real world?

The real world. She'd just been stripped of her privacy and exposed as a fraud for all the world to see. At least that's how they were spinning it.

They knew her handle was Lover Boy.

They knew she was a closet Dead Head.

And at this moment, she was dead heading without a RIG. If anyone walked into her house now, what would they find? Angie Channing passed out on the floor, mind lost in a virtual space like a drug addict tripping on some exotic mind-altering substance?

Snap out of this, Angie! Just snap out of it.

She closed her eyes and took a deep breath, knowing that if she could calm herself, she would be able to think more clearly. Mindfulness worked as a lifeline in most virtual realities.

Be there. Just wake up there. Please, wake up there in my house.

When she opened her eyes nothing had changed. Sweat was crawling past her temples. Her ears throbbed with the pounding of her heart. Otherwise, no sound.

But that wasn't true. There was a faint hum here, right?

She stilled her breathing and listened carefully. There—distant and barely audible, but definitely a hum. The power that made this room work?

Curious now, Angie stepped across the checkerboard floor toward the-truth-will-set-you-free wall. The floor under her bare feet was cold. Marble or polished granite. Maybe ceramic.

The wall was the same, she thought, stepping up to it. The moment she put her palm on its glossy surface, the vertical line throbbed with light and the hum swelled, not only in volume but in pitch. The high frequency startled her.

She jerked her hand away.

The line with the circle at the top fell dormant and the hum faded to a barely perceptible drone, lower in pitch. So the room was active. She tried again and got the same result. This line with the small hole on top was some kind of seal behind which lay the truth, she imagined. A gateway that might open if she could figure out how to operate it. No levers, no knobs, nothing but the line, the hole at the top, and the words above it: *Veritas Vos Liberabit.*

Angie turned around and faced the rest of the white room. Totally foreign and yet strangely familiar at the same time. Like déjà vu.

Why are you here, Angie? Calm down and think. Just take a stab like in any other game.

She took one. Shocked by the news that she'd been publicly exposed, she'd retreated to a place deep in her mind that had been opened by the Red Protocol. So in some ways, maybe this was home. There was something that wanted to reveal itself to her here. Something buried deep in her psyche. Hadn't her mother always told her the truth was hidden inside? "As a human, you don't see the world as it truly is, but as *you* are," she'd often said. "Discover who you are, and your perception of the world will change."

"And who am I, Mama?" she'd asked as a young child.

"Far more than you know, Angie. Far, far more."

In that way, going deep inside of her own mind was home. Still, however strangely familiar this space seemed, it also felt a bit like a tomb.

Angie walked to the wall with the words *Imago Simulacrum* inscribed above the mask and sealed hatch. When she touched this wall the hum swelled again, but this time in a much lower, growling pitch. Bass—the opposite of the truth wall.

She tried to turn the small wheel at the center but it was fixed tight. Several attempts with the buttons on the panel did nothing either. Of course not; she needed a code and a key to that code.

The books.

Angie stepped to the three books perched on the narrow white table. Real books, bound in black leather. Ancient. Each was embossed with the same title.

Play Dead.

Her heart skipped a beat. The game from Jamie's texts to Timothy and Clair. It was a real game called Play Dead? But how could that be? Unless the game had been part of her experience in the Red Protocol. Or one she'd created in her mind since emerging from that mind-expanding experience.

Either way, one thing seemed clear: This was a game called Play Dead, and these books contained either the game's rules or the code and keys to solve it.

She gingerly lifted the cover over the first book and saw that it was filled with symbols similar to ancient Egyptian hieroglyphs, but without animals and people. Meaningless to her. She flipped through the old pages, maybe thirty in all, hoping for a decoding key. Nothing but pages of foreign symbols. Images. *Imago Simulacrum.*

Hope fluttered in her belly like a trapped moth. She moved to the next book. This one contained what appeared to be binary computer code. Strings of ones and zeros. Also useless to her.

The third book was filled with fractal geometric shapes that reminded her of butterflies, each successive image increasingly complex.

Heart sinking, she set the last book back on its pedestal and glanced down the table. Three books titled *Play Dead*, one filled with ancient characters, another with binary code, and the third with geometric symbols. They had to contain whatever information was required to operate the gears or the hatch and open her mind to the truth. But without a translation key to break the code, she was dead in the water.

Dead. *Play Dead.* Was she dead? Was she in danger of being dead?

She could see a dim reflection of herself in the wall. Long dark hair down, wearing a black sleeveless top. Angie. Not dead at all. She instinctively reached out and touched the shiny surface.

The hum immediately grew in volume but was neither high nor low. It was somewhere in between. She moved her hand along the surface toward the truth-will-set-you-free wall and the tone rose in pitch. When she moved her hand back the other way, toward the wall with the mask and the round hatch, the pitch fell. The whole room was like a machine. How strange. She was in a machine of some kind?

"Hello."

She whipped around at the sound of the voice. There, seated in the white chair, wearing black Converse sneakers that didn't quite reach the floor, sat a small boy, maybe six, with blond hair and light blue eyes. He was smiling sheepishly, dressed in blue jeans and a plain black shirt. Kinda like her, she thought.

Two thoughts crowded her mind. The first was that she was making him up because he hadn't been here a moment ago, and yet here he was.

The second was that this boy looked familiar. A bit like a younger version of Jamie, who might also be the son she'd had in the Red Protocol, although that association felt even weaker now than before. So maybe this boy was just a construction of her mind based on fragmented memories and images.

All of this flashed through her thoughts as they looked at each other.

"You can call me Eli," the boy said.

Eli? Not Jamie? She meant to ask, *You're Eli?* But nothing came out.

"And you're Angie," he said. "But those aren't our real names."

She finally found her voice.

"No?"

"Nope."

"Then why did you call yourself Eli?"

The boy shrugged. "I just made it up."

Never mind that. What was he doing here?

"Do you know what this place is? How did you get here?" *You're making him up, silly.*

His feet swung back and forth. "This is the gate room and I'm here to help you."

Maybe she'd created this boy to help her break out of a psychic trap in her own mind.

She looked at the sealed hatch. "Do you know how to get out?"

"Through one of the gates," he said. He shoved himself off the chair, grabbed her hand, and pulled her toward the truth wall. Reaching it, he lifted her hand and pressed it against the wall.

The faint hum swelled and filled the room with a high tone. The line with the circle at the top glowed.

"That truth is that way," he said, releasing her hand and pointing at the glowing line. "Through the needle gate."

He was seeing the line topped by a small hole as a needle. Needle gate. Okay, that was a start.

The boy named Eli, who looked like Jamie, turned and pointed at the opposite wall with the mask and hatch. "And that way is Image Maker."

Image Maker. Simpler than the Latin. "Do you know what *Imago Simulacrum* means?" she asked.

"I think it means image. An illusion."

"Like what covers up the truth," she said. "A mask."

"Yup," he said. "Play Dead."

"What does that have to do with playing dead?"

He shrugged. "Because illusions aren't alive?"

Play Dead. Jamie's game. Jamie . . . She was here to discover the truth that would set Jamie free from prison through a game called Play Dead. Had to be!

"Are you Jamie?" she asked, turning back to the boy. Only Eli was no longer there. He'd vanished.

And with that thought, the room also vanished, leaving Angie in the plain white space she'd come to know as a whiteout. Then that whiteness morphed into colors and shapes.

She was back in her house, seated on the floor next to a fallen lamp and a shaggy dog who was staring at her, ears cocked, whining.

Her phone was buzzing on the bar.

CHAPTER
FIFTEEN

ANGIE STAGGERED to her feet and lunged for the phone with one name on her mind: Jamie. And then another: Darey. *Please let it be Darey.*

She snatched up the phone and answered with a glance at the screen. "Darey?"

"Angie, thank God. Are you okay?"

"Yeah . . ." The feed on the large 3D screen showed her headshot, the same one from the dust jacket of her book. A panel was talking about the DA's announcement, and her predicament here in the real world swallowed her once more.

"Turn the news off, Lover Boy."

The screen changed to an image of a mountain valley.

"I'm sorry, what did you say?" Darey asked.

"No, that was for Lover Boy." The same handle that the whole world now new as her own. "I . . . Never mind, I'm okay." How long had she been gone?

"You sure? I've been calling."

"Yes." Her voice was thin. "I was . . . I don't know."

"You heard?"

Angie swallowed deeply. "I heard."

"Okay, I'm almost home. Stay right where you are."

"I'm scared, Darey."

"There's no need to be. It doesn't mean a thing. I'll be right home. Don't move."

Then he was gone.

She set the phone on the wet bar and stared at the bottles of liquor set in the glass shelves behind it. Amber and clear, rum, tequila, gin, vodka—Darey liked the stuff; she, not so much, but she shared a glass with him on occasion.

On a whim, she picked up a shot glass, pulled down the closest bottle not caring what it contained, spun off the cap, and splashed the amber liquid into her glass. Then drained it in one draw. It burned going down and for a brief moment she felt like she'd made some progress. To what end, she had no idea, but she was living and that was good. She left the bottle where it was and rounded the bar, then stalled, not sure what to do with herself.

On the one hand, she had been exposed. Okay, so that would require some damage control, and Darey was the best at damage control. She might lose her publishing contract. Her involvement in Jamie's case might be hampered. Or cut off entirely.

Who was she kidding? The DA had just shattered her carefully guarded world.

On the other hand, she'd just entered a fully immersive virtual reality without using a RIG. The closet Dead Head had tripped one too many times. She was falling apart. But in that falling apart, she'd found Jamie and the game called Play Dead, which was central to the Oak Hill murder case.

She hurried to the kitchen, eager for Darey to be home, eager to grab onto something that rooted her to her old life. But she couldn't resist tapping in a quick search for the Latin words on the mask wall. *Imago Simulacrum.* *Imago* was as she'd remembered: *image.* Obvious. *Simulacrum* meant 'picture,' 'idol,' 'statue' or 'likeness.' *Illusion.* So the boy had been right.

That which makes images or masks or illusions. Image Maker. A masquerade. Like the framing of Jamie. But could a room in her mind lead her to the truth? She *was* losing her mind.

The five minutes of waiting felt like an hour. After barging through the door, Darey pulled up and stared at her, eyes wide. Worried. Then he collected himself and strolled in as if nothing was wrong.

But she'd seen the concern in his eyes. It took a lot to unnerve him.

He took her in his arms. Her composure broke the moment her forehead hit his shoulder. A week's worth of death and stress and anxiety broke free and flooded her eyes with tears, which immediately turned to sobs.

"It's okay." His large hand pressed into her back, holding her against his chest. "It's going to be okay." He kissed the top of her head. "This won't change a thing."

But she knew he was only being his optimistic self. She nodded anyway and caught her sobs. For a full minute they stood like that in the kitchen, he rubbing her back, she gathering herself and calming.

Darey looked down at her when she finally pulled back, wiping her cheeks with the heel of her palm. "It was a low blow," he said. "They're scared. Which only means we're onto something someone doesn't want us to find. We only have to figure out who's being threatened and why, and all this disappears."

She nodded. "And in the meantime . . ." She stopped, at a loss for words.

"In the meantime, nothing changes. You're not Jamie's attorney, I am. All bruises heal with time. In the end, this will mean nothing."

"They know I'm a Dead Head."

"And why shouldn't you be? You do research. It's what makes you an authority on the subject, not just some talking head who's parroting someone else's dogma. The audience will get that. Even the publisher will get that."

"This coming from the man who said you don't need to be a heroin addict to study heroin."

"Yeah, well, I was just concerned." He grinned, trying to cheer her up. "That didn't stop you anyway."

"Well . . ." How did she tell him?

"What is it? There's more, isn't there?"

Angie took his hand. "Come here." She led him into the sitting room where he glanced at the open bottle and the drained shot glass then sat on the edge of the recliner next to her. She stared at the large 3D mountain view, not sure how to tell him what she'd experienced.

"Now you're scaring me, Angie. Just say it."

"I think I tripped without a RIG," she said, eyes still on the screen.

"Tripped without a RIG," he repeated, clearly wanting clarification.

"I mean, I've been having whiteouts maybe more than I've let on. I was afraid they would take me off the case, you know? I kept thinking they would go away, but they didn't."

"They got worse," he guessed. "You had a full-blown hallucination like they said you might."

She looked into his eyes. "Not just a hallucination. A fully immersive Deep Dive without reality interface gear. I mean, one minute I was sitting here, listening to Olsen on the feed, the next I was in a white room with two gates and Play Dead books, and Jamie was there. It was real. I mean, it felt as real as this. I know it was probably just some kind of hallucination tied into what's happening to Jamie, but I was there, Darey. I wasn't here. My body was, but not my mind."

He put his hand on her knee. "Okay, slow down. Start at the beginning. Tell me about your day from the beginning. You went to meet with Susan Milton. Start there. And your lip's going to bleed if you keep doing that."

She withdrew her hand from her upper lip, took a deep breath and told him every detail she could remember. Her time with Susan. Her visit to the crime scene. But when she came to the details regarding the gate room, they'd already softened. She told him everything she'd seen and experienced there, but it was starting to feel like a fading dream. Her mind wasn't holding onto the experience. So she told him that as well.

He sat back and considered her long tale, logical mind churning. Her phone was buzzing on the bar but she ignored it.

"So you're saying that you think there might be information behind the gates that could help exonerate Jamie." His tone held doubt.

"Well, it sure seemed that way while I was in it. I mean, Play Dead. And the truth will set you free. And Jamie."

"As a boy," he said. "Why as a boy?"

"I don't know, maybe I just pictured him that way because someone like Jamie was my son in the Red Protocol and I'm making a connection that's not there. Or maybe I am connected to Jamie and don't know it. Either way, I was certain that what was happening to me was critical. Like I could access information hidden in a vault deep in my mind."

"Of course you were feeling that way. Everything you've told me comes from your experience over these last few days. Like a dream spun from the events of your life. And, like a dream, it's fading. Isn't that how all virtual experiences work?"

"No."

"Well, this one did. I don't think there's anything to worry about."

She nodded, seeing his logic. "Okay, forget the gate room," she said. "You're right. So what now?"

"Now we carry on as if nothing's happened. If we catch a break, Susan finds the key, although it's a long shot. Tomorrow we meet with Corina and we see where that leads us. In the meantime, I've filed a motion of discovery and a bill of particulars, which will slow them down unless the judge is in their hip pocket. Knowing Banister, the judge who's been assigned the case, we should be fine. He's old-school."

The phone was ringing again. This time Angie got up, crossed to the bar, saw it was Felicia, almost ignored it, but decided to answer anyway. She couldn't hide forever.

"Hi, Felicia."

"There you are! Are you okay?"

Angie swallowed. "I'm fine."

"Where are you?"

"I'm with Darey."

"Good. That's good."

The line was silent for a beat.

"How are the whiteouts?"

No mention of the DA's announcement. Maybe she didn't know. Or maybe Angie's health was more important to her.

Angie held Darey's eyes. "I'm good."

"Any more incidents?"

"Minor, but I think they're almost gone."

"That's a relief. It's critical you tell me everything, Angie. This is nothing to mess around with."

Felicia had seen Barnes and was all worked up. Angie thought about asking her how the visit went but didn't want to spend more time on the subject.

"Of course," she said.

"It sounds like you're in good hands. If you have time later this week, I'd like to sit with you."

"Sure."

"Shall we say Wednesday lunch? Noon at Garcia's?"

"That should work."

"Good. Promise me you'll let me know if you—"

"I will, Felicia. Promise."

"Okay. Good."

Felicia disconnected and Angie lowered the phone.

"I think I just lied," she said.

"Yes, you did. You'll have to beg forgiveness later."

"I will."

Darey smiled.

CHAPTER
SIXTEEN

JAMIE HAMILTON is what they called him, but for real his name was Fluffy Puppy. But not really for real because . . . Well, he wasn't exactly sure who he was, but he did know he wasn't really Jamie Hamilton or Fluffy Puppy. Those were just his handles in the games.

Jamie sat at the table in the jail they called County and looked at the red apple on his tray. Neat and brand new, like the new yellow jumpsuit they'd given him to wear. He liked yellow and in here everyone wore yellow. He could have also taken a banana, which was yellow, but it had been a long time since he'd had an apple and he wasn't sure why. Maybe his mother didn't like them. He'd ask her when she came to visit him.

Next to the red apple was some stew, not as interesting. He wondered if they had Doritos. Randy had gotten him Coke, which was nice of him. He liked Randy. Randy was a pink and pinks were smooth. Maybe he would meet someone here who would be kind to him. A new friend, maybe.

He looked up and saw the lunchroom in a single glance. Twenty-four people in yellow, five in the gray uniforms, seven in white serving the food. He didn't count the people in yellow, he just saw their shape, a polygon made of three octagons, with eight sides each, so twenty-four.

But that was the simple way to explain it, because the room was really three-dimensional, and there were no names for the complex shapes he saw. To him they weren't complex themselves, only the explaining of them, which he'd given up trying to do a long time ago.

Nine had light hair and fifteen had dark hair. Each person was also its own slightly different colored shape, depending on how they moved and were feeling. Like Randy, who was mostly pink but sometimes gray. Pink meant he was in a kind mood; gray meant he wasn't sure how to feel. Reds were the ones to avoid, because their choices were based on quick judgments. Although in many games, reds were the easiest to beat because they made too many mistakes.

A long time ago, he thought everyone saw the world the way he did. Then he'd read about people who saw colors and shapes for sounds, a condition called synesthesia. There were others who could see every word on a page at a glance and remember them all. Some saw numbers as shapes and could do math like he could, not by adding or subtracting but by just seeing the answer. They were rare, the article said.

Learning of this, he'd gone to the living room, where his mother was watching a show.

"Mom?"

"Yes, honey?"

He held up his hand. "Do you see the lines between my fingers?"

She leaned forward and studied his hand. "You have string between them?"

"Not those kinds of lines. I mean . . ." He looked at his hand, trying to think how to describe what he saw. "The invisible lines. Like light but with some color. Blue."

She shook her head. "No. Is it a trick?"

"I don't know. But I see shapes and colors."

"Really? On your hand?"

"Everywhere." He looked around. "I see three hundred and twenty-one shapes in this room in lots of colors."

She'd stared at him, lost. Then finally gave him some advice.

"Well, that's perfect," she said. "You get to see the world just like you want to. And don't never pay 'tention to anyone who says different. You're perfect just the way you are."

He'd tried to explain it to his mom a few more times after that, but it was like trying to explain to someone who'd been born blind what a city looked like.

He was seeing something real that no one else could. He saw the energy that connected everything into one huge shape.

That was his secret to winning games. He could predict what people would do by reading their shapes and colors and how they changed when they did different things. People always changed colors and shapes before they acted. Once he learned any player's pattern—which was easy—he could read them and know what they were feeling and about to do before they did it. Sometimes before they knew themselves, he suspected.

It was harder in the game of real life, because the avatar named Jamie Hamilton, which was him, didn't know how to talk to people good, so Jamie got confused and had to deal with all his own emotions, which made things fuzzy.

When things got real fuzzy, he did things that didn't make sense, like that time when he beat up some bullies. So he'd learned not to listen to his emotions too much. At least he tried. It was all a game anyway. A real game maybe, but still a game. Everyone was trying to win.

Angie was a pink with lots of blue. A rare bright blue because she was ready to be free. He'd known that the moment she came into the room. She was like the girl he sometimes saw in his dreams, the girl who was trying to figure out how to get free. But those dreams were fuzzy. Anyway, he liked her a lot. And he would trust her.

Her friend Darey, the lawyer who told him not to tell anyone about the game, was a purple, which meant he was mostly logic and facts. But there was pink there as well. And Angie and Darey were connected in one shape with golden lines, which meant they didn't have problems with each other. At least that's how he understood the code.

The other man, Olsen, was a gray. Grays hated themselves and were stuck. Like thirteen of the men in the lunchroom.

A tall, skinny bald man with arms as wiry as a corded cable plopped his tray down across from Jamie with a loud bang that made him jump. A red. Bright red. With a tattoo of a black snake coiled around his neck. The snake's jaw was wide and its beady yellow eyes glared at Jamie from a hairy chest, where the man's shirt was open.

The man stuck out a hand with the letters H-E-L-L tattooed on his knuckles. "Welcome to hell," he said.

Jamie took the hand, not sure what else to do. "Hello."

The hand squeezed his tight so that for a second Jamie thought his fingers might break. But he was suddenly too afraid to tell the man, so he just let him squeeze. The guy finally let go and grinned.

"Hello," he said, wagging his head. "Duh, hello."

Jamie smiled and mimicked him because his mother always said, *If you can't beat 'em, join 'em.*

"Duh, hello." Jamie chuckled.

Snake-man glared at him, smile gone. He didn't laugh.

Two others—a short fat man with dirty teeth, and a regular-size man with long brown hair—sat next to Snake-man. They were reds too, mostly. Together they formed the shape of a disjointed hexagonal pyramid, meaning they didn't know how they fit together even though they had. But Jamie was used to that—most people with other people formed distorted shapes glued together with black lines, which was fear. Or demon.

"What do you say, Guy?" the short fat man said. "You shake the hand that cut those kids' throats?"

"I'm shaking the hand of a dead man," Snake-man said.

They were talking about the murders of Timothy and Clair. But Jamie didn't kill them. He would never kill anyone like that. Only if his own life was at stake would he even think about killing anyone—unless it was in a game where you were supposed to kill people. He wanted to tell them that, but Darey had told him not to play the game that way. Say nothing. So Jamie kept his mouth shut.

And then his mouth wasn't shut, because he was saying something to Snake-man that he thought they might think was funny.

"Hi, Guy. Are you a guy or a girl?" He snorted once in laughter, then saw the man's face twist into a new shape made of ninety-two black lines. Jamie saw it and felt his blood go cold.

The man leaned forward and hissed, gravel like. "Now you listen to me, you little faggot kid killer." He spit into Jamie's food. "The only reason you're not locked up safe behind bars and in general population is because someone wants you dead. And now I'm gonna be the one who makes that happen, because I swear the next time I see you, I'm slitting your throat."

The black lines that made up the man's head were vibrating, and at first Jamie thought the man might do it now. Reach across the table and try to strangle him. In most games he would know, but fear was clouding his sight.

He wanted to tell the man sorry. That he meant it as a joke. That he hadn't killed anyone. That he was only trying to follow the rules of the game and was only just learning how the game was played here at County.

But he was too messed up to speak.

The man with a snake tattoo stabbed a finger at him. "Watch your back. I'm coming."

He grabbed his tray, abruptly stood, and left with the other shapes.

Jamie sat still for a long time, staring at his apple. Slowly, his mind cleared. And as it cleared, he began to calculate the odds of what might happen next. He was playing a game, and in this game he had to survive.

One thing was definite: Snake meant what he'd said. He would kill Jamie. Maybe because he had nothing to lose, because he hated himself so much. Maybe because he was already going to spend the rest of his life in prison. Maybe because he was going to die for something he did anyway.

Whatever the reason, Snake was going to try to kill him.

He'd learned a long time ago that if another player saw fear in you, they would come after you, because fear was always a weakness. Demon. Scanning the room, he saw that at least nine others had seen or heard what happened. They were watching him, searching him for fear. If they saw it, they would feel its power and use it. That's how characters played in all games, especially in the game of real life.

He had to show them he wasn't afraid, which meant he had to get rid of his fear. So he closed his eyes and went to what always calmed him.

The algorithms. The mathematics. The geometry of this scene.

Thousands of shapes and numbers spun through his mind as he allowed gaming scenarios to present themselves to him. It was all a matter of probabilities now.

If Jamie tried to befriend Snake-man, there was only a 2 percent chance the man would find the courage to step beyond his rage and succumb to what he saw as weakness. Snake-man would kill him.

If Jamie tried to win other friends to protect him, there was only a 7 percent chance he would succeed, and even then, only a 3 percent chance those friends would remain his friends, because Jamie was too different for most people to like very much.

If Jamie told the men in gray about Snake-man, there was a zero-percent chance they would care or do anything to protect him.

And so it went, dozens of probabilities calculated through a process of combining and evaluating shapes and numbers. In the end, the probability of his survival was 8 percent or less in every scenario but one.

That one scenario presented as an 82 percent chance of survival. So it was his only reasonable play.

The next time he saw Snake-man, whose name was Guy, Jamie would kill him.

CHAPTER
SEVENTEEN

ANGIE AND DAREY sat in Corina's living room the next day, drawn deeply into anguish that terrified Angie. She understood it, felt it, *was* it on some level. Here was a woman who'd given her whole life to one boy. She'd held him and loved him when no one else could or would. She'd worked two jobs to give him the best life she could. She'd cried with him, laughed with him, sung over him, and would gladly bleed for him.

In every respect, Jamie was nothing less than Corina's sole treasure. Her personal idol. Without him, she was lost.

Sitting here now, trying her best to offer Corina at least a sliver of comfort and hope, Angie was acutely aware of the fact that she was another version of Corina. She too had her treasures, without which she was only a shell of herself. But wasn't that true of the whole world? And that's what unnerved her.

The whole world was radically dependent on whatever it treasured. For some, that treasure included their country or political party. For some, a protected life. For some, a career. For some, a set of beliefs that would grant them entrance to heaven after this life. For some, money. For some, health.

For most, it was another person—family, spouse, children—in some complex interweaving of other treasures.

Humans, both personally and collectively, slaved away to possess various treasures and then spent their lives protecting them in the belief that what they had worked so hard to possess would make them whole. Possessiveness was encoded with a deep fear of loss. In so many ways, that fear was the engine of life itself.

But it wasn't life. It was a kind of death. Hell.

Angie felt the fangs of that monster called fear here with Corina more than she could ever remember feeling it, knowing that she too was its slave.

What did she fear losing? Her sanity. Darey. Her reputation. Her life. Too many things to count.

"Isn't that right, Angie?" Darey was asking.

"Sorry?"

"I was just telling Corina that we'll get through this together and while we do that, she's more than welcome to lean on us for whatever she needs."

"God, yes! Yes, whatever you need, sweetheart."

Tears wet Corina's face. She'd given up any serious attempt at wiping them away a good ten minutes ago. She sniffed and drew her arm across her nose.

"Thank you, but I'll be fine."

And then she doubled over and silently sobbed.

A knot as big as her fist filled Angie's throat. There was something especially diabolical about a young man being falsely accused. She was familiar with murder. Delving deep into the crimes of Raymond Smith while writing *Righteous* had offered her an intimate perspective into the pain of the victims' families. But in the Oak Hill case, both the accused and the victims were innocent. The real killer lived in the deep shadow, unexposed.

"We're not going to stop until we set Jamie free, Corina." She made no attempt to tame the rage in her voice. "If it's the last thing we do, we're going to find the monster that killed those kids and demand the court set Jamie free. Do you hear me?"

Corina calmed. "I hope you can. I really do."

Darey watched Angie with a look that said, *Don't overpromise.* But they both knew Corina needed promises now, even if they might not be fulfilled. He leaned back in the overstuffed green chair and crossed his legs.

"You can help us, Corina. I need you to think clearly for a few minutes and tell us anything at all that might point us to who might want to hurt Jamie for any reason."

Corina picked up a red pack of cigarettes, the old kind that were illegal to buy but not smoke. She took one out, lit it with trembling fingers, and blew out a plume of smoke.

"He was an orphan," she said, staring at an old flat-panel television. "I swore I wouldn't tell, but I didn't give birth to Jamie. No one's supposed to know. They . . ." She held back.

"Who's they?" Darey asked.

"They. The people who gave me Jamie when he was six."

Angie exchanged a glance with Darey. This was new.

"Okay," he said calmly. "Just tell us what you know."

"The only thing I ever wanted was to have a child. A boy, you know? But I can't get pregnant and I didn't have no money back then when it cost an arm and a leg to get fixed. It's all I wanted."

They let her settle.

"One day a man come up to me. I don't know how he knew 'bout me and I never cared. He said he had a boy whose parents were dead and did I want to take him? Like, legal. He said he could give me a fake birth certificate saying he was mine with hospital records and everythin' case someone come askin'. I got the papers in my room if you want to see 'em."

"We will, but later. Who was the man?"

"He never said, but he was thin, small like, with dark hair and skin. Maybe Eastern, I don't know. And he wore dark glasses all the time, I remember that. When he showed me a picture of Jamie, I couldn't say no." Her eyes darted between them. "You won't say nothin, right? You can't. They warned me."

"Warned you how?" Darey asked.

"Said if I breathed a word, they'd kill Jamie."

Angie was at once horrified and relieved. Horrified for obvious reasons; relieved because hearing about Jamie, she knew they were uncovering a significant element in the truth of the case against him.

"I shoulda' known that it would end up no good," Corina said. "But what else was I supposed to do? Someone had to care for that boy."

Darey glanced around the room. "So they're watching you?"

"You think?"

"With a threat like that, Jamie has to be pretty important to someone."

"Well, I've never seen nothin' and I certainly haven't said anything."

"Could Jamie have said something?"

"I don't think he knows. When he came to me, he didn't have a clue except to talk about the white room. Just kept wanting to know if he was going back to the white room."

Angie's heart began to pound. "What kind of white room?"

"He didn't know except that's where someone had kept him. Like in a nursery or a playroom, I figured. Best thing I could do was forget anything about where he come from and make a safe place for him with me. So we never talked about it. I asked him about it once last year and he can't remember. Good riddance, I say."

Angie looked at Darey, taken aback. Maybe she and Jamie were more connected than either of them knew. Or was it just a coincidence? A white room could be anything.

"And that was the last you heard from the man?" Darey asked.

"Uh-huh."

"And that's all? No communication? No reporting?"

"Nope." She paused. "He gave me a security system. Said it would help me keep Jamie safe. But I don't think it works. Besides, I unplugged it the day they arrested Jamie. Screw 'em."

"What kind of security system?"

She blew more smoke out and shoved her chin up at the corner. "That one."

Darey had gone still, staring up at a white fish-eye camera no larger than a pinhead. Easy to see how CSI had missed it, especially if it had already been powered down.

He exchanged a glance with Angie. His eyes shifted back to the camera then down the hall, and she knew what he was thinking.

The camera was angled to capture the living room, the kitchen, and the hall. At the end of the hall, Corina's room. On the right, Jamie's room, which they'd searched earlier. Across the hall from Jamie's room, a door led into the bathroom Jamie used.

If the camera had been active and recording, it would have captured Jamie the night of the murder.

Angie's fingers were tingling. Was it possible?

"Can you show me what you unplugged?" Darey asked.

"There's a small box in the cupboard."

"Can you show me?"

She stuffed out the stub of her cigarette. "Sure." She led them to a cupboard in the kitchen. There, behind a heap of spices and nonperishable condiments that Corina scooped up and plopped on the counter, sat a small white box the size of Corina's red cigarette box. It had been wired into the wall, but the data cord now lay beside the box where Corina had unplugged it.

Darey reached in and lifted the small processor. Turned it to reveal a slot with a half-inch data card plugged into it.

"Would it be okay if I took this card with me?"

Corina eyes were round. "You think it got something?"

"Maybe. I need to get it to a card reader to know."

"Should be easy enough," Angie said. "We have—"

"Not at our house. This goes to my safe. I don't want it anywhere near the house."

He was trying to protect her, but wasn't it a bit late for that? She was already in neck deep.

"Take it," Corina said. "I hope it's got enough on it to burn 'em in hell."

Darey plucked the card out, studied it for a second, then slid it into his pocket. "I wouldn't count on that, but if it was working, the video might tell us more about the night in question."

"I'm telling you, my Jamie was here. He'd never lie to me. If he tried, I would know. And even if he wasn't here, he wasn't out there in the dark doing what they said he did. He ain't that boy, and he don't even like walking at night!"

"We believe you," Angie said, putting her hand on Corina's shoulder. "That's why we're here."

She nodded, eyes welling with tears again. "I know. I know it's . . ." She turned and walked back toward the living room. "It's just so absurd." She shook her scrawny fists at the dead camera in the corner. "You hear me?" she cried. "I did what you told me! Ain't none of this is right! None of it!"

Darey tapped the earbud phone in his ear and held up a hand. Then, turning away: "What is it, Detective?"

Randy George.

Corina collapsed on the couch and was digging for another cigarette. "Just maddening," she mumbled.

Angie eased down next to her. "You may think this is a strange question, but do you have a gun? Or pepper spray? Anything like that?"

"No. But I know where I can get one." She lit up and sucked hard. "And I can tell you this, I'd use it too."

On second thought, maybe the gun was unnecessary. Then again, maybe not. Against professionals, no weapon in Corina's hand would do her much good, but it would give her some sense of control. She had to do something with all that fear and anger.

"Maybe not a gun but get something. A Taser maybe. Just in case."

Corina gave a curt nod and stared at the television, drawing deeply on the crackling smoke stick.

Darey faced them, expression stark. "I'm sorry to interrupt, but we have to leave."

"What is it?"

"I'll explain later." To Corina: "I want you to stay here for the rest of the day. Can you do that?"

"I got work at four. Gotta go. Staying here only makes me crazy."

"Then promise me you'll keep your phone with you in case I need to call."

"What is it? That phone call. What'd they say?"

"I just need to check this out first. Just keep your phone with you, okay?"

"Okay."

Darey gave her a hug. "Stay strong, Corina. We're going to get to the bottom of this."

"Thank you. Thank you from the bottom of my heart."

Then they were out the door, hurrying for the car.

"What is it?"

Darey glanced back at her. "Jamie just killed a prisoner at County."

CHAPTER
EIGHTEEN

THEY SAT in two of six fixed chairs in the downtown station's holo-room. Randy had set up a nonlocal interface with Jamie, who was under direct supervision 24/7, thanks to the DA. Darey had argued that as Jamie's counsel he had the right to meet with his client in person, but they were ignoring protocol on this one. No in-person meeting today. Period. Highly unusual, but nothing short of a court order would change it and there was no time for that.

Angie and Darey's drive down had been filled with stunned silence peppered with demanding questions and no answers. Randy hadn't offered any specifics, only an opportunity to connect nonlocally with Jamie in one hour. It was all being set up.

That hour had arrived. To be precise, it would arrive in nine more minutes, indicated by a countdown clock above the large 3D shadow box that would soon fill with Jamie's likeness. This model, the Convergence 2112, was the lowest grade on the market, not much larger than the 3D screen in their sitting room at home. Unlike their 3D screen, which could only receive information, the frame at the front of the holo-room generated a reasonable virtual interaction with another party, provided they were in a similar holo-room or using other RIG.

The room itself was jet black—walls, floor, and ceiling. As were the six chairs positioned in a semicircle facing the 3D frame.

At the moment the only life in the black room consisted of Angie, Darey, and Randy, who stood between them and the screen at his back.

"So let me get this straight," Darey was saying. "The guards put my client, a defenseless young man falsely accused of committing a heinous crime against two children, into general population, knowing full well the danger to Jamie in that environment?"

Randy was frowning, hands in pockets, apologetic. "Believe me, it's as objectionable to me as it is to you. I've already filed a complaint."

"Everyone knows what they do to kid-killers in prison. This isn't going to end with a simple complaint. I'll have the DA's head."

"I don't think it was him," Randy said.

"Then who?"

Randy shrugged. "An oversight."

"An oversight that resulted in a gross miscarriage of justice. My client is innocent until and unless proven otherwise. It's the state's responsibility to protect him until justice has been served one way or the other."

This was the Darey who fought tooth and nail for the accused, regardless of any doubt of their innocence.

"Agreed," Randy said. "But it's water under the bridge now." He glanced at the closed door and when he spoke again, his voice was softer. "You have to realize that you're not dealing with the law as much as optics in this case. I've never seen anything quite like it."

"I don't care about the politics of the case," Darey snapped. "The law exists for a reason. No one's beyond it, especially those who've manipulated their way into positions of government. Like I said, this isn't over."

"And like I said, I agree, but my hands are tied. Give me one piece of evidence that throws the department's case into question and that changes."

He was a good man who, like them, was a slave to a large machine that fed on its own power and crushed those who stood in its way.

"I'm sorry," Randy said. "Really, I am."

Darey ignored him. "Show us what you have."

Randy stepped over to a panel on the wall and entered a code. A 2D scene of the lunchroom at County filled the large holo-screen, which was now functioning as a simple flat-panel monitor. This was security footage from the prison, marked by a date and time stamp: yesterday, 6:39 p.m.

"This is last night," Randy said. "I've isolated both incidents for you. The full footage will be available later."

Jamie was seated at a table by himself, staring at the room, food untouched. They watched as a tall man with a snake tattoo around his neck approached the table and sat down in front of Jamie, quickly joined by two others.

"No audio?" Darey asked.

"Not here, no. I'm not sure it would help, it's a noisy room. The prisoner with that tattoo is Guy Mellinger, currently on trial for human trafficking. The case against him is open and shut."

"Everything helps," Darey said. "If there's audio, I want it."

Randy didn't reply.

The encounter was brief and ended with Mellinger leaning forward and speaking—presumably some kind of threat punctuated by a stabbing finger—before rising and leaving Jamie alone.

The boy sat in silence, staring ahead, then closed his eyes. Thinking. Thinking what?

The scene changed abruptly to an empty hallway. Date stamp today. Time 11:49 a.m.

"Second scene," Randy said. "No audio, but I doubt there's anything to hear."

They watched as the same tall man with the snake tattoo, Guy Mellinger, entered a hall and strolled toward the camera. He was halfway down the hall when Jamie hurried around the corner behind him, hands by his sides. He reached Mellinger in five long strides, wrapped his right arm around the man's neck, and jerked back hard enough to lift Mellinger off his feet.

The prisoner flailed and thrashed, but Jamie was a big boy. He had Mellinger in a chokehold that had probably cut off the man's oxygen supply and ability to cry out. No audio required.

Mellinger's body went limp in Jamie's grasp. The boy lowered the body to the floor, thoughtfully straightened his arms so they weren't caught under him, then turned and calmly walked back the way he'd come. The image froze with Jamie midstride, rounding the corner.

"His neck was broken," Randy said.

A chill snaked down Angie's spine. If this footage leaked, and she was sure it would, the public would see a man accused of strangling two teenagers take the life of another human being with similar cold, calculating power.

The countdown clock above the screen read two minutes and twenty-six seconds. Jamie would be with them soon.

"Not good," Darey breathed.

"No." The voice came from behind them. They turned to see Andrew Olsen's stocky, short frame standing in the doorway. "Not good at all," he said, staring at the screen. Eyes on Angie. "Unless you're me, that is."

Here was the man who'd dragged her out of the closet for the whole world to see. She felt Darey's hand on her knee, anticipating her rising rage.

Easy, Angie. Don't give him the satisfaction.

But she couldn't still the trembling in her hands. She faced the front of the room, took a deep breath, and settled. Which was a good thing, because the world suddenly went white.

She caught her breath, then tried to breathe as carefully as she could, aware of being watched. For two or three seconds she remained still in pure whiteness, heart beating like a tom drum. No gate room, just a whiteout.

Please come back, please come back . . .

Then she was. Back in the holo-room. She took a long, slow breath. Had they noticed?

Olsen was talking behind her. ". . . my duty to inform you that the state's seeking a summary judgment against your client for the murder of Guy Mellinger in the first degree. Trust me, I'd much prefer nailing your client to the wall for the Dead Head case, but, as you saw, this murder is open and shut. We all know that the law provides no appeals process in cases with a probability rating of 90 percent or higher. In this case, the Randal Scale calculates a guilty verdict at 98 percent, considering the video footage and Jamie's subsequent confession. We're headed for the quickest conviction and sentencing

Texas has seen. If I have my way, Jamie Hamilton will be put to death within three months. That's assuming no one gets to him sooner on the inside."

Angie twisted to face the DA, appalled by his cold nature.

"Not to worry," the DA said. "We'll do our best to make sure he's safe." Olsen turned on his heels and exited the room, leaving them in a vacuum.

Randy broke the silence.

"Sorry about that. Unfortunate. But now you know."

"And your hands are tied," Angie said, neck hot.

"Like I said, unless new evidence surfaces."

Neither she nor Darey spoke, but Randy knew how to read people.

"Is there?"

"Is there what?" Darey asked.

"New evidence."

Darey turned to the clock, which was now counting down the seconds from ten. "We're working on it," he said.

"Then I'll leave you to it. Both rooms are in full-privacy mode. I made sure of it myself."

"Good to know someone's following the law," Darey said. "Thank you."

Randy left the room, and the holo-frame brightened with a scene of a small living room—a single white leather chair, red carpet, and paintings of sailboats on the walls.

Jamie walked into the room and sat in the chair, grinning, hands on his knees.

"Hello."

There could be no doubt, Angie thought. This Jamie was an older version of the boy she'd seen in the gate room. Why was he in her head? Not because he was her son. That much was obvious—she was way too young to have a son his age. Either they were connected in some way beyond her recollection, or her mind was just populating itself with meaningful faces and symbols.

Maybe Jamie was showing up as a child because she believed he was innocent.

Darey cleared his throat. "Hello, Jamie. Good to see you."

"You're in a room with green carpet and six white chairs," Jamie said. "And large windows behind you looking at a city. It's nighttime. Pretty."

"And you're in a room with red carpet and paintings of sailboats behind you," Angie said. "How cool."

"Yeah, pretty cool. But the resolution could be better."

"Well that's what you get on a government budget. Sorry we can't be there in person."

"But this is cool. I've never been in a room like this. No RIG." He touched his face and forehead. "Ha!"

They talked briefly about the conditions in County, and Jamie seemed happy enough. He made no mention of killing Guy Mellinger until Darey brought it up. Angie wondered if he really was so disassociated from reality that he would feel no remorse for killing someone in cold blood, even if it could be established as self-defense. It was at once mystifying and disturbing, particularly in light of what they'd learned about his childhood.

Who was Jamie Hamilton, really?

"Do you want to tell us what happened this morning?" Darey asked.

Jamie's expression softened. "I had to kill the Snake-man," he said.

Darey shifted uncomfortably in his chair. "No one *has* to kill anyone, Jamie. We have laws that protect people from what you did."

"Yeah, but it was the only way I could play. Otherwise I would die."

He was still lost in game talk.

"You can't know that," Darey said.

Jamie shrugged. "I did the math. If I didn't kill him, there was a 92 percent chance he would kill me. And if I killed him, there was an 82 percent chance I would survive."

There was no way Jamie could know what he was claiming to know.

"How did you do the math, Jamie?" Darey asked.

He explained in broken phrases about the shapes and numbers and algorithms that came to him in gameplay. In games like this game. He told them that his job was to let Darey speak and not talk himself, just like they'd told him, but he couldn't play at all if he was dead. So he kept himself alive. That was all.

Halfway through Jamie's explanation, Angie's perception of him began to shift. There was something about the way he saw reality that struck her as . . . *beyond*. The whole world was code to him, and he was engaging only that. Code. He'd closed his eyes after Guy Mellinger had left him at the table, calculating the odds using that code.

In a mad sort of way, she admired him for it. He operated in an arena of pure logic, stripped of the emotions that blurred the lines of that logic. And if he was right—if Guy Mellinger really did present a clear and present danger to his life—then his actions should be accepted as self-defense by both the law and by society. If he really did have the capacity to extrapolate probabilities, he wasn't insane, he was highly evolved. A prodigy. The next step in human evolution.

But she knew no one would consider his rantings to be evidence of anything but lunacy.

When Jamie finished, they both looked at him, at a loss. What could one say to that?

"You have to know that you've made my job very difficult," Darey finally said. "Do you understand that?"

"Yeah." Still as innocent as a child. "But very difficult is better than dead. And we're not playing that game."

Angie blinked.

"We're not playing what game?"

Jamie's eyes shifted past them. Now Angie's nerves were buzzing.

"The game Play Dead?" she pressed.

He shrugged again. "Those are just words."

"Do you know anything about a gateway in a game with a white room?" she asked.

"This game?"

"No, another game with a gate room. It has books in it and gears on one wall."

"Maybe. I play too many games."

"A game in a white room, Jamie. You don't remember anything like that?"

"I think maybe I see a white room in my dreams, but I can't remember anything about it when I wake up."

"You do?"

"I think so. Is that good?"

"And you can't remember anything at all about the dream?"

"I have lots of dreams, but I can't remember them very good. Maybe I only used to dream about a white room."

Darey held up his hand, clearly not wanting to take this path. But Angie couldn't shake the feeling that Jamie knew more than what he was saying. Maybe something about his childhood or something else he'd seen was buried deep in his mind. Maybe on some level of consciousness, they were in contact with each other. A level like the space he accessed to see geometric patterns.

Or maybe there was something buried deep in *her* mind, and he was trying to help her uncover it so she could set him free. Did they know each other from somewhere else? Maybe while dead heading?

"We can't use your methods of calculating probabilities in the court. In the law's eyes, you murdered another prisoner for verbally threatening you. That's first-degree murder, subject to the death penalty. Considering the circumstances, I don't think I can mount an adequate defense for what you did this morning."

"Yeah, but I didn't kill Timothy and Clair."

"That's what we're working to prove. But what you did this morning's another matter. We're now on a whole new timeline. If we can't prove your innocence in the Oak Hill case before a judge decides on your guilt in the murder of Guy Mellinger, we're out of luck. It might cost you everything."

"Yeah. But better than being dead today."

"Do you remember anything from before you became Corina's son, Jamie?" Angie asked the question impulsively, still stuck on what made him so unique.

He looked at them in silence for a moment.

"No."

"Anything at all? Your mother told us everything she knows."

More hesitance.

"No, just empty space. And I knew that I was different."

"Different how?"

"Well . . . I can see the colors and patterns, right?"

"Only that?"

He gave them a nod.

That's all he would say. Maybe that's all he knew.

"Okay, Jamie, we'll work with what we have," Darey said. "If we can bring new evidence that clears you in the Oak Hill case, it would dramatically shift public perception. They'll see you as a victim. When all is said and done, this case will go down in whatever way satisfies the voters. It's an election year."

"Yup."

Did he understand all of that? She wasn't sure.

"In the meantime, there's a new rule to this game. No one gets hurt. Not even a fly."

"What if someone else wants to kill me?" he asked.

"Seeing what you did in there, I doubt anyone else will want to take a shot at you."

"Yup. I knew that too. People can smell fear."

Darey sighed. "Be well, Jamie. One day at a time. If anything happens and you can't get hold of us, try to reach out to Randy George, the detective."

"I trust him."

"I do too."

"Good-bye, Jamie," Angie said.

"Bye, Angie. I'll see you soon."

Soon, she thought. *As a boy in the gate room.* But that made zero sense.

TWENTY MINUTES later they were in Darey's office at Channing & Miles. As Darey had said, only new evidence would slow this speeding train. Or better, knock it off its well-oiled tracks. With any luck, that evidence was on the data card they'd taken from Corina's security system.

Darey threw his coat over a side chair, pulled the card out of his pocket, and slipped it into his desktop processor.

Angie leaned over his shoulder, aware of his musky cologne. Always manicured and scrubbed to the bone, Darey. She, not so much. They were like a rose and a thorn. He was the rose.

A soft-focus black and white video popped to life on Darey's pad. The date and time were stamped center bottom. Four days before the date of the murders.

"Well, that answers two questions," she said.

"It was working, and the memory likely holds a week's worth of continuous recording. Pretty standard for local storage."

"Something like that."

"Exactly like that," he said. Then: "Hopefully."

Darey spun through the video at 500 X until the date of the murders showed on the stamp. Then he slowed it down to 100 X, until the feed showed Jamie entering the house at 4:25 that Thursday afternoon.

"There he is." Darey scratched the time on a notepad and let the footage run at high speed. They watched as Jamie wandered around the kitchen, making himself a sandwich—lunch meat, the simulated kind, Angie thought—and pickle spears, lots of pickles and mayonnaise. He took the sandwich and a single-serving carton of Coke to his room.

Closed the door, leaving nothing other than the empty hall, kitchen and living room to be seen.

An hour later, Jamie emerged from his room and entered the bathroom. Then returned to his room, likely on the darknet, where Fluffy Puppy came to life and conquered the world.

Darey jotted down the time stamps on his notepad.

The footage showed him coming out of his room again at 7:26, this time for another Coke. Then at 8:45 to use the bathroom. Then at 9:20 to look out the living room window, maybe to see if his mom was home, although he surely knew she was working. Just a boy hoping, she thought.

It didn't matter. He came out for a bowl of cereal just after ten. Then used the bathroom at 10:40. Then took his bowl to the kitchen at 11:34, washed his dishes and grabbed another Coke. Jamie liked Coke. Then at 12:15 to check the living room window again—his mom should be home by now, maybe?

The time stamp read 12:17 when Jamie finally entered his room for the last time that night.

"That's it!" Angie breathed. "They said time of death was around midnight, right?"

Darey was grinning like a teddy bear. "Between 6:00 p.m. and midnight. We now have definitive proof that Jamie was in his house during that time."

The video was still running at high speed. It showed Corina entering the house at 1:06 in the morning, presumably after her closing shift at Local Taco. So late? She tapped lightly on Jamie's door, which earned her no response, then went to her bedroom.

Both of them emerged within fifteen minutes of each other the next morning, dressed in pajamas, his plaid, hers a lime green.

"So we have it?" Angie demanded. "This will prove he's innocent!"

Darey pulled the card out and crossed the office to a painting of an Arabian horse. "So it would appear." He slid the painting aside and opened a safe hidden in the wall behind it.

"What do you mean, appear? Can they claim we manufactured this footage?"

He placed the card inside, locked the safe, and slid the painting over it.

"Video's easy to manipulate," he said, turning back. "But it won't take much to verify its authenticity. And we'll have security footage from the school that shows him in the same clothes, carrying the same books. My only concern now is how to deliver this evidence. They're trying this case in the media. Whatever we do, it needs to be soon, tomorrow at the latest. Every hour of ranting on the feeds further solidifies the public's perception of Jamie's guilt. Everything's going to unfold in the next few days."

She settled into his desk chair. "So we give the footage to the media."

"I have to give it some thought. That data card is Jamie's only lifeline now. We have to play it right."

"Then maybe we get some help with that."

"Maybe," Darey said. "Not sure who I can trust. Randy, but he's bound by—"

"Not Randy. I mean Jamie."

"Jamie?" Then he understood. "You mean give him all the evidence and have him calculate probabilities."

"Why not?"

"You're buying that?" he asked skeptically.

"You don't? It could have something to do with the white gate room."

He snatched up his jacket. "I don't know. And I thought we weren't going there."

"I'm not, but it's his life on the line, not ours. I can at least think about it."

"True. But we need hard evidence, not unverifiable numbers. He's plucking probabilities out of thin air. It's all wildly speculative. As for the white room, you prompted him and he was still clueless."

"But you can't discount the rest of it. Twenty years ago no one would have guessed that dead heading would be possible so soon. For all we know he's dipping into a field of information we aren't aware of. We're only just beginning to understand how this world really works, trust me."

With those two words, *trust me*, the room went white. But for only two seconds before she was back.

"What?" he asked.

"What, what?"

"You okay?"

"Yup."

"It's me, Angie. What just happened?"

"A whiteout."

"The gate room?"

"No, just a whiteout. No hallucination."

Here with Darey, blinking into that space didn't scare her. She was getting used to it. No harm, no foul, just tripping. Strange. "No big deal," she said.

His frown made it clear that he disagreed. And seeing his reaction, she too realized how not okay it was. Maybe she wasn't getting used to it.

"I'll be okay," she said, rising from the chair.

Darey grabbed his fob. "I'm driving."

"Don't you always?"

CHAPTER
NINETEEN

MATTEO STEGER leaned back in his chair, studying the three screens arranged on his workstation in the dark room, as he called it. Dark, not only because he kept the light low, but because no one but he knew it existed. Not even his employers.

Information was power, and he had access to a world of information at his fingertips. The only data that was firmly beyond his grasp was their data, because they were darker than him, but that didn't concern him as long as they made his life possible. Not that he found time to use even a fraction of what they'd paid him over the last sixteen years, but he would retire soon, and he already knew precisely how he would live when he did.

Half of his resources would go to hiding himself from them, because they wouldn't take kindly to his retirement. He would spend the other half on starting a new life, this time as a family man. One with very expensive tastes. Married to someone like Angie Channing, he imagined. He knew her better than she knew herself and had always found her utterly fascinating. She and Jamie were more similar than either could possibly know. They were called 'the unveiled ones,' able to connect with reality on a deeper level. Or perhaps more accurately, able to disassociate with perceived reality far more easily than most.

He would be free soon. Very soon. As soon as the president was elected, if all went well.

So few really knew how the world worked. It was all data, really. Humanity had sold itself to ones and zeros. All movies were simply data. All digital sound. All wealth. All information, even the data locked in people's minds. All the processing power that controlled everything from electricity to weapons. Whoever controlled those ones and zeros controlled the world. And there was no technology with so many ones and zeros as the virtual reality that would one day change everything.

Truly, the technology was still in its infancy. The governor of Texas knew that and was making her play. Data led to the presidency, and there was no better platform to manipulate the world than from that office. The world had discovered as much thirty years ago during the Trump era. But unlike then, those who played the game now did so with far more sophisticated tools.

In Matteo's time, he'd put an end to the lives of sixty-three people who surfaced as threats to the organization, which might lead one to the conclusion that his greatest skill was killing. Not so. Anyone could kill. But doing so without leaving evidence that led back to the source required far more skill. A skill that depended on data.

Which was why he used redundant systems. Fail-safes.

Now one of those fail-safes had failed him. The very data he had used to secure himself in the matter of Jamie Hamilton was now working against him. He would use more data to fix the failure of that data. As always.

He glanced at the door to his right. Beyond it sat one of the most sophisticated RIGs in production. He knew the darknet as well as any but preferred screens to dead heading for the simple reason that he preferred to be in full control of his environment. Dead heading introduced a layer of disorientation that unnerved him. Still, it served him when there was no better way to pull data from that world.

There were whispers in the darknet concerning the growing realization that the human body, along with everything that existed, was only more data being expressed based on a code of fractal, self-similar geometry, which meant little to him other than its implication: the universe was digital. It was software, not hardware.

He often wondered if these discoveries were the real interests of those he worked for. Whoever they were, his power paled compared to theirs.

It didn't matter. He would play the game as he understood it. In that understanding, one rule dominated all others. Kill or be killed.

The screen directly in front of him showed footage from the Hamilton house. It was paused to show a still image of the boy's counsel, Darey and Angie Channing, meeting with Corina. The security camera he'd first installed in her house was hardly more than a red herring. A token that he'd forgotten. A rare error that would now inconvenience him.

He'd always relied on the far more sophisticated acoustic-imaging camera that used high-frequency sound waves to 'see' through paint.

Matteo spit out the toothpick he'd been chewing on and activated the landline phone, the only truly secure form of communication. The convenience of wireless data came at a price. Signals sent through the air could be intercepted much more easily than encrypted voice data transmitted though scrambled landlines.

He spoke in a soft voice. "787846309Z, connect."

He lifted the phone from its cradle and waited for the secure connection to trace itself, scanning the lines for any signal anomalies or interruptions. The receiver buzzed twenty seconds later, and his handler came on.

"What is it?"

"Hello, Katrina."

Katrina Botwilder didn't like him using her name, which was why he did. Small victories were often more satisfying than the ones that changed the world.

"I'm late for a function. What is it?"

"They know," he said.

Static on the line. But the trace indicator still showed green.

"Explain."

"The boy's counsel found footage from an old security camera CSI missed. With it, they will be able to show that Jamie was home at the time of the disposal."

A long pause ensued as she considered this information. He didn't bother sharing the fact that it was he who'd installed the security camera. None of that mattered now.

"Where's the footage now?"

"At the counsel's office."

"You're sure?"

"Quite." Again he skipped the details, namely that, unaware of a second camera, Mr. Channing had given away his intentions to hide the card in his safe. This was corroborated by the security footage from his building, which showed he and Angie hurrying into the premises shortly after meeting with Jamie. Yes, yes, the whole world was on display for those who knew how to find the ones and zeros. The data card was in the safe. And if it wasn't, Darey would lead him to it.

"Hold on."

Katrina was speaking to someone. One of *them*. She was back in less than ten seconds.

"Eliminate Channing."

"I could simply retrieve the footage."

"There's too much at stake. We don't need someone with his reputation casting doubt. Not now."

"And the girl? She knows."

"We can still use her. Besides, she's lost credibility, as you know. Kill the attorney and retrieve the footage."

He didn't like it, but when had that mattered? He found himself far more troubled by the idea of killing Angie, for the simple reason that he admired her.

"If you insist."

"Do it now and make it clean."

"I will do my best."

She disconnected and Matteo set the phone back in its cradle.

It took him an hour to breach the firewall that sheltered Channing & Miles's data. Surprisingly sophisticated for a law office.

Another twenty minutes to find what he was looking for.

Ten minutes to gather his tools and leave the house.

It was going to be a bloody night.

CHAPTER
TWENTY

THREE. THAT'S how many times Angie's world had gone white in the last hour. No more hallucinations of the gate room. They were only whiteouts, and she found some relief in that fact.

Yes, they might be dangerous. Yes, the episodes were undoubtedly connected to the Red Protocol. Yes, they unnerved her. But what if there was something specific buried deep in her psyche that was trying to assert itself?

She'd decided to accept them without resistance, curious to see if allowing them would change them.

To her amazement, it did.

She and Darey had been in their house, dissecting the case, when the first one hit. She'd been scooping takeout Mongolian chicken into a bowl as Darey explained his decision to show the security footage of Jamie to Randy first thing in the morning. A few moments later, as she blinked back into the kitchen, she was surprised to note that the world was out of focus. Shimmering. And Darey's voice sounded distant, even though he was standing right behind her, talking about Randy.

Her distorted perception lasted only for a few heartbeats, but it was definite.

The next time the world had gone white, twenty minutes later, they were in Darey's home office as he made arrangements for a video verification expert to meet them at his downtown office the following day. This time, the distortion lasted a good ten seconds, long enough to frighten her. She could still see and hear everything in the room, but it was all off. Again, shimmering.

The third time, only a few minutes ago as she sat in the living room, the shimmer lasted long enough for her to carefully take in the sitting room, breathing deep to keep herself calm.

The furniture and the 3D screen, the ceiling, the floor, the cushions—all of it was slightly distorted. Not out of focus like the first time, but . . . well . . . moving. Malleable energy that looked like it could be shaped by her hands. Lifting her right hand, she saw that it too was shimmering.

Rubbing her thumb and fingers together, she felt a slight vibration. Very slight, but there, she was sure of it.

She knew it was a hallucination—anyone who'd eaten mushrooms containing psilocybin could attest to the psychoactive effects of tripping, and this was like that. She also knew that hallucinations were bad news for her. And she also knew, having tried psilocybin with friends on several occasions in France, that resisting the shifts in perception only drew a person into a spiral of fear. Just allow it to happen, they said.

So she was allowing now, gazing about the room, watching the slight distortion linger on the wall, the ceiling, the lamp, her hands. Sally was watching her, head cocked to one side. Could the dog see what she was seeing? She doubted it. But Sally knew something was up.

"I have to run out to meet a client who's having a meltdown," Darey said, entering the room. "Shouldn't take long."

He too had a shimmer about his edges.

"You okay?" He was giving her the look that said he knew she wasn't.

"Hmmm? Yes. Just another episode. But it's fine. Go ahead, I'll be here."

He looked like he was about to say something, but then walked to her, bent over, and kissed her forehead. "Be back in an hour. Two, tops."

She was too distracted by the shimmer to ask him more.

"Okay," she said, but he was already out of the room.

You're tripping, Angie. Without drugs, without a RIG, without anything but your own mind. This can't be good.

But if she relaxed into it—if she didn't call it bad—it was kinda cool. She slowly scanned the shifting room and stopped at the 3D screen, which was especially cool. She'd been watching a panel on a national feed discussing the most recent flooding in Miami, which had gone to great lengths to mitigate rising sea levels and was still fighting a losing battle. As were all major coastal cities.

The whole screen was wavering, just barely but definitely. The panelists were in a gray conference room, seated around a white table. A screen on the wall behind them showed scenes of the Miami flooding. One of the women, Andrea Marker, who wore a red dress, was bringing up global warming, a tired subject that had long ago been settled except for all the finger pointing, which would likely last for decades.

As Angie watched, Andrea Marker's voice began to fade. The room they were in began to change. The image softened, then blurred as white pixilation filled the space in the 3D screen. Before her eyes, what had just been a news studio slowly faded to white.

Angie closed her eyes. The voices were gone, replaced by a distant hum. She knew that hum!

She opened her eyes and looked at the screen again. Still white. And then the white room began to take on a new shape and she sat up slowly, heart thumping.

It was the shape of the gate room. There was the table with the three books, the gate with the needle, the gears, all ten feet from where Angie sat, now breathless.

For several seconds, she just stared at it, sure that it would revert. But no. The 3D space in that screen showed her the gate room. And it remained that way, humming as if beckoning her to come closer.

See, Angie. Touch. Hear. Smell. Taste.

Angie put her feet on the floor and tentatively stood. Nothing changed. The screen looked like it was gone, leaving a large rectangular opening to an actual white room. She cautiously took a step toward it. Then another. Then edged up to the screen and slowly reached out her hand.

When her fingers made contact with what she thought was the screen, a vibration surged through her hand and she pulled it back, startled. Looked at her hand. No harm.

She tried again and this time pushed on the energy flowing across the space that should have been a screen. It bent inward, reacting to the pressure she applied. She pulled her hand back and it returned to its former position.

Both anxious and wildly curious, Angie tried again, this time with more pressure. Her hand and arm passed through the barrier.

She yanked her arm out again, teetering on the edge of panic.

Allow. Accept. It's like using a RIG. This is all in your mind, just like any virtual space.

It was this last thought that gave her the hairbrained courage to slowly slide her hand, then her arm, then her shoulder into the space beyond. Then her foot and her whole body.

With a faint pop, the screen itself vanished and Angie found herself in the gate room. The wall of gears on her right, the table with three books to her left, the needle wall twenty feet in front of her.

Angie gasped and twisted around. The mask wall was three feet behind her, its portal to her living room sealed tight. Above it, the words *Imago Simulacrum*. Image Maker.

"Hello."

She turned and saw the boy who looked like Jamie seated in the white leather chair, grinning. He hopped up, hurried to her, and threw his arms around her waist.

"I knew you would make it back!"

She tentatively put her hand on his head, glancing around. Nothing had changed.

"Jamie?"

He looked up at her. "That's not my real name."

"But it's you, right? You look like him, only younger. Is this you when you were a boy?"

"You can call me Jamie if you want to."

She thought about that. "Do you know anything about Jamie when he was a boy?"

He hesitated, as if trying to remember. "I can't remember. But do you want to call me Jamie?"

"If you don't mind."

"Okay."

Angie stepped away, eyes on the books called *Play Dead*. Then she looked at the truth wall, which Jamie called the needle gate. The way to the truth was narrow.

She turned back to Jamie, who was rubbing an itch on his nose. He lowered his hand and gave her a sheepish grin. Then he just looked at her, waiting for her to say something.

"You said you were here to help me, right?"

"Yup. And you're helping me."

"Then can you tell me what this room is for?"

"It's your room, but it's the same as everyone's room." He pointed at the needle. "That way leads to the truth." Then he pointed at the Image Maker wall. "That way leads to the masks that hide the truth."

"The truth about what?"

"About what we think we see and know," he said.

"See and know about what? The Oak Hill murders?"

"Yes, because the truth about who really killed Clair and Timothy is hidden and maybe can only be found beyond the gates," he said. "Just like everything in the game."

"What game?"

"Play Dead," he said.

"Is it a real game? Have you played it before?"

"I think it's real," he said. "And I think we both know how to play, but we've forgotten."

He didn't seem to know much more than she did, which would make sense if he was a construct of her own psyche. If he knew more than he was saying, he wasn't sharing it, but that was the first rule of proper gaming: no cheat codes.

Still, one thing seemed clear: the truth about the Oak Hill murders and maybe much more could only be discovered beyond the gates, even if this room was only in her mind. It was as if she already knew something, and it was buried deep inside of her memory, and this room was the gateway to that information.

That was her guess.

She stepped over to the book wall and lifted the cover of the first book containing ancient foreign symbols. What was unique about an ancient alphabet? Writing? Images? Human intelligence? History of Earth? But they could mean anything.

She set the book back on its pedestal and examined the middle book with code. Computer code rather than human code, right? All ones and zeros, right to the last page. She considered that this book conveyed its hidden meaning in digital rather than human terms.

The third book was filled with geometric shapes resembling butterflies. The images were created by fractal geometry—designs that replicated themselves, dividing infinitesimally into smaller copies. All virtual worlds were based on fractal geometry.

Did the order of the books matter? From ancient language symbols to computer code to infinite fractal geometry—a progression, maybe.

"You're saying I know this?" she asked, turning back.

He was standing close, watching on her right. "You know everything in your mind," he said. "But most of what you know's hidden from you."

It was known that over 90 percent of a person's beliefs were hidden away in the subconscious mind. Humans spent their whole lives acting out of these subconscious beliefs, which were formed, or 'programmed,' in their first twelve or so years. Most people thought they came to conclusions consciously, but many studies had shown that this simply wasn't the case. People almost always acted out of their programming. Only deep excavation could expose what lay in darkness.

So, this room was in her subconscious mind. For all she knew, it had always been here. Was it a metaphor or was it real? Had to be a metaphor, a way of seeing her mind.

"So you can't tell me how to play the game?"

"You already are."

True. And right now, the programming in her mind called Jamie, who might really be her, could only offer what she was ready to discover at this point in the game. She decided that whatever truth this room would unveil for her could only be shown if she figured out how to open the needle gate. And to do that, she had to win the game.

She had to stop trying to figure out all the whys and just focus on the game itself.

Rushing through a game never worked. You had to discover it. Here too, in this game called Play Dead, there was no rush. All of this was happening in her mind while in reality she was in her sitting room at home with Darcy gone. Besides, as she'd told Jamie, there were two ways to win at any game. By beating the opponent or, better, by just having fun. The second was the hardest way, because most people were so focused on the first kind of winning that they only really had fun if they were beating the game.

Here, the opponent was evidently herself. She was in a battle of wits with herself. Fighting herself would only slow her down. Maybe the way to win this game was simply to have fun. The boy certainly didn't seem uptight.

Angie walked up to the needle wall and tentatively brought her fingertips to the glassy white surface. The hum rose in pitch and volume and the lines glowed. She held her hand on the wall, pressing harder. The pitch skyrocketed, higher, higher, a piercing tone that made her wince. She was about to jerk her hand away when the tone soared out of her acoustic range, plunging the room into silence. No hum at all. But the high, inaudible tone was still in full force, vibrating the wall and the room with such power that her hand on the wall became a blur.

She jerked her hand away, overwhelmed by the raw power she'd activated. "Wow . . ."

"Yeah, wow. Watch!" Jamie ran up to the Image Maker wall and pressed his palm against the large white mask. The pitch fell like a rock, rumbling with increasing volume as he held his hand on the wall, casting her a daring look that said, *see?*

The whole room began to vibrate as if it were at the epicenter of a violent earthquake. The first two Play Dead books fell off their pedestals.

The third book filled with fractal geometry stayed put. Odd.

He pulled his hand away and the sound resumed its original faint drone. "See?"

"The book with the geometric shapes didn't vibrate," she said.

"Nope. It's part of the higher tone. I figured that out."

He really was still figuring the room out, just like her. They were here to help each other. Maybe he was her inner child, whom she'd made in the image of Jamie, who was trying to help her.

Low-frequency vibration, high-frequency vibration. The whole world was only vibration. All energy, all matter, all that existed was ultimately tone. Even high school and secondary-education science programs had adopted the new understanding of physics by the late 2030s, when she was a teenager.

Matter was only slowly vibrating energy. Dense vibration. A table didn't actually exist as a solid table—it was only perceived that way by humans' limited perceptual faculties called sight and touch. In reality, that table, and all matter, was mostly a vacuum called space. Take away all the empty space and all the atoms that made up the table and it would be too small to see even under the most powerful microscope. And even then, the electrons and protons that remained were just more energy that somehow arose out of an infinite quantum field of pure potential.

Maybe the game was about much more than exonerating Jamie. Maybe it was that, but also about how to heal herself from the hallucinations spawned by the Red Protocol.

"You're sure that if I beat this game, it'll help Jamie in the real world?" she said.

"Of course," he said. "And us. The game will help us so we can help him."

CHAPTER
TWENTY-ONE

THE SUBTERRANEAN parking structure was dark except for the red exit lights, a result of Matteo's handiwork with the circuit breakers which, surprisingly, he located in an unlocked panel on the third level. Dark provided cover and Matteo required as much as possible, even though it was after eight o'clock. The building was nearly empty.

The staggering predictability of human beings never ceased to amaze him. People thought they were acting independently from the collective programming, but they weren't. Even the most clever were still following the code programmed into their minds by society. Once you figured out the patterns in a man's coding, you could easily manipulate him for the most desired outcomes.

The real quandary was whether he, too, was only acting according to his own programming. He thought of himself as more evolved than those he hunted, but that could not be true if he was only another actor on the stage, playing a role. The thought often disturbed him.

Clyde Mason grunted in the back seat. Matteo turned from the garage entrance and glanced back at the man bound and gagged in his back seat.

"Yes, Mr. Mason? What is it?"

The man stared at him with wide eyes and tried to speak through the duct tape over his mouth. He managed to make a few strange sounds, that was it.

"You have to use the restroom? Is that it?" He turned back to the entrance, watching for Channing's Mercedes. "Should be only a few more minutes. Then I'll let you relieve yourself."

Another grunt of protest, higher in pitch. The man was panicking, but that was also part of his programming.

Darey Channing had recently and convincingly argued that Mason, a Lithuanian, hadn't killed his wife a year earlier. The Lithuanian Mafia had done it, he claimed, but there was no proof. A good thing for Mason, because proof would have likely forced the Lithuanian Mafia to kill him to protect itself.

But now the Lithuanian Mafia was going to assert itself.

Acting as that Mafia, Matteo had called Mason and insisted on a meeting at Rusty's Drinking Shack—an odd name for a bar—if he wanted to remain alive. Matteo had intercepted him a block from his house, climbed into the man's car, and held him at gunpoint. He forced the man to make a frantic call to Mr. Channing, explaining the threat against him from the Lithuanian Mafia and demanding to see him tonight.

Satisfied, Matteo had bound and gagged the man and driven to the offices of Channing & Miles in the man's car. He'd left his own car properly parked near Mason's house.

Lights brightened the entrance and Matteo watched as a black Mercedes rolled past them. Channing was here.

"Only five minutes now and you will be able to relieve your bladder," he said. Then, twisting back, "I'm going to take off your restraints and your gag. If you act in any way, or make any sound, that makes me think you're trying to be noticed, I'll kill you. I have nothing to lose. And remember, I'm not after you. I'm only using you to get to Mr. Channing. Keep that in mind with every step you take. If you do exactly what I say, you'll be back with your girlfriend in less than half an hour. Do you understand?"

The man nodded.

"Good."

Matteo exited the man's car, pulled him from the back seat, and affixed an adhesive disk to the man's spine, just under his collar. "There is enough directed charge in this disk to sever your spinal cord at the press of a button in my pocket. I will not hesitate. Yes?"

Another frantic nod.

To make certain, Matteo activated the device, showing Mason the trigger. The man winced, feeling a current passing through the disk on his spine.

"It's only a small current to remind you that it's there. No harm unless I press this button. Simple?"

A nod.

Matteo untied him and pulled the tape off his mouth. "Wipe the sweat off your face."

The man did so.

"Walk to the first bank of elevators."

Mason stumbled forward.

"Walk normal."

The man did as best he could.

Once at the elevators, Matteo asked him to push the call button, which he did. Ten seconds later they were safely inside. Not a soul thus far.

"Ninth floor," he said, swiping a key card over the security panel. He'd already lifted the codes from the panel when they first arrived. Technology was a beautiful thing for those who knew how to build and break it.

The man pressed the round button and they rose to the ninth floor.

"Turn left and walk down the hall," Matteo said when the doors slid open. "You're doing well. Just another minute or two and you can go home."

He walked roughly five paces behind the man, unconcerned about the cameras in each corner. He'd already disabled the building's security cameras remotely. They passed two glass doors embossed with the firm's name, Channing & Miles, and rounded a corner. Matteo instructed the man to stop. They were now out of the bank of elevators' line of sight.

Darey should arrive in one of the two elevators in the next minute or so.

"Do you remember what to do now?" Matteo asked, listening for the bell that would announce the elevator's arrival.

"Yes."

"Good. Just get him inside. I'll be right behind."

The man nodded.

The bell chimed only fifteen seconds later.

Matteo withdrew the transmitter from his pocket and held it up, brow arched. *Remember?* The man nodded again and Matteo motioned him forward.

Mason stepped back into the hall. An idiot might make a run for it, and Mason was as close to an idiot as they came, but the buzzing on his neck would keep him in line.

"Clyde . . ." Darey Channing's voice. "You look . . . Are you okay?"

Matteo slid a black mask over his face.

"No," the man croaked. "They're going to kill me, man. They're going to cut my spine." A bit too close to the truth. "Of course I'm not okay. You gotta help me, man." He was gushing, the strained voice of a small-minded man terrified for his life.

"Okay, settle down. No one's going to kill you." A beat passed. "You sure you're okay?"

There was a tone in that voice that Matteo didn't like. Unlike Mason, Channing was nowhere near the bottom of the idiot scale. So Matteo pressed the button then, before anything could disrupt what must unfold here.

The sound of a body crumpling on the floor filled the hall as Matteo withdrew his silenced pistol from the holster under his jacket. He stepped out and trained the gun on a stunned Channing, who stood over Clyde Mason's dead body.

"Step inside your offices, please," he said, calmly walking toward the attorney.

Channing was a big man dressed down in jeans and a white shirt. Loafers on his feet. He'd turned to stone.

"You have no play here, Mr. Channing. The security cameras have been disabled. One way or the other, I will leave with the data card in your safe. If you resist, I will kill you now and break into the safe using other means. If you cooperate, I will allow you to live so your wife can feel safe in your arms."

The attorney was calculating behind wild eyes.

Matteo stopped three paces from the man. "You're already thinking that I can't allow you to live. I'm wearing a mask so that you can live. You haven't seen me, have you?"

He didn't need Channing to cooperate, but it would make his task much easier. He motioned with the gun.

"Please."

Channing had already done the math, realizing that his only play really was cooperation, for Angie's sake if not for his own.

"Now," Matteo snapped.

The attorney stepped up to the glass doors leading into the Channing & Miles suite, unlocked the entry with an encrypted data key, and pushed one door open. Matteo grabbed Mason's fallen body by the hair and dragged him after Channing into the firm's lobby. Closed the door. Mason's trousers were wet—he'd relieved himself after all. A promise fulfilled.

"Thank you. Take me to your office."

"You'll never get away with this," the man growled.

"I can understand how you might think that, but so far I always have."

"It was you."

"Who killed the boy and the girl?" He shrugged. "Not really. Society killed them. I only played one role in a much larger stage play. Your office please. No more talking."

"I—"

Matteo fired a round into Mason's dead body, which jerked with the impact. "Please, no more talking. Just take me to your office, open the safe, and give me the data card."

Channing hesitated, then wisely complied. His corner office overlooked a brightly lit downtown. One-way glass.

"You must realize that this isn't the only copy," Channing was saying as he slid aside a painting of a horse and pressed his hand on the panel. The safe popped open. "If you kill me . . ."

"Card."

The attorney withdrew a small data card from inside.

"Toss it on the floor."

Channing dropped it.

Matteo tossed him another card identical to the one he'd retrieved but with altered date stamps that identified the footage as being taken a week before it actually had. Jamie Hamilton's alibi was gone. "Put it inside. Then close the safe and slide the picture back into place."

The man did so, however reluctant.

Matteo picked up the fallen card and waved the gun at the office door. "Out."

"I've already told them that I have the evidence," Channing said, desperately searching for a play.

"Not true, but that no longer matters. Out. Now."

The attorney glared at Matteo for a long beat, then walked out of his office and through the lobby.

"If you leave . . ."

Matteo shot him in the head as he approached the suite's doors, before he could turn around. The small caliber shell would remain in the man's skull. His body dropped beside Mason's like a bag of bricks. It was a merciful killing. The man was alive one moment and then gone the next, clueless that any of this had even happened. Or so some said.

Blood began to seep from the hole in the back of Channing's head, but leaving evidence here wasn't a problem. The crime would appear precisely as he intended. This was a professional hit ordered by disgruntled mobsters. They'd used one of their own to lure the men to Channing's office, then killed them both to forever silence the truth about their involvement in Mason's wife's death.

Angie Channing and perhaps the lead detective would argue that someone had come for the evidence and switched out the card, but hearsay did not equal evidence.

Matteo flipped out a knife and carved a cross, a symbol favored by the Lithuanian mob, on Clyde Mason's forehead. He then removed the disk from the back of the man's neck—no need to leave such an expensive toy behind. An autopsy might turn up the adhesive, but that wasn't a problem.

It took him less than ten minutes to scan the attorney's processing box for a local copy of the footage, on the off chance the man had indeed made one. He knew Channing had gone straight from the Hamilton house to the precinct before hurrying here to view the footage and lock it in the safe. If there was a copy, it would be here.

But there was none.

Satisfied, Matteo exited Channing's office, crossed the lobby, stepped over the two men who'd been killed by Lithuanian hoodlums in a tragic vendetta, and left the building.

CHAPTER
TWENTY-TWO

DO YOU WANT to play dead, Angie?

I can't figure it out, so I'm playing with you. If you can show me how to play dead, I'll play that game.

I am showing you.

You are?

I'm learning with you.

Are you me?

Do you want me to be you?

I think you're Jamie.

Yup. And I'm me.

A bell chimed, pulling Angie out of the back and forth. A dinner bell? It was weird, but time seemed to act differently in her dreams. She thought she was asleep, dreaming of the gate room, not actually in the gate room itself. She'd been here for a while but she didn't know how long. Lost in her mind. Seeking answers.

Mostly she dreamed of playing. And by playing, she and Jamie meant playing the game, which meant figuring out the gate game deep in her own mind.

"Time to go?" the boy said.

"Really? Already?"

"If you want."

She thought about that.

"No, I'm not done playing."

A knocking came from the back wall. The Image Maker wall. Someone was banging on it? Curious . . .

She stepped toward it, and as she did, the room began to fade. She pulled up as darkness enfolded her. Now it was dark. But the knocking was still there, out in that darkness.

Angie slowly awakened from the dream and opened her eyes. She was in the sitting room, reclined in the same leather chair she'd been in before entering the 3D screen a few minutes earlier. Or maybe longer. She must have fallen asleep while in the gate room and then dreamed about it.

She lifted her head and looked around. The shimmer was still here. Everything in the room was shifting, like she was still on some kind of trip. Oddly, she felt no concern. These were only the aftereffects of the hallucinations. Had to be.

Darey would be home soon. Should she tell him that the hallucinations were deepening? Probably, even if that meant he would try to convince her to go to Convergence for regression therapy. On the other hand, maybe she shouldn't tell him. There was something buried deep in her psyche that wanted to reveal itself and telling him might compromise her discovery of that something. Right?

Another knock sounded from the direction of the front door. Who could that be? She stood up, feeling disoriented. The shimmer was kinda cool, really, with everything shifting slightly, energy in motion and color all around her.

The bell chimed. Oh, yeah. The door. Someone was at the door at this late hour. Had Darey been locked out?

When Angie entered the hall and rounded the corner that led into the atrium, she noticed sunlight streaming in through the windows. Rainbow-colored light. It was morning?

She pulled up, staring. She'd spent the whole night in the sitting room? Darey must have come home late and let her sleep in the chair.

The floor was moving, just slightly but definitely. So strange. So curious. So wonderful. Huh . . .

Rap, rap, rap. The door.

The shimmer began to fade, and by the time she reached the front door, it was gone. A good thing, she thought. What if it was a reporter wanting to talk to the Dead Head who'd been outed to the whole world?

She glanced in the mirror over the atrium table and saw that she looked pretty much put together, at least by her standards. Same jeans and T-shirt she'd worn yesterday. She tucked several loose strands of hair behind her ears, sniffed under her right arm for body odor, then straightened. Not too bad. Presentable.

Angie unlatched the deadbolt and pulled the door open, squinting in the bright light.

Randy George stood on the porch looking at her with brooding eyes. But Randy was on their side, so whatever it was, it couldn't be too terrible. Still, he looked upset. So instead of greeting him, she came straight to the point.

"What's happened?"

"Can I come inside?"

"Sure. Yeah, I'm sorry, I just didn't expect . . ." She opened the door wider and stepped aside, letting him in. Then closed the door.

"I think Darey's still in bed," she said. "You want me to get him?"

"I just need to talk to you. Can we sit down?"

"Sure."

Angie headed for the sitting room, feeling a bit unnerved by his demeanor. Something was up. Likely with Jamie.

"Can I get you a drink?"

"I'm fine."

But his voice said he wasn't, not at all, and now Angie began to worry. Something was off. Something terrible. Something more than Jamie. Something . . .

A thought that filled her chest with dread whispered through her mind. *Darey.*

She pulled up at the archway leading into the sitting room and turned to Randy. "I think I should get Darey," she said, moving to step around him.

He caught her by the arm. "Angie . . ."

"What?" she snapped, spinning to him. Waves of heat flushed her face. "Just spit it out! What's going on?"

"Angie . . . I don't know how to say this . . ."

"Just say it!"

"He's dead, Angie. Darey's dead."

RANDY'S HANDS were trembling. Not because death was a stranger to him, but because it was such a close friend, even now, three years after the death of this wife and daughter. Responding to the call from Channing & Miles and finding Darey's body on the floor had brought it all back.

He was telling Angie, but he was also reliving that night when he'd been in her shoes. It was more than he could handle with any grace.

She stared at him, jaw set.

"What do you mean? Who's dead?"

He took a deep breath, not knowing what to say other than the bare facts.

"We received a call from the law office this morning. A man named Clyde Mason and Darey were both found dead on the floor inside the office. It was quick. A professional execution."

Her eyes were round and her lips were quivering. He continued, hating each word, knowing there was no value in sugarcoating what they'd found.

"It looks like a hit from the Lithuanian mob. Darey defended Clyde Mason a year—"

"No!" Her face was flushed and red. "No!" she screamed.

And then she was running. Down the hall, crying his name.

"Darey?"

"Angie . . ." Randy ran after her. Saw her duck into a doorway at the end of the hall, where she stopped.

"Darey?"

He could see past her into the master bedroom. The bed looked untouched. She must have slept elsewhere, why and where didn't matter right now.

For a long moment, she stood there, staring at the empty bed. He tried to think of something to say, but nothing was coming. His gut felt hollow. Sick. Only a fraction of the horror she was feeling, he knew, and it was too much even for him, because he was there again, hearing the news of his own loss for the first time.

Angie turned and rushed past him, oblivious to his presence. He let her go and followed.

"Darey?" Her voice screamed his name as she spun into the kitchen, then as she ran for his office. "Darey?!"

She ended up standing in the middle of the living room, eyes wide and lost. And then Angie's face slowly twisted into a knot. Tears filled the wells of her eyes and spilled down her cheeks.

"He went to meet someone who called," she sobbed. "He had proof and they killed him."

She staggered to the couch and collapsed. And then she was wailing. Shoulders shaking, desperate eyes fixed on him. Crying with an agonizing pain that threatened to tear his heart from his chest.

Randy stepped over to her and settled on the couch, reaching for her hand.

She sat beside him, a fractured little girl unable to think or process, much less move. Just wailing and shaking and lost.

Randy pulled her into his arms, and she lowered her head onto his shoulder as sobs wracked her body.

"I'm sorry, Angie. I'm so sorry."

Head buried in his shoulder, she feebly struck his chest with her fist as her breath vacated her lungs, leaving her silent before sucking in air and crying with renewed urgency.

"It's okay," he said.

But it wasn't.

So he said no more. Tears were running down his own cheeks and he made no attempt to hold them back. He just held her and cried with her, and a part of him wished he was dead like Darey was dead.

For a long time they sat like that, smothered by the terrible pain.

The detective in him was thinking about the crime scene at Channing & Miles. They'd found the data card in Darey's safe, which his partner had been more than willing to open. Darey had mentioned the evidence in a call last night, and Randy had opened the data card at the attorney's office only an hour ago.

The date stamps on the footage were from the week before the Oak Hill murders. Whoever had killed Darey had swapped out the data card, but there would be no way to prove it. No real case to make that Darey had been executed by anyone other than the Lithuanian mob. The DA would conclude that Darey's murder was in no way connected to Jamie's case.

But Randy was quite sure someone was going to extreme lengths to cover their tracks—tracks that led to the framing of Jamie. Most likely a party with ties to the department. If that party knew Randy's opinion, they would see him, and Angie, as a threat to their case against Jamie.

This is what the detective in him was thinking.

The rest of Randy was numb. Reeling with pain. Crying as he held Angie, who'd gone still in his arms. He was the lead investigator in the case against Jamie. Which meant that he, at least in part, was responsible for Darey's death. For Angie's loss. He didn't know what to do with that realization other than to accept it. And to help her in any way he could.

But it might be too late for that.

The doorbell chimed.

Not now. Not in her condition. Not in his.

Angie had stopped crying. She leaned against him, breathing but otherwise motionless. He took a deep breath and let it out slowly. Rubbed her back.

"I'm sorry, Angie. I know it hurts."

She didn't react. No, she was in too much pain.

"Angie?"

Still nothing.

"Are you okay?"

He regretted the words the moment they left his mouth. But now he was worried. She laid against him, stone still.

"Angie?"

Nothing. The doorbell chimed again.

He pulled back and her head fell from his shoulder like a ragdoll's, face-down. Arms limp by her side, hands folded back on the leather sofa, lifeless.

"Angie?" He gave her a gentle shake. Still nothing.

His concern deepened as he gently lifted her chin. Her eyes were open but lifeless. Her chest slowly rose and fell, but her face was blank.

"Angie!" He shook her hard enough for her head to wobble, but she wasn't coming out of it.

The doorbell rang again, this time three times in a row.

Heart pumping with alarm, Randy eased her back on the sofa so she was staring at the far wall. He ran for the front door and pulled it open.

Felicia Buckhead, Angie's agent whom he knew from interviews during the release of *Righteous*, stood on the porch. Surprised to see him.

"Detective? What are you doing here? Is everything alright?" She looked past him. "I've been trying to reach Angie."

He grabbed her hand and pulled her inside. Closed the door.

"What is it?" Felicia demanded.

"I think she's in shock."

"Who? Angie? What happened?"

"Darey Channing was murdered last night."

She pulled away from him, gasping. "Darey? Darey was murdered?"

"Yes." He took her arm and hurried her down the hall. "She . . . I don't know what's happening to her, but she's nonresponsive."

Felicia rushed past him. Rounded the corner into the living room and ran to Angie, who was still slumped on the couch, eyes wide, mouth closed.

Felicia shook her gently. "Angie? Angie, wake up, sweetheart."

When Angie only wobbled, she quickly checked her pulse.

"We should call 9-1-1," Randy said, pulling out his phone.

"No."

"No?"

"No. I know what this is." Felicia looked up at him. "She's having a whiteout. A radical disassociation from reality due to a deep dive she did at Convergence early last week."

"A what?"

"A hallucination. Long story. But she'll come out of it. No hospital or doctor can help her."

"Who *can* help her?" he asked.

"Convergence. We need to get her there as soon as she comes out." Her face was still pale. "Darey's dead? What happened?"

He considered telling her if for no other reason than to get it off his chest. Jamie was innocent. He was being framed. They were in danger. But the detective in him stopped short, knowing the information was too explosive. He had to think this through before voicing conclusions that might endanger Felicia too.

"Darey claimed to have video footage that would clear a client. That evidence is now gone. By all appearances, Darey was killed for his involvement in an old case."

She clearly saw the uncertainty on his face. "And you believe that?"

"I only follow the evidence." He nodded at Angie, who hadn't moved. "You're sure she's okay?"

Felicia hesitated. "It's her mind, not her body. As long as her vitals are strong, she's okay. Yes, I think so."

"Tell me about this deep dive," he said.

CHAPTER
TWENTY-THREE

ANGIE COULDN'T have known just how crushing the loss of Darey would be to her—only the experience itself could offer her that pain. They'd never clung to each other for meaning, or at least they'd assumed as much. Most humans used partners like drugs to satiate their own need for identity and security. Not them.

And yet even this insight did little to temper the raw pain of her loss as the mind-numbing truth of Darey's murder settled into her mind. Heaving with sobs, she gripped Randy's shirt, unable to check herself. Everything that mattered had been shattered. Nothing was left. Nothing made sense. There was no light, no hope, no purpose.

Only the bottomless void of death that seemed to be eternal. Hell itself.

In that emptiest of spaces she realized everything stopped. Numbness replaced pain. Her eyes were closed, she knew that. She had just been sobbing. Her face was pressed into Randy's shoulder, but she could no longer feel it. Even her breathing seemed to have stopped. She was dead?

Startled, Angie opened her eyes and squinted as bright light flooded her sight.

No, not dead. She was in the gate room again. Curled up on the black and white checkerboard floor this time. The soft hum droned on.

Two thoughts filled her mind. The first was that back in the real world, Darey was dead, gone forever.

The second was that his death didn't seem to be as much of a problem to her now. Other concerns had gnawed at her on her two previous visits to this place, but nothing now. No fear, no dread, no pain.

Maybe she really was dead.

"It's because you're much deeper this time," the boy said behind her. "Which is good, because I think Jamie's running out of time."

Angie lifted her head and twisted. Jamie sat in the chair, watching her with curiosity. For a long beat neither of them moved or spoke. He was there in the chair and she was here on the floor and that seemed to be perfectly fine.

She pushed her body up and got to her feet.

"I'm back," she said.

He smiled. "You never left."

No, of course not. How could she leave her own mind? This place had always been deep inside of her. Now trauma had pulled her in even deeper and in this deepness, she felt different. More at peace.

"Darey's dead," she said.

"Is he?"

"Isn't he?"

"I guess," the boy said. "But nobody ever really dies."

Because their consciousness carries on, she thought. Their soul. Whatever that essence of them was, it didn't end. Here, this simple truth struck her as obvious.

"Why don't I feel any pain?" she asked.

"Because this deep you know that nothing's really lost."

"It is for a while, while I'm in the world."

"But how long is that?"

Seventy, eighty years, she thought.

"That's less than the blink of an eye," he said.

But of course. Theoretical physicists had often speculated that time itself was an illusion. She suddenly knew that it was true. In fact, nothing was how anyone perceived it through the five senses. She was experiencing something beyond those simple senses.

Angie looked around the gate room. The large watch-like gears rested motionless along one wall. The three Play Dead books—the first with hieroglyphs, the second with computer code, the third with fractal geometry—sat on their pedestals. The two gates, one called *Veritas Vos Liberabit*, the other called *Imago Simulacrum*, were as she'd last seen them. Nothing had changed.

But I've changed, she thought. She felt so much peace now that she again wondered if she might be dead. No, she actually felt more alive than ever. Darey's death had done that, so in that way wasn't his death a gift to her?

What a strange thought.

"When you look at me, who do you see?" Jamie asked, sliding out of the chair.

"You're asking who I think you are?"

"With your eyes," he said. "What and who do you see with your eyes?"

"I see Jamie as a boy, I think." She studied him, his short hair and bright eyes, his jeans and pale skin. "Or maybe you're my son from when I was in the Red Protocol. Or maybe you're me, even though you're a boy."

"You see all of those?"

"Well, actually, I know this is in my mind, so really I don't see any of them. They're all ideas."

Even as Angie spoke, she knew she was realizing something profound. Ideas were just like images, perceived by the mind rather than the eyes. Her ideas of the world were masking what it really was.

She looked at the round Image Maker gate. Ideas were just another form of perception. Mental perception.

It was all about her perception. She was only seeing what her own mind allowed her to see. She was making the images.

"Yes!" The boy cried, pumping his small fist. "The world isn't how you think it is; it's how *you* are. How you see it. I figured that out too."

Angie already knew this because her mother used to say it when she was a child. Change the mind and you change the reality it perceives. Perception.

Dr. Crandel, her philosophy professor at Auburn University, had repeatedly made the point. At the time, Angie was fascinated, but now she knew the concept in a new way.

One person might look at an object on a woman's head and see it as a crown. A child might see the same object as a mere article of clothing. Two different perceptions of the same thing. But it went deeper than that.

One might look at a forest fire and see a tragedy; another might see the earth only cleansing itself, a blessing. But it went deeper than that.

One might look at an image on a screen and see a mountain; another might look closer and see individual pixels of colored light. But it went deeper, much deeper.

One might look at a lake at night and see a bright round object floating on the surface. Another might see the light as the reflection of a light in the sky called the moon. Another might travel to the moon and see it as a lump of dirt rather than a light. Still another might look at that lump of dirt called 'moon' under a powerful scope and see atoms. Even deeper, electrons and protons. Even deeper, bundles of energy that science called subatomic particles, which really weren't particles at all but raw energy that only manifested when observed by collective consciousness. They appeared as what was called 'moon' only in the framework of a radically limited perspective.

So what was the light on the lake? An illusion of sorts. A virtual reality.

Ancient mystics and philosophers taught the same truth: You will see light or dark, depending on how you see. Perception is everything in the world of images.

Angie had been so focused on trying to figure out the truth that would free Jamie that she'd overlooked a more obvious purpose for the room. It would lead to the truth about far more than just Jamie's unjust incarceration.

The gate room was about perceiving the truth in everything, including but not limited to the Oak Hill case. Jamie had said as much in her first encounter with him.

"The Image Maker gate is all about perception," she said.

"That part is simpler than you think," Jamie said. "So simple that it seems impossible."

Angie stepped up to the Image Maker wall and pressed her hand on the large mask. The hum dropped to a low tone that grew in volume. Dense vibration. She jerked her hand away and spun to the books, excited now.

The first book—the one with hieroglyphs, which were images—held the key to opening the Image Maker portal. The gate had to be about perception, not just images.

She took three long strides and snatched up the first Play Dead book. She flipped through it, unsure what she was searching for—something that she could understand. A pictograph that would spark insight.

Most of the images were of stick figures and animals. Peaks for mountains and wavy lines for water. Circles and arrows and patterns with dots and stripes. But nothing leaped out at her. Not until she reached the last page, on which was inscribed a large drawing of a stick figure with a single all-seeing eye above its head. The eye was maybe three-quarters of an inch in diameter, staring at her as a line drawing.

Her heart stopped. Perception. Image Maker. An eye. But how could an image help her if she couldn't decode it?

Wondering what kind of writing instrument had inscribed the image, Angie extended her forefinger to rub the etching on the page. The moment her skin contacted the eye, it crackled with energy, brightening as if made of light.

She yelped and jerked her hand away.

Behind her, Jamie laughed. "See?"

"It's . . . The book's powered?"

She slowly reached for the eye again. Again it came to life, and this time she let her finger linger. A hologram of an eye formed above the page where the image had been drawn. A small orb. A 3D virtual image of an ancient all-seeing eye, right there, at the end of her finger.

She pulled her finger back again, unnerved. The holographic eye collapsed back into the page and became nothing more than a line drawing of an eye again.

No harm had come to her, so she reached for it again and this time picked it up between her finger and thumb, feeling its gentle energy. More than gentle energy, though. It felt real. Solid. Like it had collapsed into matter. And it had, as much as any 'solid' object had. It was a fully dimensional holographic eye that felt and looked solid.

"Wow."

"Yup. Wow."

"So this is the key," she breathed.

"That's the eye."

She moved the eye over the stick figure on the page, and the lines of the drawing began to glow. The eye in her fingers seemed to be a power source of some kind, activating the images in the book.

"Cool," she said.

The stick drawing of the human glowed but it didn't move. So she tried another image—a horse-like drawing. It too began to glow. The same happened to the other images. Somehow the eye could decode the book, but how? She was still missing something.

Then again, the boy said that it was simple, so maybe she wasn't missing anything. Maybe the book was only showing her that perception made the world. Image Maker. And the eye itself was . . .

She turned to the Image Maker portal. Stared at the black panel with the concave receptacle, and the 1 and 0 below it. Fingers trembling around the solid holographic eye, she stepped over to the panel and looked at that receptacle. A keyhole of sorts. And the eye, its key.

She glanced at the boy, who was grinning ear to ear. He gave her a little nod. *Yup.*

Angie had been in a hundred puzzle rooms. The rush of excitement that always preceded solving a code coursed through her. She carefully extended the holographic eye and set it into the concave receptacle.

As if drawn by a magnet, the eye attached itself to the keyhole. Immediately, a locking mechanism clanked, accompanied by a soft hiss.

Heart thumping in her chest, Angie reached for the wheel that operated the gate and gave it a little tug. The wheel moved half a turn before slowing to a stop.

She spun the wheel again. It made two full turns before coming to an abrupt halt. The entire three-foot portal door popped out an inch. Open. But it still covered the opening.

Angie stepped back, cautious. One thing seemed certain to her: whatever was happening here, deep in her mind, would have significant consequences.

Once she opened the gate on the mask wall, something would change. Not just something small, but something fundamental. Was she ready?

"Slide it," the boy said.

She gave the gate a gentle push and it moved soundlessly to the left as if riding on air.

Immediately the hum in the room dropped in tone. The gears on the wall to her left whirred to life and began to turn, like the spinning of gears in an old movie projector.

Startled, she jumped back to the center of the room.

A thin shaft of light beamed across the room and pierced the portal opening. The beam was coming from the small circle at the top of the vertical line on the needle wall. The eye of the needle.

She'd activated the room!

A quick look at the boy confirmed he was unconcerned. Of course not. This was why she was here. She was meant to discover what the Image Maker would show her.

"You figure this out?"

"Yup."

"Is the light dangerous?"

"Try it," he said.

She lifted her forefinger and tentatively reached out to the laser-like beam of light, ready to jerk her hand away. But when her finger contacted the edge of the beam, she felt nothing. Harmless enough. So she extended her hand further, expecting to block the light.

Instead, the light went through her flesh and bones. It was as if her hand didn't even exist. Same with her arm. And then her whole body as she stepped up and placed herself between the beam of light and the Image Maker portal.

Whatever the beam of light was, matter didn't seem to affect it.

"Neat," she said.

"Do you want to see?" Jamie asked.

From where she stood ten feet from the portal, the round opening appeared to be a clear barrier, perhaps a force field or lens, flowing with energy activated by the beam. The light shone through the lens.

The whole room—the gears, the beam of light coming from the eye of the needle, the Image Maker lens—was like a cosmic movie projector, she thought. But projecting what?

She stepped up to the three-foot lens, still mystified by the beam of light passing through her body and the Image Maker portal. But she still couldn't see what lay beyond, not until she leaned in so that her line of sight was only an inch from the lens, dead center. Immediately, a world came into view, clear as day.

The scene was of her living room where she sat staring into space through blank eyes, virtually comatose on the sofa. Standing near her were Randy and Felicia, deep in conversation.

She was looking into her life in the real world. Not just a flat, two-dimensional image of her life, but a fully formed, three-dimensional representation. Or maybe it was the real thing. It certainly looked real.

As a closet Dead Head, she'd been on the edge of other worlds more times than she could count, ready to take the plunge. Which made her wonder if she could pass through the portal into her living room. That would be a trip. Like crossing the 3D screen in her sitting room to enter the gate, as she'd done last night when Darey had gone to be murdered.

She still had no concern about his death. Strange.

Another possibility skipped through her mind. What if that living room where Randy and Felicia now stood over her body really was a virtual world? What if they were all caught in a virtual world of their own making and didn't know it? Not just her, but the whole world?

This last thought set her back, not because it sounded absurd, but because a part of her believed it might be true.

She pulled back and turned to Jamie.

"Is that really me in there? My real life?"

"It depends on what *real* means," the boy said. "Is matter real or just a mask?"

Exactly. What was real? Was a body a body, or was it just energy presenting itself in a certain form so humans could experience it as what was called a body? An image. An illusion of sorts. Mask.

"Okay, but what I'm asking is"—how to say it?—"is my whole life in there part of a virtual reality?"

"In a way, everything's an illusion, because we can't see it for what it really is."

"That's not helpful," she said. "I thought you were here to help me."

"I am. But you have to experience it yourself. That's how you learn whether or not you're crazy."

"I'm crazy?"

"You have to find out."

"But the truth is that way," she said, pointing to the needle gate. "Does that mean everything through the Image Maker isn't true? We're all insane?"

"I think it depends on how you see it," he said. "That's perception."

Fair enough.

She faced the Image Maker lens again. "Is this the only scene I can see?"

"No. But you need the second book to see more."

The second book was filled with binary code. The panel under the eye that had activated the portal had a 1 and a 0 on it with a green button. First things first.

"Yeah," she said absently, staring at the living room, still wondering if she could enter the scene from here.

"That can't be right," she whispered to herself. "How could the world we know be a virtual world?"

The urge to enter the scene became more compelling. If what her mind was trying to show her could only be learned through her experience of it, she had to . . . well . . . experiment.

"Can I go in?"

No response.

"What will happen if I try to go through the portal?" she asked.

Still no response, so she turned to where he'd stood. He was gone. A quick look around the room confirmed it. She was alone.

Angie faced the portal. She had to try. So she stepped up to the portal and touched the lens. Energy ran through her fingers and up her arm. But no harm, so she reached further in, up to her elbow.

One moment she was in the white gate room, the next she was in her living room. Under the archway that opened to the sofa and chairs and lamps and carpet and paintings that she and Darey had chosen.

Only now, all of it was shifting in the shimmer. Energy.

She turned around. Her house. No white room.

Her body was there, on the couch, lost to this world. Randy was listening to Felicia, who was explaining details of Angie's experience at Convergence as research for a new book. They too were energy patterns, formed as bodies. As was Sally, her dog, who was lying by the television, watching her body with head up and ears perked.

"The whiteouts can be dangerous," Felicia was saying. "Potentially mind fracturing. Jake Barnes was clear—we have to let her wake on her own and take her to him the moment she does."

Felicia had already called Convergence. Angie wasn't sure what to think about that.

"I realize that," Randy said. "I just don't understand why." He looked at her form on the couch. "This seems . . . dangerous."

"Disturbing her in this state could create more damage to her mind than leaving her."

Randy began to pace, running a hand through his hair, eyes on her motionless body.

Seeing herself in such a lifeless state was strange, but not concerning. It really was as if the form on the couch was only a shell of her. A character that she lived as in this virtual world. Like an actor playing a role. Had to be.

So then who was she beyond that role called Angie?

She lifted her hand and was surprised to see that she had no hand. And no body. Nothing at all. No, of course not, because she had temporarily disassociated herself from that role called Angie and all the ideas that Angie had of herself.

Maybe she was caught in the in-between, disassociated from that body but not yet knowing who she was outside of this virtual world. It was the only thing that made sense to her at the moment.

She looked around, once more stunned by how obvious it seemed.

Felicia and Randy weren't simply Felicia the therapist and Randy the detective. That's only who they were in this virtual world. The whole world was lost in the roles of the characters they were playing. The whole world was dead heading.

Right? Had to be. Play Dead was the way to the truth that would set them free.

At the very least, it was the way beyond the masks that hid the truth about the Oak Hill case and Jamie and her strange connection to Jamie in the white room. Everything was somehow linked to one deep, hidden truth.

It was either that, or she really was losing her mind.

Angie moved into the living room, aware that she still had no visible body.

"The brain's a tricky thing," Felicia was saying. "The deceived don't know they're deceived any more than the insane know they're insane. If someone thinks they're insane, they aren't. The problem with a truly fractured mind is that the mind doesn't know it's fractured. In the state of disassociation that Angie's in right now, she could believe almost anything, thinking that it's real."

Or maybe I'm the only sane one in this room, Angie wished she could say. She decided then that regardless of what happened, she would treat the world as a virtual reality. At the very least, seeing the world as virtual brought her a deep peace in the aftermath of Darey's death.

"She's been out for a good five minutes," Randy was saying. "Maybe we should call Convergence again."

Felicia picked up her phone. "Let's give it another minute or two."

Angie wondered if she should try to get back to the gate room or if she should try to wake herself up.

She moved to the large 3D screen she'd entered last night, thinking maybe it would take her back to the gate room. But when she passed through it, she went through the wall to the outside of the house. Birds were chirping, the grass was green. Everything looked pristine and brimming with color.

Entering the house again, she looked about. Felicia and Randy were silent now, watching her comatose form. Angie moved to that body, not sure what else to try.

She was within a foot of her slumped form when a magnetic attraction pulled her toward it. Like smoke sucked into a return vent, she collapsed back into her own body.

Angie gasped and sat up, eyes wide, fully alert.

She was back.

CHAPTER
TWENTY-FOUR

ANGIE'S SUDDEN resurrection caught both Randy and Felicia off guard, but she was too distracted to pay them much mind. The room was still in full shimmer, energy flowing all around. This was the real reality, constructed of energy that no one else could see. Had to be. And she was going to stick with that.

Neither Randy nor Felicia seemed to be able to find words.

Angie tried to stand but her legs were weak and she collapsed before gathering herself and trying again.

Felicia was moving in to save her. "Whoa, whoa, sit back. You're still in shock."

But Angie brushed aside her extended hand and finally managed to stand. "I'm fine, really." More than fine, actually. She felt nearly giddy.

"Honey, I can only imagine what you're dealing with and I'm so sorry for your loss. Words can't express. I know how hard it is, but we have to get you some help."

Darey. Thinking of him now, an ache mushroomed in her chest. Darey was gone. Murdered.

But no . . . Well, yes, but not really. Or, really, but only here in this virtual world. The drama of the virtual world was trying to pull her back into it. She wasn't going there.

She looked around at the shimmering room. At Felicia's and Randy's bodies, which were still shifting in energy, hologram-like.

"I don't think you understand," Angie said, stepping around the mahogany coffee table. She lifted her own hand and studied the energy ebbing and flowing. "This isn't what you think it is."

"What do you mean?" They were Randy's first words since she'd awakened. His invitation was all she needed.

She crossed to him, thinking that he, if anyone, would understand. He'd lost his wife and daughter. He was a detective, used to following the evidence to truth.

"I mean this isn't real." She took his hand and lifted it in front of her, chest high. "Do you know what I see right now?"

He didn't answer. Felicia was giving her that familiar 'you're in denial' look. If anything, Felicia and Randy were the ones in denial. Right?

"I see energy, shifting, formed as a hand, but only in our perception." She looked into his eyes, begging him to believe. "This isn't all there is to you, Randy." She reached up and stroked his cheek. Stepping back, she motioned at the room. "None of this is what it appears to be."

They both stared at her as if she'd lost her mind. But of course they would. They weren't seeing what she saw.

"Tell me what you think you are, Angie." Felicia had settled into her role as therapist. "Tell me what you see."

"I see what's really here. Or at least a semblance of what's really here, because in reality, none of this is really here. I mean, it *is* real, but only here."

That kept them quiet for a few seconds.

"And where is here?" Felicia finally asked in that same therapist's voice.

Angie faced her. "'Here' is a holographic universe. A virtual reality—like a holo-deck. We're characters in a virtual reality who've lost ourselves in our roles. We believe that's all we are. But these are avatars. Just characters we're playing."

Randy glanced at Felicia, troubled. But the therapist was now in full help-the-crazy-client mode.

"If these are the characters we're playing, who are we really, sweetie?"

"You don't need to call me sweetie to endear me, Felicia. I'm perfectly sane and logical."

Felicia's brow arched. "Are you?" Meaning, *we both know that people who are insane don't think they're insane.*

Angie spread her arms. "Do I look like someone who's just lost her husband? No, because I haven't, not really. Only here in this VR. But to your question, I think that beyond this virtual world we're real people, actors. Here, we think this is the only world because we're lost in it. It's a fully integrated virtual world complete with a full history that's been running for a very long time."

"So you think everything happening is set in stone, like in a movie?"

"No, we're directing it as we go, like in any VR game. Everything we think, say and do creates our future here."

"Okay, so if this is a virtual reality, what's the real world like?"

Angie hesitated. How to tell characters lost in a virtual world that everything they held dear was only a form of illusion? Even the suggestion of it would threaten to annihilate their character's self-identity. Annihilate *them*. The *them* they thought they were.

"Not this," Angie said. "I'm assuming that the real world is like this one, but not this one. To know that, I have to enter through the needle gate."

For a few seconds, Felicia just stared at her. *Disassociation with reality is what happens when a dead head gets lost in a virtual world,* the therapist would be thinking. And true, her client was showing all the signs of a radical disassociation. But Felicia had it backward. *She* was the one who was lost in *this* virtual reality.

The first stab of doubt hit her then.

Do you really believe that, Angie?

Felicia offered her a gentle smile. "Why don't you sit for a second and tell us what happened in the whiteout, Angie."

Fair enough. So she sat. They did as well, Randy on the chair to her right and Felicia beside her, like two parents willing to hear their teenager's unbelievable explanation of why she was smoking a joint.

The shimmer was fading now, but that didn't concern Angie too much.

The change of her perception here, in the virtual reality, didn't change the truth of what it was.

Angie told them about the gate room. The portals, the books, the gears, the boy who had to be Jamie. But only in broad strokes, so it all came out in a rush. She might have given them more detail, but the more she said, the more she became aware of how absurd it all sounded.

By the time she'd told them how she moved around the room only a few minutes earlier, disembodied, she was having a hard time believing it herself.

With that doubt, the realization of Darey's murder swept back into her mind. And by then, the shimmer was completely gone, leaving only her, Randy and Felicia in the room as solid people.

"That's what you think happened?" Felicia asked kindly.

"Yes," Angie said in a thin voice. But she couldn't hold back the terrible sorrow that was swallowing her. Darey had been killed! How was that possible? He'd just been here last night and now he was gone? For a few long seconds a terrible rage boiled up from the pit of Angie's gut, interrupted only by the dawning realization that her mind really was fractured.

Panic flooded her veins. If her mind could become so easily disassociated from what was real, she was in terrible trouble. And Darey . . .

For her to think that Darey's death was okay because it was only part of a virtual reality . . . How could she return his undying love with such a callous conclusion?

She dropped her head into her hands and began to cry. "Oh, my God. Oh, my God! What's happening to me?"

She felt Felicia's hand on her back. "It's okay, Angie. This is all going to make sense to you soon. You're okay. You have one of the most brilliant minds I know. Something very good will come out of this. Just accept what's happening right now without trying to figure it out."

She was right. This was all just a part of her mind reacting to the Red Protocol experience. Right? But that wasn't much to hang on to and, either way, Darey really was dead. She felt like throwing up.

For a long minute, Angie wept. Felicia kept reassuring her in a soothing tone; Randy sat quietly; Angie let the tears flow until there seemed to be no more point in crying.

"That's good, sweetie," Felicia was saying. "I know this may sound harsh, but I need you to focus for me now. We're going to do a little exercise to get your mind back. Okay?"

Angie took a deep breath, flushing her emotions. She gave a nod.

"Tell me what you're feeling in this moment," Felicia said.

I want Darey back! she thought. *I want to kill whoever killed him!* But she didn't say that.

"Sorrow," she breathed.

"What else?"

"I feel sick."

"Okay. You feel ill. What else do you feel?"

"Revenge," Angie croaked.

"Good. Revenge. And what emotion do you feel when you think of revenge?"

"Anger!" Angie snapped. "Stop leading me with your psychobabble! I feel angry . . . God, can't you just—"

"But it's more than just anger, Angie. It's much more, isn't it? Tell me how thinking of what they did makes you feel?"

"Rage!" Her voice came out like the roar of a chainsaw. Anger was the quickest way out of fear or sorrow, they said. She felt the power of that emotion rise and swallow her mind.

But Felicia wasn't done. "That's a start but—"

"I want to find out who's behind all of this and take their head off with a sledgehammer!" she blurted, jerking her head up to face Felicia. "Is that what you want to hear?" Her whole body was trembling with adrenaline. She knew how all of this worked and she went with it gladly now, because rage felt like a soothing balm next to anguish.

"That's a good start."

"They think they can just play with our lives like they mean nothing? Darey means nothing?" Tears were coming again, fueled now by a rawness that was beyond her fury. "I'm going to burn them down. All of them!"

Felicia gave her a nod. "Good. I feel the same way. Now tell me the next step to doing that."

Angie let the thought settle in. One name emerged.

Jamie.

This was all about Jamie and the Oak Hill Dead Head murders. Jamie now had only her to protect him. Even if this wasn't a virtual reality, the solution was locked up in a white room deep in her mind. She had to focus.

"We have to find out who's framing Jamie," she said, settling.

"Okay. And what's the first step to doing that?"

Angie glanced up at Randy. "I don't know. Convince him that Jamie is being framed?"

Randy didn't seem to know how to respond.

"Not him," Felicia said. "What needs to happen with you?"

In two more breaths, Angie's anger was gone. When she answered, her voice was resolved. "Fine. I need to get to Convergence."

"Why?"

She stood and paced, thinking. "To fix my head," she said absently, then turned to Felicia and Randy. "Look, I know you think the whiteouts are dangerous. Maybe they are. But maybe they're trying to tell me something important. I mean something besides what I said."

"Tell you what?" Randy asked. "I thought we were chalking that up to hallucination."

"Maybe, but indulge me, even if it is just my way of coping. Please."

"Fair enough," Felicia said. "Tell me what you think your episodes in the white room are trying to tell you."

Angie took a deep breath. "Something about Jamie."

"Okay. What about Jamie?"

Indeed, what? The truth might be on the encrypted data key Clair had found, but that was lost to them for now, which is why the white room was so important. It was now the key.

"My episodes in the white room are trying to tell me that I'm somehow connected to Jamie, more than we know. And that illusions are covering up the truth of what's happening, meaning that Jamie is definitely being framed." She looked at Randy. "Darey and I uncovered video footage that put Jamie in his house the night of the murders. You found it?"

"Darey told me he had footage that would clear Jamie." Randy replied, face flat. "The card I found had different date stamps."

Angie felt gut-punched. "So it's useless?"

"There's no evidence that the card was swapped."

"I saw the date stamps with my own eyes!" she snapped. "Whoever's behind this isn't only much more powerful than you think, but they'll go to any lengths to pin the Oak Hill murders on Jamie. I'm telling you, Jamie's the key and I have a connection to him."

It was all coming out in a rush and she continued before they could interrupt.

"My mind might be fractured, but I don't think it's a coincidence that I'm seeing him as a child in my whiteouts. There's something about his childhood that will blow all of this wide open. He's not just another Dead Head. He knows more than even he thinks he knows, and I may be able to uncover what it is."

Randy glanced doubtfully at Felicia.

"I don't know how it all works, but I'm telling you, I'm seeing Jamie in the gate room. He's either drawing me there or I'm drawing him there. Forget all the stuff about being in a virtual reality, fine. But the least I can do for Darcy . . ." A knot in her throat cut her off, but she cleared it and pushed on. "Is to finish what he started by uncovering the truth."

"The governor stands to gain the most from Jamie's conviction," Felicia said.

Randy held up his hand. "Hold on. I'm not aware of any evidence that points to the governor or any other authority. All of this VR rhetoric is one thing, but let's please stick to facts."

"Facts?" Angie snapped. "The real question is, what facts are they so desperate to keep hidden? And she's right, it could be the governor. It could be anyone with far-reaching power."

Randy glanced around the room uncomfortably.

"Either way," Felicia said, "we need to get you back into the Red Protocol for regression therapy immediately. Please tell me you'll go with me to see Jake Barnes."

Angie considered the possibility that regression therapy would sever her connection to Jamie, but she might lose her mind if she didn't allow them to at least check her out. And now that she thought about it, going back into the Red Protocol might be a way to go even deeper into the gate.

Her pulse surged. At the very least, she could play along.

"Okay," she said.

"Thank you. I think that's wise."

"None of this changes what we know about the case," Randy said.

"After all this you still think Jamie's guilty?" Angie shot back.

He tapped his ear and motioned around the room. Then put a finger over his mouth.

Angie sat back. He was saying the house could be bugged? But of course he was. After all she'd said about how powerful these people were, her first instinct should have been to assume they'd bugged the house.

Felicia had gone pale. "Are you suggesting that. . ."

Randy cut her off with a raised hand. "I'm saying that none of what I've heard here changes the facts of the case, and all of those point to Jamie as the killer. We have motive, means, opportunity and a mountain of evidence. Regardless, he isn't being tried for the murder of the Oak Hill kids. We have him on tape killing another prisoner in cold blood. It's open and shut. Nothing is going to change that. Certainly not any crazy theory involving the government."

Randy was covering for them all, she thought. A killer who'd murdered Darey to protect the state's case against Jamie wouldn't hesitate to eliminate anyone in this room.

He continued. "I know how hard this must be for you, Angie, but the city really doesn't need you running around making wild accusations that have no bearing in fact."

She played into his dismissal of her.

"Say what you want. At the very least you owe me a full investigation into the death of my husband." Darey was dead. Emotion crowded her throat. "Dear God, have some decency!"

"You have my deepest sympathy. And you can rest assured that I'll give my full attention to the circumstances surrounding his death. But I would be giving you false hope if I didn't say that I really do think the evidence will show us what already appears to be the truth."

She felt the sting of that, even knowing he didn't mean a word of it.

"Just do your job," she snapped.

"Of course. Right now, my job is to get you to Convergence. Keeping you safe is the least I can do. I'm not a monster, Mrs. Channing."

His words and tone were perfunctory, but his eyes were filled with compassion. Randy George wanted to protect her. There was really no other reason for him to accompany them to Convergence. In her state of loss, Angie found the realization deeply affirming.

"Fine," she said.

They exchanged a long look of understanding. She decided then that she would bare her soul to this man on the ride to Convergence. He had to know everything she knew.

"Let's go," he finally said. "I have a lot on my plate today. I'll drive Angie."

BOOK FOUR

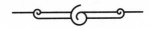

PLAY
DEAD

CHAPTER
TWENTY-FIVE

THE LAB was white, like the gate room. Reclined in the black chair at its center, Angie wondered if her mind had created a version of this room during those episodes. Both incorporated advanced technology in a white room. But the similarities ended there. The Red Protocol lab was at least four times as large, lined by an array of computer screens now being monitored by three technicians.

Regression would take her back into a virtual world through the Red Protocol, just like before, but this time for only an hour and only for the purpose of resetting her brain by clearing it of all residual programming.

"Five minutes, Mrs. Channing. Your heart rate is slightly elevated but all other indicators are looking steady. Are you still comfortable?"

"Yes."

The neural mapping and mesh alignment that had taken two days on her first visit were still viable, Barnes had explained. In another week they would have had to start from scratch due to the plasticity of the brain's neural pathways. Today, the process of fitting the wireless mesh to her head and linking to the mainframe had taken only an hour.

Angie stared up at the acoustic imaging array hovering four feet above the length of her naked body. The curved white panel with thousands of tiny black holes looked like tiny eyes watching her. When they were ready, they would lower the array until it rested inches above her skin.

Guided by the mesh on her skull, the acoustic imaging array would flood her body and brain with specific vibrations that would shut down her sensory perceptions and replace them with new sight, sound, touch, scent, and taste to create a fully immersive virtual reality.

Why the body, not just the brain? Because the body had its own memory of perception, which is why those who received organ transplants sometimes took on the preferences of the organ donor. The whole body was essentially one large brain. To create a fully immersive virtual experience, they had to interrupt the body's memory of itself or those body-memories would resist the virtual world introduced to the brain.

All internal sensation would now come from the brain, so the subject would actually feel their heart pumping, their liver hurting, their hunger growing—everything. This was a true Deep Dive. The Red Protocol. The ultimate RIG.

Angie's palms were sweating and she might have wiped them, but small padded clamps held her wrists, arms, legs, ankles, neck and waist in place. A helmet would soon be lowered over the mesh on her skull—the acoustic imaging for her brain would be transmitted through it.

"Two minutes. All indicators are nominal."

She glanced up at Megan, the short, white-coated technician with kind blue eyes who'd guided her through the first Deep Dive at Convergence nearly two weeks earlier.

"You're doing just fine, Angie. In a few minutes you'll be in another world."

The prospect drew her, as it would any Dead Head. Then again, Darey was dead because she was a Dead Head, plain and simple. A lump the size of her fist filled her throat.

"Just like the last time, right?" she said, searching for courage.

"Just like the last time except much shorter. Half an hour, hour at the most. As Mr. Barnes explained, we'll be scanning for anomalies as we bring you out. Think of it as a do-over, only this time we want to make sure every single tag from that reality is stripped clean before you come out."

"What if it doesn't work?"

"It will. And if we run into any anomalies while you're still in, we'll bring you right out, you have my word on that. But it will work because it's worked before. Trust me."

"No more whiteouts."

Megan slid the pivoting monitor she was working at out of the way and spoke into her earpiece. "We have a lock on this end, Peter. Acoustic resonance at plus or minus one thousandth. Let's set the cranial and body arrays."

Then, looking at her, "No more whiteouts. We're going to lock you into the cranial transmitter and lower the body array. Good?"

Angie gave her a short nod. She glanced up and to her left where Randy and Jake Barnes watched from behind a large glass window one story higher. She'd told Randy everything on the ride up. Including the letter she'd received from Clair, and Jamie being an orphan of unknown origin.

Randy had listened, asking only a few questions, then kept silent for a long time as he contemplated the new evidence. "Okay, so you have me," he finally said. "And that's a problem."

"How so?"

"It's a problem because if you're right, both of us really are in way over our heads."

True, she thought, *which is why I'm going back into mine.*

Looking at Randy behind the glass window now, she found some comfort. He was like Darey in more ways than one. Both dealt with the law. Both were exceptionally cool headed, unlike her. Both were strong men, easy on the eyes, gentle unless required to be firm. Both, in their own ways, out of the box, like her.

Thinking of Darey, she felt sick. But no. No, Darey wasn't really dead.

Felicia had remained with them for the first half hour but had to leave for a session she couldn't get out of, she'd explained. The world was full of emotional fires and Felicia's role was to help put them out. But she'd cleared her day from 1:00 p.m. on and would rejoin Angie then. They weren't about to leave her alone again.

"Lift your head just a bit, Angie?" Megan said.

She did and another technician slid a titanium helmet over her head, similar to those fighter pilots once wore before drones and autonomous airplanes had commandeered the skies.

"Comfortable?" Megan's question came over speakers inside the helmet.

"Yes."

"Good. We're almost there."

A whir of electric motors signaled the lowering of the acoustic imaging array. She was in her own version of a cocoon, though visible on both sides.

For a while, nothing happened. Then a high pitched but soft whine filled her ears, same as last time.

"Initiation in thirty seconds, Angie. All baselines look perfectly normal. We have a strong connection. You're going to have some fun. Just relax and enjoy it. You're a pro, remember that."

True. The whole world now knew just how seasoned a pro she was.

"We left the identity formation open, so you'll impulsively populate your immediate world with characters from your subconscious. But you won't know that."

"Right," she said. She took a deep breath and waited.

Angie heard the countdown from what seemed far away, ". . . five, four, three, two, one. Initiation. Travel well and . . ." Megan said more but the words were washed away by another sound.

It wasn't a shaking or rumbling or a noise. In fact, if they hadn't told her it was simply finely tuned acoustic waves, she might have mistaken the vibrations as heat caused by some exotic drug that seemed to melt her from the inside out. In reality, the waves were neutralizing her cellular memory. Wiping the slate clean, both in body and brain.

Her bones, her flesh, her skin—all of it was simply dissolving into a whitewash of profound sensory deprivation ending in a blackness so deep that she stopped knowing anything.

She was aware, but only of her own existence, stripped of context. No form, no world, no thoughts. Just there, suspended in pure awareness of herself, enveloped in what she might think of as an inexpressible peace, if she was thinking. But she had no words or thoughts for it.

In the next moment, Angie found herself in her home, watching a news feed on the arrest of Jamie. Jamie was her and Randy's son. He'd been arrested for the murder of Clair Milton and Timothy Blake in Oak Hill Park.

Randy? She was married to Randy George? And her name was Angie George. Their son was Jamie.

Angie blinked. *But of course not,* she thought. *I'm in the Red Protocol. This is the virtual world they put me in the first time. It's all pure fiction. I have to remember that and get to the gate room. This is just a fictional alternate . . .*

But then the Red Protocol snatched that thought away and she was no longer aware of any other reality but this one.

She turned to the television and stared at an image of her son in a yellow jumpsuit, hands cuffed behind his back, grinning innocently at the camera. The fool on the feed was talking about how his smile looked like the twisted grin of a maniacal killer.

An ocean of rage and sorrow washed over her. Tears broke from her eyes and spilled down her cheeks. How could this be happening to them? The world had been ripped out from under her feet with one impossible phone call—*Jamie has been arrested for murder*—but at times her mind still refused to accept the fact that this was happening to them.

He was her son, for heaven's sake! They'd adopted him out of the state system when he was six and never looked back. An innocent boy with ASD who wasn't remotely capable of doing what they were accusing him of.

She turned the feed off, barely able to control her rage.

A week had passed since Jamie's arrest, and each day the news had gotten worse.

Randy walked in holding two bowls of the tortilla soup he'd brought home from El Sombrero—a long-standing Friday night tradition whenever Randy's schedule allowed. They'd met in Cancun over a bowl of tortilla soup on a Friday and fell madly in love within the week. He was trying to bring some normalcy into their home. His good intentions felt oddly obscene to her. How could they celebrate themselves while Jamie was accused of murder? But Randy was in as much pain as she was, and to deny him his own coping mechanisms was to deny his humanity.

"It's hot," Randy said, setting her large yellow ceramic bowl on the tray next to her recliner. He leaned over and kissed her forehead. "Like you."

Normally she would have responded by rolling her eyes. Tonight, she could muster up only a blank face.

Maybe because of that, he set his own bowl down, grabbed her hand, and pulled her up.

She let herself rise. "What are you doing?"

He spun her around, wrapped his arms around her waist from behind, and pressed his cheek against hers, swaying in his rather clumsy way. "I'm dancing with my wife. And I know how much she loves being held by her man from behind."

Actually, she didn't. It made her feel out of control and she'd carefully organized her life to remain in control. Of everything.

"Stop it, Randy." She tried to shrug free, but his arms only tightened.

"Come on. Just go with it."

He released her and spun her by one hand, singing an old song from a band called Queen in full operatic fashion. This was the detective who'd shown her strength, kindness, and love in a way she'd never dreamed possible.

But tonight, she didn't care about any of that. She only wanted this nightmare to end. She wanted Jamie at home, where she could keep him safe from the vultures who'd singled out such a defenseless boy and would pick him apart until there was nothing left but bones.

"Randy, please . . ."

Finishing a chorus of the song, he released her and bowed. "My offering to you this fine Friday evening, my love."

"Stop it."

He straightened. "You don't like it?"

"It's not about what I like!" She shoved a finger at the now black television. "Our son is in prison for a murder he had nothing to do with!"

"I know!" Randy thundered, face flushing. Then, taking a breath. "I know, dear God I know. And I also know that we can't let this crush us or we'll have nothing left for him! I'm begging you, Angie. Please, just try it. Be the courage you want for Jamie. Be my wife, just for a few hours."

He was right. They couldn't let this tear them apart. Jamie needed them. Slowly, she let her emotions calm, eyes on him.

"It'll do us both some good," he said. "Trust me." He pulled her toward him and kissed her on the lips, gentle, like a butterfly. Her first instinct was to pull back. She decided to go with it instead.

Angie impulsively pressed into him and kissed him deeply, allowing him to hold her. The warmth of his body against hers felt like a warm blanket on a cold night, and she lingered in his embrace.

"Wow," he said when she pulled back. "See? Better already. I'm going to take it on good faith that there's more to come."

"Maybe." *But probably not*, she thought. Or maybe that's exactly what she needed. She sat down and cradled the hot bowl in her palms. Randy was right, though, she was feeling better. Jamie would love seeing them happy. Truth be told, they were suffering far more than he was.

Randy took a seat and began flipping through the feed, using a remote, old-school, clearly intent on finding anything but news.

He settled on an old reality show in which contestants spent weeks alone in the wilderness to see who could last the longest. No food, no water, no cameras but the one they filmed themselves with. Survival stuff had always drawn him, and she'd grown to enjoy it with him.

Tonight it felt like a total waste of time, but maybe that's exactly what she needed.

They were on the seventh episode and the strongest player, an accountant named Darey, had cut his foot on a root, threatening his chances of outlasting the others, each of whom were scattered along the coast of Alaska. She'd liked Darey, maybe because he reminded her of Randy. Or maybe because he was just plain hot.

But tonight, she saw none of his appeal.

Something was wrong with the soup and it hit her after the first spoonful. "No tortilla strips?"

He caught himself and stared at his own bowl. "Must have left them in the bag. I'll—"

"No, I'll get them. I need to move. Stay put."

"Want me to hold the show?"

"Watch. I'll be right back."

She strolled from the room, knowing she could miss half the show and still get the gist of it. In truth, she liked Randy's enjoyment and side comments more than the show itself.

The tortilla strips weren't in the paper bag Randy had left on the kitchen counter. Maybe the small bag of strips had fallen out in the car. Their cat, Sylvester, rubbed against her calf, wanting attention. She scooped her up and headed for the garage, scratching the cat's white ears.

"You miss Mama? Is that it? Of course you do. That's a good kitty. You love . . ."

Three paces from the door, Jamie stood facing her. As a small boy. Angie startled and dropped Sylvester.

For a moment she forgot to breathe. She blinked, and her eyes were open again, and Jamie had vanished.

Gone.

She looked around, rattled. No sign of him. She was losing it.

Get hold of yourself, Angie.

She cautiously opened the door to the garage, flipped the light on, saw nothing out of place and hurried to Randy's Mercedes. Sure enough, the bag of tortilla strips had fallen out. She scooped them up and headed back, locking the door behind her for good measure.

"I'm losing my mind," she said, tossing the strips to Randy. "I could swear I just saw Jamie in the kitchen."

Randy took a moment to respond. "That's understandable."

"No, I mean like really there." She sighed. "You're right, we can't let this crush us."

"You're perfectly fine, sweetheart. The mind just plays tricks on us now and then. Happens to me all the time."

"It does?"

"Well, now and then at least. Although it's typically things that vanish, not things that appear."

True. Randy was always losing items that were right in front of his nose. This wasn't so different, right?

Either way, she resolved to enjoy her soup, now with a layer of tortilla strips covering the hot broth and chicken. Or at least try.

"STATUS, MEGAN?"

The technician's voice returned over the intercom. "Entry looks good, stable brainwaves. We had a spike a few minutes ago but it quickly normalized. She's in deep."

Three monitors on a narrow table at the base of the window summarized Angie's vitals and a host of vibrational patterns, which reflected everything from her brainwaves to numerous other indicators that Randy wasn't familiar with.

Jake Barnes nodded. "Okay, let's give her another ten minutes at most, then bring her out. I don't want her in there longer than absolutely necessary. Everything depends on a clean extraction. We need an unattached exit."

"Understood."

Convergence's VR technology touched the lives of every soul alive and the world knew it. The man behind that company was stooped over the monitors, eyes bright in a wrinkled face, mind sharp but much older than Randy had anticipated. He had no idea the man was in his nineties. Eighties, at least.

Randy peered at the lab below, still taken aback by the sophistication of the technology represented here, deep in the walls of Convergence. He could see Angie's right side, arm and leg—the rest of her body was under the helmet and acoustic imaging array.

"So if this is the technology in its infancy, what does it look like five years from now?" he asked.

"Well, that's the question, isn't it?" Barnes said matter-of-factly. "For all we know, a lab in China has already stumbled on the advanced applications of acoustic neutralization and imaging. Most look at technology like this and worry about a future run amok. I look at it and see it as opportunity, so long as it's properly wielded. With fire you can burn a city or cook a meal. Fire is both good and bad."

"That still doesn't answer my question."

"No, it doesn't. I would say that in five to ten years' time, all the technology you see below will fit in the palm of your hand. The processing power will remain remote and fill a building, naturally, but the RIGs necessary to take someone into another world will be very small. That's the advantage of waves—they easily pass through matter, like skulls."

"Could it be used to control others?"

Barnes studied him, as if to choose his words carefully. "Anything is possible, which is precisely why it must be heavily regulated. But controlling others isn't the real danger, as I see it. We've known for decades that the world we live in is more like the virtual reality that Angie's in right now. It isn't the solid world we think it is. Theoretically, tapping into the source code beyond what we think of as reality will allow us to change reality. We'd better hope the right side controls any technology with that power."

Randy was surprised. "That sounds like something Angie would say."

"She's right. We must be very careful, which is why she's writing this book."

"I'm talking about this world being virtual."

"Yes, well, Angie's a special case. Our task is to understand exactly how our minds interact with radically immersive virtual realities, not pick apart this one—not yet anyway. Angie's perfectly suited for that task because she's so fluid in that space. But that very skill can also be her Achilles' heel if she begins to believe she can experience this world as virtual. No one can do that and remain sane. Case in point: Kevin Spencer, one of our more advanced subjects."

He peered down at the RIG in the lab below.

"While in the Red Protocol, he attached himself not only to the idea that this world is a hologram, but that he'd found a way out. The obsession eventually left him with an irreversible case of paranoid delusion. He took his own life two years ago."

"You're saying this technology *killed* him?"

Barnes's brow arched. "Heavens, no. He not only knew the risks but insisted on taking them, just like Angie. Despite our best efforts, he refused regression therapy and went on his own exploration of reality, which ended in a drug overdose. We've come a long way since then."

"What was he seeing?" Randy asked, deeply concerned. "I mean, how did he describe this reality as he saw it?"

"Hallucinations take all forms. He claimed he could see matter as energy.

Much of what he concluded came from a white room he claimed to be engaging. He was transposing the white lab you see below into an instrument of learning as he populated the virtual world in the Red Protocol. Understandable, because there's a virtual white room in the Red Protocol where we take subjects as part of their first initiation."

Heat washed over Randy's face and shoulders. "You do realize that you're describing Angie's symptoms, don't you?"

"Seeing white rooms isn't uncommon, but yes, that's why we're here."

All of this made Randy more than a little nervous. They were playing with fire. Which could cook meals or raze a city. "So she'll be okay," he said, reassuring himself.

"Of course. Like I said, we've come a long way."

Randy studied the flesh and form of Angie below and tried to imagine her in a virtual world right now. What was happening to her? Where was she? Did she know this world still existed?

"Your point is that this Kevin Spencer went too far, but it sounds like you might also think we live in a virtual world of some kind. Do you?"

Barnes glanced at him sideways. "I didn't say that. But I do know we can create a virtual world that is habitable. And I do believe that one day we'll be able to change this world by hacking the quantum field."

"If the evidence is so strong, you'd think the scientific community would be up in arms. Why isn't this common knowledge?"

Barnes turned back to his monitors and spoke in a soft monotone.

"Scientists, like religious folk, come in three varieties. The first kind hear evidence that suggests reality isn't what we think it is but refuse to seriously consider anything that conflicts with their deeply held convictions. They're in denial. The second kind are disturbed by new evidence and then jump through many convoluted hoops to satisfy themselves it can't be so. They are in rejection. The third kind of scientist is bothered by the evidence and seeks a new paradigm to understand reality rather than clinging to the old one. I am of the third kind, a minority still, but not for long. The evidence is mounting, far more than can be ignored or explained away, even by the greatest skeptic."

"Sounds a bit too mystical, frankly. If I were a scientist, I guess I'd be the first kind."

"We're all scientists on one level or another. And make no mistake, this isn't about anything spiritual or mystical. I'm talking about the nature of reality on a fundamental, quantum level. How this world works beyond the veil of perception."

He dipped his head at the scene below and continued in a soft voice filled with reverence. "And that unveiled girl down there might very well be the one who shows us the way. She's special. She's always been special."

ANGIE AND RANDY were watching a scene that showed Darey changing an improvised bandage made of leaves on his foot. But it wasn't looking good. His shirtless torso, on the other hand, was looking quite good. Not too bulky, not too thin. An amazing specimen of humanity. She could appreciate that. Distraction could be a powerful ally.

"You really think he's an accountant?" she said.

Randy chuckled. "Who knows? If so, he works out plenty."

"He's beautiful."

"I think the word is *handsome*. A stallion. Like me." He grinned.

They were a good ten minutes into the show and Angie dipped her head over the bowl to scoop up the last spoonful. She had the spoon halfway to her mouth when a man wearing a ski mask appeared from behind the recliners, calmly lifted a gun, and trained it on Randy.

For a moment, the room went perfectly still. Her mind seemed to have stalled.

The gun bucked.

She twisted and saw a small dart sticking out of Randy's shoulder. He surged out of the chair, took two drunken steps toward the intruder, and crashed to the floor, out cold.

"There are two ways to do this, both of which end in my leaving with the recordings you intend to show the media tomorrow," the man said. "The first way is for you to do exactly as I say. You will retrieve the tapes from your safe, turn them over to me, and I'll leave you both alive. There is no way you can prove I was here, so there's no need for me to eliminate you. Do you follow?"

She stared at him, heart slamming in her chest. *What recordings? What media?*

"Please respond."

Angie nodded.

"The other way is for you to resist. If you do, I will have to kill both of you before forcing the safe open on my own. This second way requires far more effort on my part, both in opening the safe and in disposing of your bodies. I strongly suggest the first option."

"I . . . I don't know of any recordings," she croaked.

"Fine, but you can get into the safe."

She was thinking frantically, knowing she really only had one option here, because she couldn't bear the thought of losing Randy. He and Jamie were her life. And if she and Randy were both dead, Jamie would have no one to help him. He too would be executed.

An image from the room's arched entry caught the corner of her eye and she shifted her line of sight.

Staring at her with a smile stood Jamie as a young boy. The same Jamie from the kitchen. She stared, fixated by the sight of her little boy, thinking he would vanish at any moment.

But he didn't vanish.

"You're running out of time," Jamie said.

She blinked. Had she really just heard him speak? Yes. Yes, she had.

"Look at me!" the hooded man snapped.

She did, trembling now. He glanced in the direction she'd been staring and her eyes followed his, expecting Jamie to be gone. He wasn't gone. What was happening?

"Jamie?" she managed.

The walls began to shimmer. And in that shimmering something deep inside of her mind recalled the white room Jamie had come from. A room with gates that led to the truth.

The man was asking her something about what she was staring at, clearly not seeing Jamie himself. But Angie now knew why. She was in a virtual reality created by something called the Red Protocol. None of this was real.

"You know what to do," Jamie said as his body began to dissolve. "If they kill me I won't win the game. Hurry!" Then he was gone.

Now the walls, the chairs, the television, her hands—all of it was in a full shimmer, vibrating into a blur. She was leaving. She was going to the gate room because that's where Jamie was asking her to go.

A strange thought occurred to her in that full shimmer: This world had felt as real as the world in which she was married to Darey. She'd seen both in full shimmer. So how could she know which one was real? Were they both virtual?

What about Randy? What about Jamie here? But she knew already—they were digital.

"You have three seconds to . . ." The rest of the man's words were garbled.

She turned to him to see that he was in full shimmer, barely recognizable. And then he was gone. As was the room they were in. And the world they lived in.

Angie found herself in the middle of the gate room, surrounded by a wall of gears, two gates and three books. Real. With Jamie's help, she'd just hacked her way out of a virtual world.

She spun around, heart pounding. No boy. She was alone.

Focus, Angie. Focus.

Jamie's last comment flashed through her mind. *If they kill me I won't win the game. Hurry.* Why was he so adamant about winning before he died if the world was only virtual? She was missing something important.

One thing was certain: Jamie was afraid someone would kill him while he was in prison before she uncovered the truth. She was here to discover what was hidden, and her time in the Red Protocol was quickly coming to an end.

She had to decode the second book while she still had time.

CHAPTER
TWENTY-SIX

FIFTEEN MINUTES had passed since the inception of the Red Protocol and all had evidently gone as anticipated. There had been some kind of anomaly roughly five minutes in, but it evidently self-corrected. They were on the cusp of bringing Angie out—the critical process of this regression, as Randy understood it.

"Thirty seconds to extraction." Megan's voice over the com sounded calm and confident.

"Okay, people." Barnes shuffled back and forth, hands in pockets, glancing at the monitors that showed all of Angie's vitals and brain patterns. "On exit, I want anything that even suggests an anomaly immediately neutralized. Don't trust the algorithms. Frank, Judy . . . Eyes sharp. I want her out clean as a newborn baby."

"Copy that."

Randy's pulse rose in response to Barnes's tension. If the creator of the technology was concerned, there was reason for it. If something happened to Angie he . . .

A soft beep on the screen monitoring her brain waves cut Randy's thoughts short. All the brainwave patterns looked as they had moments earlier, except a single line near the bottom was showing jagged spikes that reached the upper limits of the graph. A red light above the graph was blinking with the soft beep.

Barnes had gone still, eyes fixed on the screen. For a long second no one spoke or moved. Maybe they were waiting for the line to self-correct.

But the beeping didn't stop. Instead, all patterns on the screen suddenly went haywire, rocketing to the limit of their respective graphs. A dozen soft beeps chimed in a staccato pattern.

Randy's heart stuttered.

"We have a catastrophic failure!" Megan's voice snapped. "Body vitals are nominal, but her mind is splintering. I . . ."

"Check the leads," Barnes croaked, jerking his hands from his pockets as he slid into his chair. "Peter, run a diagnostic on calibration and connection. Do it!"

"Already on it, sir." Then, "Fully functional."

"We have to bring her out!" Megan's voice was strained. "She's fracturing!"

"Hold it!" Barnes was tapping inputs into a keyboard as charts and reports flew across a screen to his right. They were all nonsense to Randy, but he understood the sum of them plainly.

Something had gone wrong. Very wrong.

Randy stepped up, eyes on the screens. "What—"

Barnes snatched up his hand to cut him off. He was studying a new graph, intent on several lines of ones and zeros under his long, knotted forefinger.

"Sir, I strongly suggest we bring her out immediately." Megan's voice was urgent. "She's broken coherence with the virtual world we placed her in. She's falling apart!"

Barnes didn't seem to hear. The graphs displaying Angie's brainwaves now looked like the drawing of a possessed child.

"Sir! We have to—"

"Reboot her," Barnes snapped.

Silence.

"Reboot her now."

"Sir, we don't know how she'll respond. We've never—"

"I realize that, Megan. But we've never tried to extract a subject in this kind of disarray either." He spoke with unmistakable authority, almost dismissively. "She's far too unstable to bring out. I'm not going to risk the damage to her brain. The models favor a reboot."

"Theoretically," Megan objected.

"The whole world is theory. Neutralize the feeds to her brain, put her back in the void, let her stabilize for"—he drew his finger down a line of code—"ten minutes, then put her back into the virtual world. Once back to baseline, we extract. Do it!"

A beat.

Megan came back on, calm again. "Initiating reboot."

Randy understood the gist of what they were doing and now wasn't the time for clarification. The details didn't matter.

What did matter was that five seconds later, the graphs all went flat. It was as if someone had pulled the plug on her brain. That was good?

Barnes sat back and crossed his arms, eyes on the flatlined brainwave patterns. The same flatlines had filled the monitor when they first put her under. Her body vitals appeared normal other than an elevated pulse. One twenty-three—not too high.

"What's happening?"

Barnes looked at him. "She's in the void."

"So she's unaware?"

"Her world is black. No activity, no thought, only pure awareness, which can't be explained. We leave her there long enough to clear any residual charges, then bring her back."

"She's brain dead?"

"In a manner of speaking, yes. But not entirely. If we did a wipe, she would be permanently brain dead with zero probability of recovery. We're not doing that. We're essentially rebooting her mind."

Then, with a twinkle in his eyes and the hint of a smile, "Don't worry, this will work."

ANGIE STOOD in the middle of the gate room and stared at the gears, now still. Then at the Image Maker gate, now closed. Then at the three Play Dead manuals, all resting on their pedestals. The familiar soft background hum droned on.

She breathed steadily, collecting herself. The boy wasn't here—but he was, because he was always in her mind somewhere.

An interruption in the hum cut her thoughts short. The white room went dark and she caught her breath. Something had happened. What?

Light flooded the room again. The hum returned. Whatever had caused the interruption, nothing here had changed, but if they were on to her, time was short. Jamie's words whispered through her mind.

You know what to do.

So she would go with what she already knew.

Angie hurried to the first book and flipped it open to the end, to the stick figure with the all-seeing eye for a head. She touched the eye and felt its energy surge as she lifted it from the page, a fully formed eye. She held it for a second, amazed once more by how real it looked and felt. Squeezing it, she felt the eye's rigidity increase. Squeezing it very tightly, she saw the eye become a glass ball and stop vibrating altogether, collapsing entirely into form once again. Fascinating.

She snatched up the second book containing computer code and stepped up to the panel that operated the Image Maker portal. Set the eye into the concave receptacle at the top of the panel.

As before, the three-foot round door popped free of its seal with a hiss. When she slid it open, the room came to life. Gears along the wall began to whir as they turned; a thin beam of light from the eye of the needle on the opposite wall pierced the open Image Maker portal; beyond, a virtual world was being projected into the fabric of space-time.

Right?

Feeling a sense of urgency, she opened the second book and scanned pages filled with ones and zeros. There were no spaces between them, only what appeared to be uninterrupted lines of machine code.

Peering through the portal, she saw herself lying under the machines in the lab at Convergence, deep in the Red Protocol. That was her life now. But she wasn't interested in where she was now. She was interested in what would happen if she pressed the 1 and 0 buttons on the panel with the green button.

The book's ones and zeros represented billions of possible combinations. Selecting a random string from the center of the book, Angie entered seven numbers on the keypad only because seven seemed like a good place to start. 1001101. She pressed the green button below the numbers and peered through the portal.

The fully dimensional scene being projected beyond the Image Maker gate was of her in France. She was half dressed, racing around a room, being chased by her friend Matilda. The memory mushroomed in her mind. This was a scene from her life when she was seven! She'd dialed up a slice of her own history.

It had been a hot day and they were going for a swim. She'd stolen Matilda's favorite swimsuit and her friend wanted it back.

She watched as her mother stepped in and told them to hush. Father was sleeping. Angie couldn't hear the voices, but she had little doubt that if she were in the scene she would.

Could she do that? Could she enter the past?

She answered herself. *Yes.*

Really?

Yes, really.

Gripped with equal measures of curiosity and certainty, she pushed her hand, then her arm, then her head through the portal as she'd done before. Immediately the gate room was gone and she was herself in the room with Matilda's swimsuit bunched up in her right hand, staring at her mother in the doorway.

She was herself at age seven, reliving the past! Now, as if in a vivid, fully fleshed déjà vu. As a matter of fact, she remembered that she'd experienced a déjà vu that day as well, looking at her mother in the doorway.

Her mother's eyes lingered on her, inquisitive. "What is it, darling?" she asked in a gentle voice.

Angie stared back, unsure what to say.

Her mother walked up to her, eyes bright. She was noticing something that Angie didn't understand.

"You're seeing?" her mother asked.

Finally, Angie was able to put her feeling into words. "It feels like I've been here before. Have I?"

Her mother smiled and reached a hand to her cheek. Angie felt the warm fingers, smelled the scent of the lilac perfume her mother rubbed on her wrists and behind her ears each morning.

"One day you'll understand," her mother said. "This world is not what it seems to be, my little unveiled one."

For a moment, Angie had the strange sensation that time had stopped. And in that falling away of time, an image of a white room filled her mind. A voice was calling to her from inside her thoughts.

Close your eyes, Angie.

It was Jamie. He wanted her to go to him. So she closed her eyes.

When she opened them again, she was back in the gate room, navigation book in hand, staring at the portal. Her stomach was doing somersaults. She'd just become herself as a young girl! It was as if she'd entered a movie of her life, become her character, and played the scene for the first time. Most amazingly, when she was in herself as a seven-year-old, she had no memory of her older self. Of course not, because those years hadn't happened yet.

The book in her hand was a catalog of scenes from her role as Angie. Could she only enter her own scenes, or others' roles as well? But that would be trillions and trillions of scenes, and she saw no way one book could contain them all. This book from her mind had to be her life alone.

A new thought struck her. If she'd entered her past, could she go to her future?

Angie flipped to the last page of the book and entered the last two digits. 10.

She peered into the portal. The scene was her in the Red Protocol RIG at Convergence, busy technicians around her. Concern filled their faces. Something was wrong.

So she couldn't look into the future, because it remained solely within the realm of probabilities. An unwritten script.

She flipped the pages and entered another sequence on the panel. This one took her to a scene of her attending a mathematics class at Auburn University. Having no interest in the moment, she tried another.

This was of her writing her book, *Righteous*, late at night. She pressed on, wondering if there was anything in here that might shed light on Jamie's connection to her.

The scenes flipped by as she entered the numbers from different sections of the book. One in the first few pages was of her as an infant, crying in the crib. Hungry, maybe. There were other babies in the room, maybe ten in all. Some hospital ward, maybe. A woman lifted her up and held her close, whispering to her in another language. This was her mother? Or a nurse. No, not a nurse, because she felt deeply connected to this woman. Had to be her mother. Odd, because her mother had said she gave birth to her at home. The scene expanded and she saw that the woman had blond hair and was smaller than her mother. So then, a nurse after all. Maybe infants couldn't tell the difference when they were so young.

She was tempted to enter the scene and step fully into being a baby again, but she pressed on.

Another scene showed her with Darey on vacation at Orange Beach. She paused there, drawn to the moment, suddenly missing him terribly. But this was only a memory of a scene from a virtual world being created by those in it. She had to remember that. Yes, she missed Darey terribly, but only because she was engaging that virtual world.

Swallowing, she tried a random sequence of numbers without using the book. She was rewarded with a moment as a teenager, staring into a mirror that showed her acne. Please, not that one.

Another random string showed her riding a bike in France with her first boyfriend, a wild bohemian who taught her the finer ways of kissing.

She hurried through another dozen scenes, searching for something that might shed light on Jamie. But with each passing scene, her hopes of finding him faded. Decoding the book with any sense of order was daunting. She didn't have the time!

Breathe, Angie. Trust.

Slowly, calm settled over her. She only felt fear and concern when she was either in a scene or invested in it. Just like in the game of life. Yes, she could get caught up in the drama of death and betrayal and longing and need, but to what end?

What would happen if she figured out how to open the needle gate? *Veritas Vos Liberabit.* 'The truth will set you free.' Maybe not free from the world, but free in it.

The thought blossomed in her mind. Was that why Jamie was so interested in being set free before any harm came to him in prison? Even if the world they were in was virtual, there must be great meaning to it. Play Dead wasn't about escaping the world but being free *in* it. It was at least a possibility.

The floor began to shake and Angie put her arms out for balance. The whole room was shuddering, as if hit by a gentle, rolling earthquake. Something was happening out there. They were bringing her out? But she wasn't done!

"You have to stay sane," the boy said.

She spun and saw Jamie sitting on the floor.

"I think someone's going to try to kill me, and you can't help me if you're insane."

"Am I insane?" she asked.

"The whole world is insane . . ." he said, but even as he spoke, the white room dissolved and Angie found herself in darkness.

For what seemed far too long, nothing happened.

". . . up." The voice was faint and distant. ". . . now. Open your eyes."

She thought, *Yes, I should open my eyes.*

And when she did, she was in the laboratory, staring up at the paneled ceiling and Megan's reassuring face.

"Welcome back, Angie."

RANDY SAT adjacent to Angie in Jake Barnes's office an hour later, watching in silence as Barnes ran through his post-extraction protocol, which consisted of equal parts reassurance and simple probing questions, some of which felt rather awkward.

"How important is your body, Angie?"

She searched his eyes. "Very. I only have one so better take care of it."

"Indeed. Do you feel any shame in regard to your body?"

"What do you mean?"

"I mean is there anything about your body that, if it were different, would make you more comfortable? Something others may not be aware of?"

A long pause. "You want me to say that here?" She glanced at Randy. "Now?"

"If you don't mind. It's important."

"Well, maybe I could be taller."

"Not that. Something you're ashamed of."

She shifted, hiding discomfort. *Awkward, yes,* Randy thought. But as a detective who routinely interviewed witnesses and suspects, he knew this was Barnes's way of assuring himself that Angie had reconnected with herself in the same way all humans did. Everyone except those disassociated from their bodies held at least some shame in regard to their appearance. What it was didn't matter, only that Angie was able to feel.

"I'd rather not share that," Angie said sheepishly.

"That's fine. No need." Her reaction had satisfied him, and he moved on, glancing at his pad. "Now, I know this might be difficult, but you haven't mentioned Darey. Can you tell me how you feel when you think of Darey?"

"Darey?" Her face was blank, a protective response, Randy imagined.

"He was brutally murdered last night," Barnes said. "Did you love him? Do you miss him? Does he matter?"

The man's insensitivity surprised Randy, and he found himself wanting to protest. But Angie didn't need his help.

"How dare you?" she growled, face flushed. "I . . . How dare you!"

He lifted his hand. "I needed to see anger. That's good. That's very good, Angie."

She just stared at him. Barnes set his pad down and crossed his legs. Held her eyes for a long while as if determined to see what lay beyond. When he resumed his interview, his voice was soft.

"Tell me about the white room you visited while you were under. What did you see in it?"

"I . . . What white room?"

"The one you've been seeing. The one you just entered while in the Red Protocol."

"Those were hallucinations," she said. "I didn't see a white room this time. Only my house with Randy."

"Randy?"

She kept her gaze on Barnes. "Hmmm?"

"You said you were in your hose with Randy. Why Randy?"

"Sorry. I meant Darey," she said awkwardly. "We were discussing the recording from Jamie's house."

"What recording?"

"The one showing Jamie in his house the night of the murders. The one Darey was killed for. Jamie's innocent, but the recording was swapped."

"Really?" Barnes looked at Randy. "Are you aware of this?"

The fact that Barnes now knew about the recording unnerved Randy, because it was a potentially explosive piece of evidence. But there was now no denying it.

"It's a possibility," Randy said.

Barnes nodded. "Fair enough. It's not my concern, obviously, but if it means anything, I think there is more to the Oak Hill murders than what the feeds are reporting. Either way, please keep in mind that solving the case, however important it may feel, is nothing compared to the larger concern at hand."

"Which is?" Randy asked.

"Exposing the world to the benefits and dangers of evolved virtual reality, as I explained. Humanity is at the dawn of a new age, and our future depends on our careful and successful navigation of the discoveries we've made. Evolution is always messy and sometimes catastrophic, because the new only comes at the cost of the old. The human race can handle messy. It's the catastrophic we must avoid."

Made sense. Randy gave him a nod. His phone was vibrating in his pocket. He ignored it. Probably Rachel trying to find out where he was. He was surprised it had taken her this long. But then, they were used to him making his own way.

Barnes slowly pushed himself to his feet. "Okay, I think that does it. I'm happy to inform you that you're a real, normal human being, my dear. Let's keep it that way."

"Normal, huh?" she said with a grin. "Not sure I want to be normal."

"Better than delusional. I would like to keep you here under observation for the next twenty-four hours if that's okay with you. Just to be sure."

"No." Randy heard himself say it before he'd had time to think the prospect through. But a rationale for his insistence came immediately. "She's just lost her husband, for heaven's sake!"

"Understood, but—"

"She needs to be home under Felicia Buckhead's care. Felicia's a trained therapist, she can do the observing."

Barnes studied Angie. "Fair enough. Under one condition. Promise me that you will report even the slightest change in your sense of reality the moment it occurs. If I'm right, you won't experience any whiteouts, but on the off chance you do, I must know about it. Promise me."

She stood. "Of course."

CHAPTER
TWENTY-SEVEN

ANGIE WAITED until Convergence was a mile behind Randy's old souped-up truck before speaking, because she was far too eager to spill the beans to Randy and had to be thoughtful. But by then it became too much, and she turned to him, unable to hide her grin.

"You think he bought it?"

He gave her a side glance, brow raised.

"Then you bought it too." She faced the road. "Good."

"I'm assuming by 'he' you mean Jake Barnes. As to what you were trying to sell him, I'm not entirely sure."

"I'll explain on the way to the Milton house in Barton Creek."

"Susan Milton? Our agreement was to take you home. Do you really think—"

"Yes, I do. Clair found the encrypted key that started all of this. Now that you're on my side, we need to get back in there and find it. Assuming it's still in Clair's room."

"On your side? I've never not been on your side. I'm on the side of the truth."

"The truth? The truth's not what you think. Either way, you know better than I how to find hidden things. We have to find that key drive."

"A key no one else has been able to locate," he said doubtfully. "Assuming this key actually exists, I would guess it hasn't been found because it was recovered by whoever killed Clair and Timothy."

"Indulge me. We need to go to Susan's anyway."

"Why?"

"To bring her up to speed."

He hesitated. "I'm obviously missing something. Why don't you start by bringing *me* up to speed."

"I'll bring you up to speed when you agree to take me to see Susan Milton. I'm not your hostage, am I?"

"Of course not."

"Then you can either take me to see Susan Milton, or you can drop me off at my house so I can drive there myself," she said.

He glanced at his buzzing phone. Rachel. He ignored it.

"What happened to meeting Felicia?"

"She's not free until one. Which is it? Take me to Susan or drop me at my house."

He shifted uncomfortably. "You do understand that I'm in a precarious position here. For all I know, the DA and sheriff are in on the Oak Hill murders. Heck, the whole department might be involved. Or none of them. I'm already flapping in the wind, and I have to check in at some point or risk any chance of running under the radar with what I know. We need to think this through carefully. How am I supposed to explain a trip to the Milton house with you, a woman who's just lost her husband and should be in mourning?"

"Tell them I'm freaking out."

"Are you?"

"Tell them I'm demanding to connect with someone who's also lost the love of her life, but I'm not up to driving myself because I'm an emotional basket case. That's more true than you might realize."

He breathed out and nodded. "Fine. Barton Creek it is. Now tell me what Jake Barnes and I bought that seems to be bringing you so much enjoyment."

"I lied," she said, grinning. "Not about all of it, but in general. I pulled the wool over his eyes and I guess yours as well. Because what really happened in the regression is that I spent most of it in the gate room, working on the second book, which, as it turns out, is the key to navigating the Image Maker gate."

He kept his eyes on the road without responding.

"Cool, huh?" she said.

"Cool," he said, but she doubted he was thinking it was cool. She pressed in, determined to help him understand.

"You don't understand. The book is like a catalog of scenes from the role I've been playing in this reality. Only this is no more a reality than any virtual reality. All of this"—she waved her hand at the highway and passing cars—"it's all really a virtual world we're trapped in. I mean, I know it doesn't seem like it now, but that's how fully immersive virtual realities work. Especially in the Red Protocol. It's impossible to know you're in a world made of data. All sight, all touch, everything you hear, all of it is only information expressed through vibration, just like images of people we see on a screen, which are made of vibrations we call light. Make sense?"

"I guess from your point of view it does. What you don't understand is that this is exactly what Jake Barnes is deeply concerned about. You aren't the first person to see the white room, and the other person is dead."

"I'm not the first?" Her pulse surged. "Who?"

Randy quickly told her about a subject named Kevin Spencer, who refused regression therapy and ultimately committed suicide.

"This isn't something to mess around with," he finished. "We should turn around and take you back right—"

"No!" she cried. "No, no, no! What if this Spencer guy was seeing what was there, just like me? So he couldn't handle it, but I can. Jamie told me I have to stay sane."

"Exactly."

She ignored his jab.

"For all you know, Barnes only made up Kevin Spencer to discourage me!"

"You don't trust him?"

"I don't trust anyone who says what I'm experiencing isn't real."

"That's probably what Spencer said."

"Stop it!" she snapped. "You turn this car around and I'm getting out."

He considered this.

"Okay, but I'm not letting you out of my sight."

"Good." She sat back. A part of her was concerned with the tale of Spencer, but after what she'd just experienced, that part was like a whisper and she dismissed it.

"Pretend for a moment that you didn't know about anyone named Kevin Spencer," she said. "At least tell me if the idea that this is a virtual world makes any sense to you. Barnes himself knows it."

"Conceptually. But—"

"Well I've been in the part of the mind that projects and engages those images. That's why it's called the Image Maker. We aren't actually these characters we're playing."

"I see. So then none of this matters."

"It does, but only in the virtual world, right? Outside the virtual world, we discover who we really are."

"And you were there? Outside this . . . this virtual world?"

"No, not yet. The gate room is like a camera. A projecting mechanism. It's the in-between. To know the truth, I need to go through the needle gate. Follow?"

"The truth about what?" he asked.

"About everything. About the Oak Hill murders and this world and what's really happening to Jamie and me and *you*. Everyone and everything!"

Randy didn't answer. He entered Highway 360, headed south to Barton Creek. At least he was keeping his word.

"I mean look at me." She twisted to him and spread her hands. "Do I look like the grieving widow to you? No. And do you know why? Because now I know the truth. Sure, I miss Darey, but only here in this virtual world. That's how I was able to convince Barnes that I was angry at his suggestion that I didn't care about Darey. I just played the role of Angie. But we're making all of this up! I mean, think of it! Thousands of years of human history—wars and fortunes and weddings and nonstop drama, all gone haywire because we don't know who we really are. Tell me you can at least imagine that."

"Of course I can, but I can also imagine a moon made of cheese. You have to at least admit that you're talking and acting like someone who's suffered a profound break from reality following deep trauma and, in your case, a mind-altering trip into a virtual world."

"That's not this!" She was speaking more to herself than to him, because she knew how easy it was to lose her grip on what the gate room had shown her. This time she was going to hold on with every cell of her virtual body.

What if he's right, Angie?

Well, what did she have to lose? Darey was dead. Despite their intentions to remain married without being codependent, she couldn't bear the thought of living without him.

Then again, Darey had been a character. Just like Randy. She had to remember that.

She switched approaches, playing to his limited perspective. "At the very least, our lives in this drama now depend on you taking this exploration with me, delusional or not, because you know too much and what you know is a threat to whoever killed Clair and Timothy and Darey. Both our lives are in danger. Believe what you want about what I'm saying, but you can't deny that much."

"And you can't deny the possibility that you *are* delusional."

"Fine. If and when we find that drive, you'll know. For now, what harm is there in pretending I'm right? Indulge me!"

Again, she was speaking to herself as much as to him, because a part of her was unnerved by her own claims. Already! She needed more than talk. Experience, not talk, was the best teacher, they said.

"Don't believe me? I'll show you. Pull over."

"Now?"

"Just pull over on the shoulder."

The old truck wasn't self-driving, Randy had told her, because he didn't trust the technology. Rather than using the shoulder, he pulled off at the next exit, brought the truck to a stop, and slid the transmission into park. He was just turning to her when she leaned over, took his chin in her right hand, and kissed him gently on the lips. She pulled back, stared into his wide eyes, and kissed him again, longer this time.

She sat back, satisfied.

Randy cleared his throat, face flushed.

"That's what I was doing when I wasn't in the gate room while at Convergence."

"Kissing me?"

"We were married, you and me. It was my house, only it was decorated differently. We had some drama . . ." She decided not to share the details. "We danced, we laughed, we were most definitely in love. And I can tell you that I accepted all of it as the only reality that existed. That's how real it was. Just as real as this reality. Both are virtual!"

"You just kissed me!"

"Did you like it? It's not the first time, believe me. Although, admittedly, the others were in a fabricated reality spun up by the Red Protocol." She didn't bother mentioning that her own subconscious psyche played a major role in populating the Red Protocol's framework.

"We're here, not there. And here, in the real world, it's not even close to being appropriate. You just lost your husband, for heaven's sake!"

"That's the point! Why would I be like this unless I knew, knew, knew that this world is just like that one? Virtual! If you don't believe what I'm saying, then at least believe what you're seeing. I'm a totally free woman without all the baggage of this virtual world's drama. That's what you need to know. That's what Susan needs to know. That's what the whole world needs to know! Maybe that's what's on the encrypted drive that got Clair and Timothy killed." There was a new thought. "That's what I'm going to write about, Randy." She stabbed at the air. "I'm going to expose the truth of what's really happening, and I have to figure it out before any harm comes to Jamie. He's afraid someone will kill him in prison and for some reason that's important, even though this is a virtual world."

He'd regrouped somewhat. Maybe she'd gotten through.

"I see," he said.

"You do?"

Randy put the truck in drive and pulled back onto the highway. "I see what you think you see, let's leave it at that for now."

"So you're with me?"

"I'm taking you to Susan's, aren't I?"

True.

"But please, please . . . Promise me one thing."

"You got it."

"Don't tell Susan about any of this. Keep it to yourself. She's still grieving. You might think this is the answer to her suffering, but trust me, it's not. Not now. Can you do that for me?"

She thought about it and gave him a curt nod. "I'll only say what needs to be said. Promise."

"Fair enough."

They rode in silence for a minute, during which Randy's phone buzzed yet again. And again he ignored it.

"Did you like it?" Angie asked.

"Like what?"

"The kiss?"

He didn't answer. But she didn't need him to, because she knew that in this reality there were many levels of liking. On some of those levels, he did like it. On others he didn't.

That was fine by her. He, like her, was caught between levels.

Ten minutes later, they pulled into the Milton driveway.

"Remember," Randy said.

"I remember."

"YES?"

"There's been a change of plans."

Matteo Steger leaned back, phone to his ear, oddly bothered by the sound of Katrina Botwilder's voice, as he had been as of late. He wasn't sure why.

"This is new? Say what you mean."

"Angie Channing has become a liability we can no longer accept. I realize all of this is coming quickly, but she has to go."

The order took Matteo off guard. This was a woman he respected above most. He'd memorized every line on her face, unsure why she affected him in such an unusual way. Yes, she was special to them—an 'unveiled child,' as they called those rare ones. But this isn't what impressed Matteo. He'd been watching her for years and found her oddly delightful. Perhaps only because she was unspoiled and true, a rarity in the world these days.

"Do you mind me asking why? She's one of your most valued assets."

"Our contact at Convergence has informed us that she re-entered the Red Protocol a few hours ago, during which time she suffered a fracture. She doesn't know it, but her brain is . . . well, very broken. She's far too unstable and knows far too much."

He took a deep breath and accepted the instruction as he had so many times before.

"Understood."

"There's more. The detective knows what Angie knows. Susan Milton will soon know as well. They now present an unacceptable risk."

Matteo blinked. "I'm sorry?"

"All three of them, Matteo. Today if possible. And before you tell me how risky this is, let me remind you of the critical nature of what we're trying to accomplish here. Everything depends on the presidency. This is the path to that office. If the boy's exonerated, everything falls apart. Anyone with evidence that might compromise us must be eliminated immediately."

"This isn't possible in the same day without leaving a trail. Eliminating a problem does you no favors if that elimination leads back to you."

"It never leads back to me," she snapped. "Only to you. And if you hurry, it *is* possible. Angie Channing and the detective just arrived at Susan Milton's house. You might make it look like a despondent mother impulsively flew into a rage, then took her own life."

"That's a stretch," he objected.

"We can sell it."

She was right. They could sell almost anything that was even remotely plausible.

"One way or the other, Matteo. And while you're there, wipe the place."

"Another wipe?"

"The whole house, please."

The secure line went dead.

Matteo sat still in his car for several long seconds, mind calculating. Botwilder was right, it could be done. Assuming all three were still present when he arrived. He would have to use the police-issued handgun in his trunk and exchange the barrel with the detective's weapon so ballistics would match his gun. It would appear that Susan Milton got her hands on his gun and shot Angie in a fit of rage before killing Randy and then taking her own life. Possible.

As for the wipe—when he'd failed to find the key drive in the daughter's room following her death, he'd neutralized all data in the room using a portable EMP. No data could have survived the electromagnetic pulse he'd set off in the room. And yet they were ordering him to do it again, strong enough to neutralize the whole house this time. Just a precaution.

The detective would be the most difficult. In the event Matteo failed, he wanted the man hamstrung. Matteo tapped his earpiece and called the DA. Andrew Olsen picked up after the fifth ring.

"I told you not to call me at the office during the day. You're going to get me crucified!"

"Your detective, Randy George, is on the loose. Discredit him. If you can't, we will discredit you."

He disconnected, started the car, and pulled onto Highway 180. He had to make sure the maid was called out—easily done. When he went in, he would go quick, without finesse, and clean up later. Dead bodies were much easier to deal with than living ones.

Especially three.

CHAPTER
TWENTY-EIGHT

JAMIE HAMILTON sat upright in his bunk and looked around, disoriented. White brick walls, one sink, one bed and him. No white room.

He slid his feet off the bed and stood. No white room, but he'd dreamed of it again. The white room Angie had asked him about. She'd seen it too. So what did that mean? Ever since she'd asked him about it, he tried to remember what he was dreaming, because it somehow seemed important. She seemed to think so.

She was a pink. He loved pinks.

Jamie stepped over to the sink—a step and a half, actually—turned the faucet on, and splashed water on his face. Nine ounces of water, give or take, that's how much he used based on the shape of it. He'd learned how to calculate volume using his mother's measuring cups at the sink.

He lifted his arm and wiped his face with the yellow jumpsuit's sleeve. Better to keep the small towel clean and dry on the rack. He didn't like a messy room.

Staring at the white wall again, he thought about the dream. But he couldn't remember anything about it except that it was a white room, and even that might be because this room was white. The only thing he remembered, and this was only a hint, was that he was trying to help Angie because she was in danger.

In danger from what?

He'd rescued people in Deep Dive before. If a player was super thin, meaning if they saw the world's thinness, they could get stuck in their own brains and start to fall apart. Maybe Angie was in danger of falling apart and he was trying to help her.

But that wasn't possible because he was in here without a RIG and she was out there.

A bang on the bars startled him. He spun to see Claude the guard outside his room.

"Ten minutes to yard time, Terminator," Claude said. "You okay in here?"

Claude called him Terminator because of how he'd killed Snake-man. They said he was from the future.

They'd moved him to this hall where he was all alone. Here, all the guards were his friends because they didn't like Snake-man, and besides, he helped them pick out winners in boxing shows. They bet money and they usually won because he could watch the players before they entered the game and calculate probabilities based on how they acted. Just like he had with Snake-man.

"Hi, Claude! Yup, I'm good."

"You need anything?"

Jamie thought about that. "Do you have Froot Loops?"

"Well, I don't know. But if we do, I'll make sure you get some."

"Okay. Have you seen Angie?"

"Angie? You mean Angie Channing?"

"Angie Channing."

Claude looked concerned. "You haven't heard?"

Heard what? "I don't think so."

"Her husband, Darey Channing, was found dead this morning. He was your attorney, right?"

"Yup. So he's done playing."

Claude squinted. "Done playing? You mean dead."

"Dead."

"Then I guess he's done playing."

"That's too bad. I like my attorney."

Maybe that's why he was trying to help Angie. Maybe when Darey died, her mind broke and she needed help getting back.

"Is everything just a game to you, Terminator?" Claude tapped his head. "Up there the whole world is just one big game?"

"Yup."

"Well, maybe you could help a couple of us play a game of football tomorrow. You know . . . pick out the winners before the game."

"I don't know football."

"Not to worry. You're going to love it."

"Okay."

FOR THE THIRD time Randy read the copy of Clair's letter that Angie had left with Susan, curious as to why Darey hadn't submitted it into evidence as soon as it surfaced.

Angie was right about the key drive. It was likely the one piece of evidence that would blow this case wide open, assuming it still existed and could be found. The letter itself offered no proof of Jamie's guilt or innocence.

Susan sat on the sofa, face blank. Angie watched her with kind eyes, like a sympathetic mother.

She and Darey had been right about one thing: Jamie Hamilton was almost certainly being framed for the Oak Hill murders and someone in law enforcement was almost certainly involved. Nothing else made sense to him any longer.

Which put him in a precarious position. As far as he knew, no one at the station suspected his reservations about Jamie's guilt yet. Their ignorance could play into his hand if he stayed under their radar.

Angie was in far more danger than she realized, especially in her fragile state. Her safety was as important to him as the case itself. There was something unique about her, but there could be no mistaking the fact that she was delusional.

No human in their right mind could possibly carry themselves as Angie did following the death of a loved one. She'd kissed him! It wasn't normal, it wasn't right, it wasn't conceivable, not to him. And what about the fact that she'd created a virtual reality in which she was in love with him? Dear God, it was all madness.

But he couldn't deny that he was drawn to her.

He looked at Susan. "You're saying your husband was here yesterday, in Clair's room, for an hour with the door shut. Your husband didn't say what he was doing? If he was searching for something?"

"No. But he was beside himself. I've never seen him so distraught. I figured he was finally getting around to mourning. He's a beast, you know?"

"He showed no sign of finding anything?"

"He left even more upset than when he got here. You're not suggesting that he knew about the drive, are you?"

"Could he have known?"

"I don't see how. Maybe. He's neck-deep in that dumb company of his. Mistletoe. He's always meeting with all kinds of tech companies. Used to take Clair with him now and then when she begged him. She might have hated him, but she was mesmerized by the tech."

Randy glanced at Angie, who was still fixated on Susan. Depending on perspective, she looked either angelic or unhinged. The latter, he thought, but she still had an angelic glow about her.

Back to Susan: "Can you remember any of the companies he might have visited with her?"

"No. I never paid any attention to that stuff. You think she found the key at some company Steve took her to?"

"Just considering the most obvious possibilities. How else would Clair have stumbled on something like this?"

Susan just looked at him.

"Is there any chance your maid might have noticed something?"

"I asked her, but feel free to ask her yourself. She's out running errands right now."

"Thank you, I may do that. I'm assuming you've searched for the key?"

"Not just in her room, but everywhere."

"Fair enough. Did you notice any recent changes in Clair's behavior?"

Susan glared at him. "If you had a teenage girl of your own, you'd know how dumb that question is. Her behavior changed every week."

That hurt. He knew exactly how temperamental teenagers could be, especially in the throes of puberty. He moved on.

"Do you mind if we look in her room again? I know it's been searched, but if you wouldn't mind."

"Be my guest." She motioned at the hall. "You know where it is."

He stood, expecting Angie to follow suit, but she remained seated.

"Go ahead, Randy. I'll be right here."

He gave her a nod. "I won't be long."

At least four different parties had searched Clair's room since her death. CSI, the killer, Steve, and Susan. By all appearances, all of them had turned the room inside out, scattering clothes, books, posters, bed sheets, and personal items every which way.

Unless CSI had reason to believe a key had been hidden, they wouldn't have used penetrating scanning technology. But a sophisticated tech-head who knew what they were looking for would have.

Assuming the key was still in the room somewhere, and assuming that a thorough sweep hadn't turned it up, Randy believed Clair had placed the key in a shielded sleeve and hidden it in the walls, ceiling or floor. Or in the bed's frame. It could be anywhere—she was a clever girl. The killer would have known that. They might have even wiped the room with a local EMP.

All things considered, a search seemed pointless to him, but he was here.

The baseboards were the most obvious to him, maybe under the carpet along the edges. Randy headed to the farthest corner, knelt on one knee, and ran his hand along the carpet, tugging at the low-pile wool fibers, checking for any signs the carpet had been tampered with.

He'd made one pass down the far wall when his phone buzzed. That made ten calls, at least. Ignoring his partner any longer might raise suspicion in and of itself.

He stood and slipped the phone from his coat pocket, expecting to see Rachel's ID. It wasn't Rachel. It was the chief, Renee Dalton. They were serious.

"What is it, Renee?"

"Where in God's green earth are you?" she snapped.

"I assumed you knew. I left Darey's office and headed out to inform Angie Channing. As you can imagine, she didn't take the news lightly."

"That was five hours ago! Rachel says she's been trying to reach you all morning. Where are you now?"

Easy, Randy. Just another day. No concern here.

"Yeah, I'm sorry about that. Angie suffered a hard crash. Felicia Buckhead, her therapist, and I took her to Convergence."

A beat.

"Convergence? What for?"

"Turns out she was the subject of experimental virtual technology that compromised her mind. Research for her latest book project. They put her through a regression. Sorry, it's been a hectic morning."

She absorbed the information for a moment.

"Where are you now?"

Why was she asking? His GPS transponder would tell them where he was.

"I'm at the Milton house. As you can imagine, Angie Channing's in a tough place. She wanted to talk to Susan. Both are grieving and—"

"I have the DA crawling down my throat and you're holding hands with two distraught women? Olsen's convinced you're conspiring with the defense in the Oak Hill case, and he's demanding to talk to you immediately. So here's what you're doing. You're dropping your charade there and getting your butt back here immediately. Do I make myself clear?"

Olsen? What did the man know? More to the point, *how* could he know? Even if the DA was on the inside and privy to whatever a bug might pick up in Angie's house, Randy had said nothing there that would cast suspicion on him. If anything, his had been the voice of caution.

"You do," he said. "And for the record I never have nor ever will undermine any investigation. I only follow the evidence. You tell Andrew Olsen to review the code of conduct for a detective in the state of Texas before I get to the station. He clearly needs a reminder of what uncovering the truth looks like under the law. I'll be there before three."

"I said now, not in two hours."

"I'll be there as soon as I can."

He hung up. This wasn't good. Not good at all.

An anguished cry from the living room cut through the silence and he jerked to the door, alarmed. Nothing for a moment, then another cry arose, furious now but too distant for him to make out the words.

Randy hurried from the room and ran down the hall toward the living room.

"Get out!" Susan, jabbing her finger at the door, faced a stunned Angie. "Have you lost your mind? How dare you come in here and tell me Clair wasn't real?"

Dear God . . .

"Get out, both of you!" Susan turned on Randy. "Now, before I call the police!"

Randy held out his hand. "Easy. I *am* the police and we're on your side. Don't worry about what Angie—"

"Out!" Susan shrieked. "Now! Get out!"

"Okay, easy. We're leaving." Randy motioned Angie toward the front door.

She looked like a child who'd been slapped for no reason. "Yeah, we're leav—"

"Shut up!" Susan cut her short, face beet red. "Out!"

The claim that his own wife and daughter weren't really who he thought they were would have been his undoing as well, he thought, especially in the weeks following their deaths.

He gave Angie a pointed stare and spoke to Susan in a calm, defusing voice. "We're leaving, Susan. Angie's husband was murdered last night, I'm sure you can understand the pain she's in. We all have our ways of coping. Please forgive hers."

That quieted Susan, who was now studying Angie in confusion. For a moment, Randy thought she might offer a retraction.

"Just get out," she croaked.

CHAPTER
TWENTY-NINE

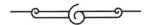

MATTEO STEGER stood in the shadows near a door that led into the master bedroom, rehearsing his situation. He'd parked his blue BMW half a block away and approached the Milton house from the natural greenbelt behind the mansions set into this hill country. Botwilder's intel was good, as expected. All three were here. The detective's old pickup was the only car in the driveway, which meant the maid had gone out in a response to the call from her daughter's school, also as expected. She would be gone for at least half an hour.

Matteo slipped the police-issued side arm from his waist and attached the silencer without thinking through the process. His kit rested by his feet, ready with rope and the other tools he would need.

This was his second visit to the house, so he knew the basic layout well enough. He'd already freed the lock on the door to his left. His approach would take him through the master bedroom and into the living room from the side. He would take the detective first, then Angie, both with head shots. Then the mother, who was going to hang herself.

Matteo put his hand on the doorknob and was about to enter when a cry from inside the house reached through the tall windows overlooking the backyard pool. The mother was upset.

He released the knob, sidled along the wall, and quickly glanced inside before pulling back. The enraged mother was screaming at Angie. The detective stood at the entrance to the hall.

The mother cried out again and this time her words were unmistakable. "Get out."

Matteo considered his options. He couldn't afford for them to get out.

He briskly stepped to the master bedroom door, slipped inside, and strode for the main house on soft soles. Not a sound. The living room drama seemed to have resolved for the moment.

The front door shut with a loud crash.

Matteo pulled up, weapon by his side. They had left. Under no circumstances would he risk confronting or killing them on the driveway. The opportunity was spoiled.

He took a calming breath and waited for the sound of the detective's pickup to fire up and pull away. So be it. He'd deal with the mother now and call in for further instructions.

Matteo found the mother standing on the stone floor next to one of two towering pillars, arms crossed, staring out through the glass sidelight. He took a moment to study her grief and rage.

Curious. What had they told her? He had to know because they were now his prey. But he was also best served by moving quickly before that prey got too far.

"What did they tell you?" he asked, weapon still at his hip.

The mother gasped and jerked around toward him. Her eyes dropped to his gun and she took a step backward, eyes bulging.

"I'm not going to hurt you, Susan," he said calmly. "I just need you to tell me exactly what they told you."

She blinked. "Who . . . Who are you?"

"FBI," he said. "Investigating corruption at the highest levels. No one can know I was here. To that end, I need you to step away from the windows and join me in your bedroom sitting room."

"The bedroom?"

"Yes, there's something I need you to see."

She stood frozen, tears snaking down her cheeks.

"Quickly please. Before they get too far."

"You . . ." She glanced at the front door. "You're investigating them?"

"I'll explain." He shoved the gun in his belt, wagged his head back toward the bedroom, and turned away from her. "This won't take a minute."

She came willingly then and stopped under the large beam at the center of the large bedroom. A good place for a hanging.

He smiled. "Thank you. Now tell me what upset you so much."

She hesitated, then answered with a scratchy voice. "They . . . I'm not sure how to say it."

"Just say it. Speak the words one at a time. It's not hard."

"It doesn't make sense but . . . she said that none of this is real."

When she stopped there, Matteo motioned with his fingers.

"You want me to come over there?" she asked.

"No." He beckoned again. "This can also mean 'continue.' I need you to continue. What isn't real and why?"

"The whole world," she said. "Something about us all being caught in a virtual world and not knowing it. That Clair wasn't really my daughter because she was just a holographic image or something like that. It was nonsense."

"If it was nonsense, why did you react so violently and ruin my plans?"

"What plans?"

"My investigation. Your outburst cost me an opportunity, which upsets me, I won't lie. When someone says something ridiculous, we, as adults, are always best served by not overreacting to it, yes?"

She stared at him.

"So why did you react like a child?"

"I . . ."

"Never mind. What else did they want?"

"They came to look for the drive in Clair's bedroom."

So they knew about the key. It was why the detective had to go. Question was, how did they know?

"Do you believe there's a key?"

"Well . . . Clair wrote . . ." she stopped, clearly not wanting to break confidence.

"We know about that. Can you show me?"

The mother slipped a piece of paper from a pocket over her chest and held it out. "No one's supposed to know."

Matteo took what appeared to be a handwritten letter. This was the first he knew such a piece of evidence existed. Botwilder's concern made more sense now. And this was only a copy, which meant someone still had the original—likely Angie or the detective.

He scanned the letter and shoved it into his front pocket.

"Thank you," he said. "I would be upset to learn that I was only a character in a virtual reality as well." He found himself amused by the thought. "But you have to offer Angie some grace, my dear. She's had a long, hard life and she's just lost her husband. I'm going to tell you what's really happening, but you have to keep it to yourself. Can you do that?"

She gave him a nod.

"Angie isn't a normal woman. She's touched, just like Jamie is touched. They're called 'unveiled children.' The unveiled are subject to wild swings of fancy and exotic hallucinations that distort reality. They think things like what Angie told you. It's not their fault, they just don't know. Do you follow?"

Again she nodded.

"We've been watching both Angie and Jamie for a long time, monitoring every move they make in the darknet and in the virtual worlds they enter. Understanding how their minds work will one day make possible fully organic mechanisms for entering virtual worlds. It's critical that the right authorities are in control of that emerging technology. In the wrong hands, it could destroy society as we know it. Your daughter stumbled into highly sensitive information embedded on an encrypted key. We believe that's what got her killed."

The mother's lips were trembling. He felt a pang of pity for her. It was good to speak the truth, but there was no need to inform her that he was the one who'd killed her daughter.

"Angie's mind recently suffered a critical break while in an experimental protocol. An attempt to heal that break earlier today made it worse. She's suffering from severe dissociative delusions, which have become dangerous to her and those around her."

"Why are you telling me this?" Susan asked, now stricken with fear. She wasn't too far gone to realize that she had no business knowing any of it.

"I just thought you should know the truth about your daughter. It's healing to have closure before you die."

He could see her mind spinning behind wide eyes.

"Thank you," she whispered with no conviction whatsoever.

"Of course. Now wait here for just a moment. Don't move."

Matteo stepped to the door leading out to the balcony, retrieved his kit, dropped it on the bed, and withdrew the quarter-inch rope with its neatly fashioned loop on one end. He tossed it to her feet and lifted his gun.

"Place the loop over your head."

It took the mother only two seconds to comprehend his intentions. She whirled to the door and had taken three steps before Matteo caught her by the neck from behind and choked her out.

Three minutes later her body hung from the beam, unmoving. She was finally at peace.

Satisfied, he withdrew his phone and made the call.

Botwilder answered immediately. "They're on the move. What happened?"

"The detective and Angie left before I could stop them. The mother hanged herself."

The connection hissed.

"Where are they now?" Matteo asked.

"Headed northwest toward Lake Travis. He's defying a direct order to return to the station. We don't want to involve law enforcement unless we have to. The trace will be patched into your GPS. Please hurry."

"You should know that there's a letter from Clair that discloses her discovery of the encrypted key drive. I have the mother's copy. I do not have the original."

Botwilder's hesitation said she hadn't known about the letter.

"Hurry," she said.

"And the wipe?"

"No time. You already did it once. Just go."

CHAPTER
THIRTY

ANGIE FELT disoriented, as if she'd woken from a foggy dream and couldn't place herself in the waking world. The image of Susan's outraged face, bony finger stabbing at the door as she screamed for her to get out, had snapped her out of a reality that was certain. Now she saw it for what it was. Insanity.

Her confusion was no longer about reality. It was about how she could have so fully accepted something that was so clearly false. If her mind really was that fragile, how would she ever know if she was sane?

Stay sane, Jamie had said. But how could she know if she was sane? It was maddening!

Randy hadn't spoken since they left the house. She had no clue where they were going and honestly didn't care.

"I thought we agreed," Randy finally said.

She glanced at him, feeling foolish. She wasn't sure what he was talking about.

"Susan was off-limits."

Right. That. And she felt even more foolish. "She was in so much pain. I just . . . I just wanted to help her. I'm sorry."

"Even if you are right, which you're not, people need their pain, Angie.

They don't want you to take if from them until they feel they've paid the price they think they deserve to pay."

"Yeah." She wasn't properly processing his explanation, but she didn't want or need clarification. She only wanted out of this. Darey was dead. She might as well be too.

He let out a long breath. "It's okay. Forget it. We have bigger problems right now."

"Yeah."

He looked over at her. "You okay?"

"No."

They drove in silence for another mile or so. She noted they were on Highway 71, headed northwest.

"Where are we going?"

"To the lake. I just need time to think. The chief ordered me back to base. The district attorney is accusing me of working with the defense to undermine the state's case. If I tell them what I know, things could get ugly, and I'm not prepared for that right now. So I have to think. Water helps me do that."

"What defense? Darey's dead." She stared forward, making no attempt to stop the fresh tears slipping down her cheeks. This was her fault. All of it.

"I'm sorry," he said.

"I'm the one who's sorry," she said in a voice far too pathetic for her liking. But she could muster no courage.

"Don't be. If not for you, we wouldn't know what we know about this case. Whoever's at the bottom of it has much more in mind than killing two innocent teenagers. When all is said and done, the country may owe you far more than it can ever pay."

That brightened her spirits a little. And maybe he was right.

"If I'm a mad genius, I don't want to be."

"Well maybe you are. And maybe it's the price you pay for the good that will come of this."

"You think?"

He looked at her, wearing a gentle smile. "I do. I really do. What happened, happened. Now we get to figure out what happens next. Time's running out for Jamie, and he's at the heart of this. So I need you to do something for me."

The dread she felt in her gut softened enough for her to redirect her energy to Jamie's predicament. "What?"

"To the extent that you can, forget you ever thought this is a virtual world. Right now, I need your brilliance focused on what's happening here, not in a white room. Because I think you may be more connected to Jamie's case than even you know."

She faced him. "How so?"

"I don't know. Something Jake Barnes told me. The reverence in his tone when he spoke about you. As if you're special, not because you wrote a book he promoted, but because of who you are. Who you've always been."

Why did that feel true to her? She and Jamie, connected, sure, but how? Or maybe Randy was just saying that to keep her on the narrow road.

His phone buzzed and he glanced at the dash screen. Rachel, his partner. Not one for earpieces, he motioned for Angie's silence and opened the connection over the car's speakers.

"Sorry, Rachel. It's been a busy day."

"Where are you?" she demanded, voice strained.

"Running an errand. Headed in soon. What's up?"

"What's up? The whole freaking world is up! Chief Dalton is raging. I'm assuming you heard about Susan Milton."

Randy exchanged a look with Angie.

"What about Susan Milton?"

"Her maid returned home to find her dead. You're not watching the police bulletins?"

"Susan Milton was *murdered*?"

"Don't know. She was hanging from a rope in her bedroom, apparent suicide. The chief says you're the last person to see her alive." A beat. "You need to get back here, Randy. Now."

Angie stared at him, sickened. Randy must have noticed because he calmly reached over and gave her hand a squeeze, nodding as if to say, *It's okay, I got this.*

"I'm sorry, but I can't do that, Rachel. Not yet. I can't go into detail, but I need you to cover for me. Just a few hours."

"You're not listening! We're beyond that!" Then, "Cover how? There is no cover!"

"I don't know. Tell them I received a phone call from someone who claims to have information related to Susan's suicide. It's time sensitive and I'm on my way to check it out. As soon I have some answers I'll be in, but I'm not going to drop my duties as an investigator to smooth the DA's ruffled feathers. Tell them that."

"The DA? What does Andrew Olsen have to do with this?"

"Figure of speech. I'm only doing what the state hired me to do. Gotta go."

He disconnected. Then swore.

"I did that," Angie rasped. "Me and my insanity."

"Not for a second." He braked hard and took a sharp right on Bee Creek Road. "They were the ones who got to her. It wasn't you. Anger doesn't push people into suicide, quite the opposite. She was ready to kill, not be killed. It was no suicide." He glanced at his phone. "We're being tracked."

"How?"

"Phones. We need to ditch them."

Angie's head spun. Something she'd said at her house or at Convergence had been overheard or reported.

"The encrypted key," she said. "They've discovered that we know about the key Clair found."

"That and more, I would guess."

Angie stared out the windshield, stunned. "They're killing anyone who stands in the way. Darey . . . Now Susan. It's horrible!"

"Susan wasn't the only target," he said. "They just missed us. Like I said, we have to get rid of these phones."

"Who?" she demanded. "Who's *they*?"

He veered onto Highlands Boulevard, pushing the truck to its limit. "That's what we're going to find out, and until then we can't trust anyone at the department. Friend of mine has a cabin near Marble Falls I use sometimes to get away. We ditch these phones here and then cut back west. With any luck, we get to some cover before the drones get involved. There are weapons there. Food. We go from there."

This was the Randy feared by those on the wrong side of the law. The one who'd been celebrated by the very people who now pursued him. A pit bull who, once latched on, wouldn't let go.

Well, he was latched on now. And she was with him.

"ACCEPT," MATTEO said. The BMW's speakers filled with Botwilder's voice.

"They ditched the phones." Botwilder's voice was tight. "Trace is useless."

He'd guessed as much—the signal had ended on a backroad just ahead and hadn't moved in five minutes.

"No vehicle trace?"

"GPS is disabled but we'll have a location in the next thirty minutes. We're pulling all GPS data from his movements over the last five years and will feed it through our algorithms."

"Understood."

"In the meantime, head northwest, the direction he was headed before—"

"Yes, yes, Katrina. Just tell me if I'm alone on this."

She wanted to snap at him, of course she did. And that was nice, he thought. He might do what she paid him to do, but that didn't mean he had to like her or make her life comfortable. One day she would pay for all her sins. Wouldn't they all?

"For the time being. An APB will be issued in the next half hour. The police—"

"No police," he said. "No drones if you want me to go in. I'm not interested in playing on their turf."

"Don't interrupt me! You have an hour. I don't want this to go public any more than you but we can't afford to lose them. One hour and the search will go public. Head northwest and wait for a target. And please remember who you work for."

Then she was gone.

Maybe one day he would meet Katrina Botwilder. And maybe on that day he would teach her that, in the end, he worked only for himself.

THE CABIN WEST of Marble Falls was owned by a Special-Forces-turned-SWAT friend of Randy's named Joseph Conrad. After following a gravel road that wound through thick trees and underbrush, they'd come to the gate, which Randy opened before uncovering a small keypad in the grass and punching in a string of numbers. Disarming perimeter alarms, he said. Conrad was a survivalist, and this was his safe place.

Safe from drones because of the heavy tree coverage. Safe from overhead heat sensors because of its lined roof. Safe from intruders, due to the security system. Safe from digital tracing, thanks to complete isolation from the grid. The only connection to the outside world was via an Iranian satellite Conrad had hacked.

Fifty yards away over a small knoll, hidden from the cabin, was an old shed among the trees. Never used, Randy said, but there just in case. Angie didn't press for specifics. The details of the main house were striking enough.

The main floor consisted of what she would expect to see in any rustic cabin with a few upgrades under the hood: A small kitchen with a fuel-cell refrigerator. An old wood-burning stove retrofitted with a recycler that stripped the smoke of the hydrocarbons that gave it an ashen color. A round wood table with four chairs. The living room had a couch, one leather chair, a round woven brown rug, and two lamps.

One bedroom with a queen bed, one bathroom, a loft with another bed. By all appearances, that was it.

They accessed the real treasure in Joseph Conrad's safe place through a hidden door in the bedroom closet. Steps led down to the bunker, as Randy called it. In that bunker was enough food and water to keep four people healthy for six months and enough firepower to fight a small war: old-school weapons long ago banned, including M-16s, three sniper rifles, a dozen handguns, pressure mines, and other explosives.

Randy gave her the quick tour, snapping off facts and figures so familiar to him that Angie wondered if the cabin was actually his. But no, he insisted. He just liked old-school stuff. Like his truck.

The electronics were anything but old-school. 10G phones, rerouters, electronic jamming packs, even false digital IDs linked to accounts with balances. The solar-charged batteries here could run everything but the stove indefinitely, assuming they had sun, which in these years of draught wasn't a concern.

Randy slid behind a small desk and flipped open a pad that came to life with the touch of the screen. "Anyone approaching can get through the gate no problem," he said as she stood over his shoulder, "but motion detectors fifty feet inside the perimeter will sound an alarm in the cabin if triggered by anything containing metal, like a weapon or a car. Heck, even keys or a belt will set it off. Not likely anyone in these parts would be walking around naked. Not foolproof, but pretty darn near."

"Darn?"

He grinned. "Darn." And that was the last of his humor. He worked and spoke quickly, all business, arming the security with a tap on a red square.

"There's a pad like this by the front door—perimeter can be activated and deactivated there as well."

With another tap, a feed popped to life and he scanned the media. "No mention of Susan. That's good. The governor is leading all polls in the presidential race by double-digit margins. Maybe not so good."

"And us?"

"Nothing in the public feeds." He brought up a secure police portal and entered a password. "They'll know I was in here, but the signal will come from Iran or somewhere, not . . ." He stopped.

"What?"

"An APB. We're officially on the run."

Angie stared at the bulletin on the screen. "So now we're not only dealing with whoever hanged Susan but the whole state of Texas."

He leaned back in the chair. "Just got real. We don't have much time."

"But we're safe here, right?"

"Maybe, maybe not. They have data. Conrad never comes near this place with a phone, but I have. If they're on their game, they'll run the history from my GPS."

"I have contacts in the darknet who can make life—"

"No chance," he said, rising. "The darknet's no more safe than public feeds, not when you're dealing with the NSA. Those days are long gone. We have to assume the worst."

He cracked his knuckles and paced, lost in thought. His gentle face and soft eyes hid the hard life he'd lived as a detective. Pacing now, he carried himself like an athlete. Strange how she yielded to him in this environment— she'd never yielded to men. But not so strange considering her fractured state of mind. She wanted someone to trust, and Randy was that person.

It struck her that she hadn't experienced a whiteout since coming out of the Red Protocol regression. That was good.

"APB means drones. Drones will find my truck in no time. We have to stay away from any electronics, any transactions of any kind, all cameras. We need intel. Not the kind of intel available on feeds or the darknet. We need live intel."

She thought about that. *I'm intel*, she thought. *This is about me as much as Jamie.*

Randy strode to a tall shelf that held several empty backpacks. Snatched one up and tossed it to her. "Fill that up with food. Anything that doesn't require fire."

He grabbed another and began shoving survival gear into it—batteries, lights, space blankets, other electronics.

Angie hurried to the food pantry and picked through cans of meat and fruit. "What exactly did Barnes say about me?"

"I'm not sure. Something about how the unveiled one would show the way."

She emerged from the pantry and lowered the backpack. "He said that? Unveiled one?"

"Something like that, yeah. Why?"

"That's what my mother called me! I mean when I was reliving scenes from my life in the regression. I was in France as a young girl and she asked me if I was seeing. She called me her unveiled one and said that one day I would understand."

He was examining a rifle, not as captivated by the coincidence as she was. He gave her a nod. "Right."

"So what if now is that day? What if I'm like Jamie in that I can see easier than most? And I saw something else in there. I was an infant in a room with other infants. My mother picked me up, but she wasn't my mother. What if I . . ."

A wall of confusion hit her hard, and she couldn't utter the words that were whispering through her mind, as if saying them would make them more real.

Randy stopped what he was doing and faced her. "What if your mother wasn't your birth mother," he finished for her. "You think you were an orphan?"

She didn't understand why that possibility affected her so much. Her father and mother had died in a boating accident ten years ago. Even if she had been an orphan, they were and always would be her parents. What difference did it make who gave birth to her?

But it did make a difference.

"Yes," she said.

"You're suggesting that both Jamie and you were part of a program for so-called unveiled children able to engage perception in a unique way."

"Who said anything about perception?"

"Jake Barnes," he said. "That's what the Red Protocol is all about. Changing perception."

"He's right. And in the white room, the truth is beyond the masks that hide it. I'm the one who—"

"Forget it. In fact, forget I said anything about intel right now." He resumed his packing, moving deliberately. "Right now, we need to survive. We can't do anything if we're dead. Even if you are right, there's no way we're getting back into Convergence. For all we know, Jake Barnes is at the center of all this. Absolutely not."

"You think so? Jake Barnes? What does he stand to gain?"

"I'm not saying he's involved, but I am saying we can't afford to trust anyone, and I do mean anyone. First we survive, then we get intel. The only way we survive is . . ."

A sharp beeping cut him off, and he jerked his head to the monitor. A red light was flashing on the wall behind the desk.

Randy swore.

MATTEO APPROACHED on foot along the tree line ten feet from the gravel road, moving quickly. The hill country was peppered with survivalists who disdained the government and sought to stake out their independence from the system. It was a sentiment that he appreciated. Soon, he too would vanish from the all-seeing eyes of the system.

In the meantime, it was his business to work in that system, and it benefitted him to understand the thoughts of those who tried to escape it.

He assumed the cabin that Randy George had visited eleven times in the last three years was one such escape, built by someone who knew how to remain hidden and safe. It likely had a perimeter security system, which he'd already tripped.

Thus, the grenade launcher slung around his shoulder.

On occasion, surgical precision didn't serve the goals at hand. This was one of those times. Raw power would ensure a quick end. Any collateral damage was inconsequential considering the stakes.

There was no direct evidence that Randy George was here, naturally. The algorithms put that probability at 89 percent, based on the terabytes of data that had been collected from his life profile—every purchase, every movement, every online search, everything tied into a world that was run by ones and zeros.

He rounded a bend, still moving quickly, bent over now. There, roughly seventy paces ahead, nestled among tall trees, stood a cabin. One look at its roof and he knew he was right—this was a structure built to hide its heat signature from drones.

The old Ford pickup truck was parked twenty feet from the cabin. They were here.

Matteo dropped to one knee, shouldered the launcher, aimed it at the right window, and squeezed the trigger. The three-inch shell left the barrel with a soft roar, streaked for the cabin, crashed through the window, and detonated as designed.

A ball of fire swallowed the cabin. No living thing could have survived the blast. But any cabin with a thermal insulating roof would also have a bunker. They would be there, underground.

Matteo shrugged out of the pack on his back, withdrew a second shell, and dropped it into the receiver. This projectile was designed to home in on the specific heat signature of the first shell, bury itself deep, and detonate below ground.

He lifted the launcher and fired the second shell. It vanished into the inferno. Three seconds later a muffled explosion punctuated the roar of the blaze. The ground shook as what remained of the cabin rose off its footings before collapsing into the depression created by that second detonation.

Matteo stood, satisfied. The old truck had escaped the attack, but this was no longer of consequence. The only remaining task was to find the escape route. A seasoned survivalist always had one.

To this end, Matteo pulled a small surveillance drone out of his pack, spun up the four blades with a flip of a switch, and released it into the air. The drone was preprogrammed to rise above the trees and conduct a search for any signs of life as it flew in concentric circles out to a distance of five hundred yards.

"Fly high, my darling," he muttered.

"STAY LOW!" Randy whispered. "Run!"

Within twenty seconds of the alarm's first beep, they were out of the cabin and in a narrow tunnel. It led out the back of the bunker and spilled into a deep draw twenty yards beyond the tree line.

Randy led, bent over, carrying the sniper rifle and the backpack filled with supplies and weapons. Angie ran behind, lugging the food. Pushed by adrenaline, she hardly noticed its weight.

The first detonation came when they were less than thirty yards from the cabin. Angie spun back to see a ball of fire fill the sky.

"Don't stop!" Randy snapped. They were going for the shed, she knew that much. He hadn't explained why, but her imagination was already seeing them in a tiny shack, firing weapons out of windows at a SWAT team swarming the place.

Angie pushed the thought away and ran. Randy knew what he was doing. He had to.

A second explosion shook the ground hard enough to knock her to one knee. Randy's hands were already pulling her to her feet. Whatever that was, nothing was left back there. Not a scrap. But they were free.

"We're almost there!" Randy held her arm in a vise grip and dragged her forward.

"I'm good," she panted, pulling free. "I'm good."

He veered up a small embankment, crouched low. "This way." They topped a barren knoll and had just turned north to head back into the trees when Randy pulled up, listening.

"What?" she whispered, following his eyes to the sky.

"A drone."

She heard the high-pitched whine then.

"Get to the trees!" He motioned for her to go, so she went. Ten paces and she was into the trees, spinning back.

Randy had dropped his pack and shouldered the rifle, which he'd trained on the sky. Breathing heavily, Angie dropped to her knees and studied the sky. She couldn't see a thing. But if they had one drone, they probably had more. They would hear the rifle and spread out to trap them in the shack.

The rifle bucked. Its report echoed through the trees. A small detonation farther south lit the afternoon sky. Okay, so one down. He was a good shot; she would give him that. But there would be more.

Randy was already by her side, rushing past. "Hurry!"

The shack was tiny, maybe ten feet by fifteen feet, with a single door, no windows.

"What good—"

Randy snatched a finger to his lips and motioned at the door. *Inside.*

Inside was nothing. Some shelves and a floor covered by straw. Several hay bales covered in chicken poop. A coop?

"Stand by those hay bales," he ordered. "Off the straw."

"What are we doing?"

"No time, just do it."

So she did, watching anxiously as he stepped to the far wall and pulled on a rope. The floor budged. Then lifted off the foundation as he kept cranking.

She took another step back and watched the floor rise, revealing a Jeep parked on sloping ground. The shack was a garage of sorts. Hope surged. But what good would a vehicle do in the trees?

Her question was answered when Randy unlatched the front wall and let it fall to the ground outside the shack. An old overgrown fire road led from the shack into the valley.

Randy dropped into the Jeep through the open roof, fired the engine—which caught after several long seconds—shoved the transmission into drive, and roared up the steep slope.

"Bags in, hurry!" He went for the rifle, which he'd leaned on the shed's outer wall.

She threw the backpacks into the back seat and climbed in.

Randy slid behind the wheel, dug into his pocket, and tossed a phone through the window. "Just a little gift," he said.

And then they were moving, bouncing and jerking but fast, like a rabbit freed from a snare.

CHAPTER
THIRTY-ONE

SEVEN HOURS and nothing. No bodies in the cabin or in the woods. Vanishing wasn't as easy as it had been even a decade earlier and yet, at least for the time being, the celebrated lawman had done just that. And he'd taken the unveiled one with him, beyond the reach of both those he worked for and the law itself.

Matteo sat in the BMW, parked on a hill overlooking Lake Travis, south of Marble Falls. Dark was fast approaching. The authorities had joined the hunt within the first hour, as Botwilder said, but they'd turned up nothing. Without a digital trace, they were limited to visual surveillance of the region.

And yet, nothing.

Matteo had hidden a small tracker on the man's old Ford pickup truck in case he or the woman returned for it. Then he retreated from the scene and set himself up here on the hill, waiting for contact.

His employers had taken care of the cabin blaze without involving authorities. An APB was in full force. Under the watchful gaze of heat-sensing drones, every living creature larger than a child was now being tracked. Every square inch of greater Austin was now being searched.

His prey could remain hidden in these hills only for so long.

He held the new flip phone he'd found in the grass beside the old shack, turning it over between his thumb and fingers. It was an old burner phone. Unused and unlocked. Had the phone been lost or had its placement been intentional? He was leaning toward lost because of its haphazard location in the grass. If the man had wanted to guarantee he found the device, he would have put it in a more conspicuous location.

But being a master of the game, Randy George might have known his adversary was thorough and would eventually find it. If so, he'd left it for the sake of eventual contact. The possibility intrigued Matteo, because he had no interest in the law finding them before he did. If his prey were taken into custody by some harebrained officer, eliminating them would be much more difficult, and elimination was now paramount. Even a few words from Randy or Angie to the media could cause disaster.

To this end, Matteo would keep the phone charged and on, hoping the lawman would reach out to him. Why would the man do so? To negotiate. Or to deceive him. Or to fish for information. It hardly mattered. In any case, Matteo, not the law, had to find his prey first.

He carefully set the phone on his dash and stared out at the glassy lake.

"There is nowhere to hide, Randy George," he muttered. "Your days are coming to an end."

THE NIGHT was warm, even in the cave. Better than trying to stay warm in the cold months, Randy thought. It was a small gift, and they needed every break offered them.

The escape route from the cabin had crossed sparsely treed terrain before intersecting a gravel road and joining a service road that led to the valley they were now in. They'd moved quickly, knowing that state drones would cover the surrounding hills within the hour, using both cameras and heat sensors to track all movement.

Ignoring Angie's questions about his plans, because he didn't have any, he'd stashed the Jeep in a thicket and covered its frame with leafy branches and its engine with a space blanket that would block its heat signature until it cooled.

Randy had then led Angie a hundred yards up the hill to the entrance of a small cave covered with overgrowth. From there they could see where the Jeep was hidden.

Conrad had done his homework in laying out the escape route. Tracking them on foot to the cave would be difficult. They were safe here. For now.

Randy knelt on one knee at the entrance, peering out at the starry night. The gentle whine of a drone came and went, headed south. They'd heard at least a dozen passes and with each failed attempt, Randy breathed a little more easily. Conrad's getaway plan had worked. Unfortunately, his cabin was now gone. If they survived, Randy would make sure the department repaid the cost and more.

He replaced the branches that blocked the cave's entrance and, head bent to avoid hitting the low stone ceiling, retreated to where Angie was seated beside an LED lamp. No fire, but at least they had light.

They'd pulled out the contents of the bags and made a quick inventory of the supplies: Three more space blankets, which might come in handy to mask their body heat outside the cave. Two battery-powered lanterns, one of which was hardly more than a flashlight. A hunting knife. Two wafer batteries that were probably drained. Two burner phones like the one he'd left at the shack. A compass. A signal scrambler, which might be useful. A ball of twine. Four flasks of water. Four cans of peaches. Four tins of Spam. Two sardine cans. Three meals ready to eat, better known in the military as MREs.

That and the weapons, which were still in the second backpack, except for the sniper rifle leaning against the cave wall near the entrance.

He settled down opposite Angie, who sat with legs crossed, watching him. "Why only three?" he asked.

She gave him a blank look.

He nodded at the small store of food. "The MREs. Why only three? I would think they have much more value than heavy cans of peaches."

"Seriously? That's all you can think about?"

"Not at all," Randy said. "I have more thoughts than I can begin to express. Beginning with the stray thought that's asking me what in the world I'm doing in a cave, running from the law, which is myself."

"I can offer you some clarity on that thought. You're not running from the law, because you're on the right side and Andrew Olsen is on the wrong side."

He preferred this spirited Angie over the one who was lost in confusion. They'd discussed his suspicions that Andrew Olsen played a role in this trouble—why else would he fly off the hook and demand to haul Randy in? And if the DA was complicit in framing Jamie, others in the government likely were involved as well.

"Well, that clears that up," he said. And he meant it.

"And?" she pressed. "What other thoughts are crowding your mind, because I'd really like to know how you think we're going to get out of this mess. I don't like being in the dark. And I don't mean the cave."

"I'm not one to throw ideas at the wall to see what sticks. Still thinking."

She took a deep breath and settled.

"Fair enough. But it's been what? Eight, nine hours? Surely you have some clue by now. Or are we really that screwed?"

"Maybe."

"Just say it, for goodness' sakes! I realize you've shut yourself off to cope with your own tragedies, but when lives are at stake, like mine, sharing's appropriate, wouldn't you say?"

Her words cut deep. But she was right, he thought. Since Andrea's and Stacy's deaths three years earlier, he'd remained hidden in his own cave, sorting through his pain.

Her face softened as she studied him. "Sorry. That was uncalled for."

"It's okay. And you're right, I don't let anyone in. It's easier that way."

She nodded. "I can understand that. But I think maybe you're wrong. It might do you some good to come clean. Either way, I'm not asking you to bleed on the ground for me. Just tell me what you're thinking."

"Andrea used to say that when I focused on a challenging case, I vanished. Nothing mattered but solving that case." He shrugged. "Not an excuse, just sharing."

"Good. See, that's not so hard." Her voice was gentle. Teasing.

He gave her a thin smile. "True enough. So . . . As I see it, we're going to be here for a while. Long enough for them to think we've slipped through their net—they know how familiar I am with all the holes in their surveillance capabilities. Unfortunately those holes are admittedly few."

"How long?"

"Best case, only two days. That'll give us—"

"Two days? In here?"

"We only have enough water for two days, but by then the heat will have moved off these hills and they'll focus more of their resources on borders, flights, longer-range possibilities. Whoever framed Jamie and is going to such lengths to cover it up won't stop until they put an end to any threat."

"Sounds grim."

"It's the rogue element that concerns me," he said. "If I were part of a conspiracy, I would limit my exposure by vastly reducing the number of people involved. My guess is that whoever took out the cabin was working alone, following orders. The drone wasn't government issue."

"Probably the same assassin who killed Clair and Timothy," she said. "And . . ."

Darcy, he thought but didn't say.

"And Susan," he finished for her. "They wouldn't want the state to take us in. They need us dead so we can't talk."

The lamp lit pools of tears in her eyes. He could only imagine the anguish she was in. Dealing with a fractured mind and the loss of a spouse at the same time would break most people. She seemed to have an extraordinary capacity to compartmentalize, ignoring what didn't serve the task at hand. Maybe that was part of what made her mind so special. Unveiled. Maybe she could see beyond a situation by limiting her attachment to the situation itself, unlike most humans.

"Sorry to put it so bluntly, but you wanted to know my thoughts, unfiltered."

"No, that's good." She looked away, swallowing. "So two days. And in the meantime, Jamie's flapping in the wind. In two days he might be on death row."

"Not a chance."

"I'm just saying."

She was absently picking at her lower lip but dropped her hand and looked at him. "We should call the media. You, I mean. They'll listen to you! Tell them everything, that'll slow things down."

He shook his head. "That'll speed things up. The state will spin it and turn us both into monsters. Fact is, we have no evidence. The only way to deal with this is to cut off the head."

"And the head is the one who stands to gain the most by Jamie's conviction," she said. "The governor? Judith Patterson?"

"She stands to gain, true, but if she's involved, she's a pawn. Has to be. This has to be about more than just getting one person elected to office."

They sat in silence for a few long seconds.

"We need intel," he finally said. "The one person who can give us that intel is the party who's hunting us. We have to make contact, which is why I dropped the burner on the ground next to the shack. With any luck, he found it."

"Call him?"

"Not sure yet."

She rose to her feet and paced. Being shorter than Randy, she didn't have to stoop under the cave's low ceiling. "You thought to leave a phone, huh? So you were already thinking ahead. Smart. Real smart." Then, "Okay, that's good. It's a start, anyway. And don't worry, I won't ask how you think you can get intel from a ghost who seems to be able to kill anyone at any time with impunity."

He left the statement alone.

She walked to the cave entrance, pulled the brush aside, and looked out at the night sky.

"I do have some ideas," he said. "We have to lure him in."

"Naturally," she said, pushing the branches back into place. "And I have an idea as well." She returned, picked up one of the space blankets, flapped it open, and laid down on it, facing the ceiling, arms crossed over her belly.

"Which is?" he asked.

"The Red Protocol," she said.

"You just can't let go, can you?"

She shrugged. "I'm trying."

"The Red Protocol's out of the question. For starters, we'd never make it to Convergence. Even if we managed, Barnes would never agree. Based on my limited understanding, going in again might kill you. Or worse, leave you in a vegetative state. You'd be no fun that way."

She arched her brow. "And what do you care if I'm any fun?"

"I don't," he said quickly. Then, realizing how insensitive that sounded, "I mean I do, but not really. Just a figure of speech."

Her eyes lingered on him for a few seconds before returning to the ceiling. She lifted her hands and covered her face. Her body shook with a silent sob. Tears trailed past her temples.

Randy wondered if it was something he'd said. Surely not his comment about her not being fun. Of course not, she was just in deep suffering. And he was powerless to help her.

But that wasn't true. He could comfort her; however feeble any attempt might be.

Randy rose, stepped to her side, and settled on the ground. He put a hand on her shoulder, feeling awkward but not knowing what else he could do.

"I'm sorry," he said.

She blew out some air, gathering herself. "Do you still miss them?"

Andrea and Stacy. "I can hardly stand the thought of living without them," he said.

Her eyes were closed and she was struggling not to cry. "Me too," she managed in a ragged whisper. "I wish I'd been right."

"About what?" he asked softly.

"About this world not being real."

In that moment, Randy understood on a deeper level how her delusion could be such a balm. Instead, Angie was in the difficult position of accepting a reality in which the man she'd clung to for identity and security was now dead.

"I hate it," she said.

And then she rolled over, hugged his folded leg as if it were her last lifeline, and sobbed openly.

CHAPTER
THIRTY-TWO

ANGIE LAID on her back, staring up at the stars, which looked much brighter out here in the country than when viewed from the city. Amazing how even thirty miles could make such a difference. She knew that many of the pinpricks in the black void were actually galaxies containing hundreds of millions of stars. What was happening in them? What did Earth mean to such a distant place? From those galaxies' perspectives, the year-in, year-out endlessly repeating drama of the human race on a distant planet was totally insignificant, if known at all. From that vantage, Earth didn't even exist.

These thoughts reflected how she was feeling about the drama that had swallowed her life back in Austin. Sorrow over Darey's death had deepened in the cave. She'd shed more tears in the last two days than she had in the last two years.

But even Darey's death had become oddly distant to her out here. She felt numb.

Randy laid on his back beside her, staring up at the same stars, mind working as it always did. Figuring, solving, rethinking the same thoughts that had consumed him for only God knew how long. *Can I, should I, will I? No, yes, no, yes*—an endless cycle that never really went anywhere before the body finally gave up in death.

They were side by side on a large slab of stone, bodies pressed close so, if spotted, they would appear as one nondescript form too large to be human. But they wouldn't be seen from above—the earth-toned space blankets draped over them blocked their body heat, and the rock they laid on was still warm from the day's sun. Knowing the drones' limitations, Randy finally agreed to her need to come out of the cave for some clean air. After two days and nights, it had become a prison. Considering the real danger they would face later tonight and tomorrow, it seemed like a good idea to experience some normalcy, if only for an hour or two.

Randy spoke in a gentle tone. "I just want to point out that there's no guarantee this will work. The more I think about it—"

"Then stop thinking for a minute and take in the sky," she said. "I already know how dangerous it'll be. Right now, I just want to be here."

His chest rose and fell beside her. What if Randy were the only person left on Earth? How would she view him? Would they love each other? Yes. Of course they would. And did anyone else exist right now? No. For all she knew, she would be dead tomorrow.

"It's just the stars and us right now, Randy. Nothing else matters. None of it's even real for us unless we make it real. So let's just be here for now."

He seemed to consider this and finally said, "Fair enough."

"No death," she said. "Nothing to miss. Only us lying here on the rock, right now. Everything that's happened was only a bad dream. This is us."

She wasn't sure he could go there, and a part of her suggested that she was going there only because she didn't want to face the truth, but oddly this didn't concern her. She found the process of disassociating from the world of drama surprisingly easy.

"Want to hear one of my favorite truisms?" she asked.

"Sure."

"What happened to you couldn't have happened any other way," she said, and waited for him to react.

"Why do you say that?" he finally asked.

"Because it did," she said.

He hesitated. "That's it?"

"Think about it. Acceptance goes a long way."

"It's not that easy for me," he said. "I can't disassociate like you."

"But think of how much peace can be found there."

"We don't all have your gift," he said.

"Well then, maybe it pays to be insane."

She reached over and found his hand under the thin blanket. "So be just a little bit insane with me, Randy. Maybe it'll do us both some good."

They laid in silence for a while and she wondered if her hand on his made him uncomfortable. Maybe he'd frozen up, feeling awkward. But then she felt his fingers tighten ever so slightly on hers and she thought, *He likes it*. Who wouldn't? All it took was letting go.

"I love you, Randy," she said.

When he didn't reply, she offered him more.

"It's not what you think. I just love being here with you right now."

"I love it too," he said.

"Really?"

"Yeah. I mean . . . Yeah, I do. It's been a crazy few days and I feel at ease here with you. Maybe the calm before the storm."

"Maybe," she said.

They laid like that for a long time. Every time she thought about saying something, she quickly decided that saying it would spoil what they had. Maybe he felt the same way. She tilted her head so that her cheek pressed against his shoulder. There was nowhere else. There was no history or future. There was no agenda or drama. Words might make drama.

Finally, he said, "It's late. I need to go."

Slowly, and then like a flood, the danger of what they were about to attempt swallowed her.

"You're sure about this?" she asked.

"No. But I don't see another way."

"It still seems too simple."

"The best plans always seem too simple," he said.

"That's what you said."

He drew a deep breath and let it out. "Tell me again what we're doing."

Angie cleared her throat and released his hand. "We're using three phones on the 8G satellite mesh network. Once the phone numbers are identified, their exact locations can be isolated as long as they're on. You're going to go back to the cabin to lure him into a trap. Right?"

"More or less."

"It's assuming a lot."

"It's assuming I'm thinking the way he thinks, expecting a trap. Once we've given up our location, it's only a matter of time before this hill is swarming, even if we do neutralize him. *Especially* if we neutralize him. His people will be tracking him. As soon as I make the call, this is a one-way ticket."

He wasn't sugarcoating it.

"I'm going now," he said, but he wasn't moving. She didn't want to move either. The world was so serene and hopeful out here. That was about to be shattered.

Randy finally sat up. "Here goes nothing."

RANDY WALKED carefully, headed south to the gravel road, which would lead him to the service road they'd used to escape the cabin. He wore the space blanket like a poncho over his head and under the backpack, blocking most of his heat signature, and he moved under the trees. The drones were still up there somewhere, but, as he'd expected, the coverage wasn't as heavy as it had been even earlier in the day.

Keeping to the trees and moving mostly by memory over unmarked terrain, it took him nearly two hours to find his way back to Joseph Conrad's property, roughly five miles southeast. Moving as silently as possible, he skirted the area, aware that they likely had eyes on the place. But one full circuit of the area satisfied him that there was no human surveillance here.

As hoped, the phone he'd tossed in the grass by the old shack was gone. It had been found. That was good.

The large hole in the ground where the cabin had once stood had been bulldozed. Only Randy's truck remained. The paint on the side facing the cabin was charred but otherwise the truck appeared undamaged and usable. Also good. Very good.

If he were the killer, he'd have hidden a transmitter on the truck, hoping its owner would return to reclaim it. Finding that transmitter, if it existed, was his first objective.

Using a digital tracer he'd taken from the cabin, the task took him no more than a few minutes. The small disk had been placed on the frame under the battery bank. He pried the transmitter off and carefully set in on the ground directly below its former position. Moving it now would only alert whoever was monitoring it.

He rose beside the truck and listened. Nothing but a few crickets. He was alone out here. And if not, he was already spotted.

Moving quickly now, he hurried to the gate and strung a wire low to the ground, ten feet past the entrance. On either side of the road, he placed two directional charges facing the driveway. Once armed and triggered, the explosives would shred anything that passed.

But Randy had removed both detonators back in the cave. Despite the appearance of being fully functioning charges, they were useless.

Retreating to the trees, Randy sat on a log, withdrew the first phone from his pocket, took a deep breath, and turned it on. Then he called the phone he'd left at the shed to be found.

His exact location at the cabin's gate was now accessible to whoever had that phone. As were the full contents and contacts of the phone in his hand, assuming they knew how to break into a phone remotely, which Randy was counting on.

Most critically, they would discover only one number in the contacts of his phone. That number belonged to the third phone, which Angie had back at the cave. It was important that their hunter discovered that number.

There was no turning back.

He wiped at the sweat beading on his forehead and cleared his throat. Two rings. Three. Five. Connection was established on the eighth ring.

"The celebrated detective wakes from the dead," a male voice with a slight Mediterranean accent said. Greek, Randy guessed. If he was right, he was on the phone with the man responsible for more than one murder in the last two weeks.

"Who is this?" Randy asked.

A long beat.

"The one you left the phone for," the voice said.

"Good. I have something for you at the cabin. By now you've traced this call and know I'm here. Meet me here at 7:00 a.m. If you come earlier, I'll know and you'll never see us. If you're late, I'll be gone. Seven a.m. Alone."

"And what exactly do you have for me?"

"Information about the people you work for," he lied. This was the game. "I know about Jamie and Angie. I know how they're special and why. I also know why you can no longer allow them to survive. But more, I know how your own life is in danger. Meet me at seven and you'll understand everything. Not a moment later."

He hung up and lowered his hand, noting the slight tremble in his fingers. Then he walked back to the cabin, unlocked his truck, and set the phone on the seat, leaving it powered up. The Mediterranean man would keep an eye on the signal, but he wouldn't expect them to be here. He was too smart for that. Instead, he would try to outsmart his prey.

Randy was counting on it.

With a flip of the privacy switch on the dash, the glass windows darkened. No one could see inside without breaking in, which would be virtually impossible considering the truck's security system, which he'd modified with the latest tech himself. He locked the truck, shoved the key into his pocket, glanced around to make sure he wasn't forgetting anything, and headed north.

The game was on.

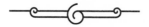

MATTEO IDLY tapped his pad screen, considering the call. The detective knew he was being hunted by an assassin. He probably assumed it was the same assassin who'd murdered the Dead Heads in Oak Hill Park. And executed the attorney in his office. And hanged the mother in her bedroom.

But the call was a bluff that would undoubtedly lead to a trap.

Whatever the man was up to, it did not involve offering information related to those Matteo worked for. Not even he knew their true objectives or identities. Only Angie knew the truth, they said, and that knowledge was buried deep in her psyche.

Then again, her regression at Convergence had jarred some of that knowledge loose. It's why they wanted her dead.

Two days had passed. The district attorney and the governor were climbing the walls. As was the chief of police, Renee Dalton, although she was a clueless puppet. Randy George and Angie Channing had escaped him once, and they had a clear plan, which made them a threat. It was one thing to take unsuspecting prey, and another thing to stalk seasoned prey that knew it was being stalked.

A chill snaked down his spine, the first he'd felt in a very long time.

He could inform Botwilder of the call, but far better to deal with this on his own. There was only one solution and it was unchanged: both the detective and the unveiled one had to die, taking all they might know with them.

Matteo studied the tracking program. The phone Randy had called him from was in a location that matched the position of his abandoned truck. They were sleeping there, in the vehicle. But the call had been placed near the gate, a hundred meters south. Why there?

He accessed the stripping tool and let the application break into the phone at the truck through the back door required by law. It took only ten seconds for the phone's contents to appear on his screen. The activity log showed that the phone had been used only once before, earlier in the day. A text sent to another phone of the same area code.

Matteo brought the text up.

"Where are you? Return to car."

No response.

He considered the meaning. This was likely Randy texting Angie, telling her to get back to the car. They must have been separated. But none of that mattered. What did matter was that he now had the numbers of both phones.

He quickly ran a search on the second phone number, but there was no signal. It was currently off. They were together and had no need for two phones. Made sense. He put a trace on the second number and told the system to record GPS coordinates and report back the moment the phone was powered up.

His only logical move now was to put eyes on the cabin and play along with whatever game the detective had fashioned. He had no intention of meeting or talking to either of them, naturally. His only objective was to silence them.

The sooner they were dead, the better.

THE FIRST gray of dawn was already creeping up the eastern sky when Randy finally made it back to the Jeep in the valley below the cave. Just after six in the morning. He looked up the hill—too dark to see anything. Even in full daylight, the cave couldn't be seen from this vantage unless you knew precisely where it was, and then it was nothing more than a tangle of brush among a hundred other tangles of brush on the rocky hillside. Anyone approaching the Jeep, on the other hand, would present a clear target from the cave entrance.

He prayed Angie had managed some sleep. She would need it today.

No drones in the sky that he could hear. That didn't mean they weren't there.

Withdrawing the second phone from his backpack, he powered it up, waited for the screen to come up, then powered it back off. He quickly removed the foliage that hid the right side of the Jeep, tossed the cell on the front seat and locked the door.

Five minutes later he was in the cave, breathing heavily from the climb, facing Angie who stood by the lamp, eyes round.

"Thank God!" She hurried forward and flung her arms around him. "I've never been so happy to see anyone in my life." She pulled away, eager to hear. "So? How did it go? Did you get through? Are we good?"

Randy thought he could love this woman.

"I got through," he said. "We'll know if we're good in under an hour."

"But what happened? Tell me!"

He did, quickly.

"So that's it? We just wait?"

He nodded. "If I'm right, he's already either accessed a drone or used his own to scope out the cabin property. He knows the phone is in the truck, but he won't be able to verify our presence there because I activated the privacy windows. He's also likely scanned the ground and found the charges, so he knows it's a trap."

"And that's what we want."

"Ten minutes ago, he received notification that the second phone was turned on to check for messages, and he'll assume it was you, looking for me. That phone's in the Jeep now. With any luck, he's already on his way, realizing at least one of us is here, at a new location, rather than at the truck. He'll assume we only want him to think we're at the cabin, which is why we left the phone on there."

"And we'll have the advantage because he doesn't realize we know he's coming here." She was only repeating what they'd discussed numerous times, reassuring herself. "And if he doesn't show, we go anyway, like we decided," she said. "Like a bat out of hell."

"Well let's hope that doesn't happen, because without him, we have no case. We have to take him alive. It's our only shot."

CHAPTER
THIRTY-THREE

MATTEO LAID on his belly, high-powered digital binoculars trained on the clump of trees below. The GPS coordinates of the second phone were there, at the center of those trees. The phone had been powered down quickly, so he couldn't be sure it was still at the same coordinates, but whoever had turned it on—either to check for messages or as a ploy to lure him here—had been in that precise location an hour earlier.

Brush and trees. Nothing more. He flipped the sensor toggle to measure density and only then saw the mass hidden by branches and brush. Switching back to standard visuals, he increased the magnification to 100 X 1, engaged vibration control, and studied the dense underbrush more closely.

Without knowing something was under the trees, no surveillance would have picked up the black smooth surface just visible between the leaves of two thick branches. Metal. A vehicle. And now he saw its basic outline—a sport utility of some kind. Perhaps a truck.

His pulse was steady, albeit elevated. Deploying a drone at the cabin, he'd found the hidden charges at the gate. The Ford's privacy windows had been activated so there was no way to determine if the detective and the woman were inside, but if it were him, he would have established the entire scenario as a decoy.

A less skilled hunter might have triggered the charges entering the compound, assuming those charges were armed.

A more skilled hunter might have considered the cleverness of his prey, realized that the Ford was a decoy, and followed the signal from the second phone to this spot, thinking the discovery of the decoy gave him the upper hand. He would likely descend on the hidden vehicle below, assured of success.

But Matteo was neither of those hunters. His edge came from assuming his prey was more skilled than him and, from that vantage, anticipate their next move.

If the detective was as accomplished as his decorations claimed, he might expect his hunter to descend on the vehicle, where he could be easily taken out with a single round.

Randy George was hunkered down with a clear view of the vehicle below. But where?

He lifted the binoculars and began a systematic search of the three slopes that led down to the hidden vehicle. They were covered in scrub oak and smaller trees, peppered with craggy rock. A thousand places to hide.

But time was on his side. The seven o'clock hour had come and gone, but that hardly mattered now. They would eventually conclude he hadn't taken their bait and show themselves. He would simply wait them out. Without increased surveillance from drones, they would have no clue that the hills were being watched.

Patience.

He'd left his BMW in a pull-off at the gravel road and walked in on foot from the south, keeping to the trees. His clothing impeded infrared and sonic detection from above but there was no way to avoid visual contact other than by using overhead cover.

Approaching the valley, he'd picked his way up this slope with care in the event they were hidden here. They weren't. He, however, was. All he needed was in his pack, which lay to his right.

An hour passed, and the sun was bright on the eastern horizon when he first saw the small glint of light in the brush across the valley. It was nondescript, just a reflection that could be the result of dew or crystal in the rock behind the brush. But after a few minutes of scrutiny with the aid of the density sensor, he concluded differently.

The brush covered what he thought must be a small cave or depression in the hill. It would have hidden them well from overhead surveillance. Only then, armed with this assumption, was he able to see the barrel of a rifle pressed against the side of a long branch that almost completely hid it from view. Smart.

But smart wasn't good enough.

Matteo marked the cave's precise GPS coordinates, then withdrew and rolled over onto his back, considering his options. One, he could send a guided shell into that rifle barrel, destroying whatever hid behind the brush. But the explosion would be noted from the sky and the place would be buzzing with drones long before he could verify that he'd made the kill.

The other option was to make his way to the back side of the far slope and descend to the cave from above. Being so close, he could either use a shell or a silenced weapon, verify his kill, and make a hasty retreat to the trees before the drones arrived.

The latter was his only safe option.

ANGIE BREATHED in the still air behind Randy, otherwise silent as they'd agreed. The binoculars were set to offer the broadest possible view of the approaches into the valley. He'd tracked a dozen squirrels, twice that many birds, and one small deer, but no sign of human activity yet.

He glanced at his watch. Nearly eight. It was possible the man had missed the ping on the second cell phone and was oblivious to their location. More likely, the killer was hidden in the hills now, watching the Jeep from safety. Or making his way to the cave.

"How long—"

He cut off her whisper with a raised hand. Shook his head. She closed her eyes and nodded, steeling her nerves.

Nevertheless, it was a good question. How long would they wait in this cramped space?

If need be, until dark. Eleven hours. If there was no activity by then, they would assume the ploy had failed.

Eleven hours was a long time to remain hidden without moving.

IT TOOK Matteo thirty-seven minutes to work his way west, then north, and back south to a boulder at the top of the hill. The cave was roughly thirty meters below. Being so close, sound was now his greatest enemy.

Breathing steadily, letting his body relax, he considered his next move. From this location, he could flee under thick trees due west with only some risk of being spotted before drones arrived. Once they did, he would be forced to keep to cover. Quick movement ran too high of a risk even under heavy foliage.

He was sorely tempted to end this charade by firing a GPS guided shell from where he sat, quickly descend to verify the kill, and then cut for the road. Firing from here would remove the danger of him knocking a stone loose or making some other sound that might alert them. But using a shell still came with that risk, however minor, of alerting the drones and being spotted. There was a better way.

The cleanest kill would be a direct assault on the cave entrance using a silenced, automatic shotgun with scattering shrapnel. A stealth approach followed by a ruthless barrage of shells that would reduce anybody in the cave to ribbons of flesh.

He pulled out the shotgun fitted with a two-inch silenced barrel, hid his pack under the boulder, and checked the side arm at his back. Chamber loaded, safety off. Satisfied, he picked his way down the hill, breathing shallow.

He was within ten feet and could see the barrel of the rifle below when his foot nudged a small stone, sending it clattering down. Without thought, he threw stealth to the wind and took those last ten feet in two bounding leaps, shotgun already trained on the brush.

The shotgun bucked with a dull whump and his first salvo ripped into the rifle's barrel before he landed, four feet from the entrance. Six successive shells ripped through the opening without discrimination, shredding everything in their path but rock. The brush that had concealed a cave became a gaping hole filled with dust.

No screams, no grunts, no signs, either human or animal. The sniper rifle lay on the ground, protruding from the cave, scope and stock shattered.

Matteo surged, firing three more rounds into the cave, and was just leaning into the entrance when a voice stopped him cold.

"Drop it."

He jerked his head to his right. The detective stood before a rock overhang ten feet away, handgun trained on Matteo's chest. Angie Channing crouched behind him under the ledge, staring.

The cave, too, had been a decoy.

"I can kill you," the detective said, "but I think we may both be on the same side here. Drop your weapon and I'll explain. Or don't and you'll die here. Your call."

There was no indication Randy had seen the gun tucked under his belt at Matteo's back.

RANDY HELD his side arm on the wiry, olive-skinned professional, finger on the trigger, tempted to end his life. And he might have if the man hadn't dropped the shotgun and straightened. A thin smile curved his lips.

"Not bad," he said. "You should consider changing professions. They pay well for those with your skills."

"What's your name?"

The man considered the question.

"I suppose you've earned at least some honesty. My name's Matteo Steger. And yes, I killed both Dead Heads in the park. As well as Susan. But not the attorney. That was someone else."

It was a lie, Randy thought. And the only reason for him to lie was to retain at least some good grace with Angie. Steger wouldn't care about that unless he needed that good grace. Which meant he was either giving himself up or feigning surrender.

"Why did you kill Clair and Timothy?" Randy asked.

"I only follow orders, you understand. But evidently they stumbled upon an encrypted key drive that might put those I work for in dire straits. I think you already know this."

"Keep talking. Who do you work for?"

"First you must tell me why we're on the same side."

"You're a pawn. So is Angie. We're all pawns, and the only way any of us survive this mess is to bring down the players moving the pieces. But I think you already know that."

Matteo smiled. "Well, that's a problem because I don't know who's moving the pieces. I receive my orders from a woman named Katrina Botwilder, although I doubt that's her real name. I can tell you that whoever's pulling the strings has virtually unlimited resources and is fully committed to controlling virtual technology at the highest level."

Randy could hear Angie's steady breathing five feet behind him. She was staying put as agreed. Good.

"Control VR, why?" he said.

The man shrugged. "This whole world is already ones and zeros. It doesn't take a genius to understand that whoever controls them controls everything. This is especially true as it relates to virtual technology, which will one day soon be the world. It's a guess, mind you, but a pretty good one." The man paced to his right, hands on his hips. "Now tell me how we can help each other."

Randy wasn't done.

"Who can we trust at the department?"

"No one. At this level, it's far too dangerous."

"No one, but who doesn't know?"

"Few of them know. That's doesn't mean they're not puppets."

"What about Renee Dalton? Andrew Olsen. Bill Evans, the prosecutor."

"The chief is oblivious," Steger said. "The other two are on my payroll."

"And the governor?"

"Ah, yes, the governor. Would you expect anything less?"

If the man wasn't lying, Renee didn't know. Randy had little choice but to believe him on this point.

"Why Angie?" he asked.

Matteo's eyes moved past Randy, lingered on Angie, then reacquired him. "That's the real question, isn't it? Why Angie, the unveiled one? Why has so much energy been exhausted following her every move for over two decades? Were she and Jamie born this way, or were they intentionally broken as children and turned into unveiled ones?"

A chill washed over Randy's back. So Angie had been right about her connection to Jamie. A whole new line of inquiry had just opened up. Matteo eyed him steadily, daring him to react. Randy let the silence stand.

"We both know you can't kill me," Steger said. "All the evidence, including the key drive, is gone. I'm the only one who can point the finger away from Jamie Hamilton. Without me, you have nothing. With me, you'll have enough information to blow the lid off all of this, but not until you tell me how you can help me."

True enough. But the man was playing ball. They had their intel.

"Full immunity," Randy said. "Assuming we can put ourselves in a position to . . ."

The man's arm moved like a flash of lightning while Randy was distracted by his own reasoning. In the space of half a breath the man had withdrawn a weapon at his back and was firing.

Randy fired before Matteo could, but the man was lurching to his right. The two silenced detonations came nearly as one, like two pieces of corn popping.

A slug tore into Randy's right arm, spinning him around and knocking his gun from his grasp. A second bullet whipped through the air inches from his left ear. And then Randy was charging, roaring full-throated.

Two long strides and he was there, even as another slug cut into his side, jerking him around. Randy's fist managed to land on flesh, but he was falling.

The world slowed and his thoughts came with surprising clarity. He'd beat the man. Lured him in and forced him into a corner. Angie had trusted him and he'd delivered on that trust. But the wiry Mediterranean had moved faster than he thought possible. In three seconds from start to finish, their roles had been reversed and he was falling to the ground without a weapon. Bitter regret clawed at his chest.

Randy landed hard and rolled, uncaring of the pain digging into his side. When he jerked up, desperate to get to his feet, he found himself staring into a black barrel. Behind it, a killer with cold, dark eyes.

The smile had just begun to form on Matteo Steger's lips when the right side of his head disintegrated, taking one eye with it. At first Randy thought the explosion that ripped through the air came from that head blowing up. But of course that wasn't the case.

The case was Angie. She was standing ten feet to his left, gun raised. She'd shot Matteo through the head.

Matteo Steger, head half gone, teetered on his feet for a full second, already dead to this world, then collapsed into a pile, limp and lifeless.

"Now who's the Dead Head?" Angie bit off, glaring down at the man who'd executed Darcy.

Randy staggered to his feet, aware that the gun Angie had pulled from his pack wasn't silenced. If there were any drones nearby, they would be programmed to alter course and fly over the anomaly.

He quickly checked his side. Not too deep. His right arm was bleeding but he didn't think his bone was broken. There was no time.

He turned to see Angie, staring at the dead body, eyes wide. Then she looked at Randy's arm.

"Oh no!"

"It's okay, just a flesh wound. We have to go."

"To the station?" she asked.

"We'll leave the body for the drones," he said, twisting back to Matteo's crumpled form. "You saved my life." He faced her. "Thank you."

Her eyes were glued to the fallen body with half a head.

"It was self-defense," he said.

She looked up at him. "I've been thinking."

Ignoring the pain in his shoulder and side, Randy hurried for the pack lodged under the small ledge they'd squeezed themselves under. "We've had two days to think. We go straight to the department and hold a press conference. It's our only shot."

"You're wrong. *I'm* the only shot we have now. Without Steger, we have only me."

He spun back. "There's no way we're going back to Convergence! Even if we did make it there and past the front gate, drones will be everywhere. Barnes will never let us in. Even if he does, the police will be all over the place."

"Barnes will let me in because I'm valuable to him. You said so yourself."

She paused for only a moment, then hurried on before he could disrupt her.

"I've been tempted to think that if this world is virtual, then nothing here matters, but that doesn't feel right anymore. Everything that happens in this world is somehow critical. Everything is linked. That's why we can't let them convict Jamie. And it's also why I need to stay alive. It's critical."

She walked up to him, calmer now.

"I've sat alone all night thinking about who or what could be so critical, and one name kept coming back to me. Jake Barnes. His technology is at the center of all of this. So is Jamie and so am I. You heard the man. This goes way back to our childhood. We've been so focused on the Oak Hill case that we've missed the underlying problem. Like treating a rash while ignoring the poison in the blood that's causing the rash. We need to get to the real point."

Her eyes were bright and her face resolute.

"*I'm* the point, Randy. Jamie's the point. Our connection is the point and only Barnes has the technology to make something like that happen. His tech will change the course of history. What if the authorities aren't using him? What if he's using *them*? He needs the right people in place so his plans aren't compromised."

"That doesn't make any sense. Technology to do what exactly? Drive people insane?"

"That's a low blow."

He held up a hand apologetically.

"I don't know what's happening behind the scenes, but I can't shake the feeling that deep down, I do know. And if I do, I'm the only shot we have of uncovering it."

"If Barnes is behind all of this, and I think that's a pretty big if, then going to him's out of the question. What do you expect me to do? Arrest him on the spot? I'm a fugitive, for heaven's sake!"

"Not we, Randy. And not you. Me. You've broken the law; I haven't. Technically, you're the fugitive. I'm not. So I go to Convergence on my own while you lead the drones south."

Desperation settled over him.

"There's no way I'm letting you out of my sight, not now. I can't allow that."

She took his hand. "I know. I get it. But this is my call. I have to get back into the Red Protocol, Randy. If I'm right, Barnes will allow it, especially if there are no police. I have to get in there and find out what I know, deep inside."

What she said made an absurd kind of sense but was far too risky. And that risk? Losing her. But that was absurd too. She wasn't his to lose.

"It's too risky," he managed.

"And racing for downtown Austin with an armada of drones overhead isn't? You really think that's safer? This is our best shot."

For a few long seconds Randy stood still, his hand in hers. Who was she really? What great mystery hid in that mind behind her eyes? What did Barnes know about her?

The more he thought about it, the more he realized she might be right. Something way beyond his paygrade was happening here.

Randy stepped away and ran his fingers through his matted hair. Closed his eyes and took a deep breath, resigning himself to the stark reality of their predicament. The drones were on their way. There was no safe course.

When he faced her again, he saw she hadn't moved.

"We have to go before the drones come."

"Where?"

"To the Jeep, then to my truck. I have to get to Renee Dalton and make some noise." He grabbed the last burner phone from the pack. "Leave the rest, there's no time."

She was staring down at Matteo's head, eyes wide as the stark realization of what she'd done set in.

"Now, Angie! We have to go!"

"Where am I going?"

He hesitated, because even now, knowing it was their only decent shot, he loathed the thought of her going alone.

"I'm going south in my truck," he said. "You're going north in the Jeep. Get to Convergence and get in your head. Dear God, I hope you're right about this."

BOOK FIVE

THE
UNVEILED
ONE

CHAPTER
THIRTY-FOUR

ANGIE KEPT her eyes on the analog speedometer because she dared not break the speed limit, with sensors tightly monitored on all roads. The Jeep was ancient, retrofitted with an electric motor but no GPS, no holographic displays, no link to the net or devices connected to the net.

Randy had been adamant that she drive normal, like a sane person. But she wasn't sane, not really, so it took all her concentration to stay focused on the road rather than on what might be happening to Randy or what might be waiting for her at Convergence.

They'd beaten the drones to the Ford, at least that much was in their favor. Both of his wounds were flesh—one just under his shoulder bone, the other an inch below his ribcage on the right side. She'd quickly dressed both using a first-aid kit from his truck. Randy was in pain but assured her he would be okay.

He'd embraced her awkwardly and, with a few parting words of caution, none of which helped her, roared away from the cabin, headed south, hopefully attracting all the heat. This would provide cover for Angie, who drove straight north on Highway 281 to Burnet before taking Highway 29 east to Georgetown, then heading to Convergence. While the city focused on Randy heading south, she would be free to make her way north. Simple. Not easy.

He would wait ten minutes and then call Renee Dalton to inform her that he was bringing Angie in on the condition that he meet her, and only her, at the station.

Not counting Matteo's death, which no one knew about, technically only he, not Angie, had broken the law. Once in custody, he would persuade the chief to check out Convergence with him, hopefully while Angie was still in the Red Protocol.

At least, that was the idea.

What would happen then was anyone's guess. It all depended on what happened to Angie, assuming she was able to get into the Red Protocol.

To her relief, no drones swooped down on the old Jeep as she blazed north on 281, picking at her lip and trying not to look up at the sky.

No cruisers intercepted her driving east on 29. Or along the back-roads that led to the sweeping grounds that accommodated Convergence's international headquarters.

Angie pointed the Jeep up the split-lane driveway that ended at the secu-rity gates. Genetically engineered palm trees that could survive Texas's mild winters were planted along the causeway between the lanes as well as on either side of the driveway. The entire compound was protected by a tall red brick wall, but the unseen forcefield extending above the wall provided the real security. The only way in was through one of the armed gates.

She pulled behind two other cars, both Mercedes, and waited her turn. The driveway was still clear behind her. Worst case, she could spin the Jeep around and make a run for it. But she discarded the idea. This was a one-way ticket. If they didn't open the gate for her, she would ram through it.

That's smart, Angie. It would be suicide.

Okay, she wasn't sure what she would do if they turned her away. She hadn't really spent any time thinking about the possibility because she'd been so sure Barnes would see her. Thinking that she might be wrong filled her with a sense of dread. Not only because Convergence was her only chance at solving the drama of these last few weeks, but because Barnes might make her feel dismissed. Rejected. Abandoned.

She swallowed, taken aback by the sentiment. It was the feeling that came with being thrown out by your own family. Almost as if Barnes was like a father to her.

Was he?

A guard dressed in white with patches bearing the Convergence logo above its motto, *A Whole New World,* on both shoulders was waving her forward. She edged the Jeep up to him and rolled down the window.

The moment the guard saw her, he stalled, as if unsure he was seeing what his mind told him he was seeing.

She glanced at the name on his right breast pocket. "You know who I am, don't you, Brit?"

Without responding, he tapped his earpiece to report her.

"Call it in, but only to Jake Barnes," she said, heart crashing. "And you'd better know what to say to Barnes when you speak to him. You make the wrong move here and he'll have your head, I can promise you that."

That gave the man pause. "Never mind," he said to whoever had picked up. He disconnected, then glanced around. "You do realize that you're being recorded."

"So are you, so listen close. Tell Jake Barnes and him only that I need to meet now, in the next five minutes. Tell him I have information that was encoded on an encrypted key drive. Tell him I know. Call him."

"That's not the way it works here, ma'am. I need you to get—"

"Call him!" she snapped. She gripped the Jeep's steering wheel to calm herself. "Just do it."

He hesitated for a few seconds, then retreated to the gatehouse, where he tapped into his system and eyed her sideways before straightening and speaking into a landline. A nod and he was back out.

"Forgive me, this isn't the way we normally—"

"We don't have time," she said.

"Right. Head to the end and then take a right. Follow the signs to the underground . . ."

The gate was lifting and Angie pulled forward before he could finish giving her directions. She'd been here more than once and knew exactly where to go.

It took her less than five minutes driving like a maniac to reach the south building's basement lobby. Leaving the Jeep by the entrance with its door open, she hurried up to the guard on duty and gave her name, praying he'd been informed.

The guard rose without asking for more detail and led her to a bank of elevators. He swiped his card over the access panel and punched the tenth-floor call button.

"Ask for Clarice."

Thirty seconds later, she stepped into the tenth-floor lobby of the south building. The receptionist named Clarice, whom she'd met before, was waiting by the elevator.

"Good to see you again, Angie. Right this way."

No guards, no sign of security at all. Clarice was asking how her day was, as if nothing out of the ordinary was happening. And maybe nothing was out of the ordinary for the receptionist. Her job didn't involve knowing the guests, just caring for them.

"Good," Angie finally answered.

"That's good," came the reply in a friendly voice. It was all a bit surreal.

Clarice pushed the door to Jake Barnes's corner office open. "He's waiting for you."

The old man was standing at the center of the expansive white room that overlooked the grounds, one hand on his desk for support. This was his ivory tower, a monument to humanity's farthest-reaching technologies. Like the one that maybe made her who she was.

He picked his way forward as the door closed behind her. Approaching, he took her right hand in his knotted, quivering fingers. Kissed her knuckles.

"Thank God you're okay! Can I get you anything? Water? A soda?"

"I'm fine."

"Come, come." He indicated the white leather sofas to their right. She followed and eased into the closest seat. Barnes also sat.

Looking into his pale eyes, she tried to imagine him breaking her when she was a child, as Matteo seemed to suggest. But she couldn't imagine it. All she saw sitting before her was a kind old man who had given the world the gift of dead heading.

"They're saying you went on the run," he said. "You can imagine my concern. I'm assuming the hallucinations are back and if so, I'm terribly sorry. But you came to the right place."

"If I'm not mistaken, this is where I got those hallucinations," she said.

He dipped his head. "Indeed. I can understand how you would draw that conclusion. So then your hallucinations *are* back?"

"No, but I think you knew that."

"On the contrary, nothing else could explain what the feeds are saying."

"Lies," she said. "But that's not the point."

"Then why are you here?"

"My brain is broken. I need to fix it. I don't even know who I am anymore. I was told that maybe my mother wasn't my real mother. Like Jamie, I was an orphan."

He looked surprised. "Jamie Hamilton? The one being accused of killing those two kids? I didn't know he was an orphan. And I don't know about your past other than what's in the file we have. We vet our subjects, and I don't recall anything that remotely suggests you aren't your mother's daughter. Who told you this?"

She had to remember that she was here for the Red Protocol and nothing else.

"One of my hallucinations told me," she quipped, rising. She walked to the windows and studied the bright Austin sky to the south, where Randy was neck-deep in his own drama. She had to keep this simple and quick. And for that, she needed Barnes's trust.

"You have to forgive me," she said. "It's been a rough few days."

"I understand," he said, walking up behind her. "I'm surprised to see you here. Do the authorities know?"

"No." Angie faced him, resolute. "And I hope you can keep it that way."

"Of course. Our people are accustomed to absolute discretion. Tell me how your mind has been since our regression therapy."

"Like I said, broken. I can hardly tell what's real and not real anymore, which is why I need to go back in."

He studied her for a while, then stared out the window.

"I don't think that's wise," he said. "Not so soon. The risks are too great."

He was discouraging her. Maybe she'd been wrong about him.

"Do you remember telling me about how genetic expressions can be affected in a Deep Dive over time?"

Barnes didn't answer quickly, making her think she'd struck a chord. "Epigenetics," he said quietly. "We've been testing it for years."

"If a body can change its form in this world through belief alone, like the kind of belief that comes in a fully immersive Deep Dive, then the mind can change itself as well, because really, the brain is just part of the body." She faced him, hoping he would accept her explanation. "Right?"

"You think you can repair your own brain in the Red Protocol."

"Can't I?"

Another long pause. "I tried," he said. "I've been in the Red Protocol more than any other soul, long before we refined the technology. If you'd done your homework, you'd know that I'm currently only fifty-nine years old. My body is aging at many times the normal rate. I somehow damaged the telomeres in my DNA and haven't been able to reverse that damage."

He turned his blue eyes on her.

"I have less than two years. In that time I will either heal myself or die. So you can understand why I don't think you'll have much success repairing your brain, my dear."

His admission stunned her. The ancient wrinkled man standing beside her had been irreversibly damaged in the Red Protocol. She didn't know what to think about that.

"Truth be told, I don't think there's anything wrong with your brain, Angie."

"Of course there is. Even if it's just my thinking that there's something wrong. I can't keep living like this. Nothing is what it once was. I'm as broken as they get."

"I see. And what makes you think you can change your brain in the Red Protocol? You would only be in another virtual reality, believing it to be real. There would be nothing to tell you this reality even exists, much less that you have a brain that needs to be fixed."

"*Another* virtual reality?" she said. "You say that as if this world is also virtual."

"Yes, well, it's a figure of speech. Aren't all realities virtual on one level or another? Nothing is what it seems. Our perception is radically limited and shows us only illusion. In that sense, everything is virtual."

He looked away.

"Now tell me what makes you think you can do anything constructive while under?"

He was still holding back, she thought, so she pressed in, eager to say enough to make him think she was only a desperate subject who needed her fix.

"I lied to you," she said. "When I was in three days ago, I was only in the reality in which I was married to Randy George for a little while. The rest of the time I was in the white room."

She watched him but he didn't seem surprised.

"Yes, well, that's quite common. When we insert you into the protocol the first time, we park your brain in a white room as part of the acoustic neutralization. Hallucinating a white room is only—"

"I don't think it was a hallucination," she interrupted. "I think it actually represents my inner psyche. My brain. From that white room, I can select different scenes from my life. It was by going into those scenes that I heard my mother calling me her 'unveiled one.' Does that mean anything to you?"

He shook his head. "Unveiled one? No."

"Randy George says you called me that as well."

"I may have. It's a reasonable designation for those who are fluid in altered states."

"It was also there that I saw another woman who appeared to be my real mother."

"I see," he said. "And yet neither of those experiences happened to the real you. Both are likely figments of your imagination."

"I was in the Red Protocol, where I was supposed to be experiencing another reality like this one, but I was in the white room. I think it's the key to fixing me. I'm begging you, let me back in. Worst case, I fry my brain. I'm willing to take that risk because it's already fried."

For a long time, Jake Barnes just stared out the window, lost in consideration.

"Do you think it's possible for the human mind to enter alternate realities without a RIG?" she asked impulsively. "I mean, what if ultimately *we* are the RIG?"

"Yes," he said quietly. "I do. We're not there yet, but . . ." He stopped himself.

"What if I'm one of the first ones to do that? I still need the Red Protocol now because I don't know how to get there myself, but what if I can learn? And what if I can figure out how to reverse the damage to your DNA while I'm in that space?"

He didn't respond and she immediately chided herself for straying. This was about discovering the truth about both her and Jamie, because the truth would set them free and expose something far more explosive than murder. Something that would justify hiring an assassin to kill Darey and Clair Milton and Timothy Blake and Susan and dozens of others for all she knew.

"Okay, forget all of that," she said. "Just a crazy thought. I only know that I have to get back inside and put things back in order."

"The fact is, you may be right. Everything is only an idea until someone does it." His voice was reverent, which made her think of what Randy had said about Jake's awe of her.

"But to be clear, that's not what I'm doing right now," she said. "I just need to find some stability. Maybe you can use me as your lab rat later, but right now, I just need to find normal."

"I would never want to use you like that."

"Of course not," she said, sure that he was lying.

His shoulders seemed to relax and she knew she'd won. "I'd need you to sign a new release. As I said, what you're suggesting's quite dangerous. No one's ever entered the Red Protocol so soon after—"

"I'll sign whatever you want. But we have to do it now."

He gave her a nod. "Very well. I'll do the procedure myself."

RANDY SAT across from the chief in the conference room adjacent to her office, palms sweating. He glanced up at the clock. Two hours had passed since he'd left Angie at the cabin and not knowing her fate concerned him more than the consequences Renee assured him he'd face.

As things stood now, those consequences would include repercussions for his defiance of direct orders and criminal charges based on evidence that had come to light. Namely, surveillance video that put him in Susan Milton's house at the time of her death. He did not have time to explain how easily someone like Matteo could have fabricated that evidence and handed it off to his puppet, Andrew Olsen, the very district attorney who had miraculously uncovered the footage.

He knew how tenuous his predicament was. In this world, even a shadow of doubt could destroy a man's reputation.

Never mind that he had no motivation. Never mind that his cell tracking data had him north of the house at the time the footage put him at the scene. For that matter, never mind any defense—the story that would survive was the story the media would sell, and the media was ultimately in the pocket of the powerful.

"I *am* listening, Randy," Renee was saying. "And what I'm hearing makes far less sense than what the evidence is showing me. Just listen to yourself. Hear the evidence from my perspective, for heaven's sake. You really expect me to believe there's some conspiracy to frame Jamie Hamilton? One that involves the governor?" She stopped, exasperated. "Dear God, it's insane. Andrew Olsen? And all this discovered by a closet Dead Head? Not only is it beyond the pale, even *hints* of a conspiracy would destroy the department."

Yes, it would, he thought. *And if you knew what Angie really thought, you'd lock her up and throw away the key.*

He hadn't implicated Jack Barnes or Convergence because Angie was right—if Barnes was complicit, there was no telling what he would do if police swarmed the place. Police presence would endanger Angie.

As expected, the moment he placed his call five miles south of Marble Falls, an armada of drones and cruisers had joined an escort to deliver him to the station. As expected, Renee had agreed to deal with him personally.

After all, he was under her authority, a liability for her. She'd brought a doctor in to dress his gunshot wounds, but once assured that he would be fine until they could get him to the hospital later, she got right down to business. When she finished, Randy had mere seconds to make his case.

"Forget about any of this being discovered by Angie for now," he said. "This is me, telling you what I've uncovered, including the confession of a killer named Matteo Steger, who managed to put two rounds into me before I took him down. By now you've dispatched a drone and found him missing half a head at the entrance to the cave where Angie and I spent the last two nights. Was I lying about that?"

"Unfortunately, he won't be talking, and preliminary identification comes up nada so there's nothing there to confirm your claims. We have little choice but to classify it as a crime. At the moment, you're the only suspect."

He'd expected nothing less. As long as they kept Angie out of it.

"You found his car? His phone?"

"All clean."

"Clean as in no corroborating evidence or clean, clean?"

"I mean clean as in no data."

His handlers, Randy thought. "How do you explain that?"

She shrugged. "I don't. Absence of evidence isn't evidence. If and when hard evidence does surface, I'm all ears. But you're not giving me anything to go on here, Randy. I respect you, always have. But this . . ." She shook her head. "It's too much."

It was a lost cause. Nothing he could say or do in here would shift her mind.

"Do me one favor then," he said, settling back in the chair. "Just one."

"Depends," she said.

"Keep me here. Cuff me to the table if it makes you more comfortable but keep me here for the rest of the day, alone. No DA, no prosecutor, no other officers, just me. If no new evidence comes to light by then, do what you like."

She glanced at his bandaged arm.

"I'll be fine," he said. "I have to stay here."

"Why?"

"Because someone wants me dead and I'm not ready to die yet, Renee."

She looked at him for a full ten seconds, then stood, crossed to the door leading into her office, and turned.

"Dear God, I hope you're wrong about this, Randy. I really do hope you're wrong."

So do I, he thought. *So do I.*

CHAPTER
THIRTY-FIVE

AN HOUR, MAYBE LESS, Angie thought. That's how long it took Jake Barnes to establish Angie's interface with the Red Protocol RIG in the white laboratory and establish a coherent connection to both the acoustic imaging array that now hovered over her body and the helmet that covered her head.

He worked alone, hurrying between terminals and the RIG itself, then retreating to the command room overlooking the lab, where he and Randy had watched her only three days earlier during her regression.

He was inserting her into the Red Protocol by himself because no company guideline allowed for what they were now doing, he explained. Thus, the release she'd signed. Involving others would complicate the process.

The fact that others—like Megan, whom she trusted—would protest, bothered Angie more than a little, because it highlighted the danger of her choice. She contended with the stress by fixing her mind on the white gate room. The answers were there, deep in her mind, and this was her only way to get there.

Now, staring up at the mesh over her eyes, cocooned in the acoustic imaging array, strapped onto the reclined chair, doubt lapped at her mind. What if this really was the end? Randy had explained how she'd experienced a fracture the last time, remedied by a reboot of some kind. It was evidently like putting the brain in a coma and resuscitating it. She should have experienced the void during that reboot.

She hadn't.

Instead, the light in the gate room had only flickered for a second. Nothing more than a glitch.

She'd explained this to Barnes as he ran through his checklist earlier, and he went still. A new light filled his eyes.

"Could it be?" he mumbled. When she asked him to explain his interest, he deflected, saying they could speculate later. "But it's good, Angie. You might be more gifted than even I realized."

"Unveiled?" she said.

He looked at her curiously. "Yes. Unveiled."

And that was that.

But now she wasn't sure of any gifting or special unveiling. Now she was only staring up into darkness and feeling like she might be on a one-way trip.

Barnes's voice filled the helmet. "All systems are in alignment, Angie. Are you comfortable?"

No, she thought.

"Yes," she said.

"That's good." His voice took on a more distant quality. "Now I need to explain something that might disturb you a little, but it's important you don't panic."

Her pulse surged. Panic? What did he mean?

The whine from the acoustic array filled the room as it powered up. They were already in the countdown. She could feel her skin tingling as the first waves worked their way into her body.

Panic about what?

"The last time you were in we rebooted your mind, apparently to no effect. The only way to do this properly now is to initiate a full wipe. I've never pushed anyone to brain death, but it might be the only way to know if the white room can be breached. The wipe will either make you or break you." His voice was fading but her heart was pounding like a hammer. "Either way is fine by me because I need to know as much as you do, my dear." *Know what? What does he mean?! He's going to kill me?* Dread swallowed her. His voice was distant. "It's been . . . long time . . ."

And then his voice was gone as her bones, her flesh, her mind itself dissolved into a whitewash of nothingness that replaced any sense of individuated identity. There was no form, no thoughts, just existence. For Angie, the universe had ceased to be.

In the next moment, she found herself standing in the middle of the white gate room, breathing hard, planted solidly on two feet in the familiar space. Clarity came quickly.

She was back.

Barnes had said something about a wipe, and she knew that was a very big problem out there, but in here, it felt strangely inconsequential.

"He knows about the gate room," Jamie said behind her.

The sound of that voice filled her with joy and she spun, took two long steps, and wrapped her arms around him. "Thank God, you're here!" she said, lifting him off his feet.

He gave a short laugh. "And thank God *you're* here."

She set him down, mind swimming in what she knew about both of them. How much should she say?

"You're dreaming right now, aren't you?" she asked.

He thought about that. "I am?"

"Maybe that's why you keep coming and going. You disappear when you change dreams or wake up."

He shrugged. "Maybe. I just know that I have to figure out how to open the needle gate, but I can't. So maybe we can do it together."

"I used to wonder if you were just part of my own psyche, but now I think you're actually Jamie's psyche, here with me right now," she said. "Do you know why we're connected?"

"Yup. We're both in our own minds right now, but we're joined, and I don't know how that works. *That* way"—he motioned at the needle gate—"is the only way to know the truth about everything. And I think we're running out of time."

Yes, because Barnes is going to wipe my brain and I'll be a vegetable.

She reached out her finger and gently brushed his bangs to one side. "My guess is that we're connected because we were both orphans whose minds were altered in a virtual reality. The Oak Hill murders are the latest link in a chain of events that goes back to us, a long time ago. If we figure us out in this room, we figure everything out. If we figure everything out, we'll be free."

"Yup. But we have to hurry."

"Do you have any memory of what happened to you before your mother adopted you?"

He slowly shook his head. "I just know that if we don't get out, something bad will happen. Maybe Jamie will die in prison."

Yes, if Barnes wiped her brain before she solved the room, Jamie probably would die in prison. The evidence that might set him free was all gone.

Angie looked over at the needle with the words *Veritas Vos Liberabit* imprinted above it. The truth will set you free. She'd come with one task on her mind: to learn what had happened to her and Jamie and who was behind it. To unravel the truth that those responsible would go so far to hide.

There were two paths to follow. One was to navigate the Image Maker gate and find the scenes of her as a child that would shed light on who she really was. The other was to work only on the needle gate with the hope that the full truth would be unveiled beyond it.

"Okay, so this is what we know," she said, walking to the books. "Three books in progression. One with images and an eye that operates a portal into our lives in the world we know. Evidently, those lives are masked by illusion. False evidence appearing real. Nothing is what it appears to be, right?"

"Right."

She opened the first book, lifted out the eye that activated the Image Maker lens, and crossed to the panel. Once again, she set the eye in its receptacle. Once again, the portal's seal released with a hiss. Once again, she spun the wheel and slid the gate open.

The hum dropped to a low drone and the entire room came to life. The gears on the wall turned; the piercing beam of light blazed from the eye of the needle; the Image Maker lens flowed with energy; a virtual world formed beyond the lens. If she peered directly through the portal, she might see herself at Convergence right now.

Angie stood next to the boy, looking with wonder at the room in motion. "Cool."

"Super cool," he said.

"Super cool," she mumbled, stepping to the middle book with the ones and zeros. She opened the cover.

"Machine language. Raw information, which provides coordinates for the images."

She paused, wondering if she'd missed something about the book.

"Information," she said. "Maybe not coordinates but the actual coding of those images." She spun to Jamie. "In . . . formation. You get it? In-to-formation. The code that becomes form. Images. Everything in the universe is just information somehow manifested in form through a process no one fully understands yet. Does that make sense?"

"Information becomes formation," he said. "Data becomes form. That's what I figured out too. And information is just ideas. Everything is just the idea we have of it. Change the idea about something and you change how you see it."

He was just a boy, but this boy knew far more about philosophy and science than most adults. Maybe any adult.

"Smart," she said. "Ideas are just another kind of image. Both are just masks that hide the deeper truth."

"Yup."

There was no need to navigate scenes in her life because the truth they were looking for had to be through the needle gate, beyond the world of masks.

"So that's what we know. What we don't know . . ."

They both looked at the last book. The one with geometric patterns. Then at the needle wall with the Latin inscription at the top. The room seemed far more significant than just a program in her brain that was hiding suppressed memories.

"If formation, or mask, comes from information or ideas, what comes before ideas? If it's a progression, then this isn't about discovering the truth in the world we know, but the truth beyond it. Like . . ." She felt her fingers tingling. "Like the secret to everything, not just our lives in the world."

"Yup. And that's going to set me free. So the truth is both beyond the world and in it. At least that's what I think."

Made a strange kind of sense to her.

"What's before ideas?" she muttered, opening the last book. "I'm assuming this book operates the needle gate once the Image Maker is open."

"Has to be," he said. He was just a little boy now, looking to her for answers. In that way, he was like a son to her.

She traced the title on the cover. "*Play Dead*," she said. "Dead. Dead Head. Dead heading is essentially dying to one world to experience another."

He'd stepped up beside her, looking at the book. "That's what I thought."

"You still do?"

"It must be."

"Okay . . ." She opened the book of fractal geometric shapes resembling butterflies and scanned them. "Butterflies. What do we know about . . ." She was on the last page and stopped. The large image on the page was as she'd seen it before with one significant change. Between its spread wings, the butterfly's body was glowing. As was its head. But the body was now a straight, vertical line and the head was larger, and its eyes were large, even exaggerated.

"I've never seen that," the boy said, staring.

"It's the needle gate," she breathed. "It must have been powered when we activated the Image Maker."

"What does it mean?"

"It means we're getting close."

"Touch it," Jamie said.

She reached her hand out and placed a finger on the glowing line. Nothing. Same with the large eye-head. She withdrew her hand.

"Okay, we need to back up. What do we know about butterflies?"

"They come from caterpillars who crawl on the ground," Jamie said. "But a butterfly sees the whole world from up high."

At least it had a more expansive perception of the world.

"And to become a butterfly," she said, "a caterpillar has to liquify itself in a cocoon so it can be remade. A butterfly re-knows itself through a death and re-formation."

"From one perception, through a death, to another perception," he said.

"So playing dead is dying to what is known to re-know it as something else. Which is what the butterfly does. And in this book it's represented by fractal geometry. Infinite patterns."

Her heart was hammering now. She believed they were on the edge of some great knowing that would change everything they thought was true. And that truth was beyond the needle gate, a narrow way that not even Jamie had been able to enter.

"So . . ." She stared at the eye of the needle, crackling with power as its thin beam of light sliced through the room, struck the Image Maker lens, and formed her world.

"Maybe the world we know really is like a holographic reality," she said. "I . . . I was right. Like a fully dimensional virtual reality that we're trapped in."

"We're like caterpillars," he said.

She slowly turned to Jamie, who was staring at the needle gate.

"The only way out is to die."

He looked up at her with wide blue eyes. "But what does it mean to die? And why is the last butterfly glowing?"

She slowly approached the beam of light. Source. "Not physical death, right?" She ducked her head under the light and eased to the other side. Then lifted her hand and passed it through the focused beam, maybe a quarter of an inch in diameter, unaffected by her fingers.

"If the images through the Maker gate create the world as we know it, then death must be the death of images. Mental images are also called ideas. Old ideas have to die for the new to take their place."

She faced the portal, hand still in the light.

"Every idea we have of every image in that world makes up a piece of our identity in the world. We're bound to those images because we think they make us who we are."

She was speaking to herself more than to Jamie, processing her thoughts aloud.

"Our bodies, our relationships, our lives. We're terrified of losing those things because we think they make us who we are. Fear of loss keeps it all in place. Dying means letting go of all of it, our entire life in the world, to know ourselves beyond the images and relationships apparent in this world."

It made perfect sense to her now. It was as if she'd known all along. She wasn't ultimately Angie. That was the role and personality of a character being played in a fully dimensional experience called 'the world.'

"But how?" Jamie said. "I don't know how."

Angie looked back at him. "What sees the images?"

"Perception," he said. "The brain."

She nodded. "Perception. The brain decodes it all but it's only radically limited perception."

He blinked.

"So . . ." she said, facing the Image Maker portal again. "The old perception has to die." It seemed so obvious now. "The idea we have of ourselves has to die. Everything we perceive gets to die, just like dead heading. Out of one world and into another. Only in this case . . ."

"It's out of the virtual world, into who we are beyond it," he said.

"That's right. So how's our perception changed in a Deep Dive?"

Jamie answered immediately. "Acoustic neutralization."

Now she was leading him, she realized.

"That's right. But acoustics are vibration, just like light." She drew her fingers through the quarter-inch beam of light, playing with it even though it was unaffected by her. "So what if this light, the source before image making, can act like acoustic neutralization? What if the light itself is the truth? What if only the light can neutralize or purge the old images?"

His eyes were as round as quarters. "How?"

"Maybe just like everything in this room. We're still in the world of images. So in the world of images, what perceives them?"

"The eye," he said.

They both turned to the Image Maker book with stick figures. The one that had the eye they lifted out of the page.

Angie rushed to the book, flung the cover open and stared at the eye that operated the Image Maker gate.

"The eye has to play dead and be reborn like a butterfly!" she said.

Jamie put his small fingers on the eye, which quickly solidified in his hand. Then he hurried to the butterfly book. Flipped it open to the last page.

Angie stood over him, barely breathing as he brought the eye in his fingers to the glowing image of the butterfly's eye-head. The page seemed to suck the round eye into the image of the eye-head so that it became embedded halfway in. It fit! This was it!

Immediately the room's hum rose in pitch and volume. She spun to see that the focused beam of light flowing from the eye of the needle on the wall to the Image Maker portal was now at least six inches in diameter, blazing as a shaft of raw energy.

Like a massive arc of electricity from a welder's rod, the light hissed and crackled.

Too stunned to speak, she turned to Jamie. But Jamie was nowhere to be seen. Like a phantom, there one moment, gone the next. Had his mind skipped out of the dream or had he awoken in the prison cell? Either way, she was on her own.

The light was now in full flow, but the needle gate was still closed. So what would open it?

"The eye showed me what to do," she heard herself say. "I have to surrender my perception to the needle gate. My mind. My . . ."

The truth was now clear to her, but it seemed terribly dangerous.

"Everything," she said.

How could she surrender everything? It would kill her!

Then she remembered what Barnes had said. He was going to wipe her mind. Put her into a vegetative state from which she would never recover. So what did she have to lose?

Nothing.

She moved before she lost her nerve. Two careful steps and she was next to the crackling shaft of light where she pulled short, feeling the heat from the light radiating over her face.

"Everything, Angie. Everything!"

But her self-encouragement didn't get her moving. The light was searing hot and looked like it could cut through steel. She spread her arms wide, staring at the blazing shaft, rooted to the checkerboard floor. The gears whirred, the hum whined, the light raged. Angie could hardly think straight.

Barnes was going to wipe her brain. Or she was going to kill her brain. One way or another, her life would never be the same. She could trust the light, or she could trust . . . what? What else was there to trust but her own broken life?

"God, help me," she breathed. And with that breath, she faced the Image Maker portal and stepped into the shaft of light, half expecting it to burn straight through her skull with searing pain.

Like a supernova erupting from the core of her brain, searing light immediately blinded her to all but that light. She felt no pain, experienced nothing except whiteness that felt radically disorienting. Like a mind wipe.

Panicked, she was about to tear herself away when the vast sea of white light morphed into an image of the large mask on the Image Maker wall. Not just a plain mask this time, but a mask of *her* face.

The shaft of light blasted through her head and slammed into the mask dead-center before spreading out like a white flame. Immediately the surface of the mask began to flake away, as if under the full force of a powerful sandblaster.

Angie began to scream. Not from physical pain, but from a deep anguish she'd never felt before. It was as if her mind was being dismantled from the inside out.

Chunks of the mask began to disintegrate, leaving ragged gaps in the once-smooth surface. The whole facade that was her identity in the world was being stripped away. *Imago Simulacrum.* Image of statue. Idol. Mask.

Her character was being unmade.

Fully formed scenes emerged from those holes in the facade of her life and rushed toward her. It was as if the whole movie of her life, in millions of frames, was being replayed. Reversed. Relived.

The mask was gone, leaving only the flood of images flowing from the Image Maker portal back into her mind.

They came in full dimension, thrust upon her consciousness so that she relived them in their purest form. Every moment that she'd ever experienced, flowing with a raw power that took her breath away and shook her body from head to feet.

Every nightmare, every fear, every tear, every joy, every thrill, every thread of hope, every flower of love, every shard of rage—the full spectrum of beauty and suffering and anxiety and dread, relived in brutal clarity. She was shaking from head to foot, screaming without any capacity to silence herself because every experience of love was immediately smothered by ten of darkness and fear.

This was Play Dead. She was being deconstructed from the inside out like a caterpillar being liquified. This white room was her cocoon.

Caterpillars become butterflies, she thought. *They are reborn.*

With that thought, she surrendered to the light.

And as soon as she surrendered to the light, her fear vanished.

Still the fractals of her life came. Still the searing light blazed. Still her body shook, and now she floated off the floor. The light had pinned her in the air like a rag doll, unmaking her.

I'm dying, she thought. *I'm dying and I have no fear.*

CHAPTER
THIRTY-SIX

JAKE BARNES stood at the control console that overlooked Lab 23, the private lab in which he explored the boundaries of human existence and consciousness. The Red Protocol had taken Angie deep, beyond anything conventional neuroscience had yet discovered this side of the quantum field. There, she would find the white room.

To his knowledge, she and Jamie were the only two people in the world other than himself who'd found the white room, and even then, Barnes couldn't be sure of Jamie. He hadn't entered the Red Protocol per se, but the boy had mentioned the white room many times in his nightmares. It seemed he might have found a way to the back door in his dreams but was unable to retain the knowledge in a waking state.

But it wasn't only Jamie's mention of the white room that led Barnes to believe the boy had found it. It was more the fact that Angie and Jamie seemed to be connecting there. He knew this from Angie's conversations, most of which had been bugged and recorded.

Angie had called the white room the gate room, which was more accurate than she realized. He'd always understood the room as a piece of code—the back door into the infinite quantum source code, which allowed for this reality to be experienced as it was by those in it. A gate into or out of the whole virtual world.

Although he had no definite proof, Barnes was convinced that it was also the mechanism that could make, unmake, or modify the experience of that reality. A kind of hidden control room. Perhaps one that was meant to be discovered before the whole world annihilated itself.

Barnes scanned the sensors on the three monitors before him, analyzing the hundreds of data lines as if they were a part of him.

Of the many subjects he'd studied and watched over the past twenty years, Angie's shift into a subconscious state had always been the most fluid, and the data on the screens bore that out now. Like riding a wave deep into her own psyche, she'd dropped in effortlessly less than ten minutes earlier. Without exception, every other subject retained stable infra-low brain wave function while in the Red Protocol. Normal brain function.

When Angie dropped in, however, her infra-low waves indicated hyper rather than stable activity. Between eight and ten times as active as any other human brain. This could only mean that she was experiencing something far more profound than a virtual world.

It was as if she was more alive while under.

Fitting, he thought. Angie was Subject 1, the very first child he'd introduced to full immersion. She'd come from Lithuania, an orphan facing a life of suffering in a cruel world. She was only three when he'd taken her into the safety of his care and opened her mind to virtual worlds for days and weeks at a time, thus unveiling her. That was twenty-four years ago, when the technology was still in its infancy, but Angie had responded more profoundly than any other subject besides Jamie Hamilton. There had always been something unique about each of them.

He'd arranged for Angie to be adopted to unsuspecting parents when she was five and studied her every move to see how her mind reacted to various circumstances in a normal life. A life that he manipulated behind the scenes when his research called for it.

It was Barnes who facilitated Angie's experience of radically different cultures while growing up. Her father's appointments to France and Saudi Arabia were not coincidental. Neither were the brutal Dead Head murders that Angie investigated for her book, *Righteous*. Barnes engineered those to sow fear of VR technology into the public mind.

Nor was her parents' boating accident, a decision made when it became apparent that the mother was awakening to the truth about her daughter. In fact, it was the mother who first used the term *unveiled one*, which Barnes adopted in referring to all of his successful subjects.

It had all culminated in this, Angie Channing's final journey into the Red Protocol.

He was torn about his intention to initiate the sequence that would irrevocably wipe such a stunning mind. There was still so much to learn from her. So much she could show them about the boundary between this world and the real world.

It was critical that he understand the exact mechanism that would allow any mind to rise above the character they were playing in what was known as the world. Critical not so he could help others transcend their character, but so he could limit humanity's ability to do so. Someone had to be the gatekeeper.

And yet she presented a risk far too great to accept. Decades of research and technological advancement would be wiped out if she discovered the truth. His own life would end within two years if he couldn't crack the code, but it would be gone today if she exposed him.

Either way, he'd established a program within the Red Protocol directly tied to a pulse monitor embedded under his skin. If his pulse stopped for longer than one hour, the entire program would erase itself and be no more. He wasn't about to leave the world with a technology that it couldn't fully grasp or properly utilize.

Barnes was only forty-five when he first uncovered the mathematical proof that the reality they lived in was holographic, not only in theory, but as a matter of fact.

He couldn't accept this conclusion, naturally. Not without the extensive research and modeling that consumed him for the next decade. Only then was he able to surrender himself entirely to where the data had taken him.

He didn't know about other worlds, but in this world, all of 'humanity' was living in a virtual reality, a fully dimensional world, directed by those in it.

Who or what was behind it all? What was happening beyond this universe? Why did this virtual reality exist?

With abandon, he'd pursued deep spiritual realization, thinking maybe he was bumping up against a spiritual reality spoken of by the mystics. But this wasn't that. They, too, were simply characters lost in their roles.

He quickly understood why the characters in such a virtual reality would so strongly resist any notion that they were in a phantom world. It would rob them of their identity at a fundamental level, which was tantamount to death.

The daunting realization that he wasn't who he thought he was had wreaked havoc with his mind. Who was the real him, now playing the role of Jake Barnes in this virtual reality?

For several years he spent endless days and nights attempting and failing to find a way to break free from the illusion they were all in. It was then that he had first encountered the white room. It was then that he damaged his telomeres and began aging prematurely. Only after crushing defeat did he finally consider another option. And upon reflection, perhaps a better one.

Rather than escape it, what if he could manipulate it for the better? Transform it.

He just had to intercept, decode, and then recode the stream of information that formed the world as they knew it. Whoever did so would have the power to offer humanity a narrative that replaced the world of suffering they knew.

Conversely, they could manipulate the world's narrative for their own gain.

None of the characters on this world's stage would believe the truth, naturally. Even considering the truth would throw all but the most expansive minds into rage and confusion, inviting terrible chaos. They would crucify the messenger, surely. The information and technology had to be closely guarded.

So be it. This was his destiny and always had been.

Barnes took one last look at the beautiful form under the acoustic imaging array in the lab below. Right now she was likely in the gate room, desperately trying to free herself before he put her in a permanent vegetative state. Her last gift would be giving up her mind entirely in the service of humanity.

He reached for the wave modulator that would strip all neural networks attributed to cognitive function and leave her alive but in permanent darkness, utterly unaware. This was the Black Protocol—red for life, black for death.

"I'm so sorry, my dear," he breathed. "It's been a long journey."

He turned the dial until it would turn no farther and let out a sigh. He felt sorry for her. He really did.

The first indication that the Black Protocol was doing what it had been designed to do was reflected by a flatlining of all brain activity except the infra-low waves, which continued spiking in her active subconscious brain. Within five seconds, those waves were suppressed. And then they, too, flat-lined.

Angie was no more. The body in the chair below was still breathing, still alive, but in every other sense of the word, dead.

For a long minute, Barnes stared, feeling both sorrow and calm. He would have to find another suitable mind. His own was evidently too secure in its fundamental beliefs to accept full release from itself.

Barnes left the control room, made his way down one floor, and entered Lab 23. He would need to call the authorities and report the regrettable accident. Inquiries would be made and accusations leveled, but considering her profile and the release she'd signed, they would soon accept her fate.

She was a Dead Head who'd lost her husband in a tragedy. She had fractured and subjected herself to an experimental procedure that might have healed her but had instead rendered her brain-dead. This was an old story in the world of medicine. In time, even the negative press given to the procedure itself would be forgotten.

He walked to the RIG and pressed the canopy release. The acoustic imaging array over her body rose with a pneumatic hiss. He watched her lungs fill and empty—a body with a brain that allowed it to function, but no mind.

"What's happening?"

Barnes turned to Megan, who stood in the doorway, eyes wide. She looked at Angie's body, then at the monitors. Those that showed no brain cognition.

"What's going on?" she demanded, walking up to him, eyes still on the screens. "She's . . . Is that right?"

Barnes swallowed, momentarily overwhelmed by the finality of his decision.

"I'm afraid so. She was beyond herself and deeply fractured. I didn't have time to assemble the team. I don't know how it happened. It was almost as if she did it to herself from the inside. I . . ." He faltered for effect.

Megan's face was white. She hurried to the far side of the chair and quickly cycled through several screens. "She's . . . She's brain-dead?"

"We have to call . . ."

His eyes were on Angie's naked body, lying in peace not three feet from where he stood.

She was there, in the flesh, breathing gently.

And in the next moment, she was gone. Just gone, leaving an empty RIG.

Megan jumped back, throwing a hand over her mouth to stifle a cry of alarm.

Barnes stood frozen. She'd vanished. Yes, but . . . He glanced around as if he might find her, even knowing he wouldn't. How could...?

And then he knew how she could vanish. She'd exited this world. Her character no longer existed here. He'd surmised that bodies didn't vanish when people died because they were still playing the role of the dead. But Angie hadn't died. She'd done what no other character had ever done.

She'd found the way out of the virtual world while alive in it.

"Dear God," he breathed. "She's done it."

CHAPTER
THIRTY-SEVEN

ANGIE SLOWLY opened her eyes and stared up at the white ceiling as her mind found itself. Where was she? She jerked up and looked around to see that she was in a room, maybe five by eight. She wore a black robe and was lying on a spa bed. The walls were white, bathed in a warm blue light. Nothing else except for a small bowl fountain in one corner and a side table with what appeared to be her clothing—jeans and white T-shirt—folded neatly on top of it.

Something was stuck on her forehead, and she lifted her hand to feel a small round disk. She scraped it off. A single white disk throbbing with green light. She couldn't remember what it was, where she was, or why she was here.

She set the small disk on the pillow, swung her legs off the bed, and walked to the door. Pulled it open and stepped out of the room.

The hall outside was empty. The words *Play Dead* were inscribed on a small black plaque that identified the room she'd emerged from. The hall ended at a thin veneer of water silently flowing down the wall from the ceiling to the floor. Three more doors lined the hall, all closed. An archway led from the hall next to the waterfall.

The place was like a day spa, she thought. And even though she couldn't remember why she was here, she felt perfectly at ease. Fully rejuvenated.

Overwhelmingly grateful just to be alive despite being at such a loss. Whatever treatment she'd experienced in this spa seemed to have done wonders.

Angie walked down the hall, stepped through the archway, and entered a large white room with a black desk at its center and tall windows that over-looked an arid landscape. Memory tumbled into her mind. This was Jake Barnes's office overlooking Austin.

She'd been in the gate room with Jamie, who'd vanished. She'd stepped into the light and woke up here, in Barnes's office. Why? And what were the spa rooms? Even more, why did she feel so at ease despite feeling so disori-ented? Was this the real world beyond the virtual world?

"That was quick."

She turned her head and saw a woman at the head of a conference table to her right. Four others were seated casually on adjacent chairs—two women and two men. She recognized them all.

The woman at the head was her mother, Sarah, dressed in a white busi-ness suit. But that was impossible because her mother was dead. The other two women were Felicia Buckhead, her therapist, and Judith Patterson, the governor of Texas.

Angie blinked. They were here?

The man closest to Sarah was Darey. That, too, was impossible, Darey was dead. And the other was Randy.

"What's happening?" she asked, barefooted on the marble floor.

Her mother smiled. "Take a deep breath, darling. The aftereffects will wear off in a few minutes."

"You . . . You're alive?"

The woman who was—but couldn't be—her mother offered the others an amused glance. "Last time I checked. Join us, Eve. Take a seat."

Eve. With that one word, Angie's mind began to clear. She'd entered a virtual world nearly identical to the real world through a game called Play Dead—the game of life. The disk on her head was the interface to that world.

More details fell into her mind half-formed. She was in her thirties, single, dedicated to following in her mother's footsteps. They were in the Temple, a center for higher learning and spiritual development established by her mother. But she couldn't place the others in the room. She recognized them from the game, but she couldn't remember who they were here.

"You're still attached to the narrative of the Practice," her mother said. "The shock will pass as you remember yourself in this world." Her mother nodded at a chair, eyes bright. "Sit with us, darling."

Was she still attached? She remembered all the details from the game—the Practice they called it—but she felt strangely unattached. Free.

Angie walked to the table and slid into the seat opposite her mother.

"Sarah?"

"That's who I was in your Practice?" her mother asked.

Angie nodded. "You were my mother."

"Wonderful. Well, that's who I am here as well." She nodded at Darey. "You remember Sebastian?"

She glanced between the two men, mind still swimming in the relationships she'd had with them. In the Practice, she loved them both in different ways. But she was still having a hard time placing them here. Her connection to Sebastian, who was Darey in the other world, confused her the most. She felt little for him here even though he'd meant the most to her in the other world.

"Kind of," she said, eyes on Sebastian. "Only you were Darey. I was married to you."

His brow arched. "Lovely. But I can assure you we've never been married. I was transferred from the Brussels temple last week, which was the first we met. But thank you for populating your world with me in such an insightful way."

A few chuckles. Now the details filling her memory took richer form. She looked at the man who'd been Randy in the virtual world.

"And you're Daniel."

"As you well know," he said. Hearing his voice, Angie remembered that she'd developed somewhat of a crush on Daniel, the first in a long time. She even imagined Daniel as a husband and father. She hadn't whispered a word of this to him, naturally. They'd been close friends for over ten years and she'd been afraid to mess that up.

Looking at him now, she saw no reason why she shouldn't share her feelings with him. There was nothing to fear.

The other two women, Felicia and Judith, were watching her with interest.

"You were my therapist," Angie said to Felicia before turning to Judith. "And you were Judith, a governor."

"Politics? Please. I would rather swallow razor blades than run for office. And in case you haven't placed me, I'm Casandra." She nodded at Felicia. "She's Loren. Plays a mean violin."

Angie remembered. Casandra was a playwright and Loren was a world-renowned musician.

"How do you feel, Eve?" her mother asked, eyeing her curiously.

"I'm still a bit . . . It's coming back."

"Yes, but how do you *feel?*"

Angie thought about it. "I feel grateful. Actually, I feel . . ." She wasn't sure what words to use to describe the deep calm in her veins. "Peace," she finally said.

"No concern or anxiety?"

Angie shook her head. "No. Just a little fuzzy on the details."

Her mother exchanged a look with the others, who also seemed curious. Was she supposed to be feeling anxious?

"Start from the top, darling," her mother said, voice now softer. "Tell us what's happening, not in the virtual world, but here, in Prime. Speaking it aloud is the fastest way to anchor back into reality."

"This is Prime," she said, remembering. "It's Earth but we call it Prime to distinguish it from the virtual Earth in Play Dead, which I just came from."

Daniel had risen and was walking toward a table with fruits, pastries and water. Beyond the table, a server walked in carrying a plate of cheeses. Angie knew her as well.

This was Susan Milton, the woman Matteo had hanged—the poor mother who'd suffered so much in the last few weeks of her life in that other world.

"Susan?"

The server looked at her as she set the tray down. "Susan?" She smiled. "Yes, I lived that life in the Practice a month ago. Just coming out, huh? We aren't encouraged to discuss our experience in the Practice, but I assure you I felt no lingering effects from that nasty hanging. And, as you know, there's no time correlation between what happens here and what happens in that world."

The server glanced at her mother. "Do you need anything else?"

"That's more than enough, Kristen. Thank you."

Kristen dipped her head. "Enjoy." She left the office the way she'd come.

"Please continue, darling. Tell me who you are."

Angie said what she now remembered about herself.

"My name's Eve Channing and you're my mother. My father's name is Theo Channing, a philanthropist known the world over. I love horses and water skiing and speak three languages other than English, French fluently because I was born in France. You and I returned to the United States ten years ago, leaving Father to oversee operations in the eastern hemisphere. I'm very close to him and see him as often as I can. The year is 2061, and we are more advanced than the world in Play Dead, which is a virtual reality created by the Temple as a practice of transformation. How am I doing?"

"Perfectly. What is *Temple*?"

"Temple is symbolic of incarnation. Our bodies are temples of spirit or consciousness. It used to be called religion. The game Play Dead is like a meditation. Millions enter the game—the Practice—each day. The most devout enter the Practice every day. The virtual technology is similar to the Red Protocol in the virtual world, but far more advanced."

With each passing breath, it became clearer.

"The only way to complete the Practice, or to win the game so to speak, is to awaken to who you really are beyond that world while still in it. We do this Practice because it mirrors our own spiritual journey here, which is to awaken to who we are both in and beyond this world. It's difficult because in the Practice, an initiate becomes their character without any memory of who they were before entering the game. When we enter, we can enter at any point in the history of that world, and we often blueprint our lives to meet up with other players we know here, although once in the game we don't know we've set it up beforehand. No one's yet succeeded in waking up to the full truth while in the Play Dead world."

Was that true? Daniel set a glass of water and a small plate of strawberries and cheese on the table. She gave him a thin smile, *thank you*, and went on, emboldened. He had such a beautiful spirit—it was no wonder she'd been drawn to him, both here and in the virtual world.

"There's no correlation of time between this world and the world we created, because Play Dead creates its own space-time. One or two hours in the game here is experienced as an entire lifetime in the Practice. When you enter the game, you're born as an infant in that world and live until you die, at which time you wake up from the Practice, leaving only a trace program that manifests as a corpse, which is buried and mourned in that world. "

She stopped, but her mother urged her on.

"Go on. Speak it out."

"Those who use the Practice often go back many times, each time as a new character, which is why the virtual world is populated by billions of people. Virtual people. The storyline of that world can only be changed by those in the Practice. No one's ever woken up while in the game, but each time they go back, they retain subconscious knowledge that pulls them closer to the truth."

She'd said no one had ever woken up while in the Practice. But that wasn't true, was it?

Daniel was wearing a whimsical smile and clapping. "She's back. Just in time to hear the president's address to the nation."

She'd forgotten about that. "When?"

"Ten minutes. Word on the feed is that she's going to declare war on the United Nations. You don't remember?"

Of course she did. "It's coming back," she said. "We might find ourselves in a world war over the inequitable global distribution of wealth. This day was always coming."

"As long as there's money, there's war," he said.

Angie made a correction without thinking about it. "Until humanity wakes up beyond fear and judgment, there will always be war. It has nothing to do with money itself, only the meaning we give to money."

He dipped his head. *Touché.* "Even truer."

"What did you learn in the Practice, Eve?" Sarah asked, studying her closely.

"I learned what I always learn, that all the suffering we experience here is just like the suffering we experience in that world. It's all rooted in a radical misperception of reality powered by fear."

Angie glanced around the table. "Have any of you . . . Did you ever find a white room?"

They looked at Sarah.

"Can you describe this white room to me, Eve?" her mother asked. She was settled back in her chair with one leg folded over the other, hands in her lap, but there was nothing relaxed about her focus.

"There were two gates, the *Imago Simulacrum* gate and *Veritas Vos Liberabit* gate," Angie said. "I called the first one Image Maker, and the second one, the needle gate because that's what Jamie called it. Jamie was a boy in the room. We were working together to solve it."

Were they all aware of the gate room? She thought so, but maybe no one else knew how it worked. Or maybe they'd all found it and she was just late to the party. But she couldn't remember any mention of it.

"Were you able to open either gate?" her mother asked.

Angie nodded. "First the Image Maker gate, which showed me what I thought of as the movie of my life. Then the needle gate, which opened when I died. But . . ."

Had she died? She must have, because it was the only way out of the Practice and she was out.

"Eve?"

"Yes?"

"Did you *die* in the Practice?"

"The light went through me and . . ." She looked from one to the other, only now fully recalling what had happened.

A tingle ran over the crown of her head, over her shoulders and down her arms. She hadn't died in the game, had she? No, she'd transcended it.

"Did your *body* die, Eve?" her mother pressed.

"No. Not my body. Only the images that were me died."

Silence thick enough to suffocate settled over them all. Their eyes were on her as they took it in. They knew too. Maybe it was the look on her face, maybe the fact that her body hadn't died. But they knew. She'd done it.

The images that were identity had been consumed by the light. She'd died to the dramas of that world by surrendering her whole self to the light.

Suddenly overwhelmed, Angie lowered her forehead into her hand, half covering her eyes as tears slipped down her cheeks. She couldn't comprehend what she'd done, really. Only that in transcending the Practice she'd somehow changed everything about her life forever.

"Would you mind giving us a moment alone?" her mother said quietly.

The others pushed back from the table and rose, each dipping their head to Sarah, their matriarch. Daniel, who was as much Randy to her now, put a hand on her shoulder as he passed. "I always knew you would be the first," he said.

But Angie didn't think she was the first.

The door closed, leaving them alone. Angie sat in the lingering silence, head bent and eyes closed now, allowing her emotions to fall away.

"I'm so proud of you, my darling."

She didn't know how to respond to that because she couldn't find any pride. Only gratefulness.

Her mother stood. "Join me," she said, walking to the tall windows that overlooked the city to the south. Angie pushed her chair back and followed.

For a few long seconds they looked at the skyline. And such a beautiful skyline it was. She'd never seen it so blue. Everything looked more alive to her. In that moment, there were no problems, nor had there ever been. She could only imagine what her life back in the Practice would be like with this awareness.

"Tell me about the light," her mother said.

"I gave myself to it," Angie said. "The Image Maker portal showed me everything I'd ever done or thought. Every experience, every scene. It took me apart from the inside and then I woke up here." Her mind was still swimming in an ocean of wonder.

Her mother faced her. "The reason so few find the narrow way is that their brains are part of that world's encoding and, as such, must operate within the logos of that world. They are in the world and *of* its logic, and that logic demands judgment of self and the world. The others know about the white room, but even knowing, they can't find it, because when they're born into that world, they have no recollection of it. They're immediately fragmented, separated from their true identity, lost. In that state, the need to belong to something becomes primal. Fearing that they will never measure up to the conditions of belonging in a world of judgment, they try even harder, desperately clinging to anything that feels fulfilling. Wealth, relationships, family, politics, country, religion, vices—everything and anything. It's everyone's story in that world and this."

So simple, really, Angie thought. She continued for her mother.

"In the end, transcendence—winning the Practice we call Play Dead—comes only as we release the logic of our own ideas and all of the judgments that those ideas demand," Angie said. "This can only be known and experienced through a kind of death and rebirth while in the Practice. Few are willing to take up that cross."

Sarah took Angie's hand and kissed her knuckles.

"But when we do, the caterpillar dies to what it was in its tomb and awakens as a butterfly. It's fitting that your name is Eve. You are the first."

"But I'm not the first, Mother," she said. "You have as well, haven't you?"

Her mother's kind eyes held her. There was no denial in them.

"When?" Angie asked.

"Two hundred and ninety-two days ago," her mother said quietly.

Angie remembered that time clearly. Her mother's urgency had vanished, replaced by a surety of their purpose without any concern. Now she understood why.

"And now that you've transcended the virtual world, can you transcend this world?"

"Of course, darling. That's the whole point of the Practice."

A part of her wanted to ask her mother if she had transcended this world, but the rest of her knew it was a sacred experience where mystery could be known but not explained.

"But there's more, Eve." Sarah looked at the horizon. "The choice that confronts you is the most important one you will ever face."

"What choice?"

"Walk with me." Her mother stepped lightly along the towering windows. Outside, sparrows had built a nest under the eaves. No fewer than five swooped and dove, doing what birds did to live and feed their young and experience their world. What might have seemed rather haphazard before now struck Eve as a perfectly executed, divine dance.

"Beautiful, isn't it?" her mother asked, her eyes following the birds.

"I've never seen them so beautiful."

"When you change the way you see the world, you make a whole new world," her mother said, repeating one of her favorite truisms. "You and I both know that intimately now. The world of Play Dead is blind to the only thing that can save it."

Angie briefly wondered what was happening to Jamie in the virtual world. The thought filled her with a strange mix of emotions.

"If I've transcended, why do I still feel some things so strongly?"

"Because you're still in the world, darling. As long as you're in any narrative, you'll experience that narrative with emotions. We never find ourselves as robots. We always have choice. And now you have one. Would you choose to know your truest self out of that world . . . or in that world?"

The question confused Angie. *That* world, as in the virtual world? But why? She'd just transcended the world of Play Dead.

"I don't understand," she finally said. "I thought discovering reality beyond the virtual world was the whole point. Play Dead isn't the real world."

"But that's where you're wrong. The virtual world *is* real. Not in the way we think when we consider absolute reality, but as an experience of a lifetime that is real, very real. And it has a direct effect on people's lives here."

"But that doesn't mean it's really real, right?"

"As real as anything we think of as real. How one navigates their experience in Play Dead has a direct effect on their lives when they emerge from the Practice. Those who learn deeper love in the Practice demonstrate it here. The race wars of the 2020s, for example, were experienced by those in the Practice here, and as a result, racism in Prime is nonexistent. We know firsthand how insane it is to put significance in the shape or color of one's avatar. In these ways, Prime has already been massively impacted by the Practice of Play Dead."

"You learn love there and it becomes a part of you here," Angie said.

"Indeed. Everything in the Practice affects life here, because it changes the one practicing. If one were to commit suicide in the game, their lives here would become very difficult. All of the suffering and war and darkness in that world are experienced as real there and directly affect life here."

Her mother took a deep breath.

"Which is why I've given every waking breath of my life for the sake of this world. You can do the same. That will be your choice."

Angie was still somewhat confused.

"You want me to work with you?" Together, she and her mother could change everything here. "Of course I will."

"No, Eve. This world already has its witness of truth beyond illusion. The world of Play Dead doesn't."

The idea collapsed into Angie's mind as a fully fleshed story. Re-enter Play Dead as an awakened one. Her fingers trembled as her memory of her life in Play Dead blossomed, drawing her with deep compassion for that world. She'd been so lost, so fractured, so laden with lies of unworthiness. So were all who lived there, even if they'd buried their fears so they wouldn't have to deal with them.

"There's something else you should know," her mother said. "All of our forecasting models, which have proven to be accurate, predict that the Earth in Play Dead will end with cataclysm in the next twenty years if humanity remains on its current trajectory. The suffering and horror that will come to that world will be far greater than any experienced in its history. Humanity seems determined to destroy itself, both there and here. If we can change that course there, we can surely change it here."

The revelation surprised Angie. "Only twenty years?"

"So you see, Play Dead is a virtual world, but every soul there will endure increasing suffering unless they turn to the truth, which replaces fear with love. Jamie still needs your help. So does Randy. So does this world."

Anyone who transcended in the virtual world would affect the awakening of Prime. Her mother would bring the light here, she would bring it there. Her pulse surged.

She turned her head. "Do you know who Jamie is here?"

Her mother shifted her eyes. "I believe I do."

"And?"

"In the current narrative, Jamie is your father."

Angie gasped. "Father?"

"Theo Channing, my dear husband and your father."

The revelation stunned her. Jamie, her father, right now incarcerated in the virtual world! Her pulse surged.

"How would I do it?" Angie asked.

"There would be a great cost. It's never been done before, and we have to put you in within six hours or the window for reentry will collapse. But I—"

"Tell me how."

"Once there, you won't know fear, but you'll have other emotions that can be difficult to navigate."

"Of course. But how, Mother? Just tell me."

Her mother hesitated, then smiled and took her hand.

"Follow me."

She led Angie from the office down a long hall that overlooked a large atrium bustling with a dozen staff. Angie recognized many of them now, but one stood out like a beacon of light. Clair Milton was walking through the atrium with a young man her age, deep in passionate discussion about something that clearly excited her. She couldn't see the young man's face or remember Clair's name here, but there was no mistaking the girl.

How beautiful. How wondrous. Clair was alive here if not there. And so was her mother, Susan.

They turned down a second hall and approached a large steel door. This was the Hub, the main control center for Play Dead, Angie recalled.

Her mother was reaching for the panel that would grant them access when the door swung open from the inside. A janitor with gray hair emerged. Angie blinked twice. The man in the blue coveralls was Jake Barnes, looking twenty years younger than the head of Convergence in Play Dead, but surely him. Or the one playing him.

"Thank you, William," her mother said.

"My pleasure, ma'am."

"Give my blessing to your daughter. I hear she's passed the bar."

Barnes, who was actually William, grinned wide. "Sharp as a whip, that one." He turned back to the room he'd come from. "Coming, Frank?"

"Coming."

A second janitor emerged from the room. It was Matteo, younger and with blond rather than dark hair, but most definitely Matteo—the same man whose head she'd blown off outside the cave in Play Dead.

"Mind the storage light," he said to Sarah. "I'll have it replaced today."

"Of course. Thank you, Frank."

Matteo, who was Frank, dipped his head at Angie. "Ma'am." He followed William away from the Hub.

Barnes and Matteo were both janitors. Go figure. She would have to remember that if she went back.

The back wall in the small twenty-by-twenty room was lined with panels of blinking green and yellow lights, behind which hid the main quantum processors, which powered Play Dead. It was by far the most powerful processor in the world.

Sarah walked to three chairs facing four large screens that monitored critical operations.

"The interface changes once you've transcended Play Dead as you have. You can go back using the portal, but you personally won't be able to find the gate room again. You can point others to the white room—it's encoded in every mind—but once there, only physical death will take you out again."

Her mother pressed a small black button, and a tray holding a single red disk the size of a poker chip slid out.

"Normally, when you go in, you would start from birth without any memory of any prior experience. But if you choose to go back now that you've transcended, you'll pick up exactly where you left off, fully aware of everything that's happened to you. You'd be the only one in the virtual world to truly know yourself as you are, in the world but not of it. Reborn as the unveiled one."

Angie tried to imagine what that would be like, but her mind faltered.

"So Randy and Jamie and the others from that world would be as I left them," Angie said.

Her mother withdrew the poker-chip-sized disk from the tray. Its translucent skin pulsed with red hues. A quantum data chip. It was said that all the data in the world could be stored on even one such chip.

"Exactly as you left them. Only a few moments will have passed."

"And what about here? How much time will pass here?"

Her mother took a deep breath and closed her eyes for a moment. When she opened them, they were swimming in tears. She took Angie's hand in trembling fingers.

"That would be the cost, my darling. The only way to incarnate now that you've transcended the code is to wipe your mind here, leaving you in a lifelong coma."

Angie wasn't sure she was understanding. "Going under is always like going into a coma," she said.

"But only for an hour or two. If you return to the Practice, you would never again awaken in this world. When you finally die there, you'll find yourself in the world of souls."

"But . . ." She would never see her mother or father again? "What happens to my body here? It's just in a coma and then dies?"

Tears slipped down her mother's cheeks. It was answer enough.

Angie didn't know what to think. Deep emotions seeped through her bones and filled her chest. It wasn't fear. It was sorrow and compassion. Compassion for herself and her father and for the mother standing before her with tears in her eyes.

They were like twins. That would end? And what about her father here?

The emotions flooding her chest broke through and she lowered her forehead on her mother's shoulder, suddenly weeping beyond her control.

Sarah placed a hand on the back of her head and held her without speaking. Mother and daughter stood in the hub of Play Dead, overwhelmed and for one reason only.

The both knew she would go back.

"I love you, Mother."

"You don't have to do it, Eve. You can stay here with me and we can change this world another way."

But Angie already knew that this was her path. As the sorrow bled from her body, a deep resolve replaced it. She had to go back for the sake of both worlds. She swallowed the lump in her throat.

What was it like to live in a world one had transcended? What was it like to have entered a cocoon as one creature and then emerge as a new creature to live in that same world? A butterfly on the wings of love in the world of caterpillars crawling through fear.

The calling drew her.

Angie lifted her head, took a deep breath, and slowly exhaled.

"I have to go within six hours?"

"Unfortunately, yes. When you came out, you left a phantom trace. It will be gone within six hours and you won't be able to return as Angie."

"You always knew this day might come, didn't you?"

"Yes. And I would go myself but I'm not sure this world can survive without me. You'll be going as me, so I'll always be with you. You understand that, don't you?"

Angie nodded. "I need to do this."

"Are you sure? You really don't—"

"Is it what you want?" Angie asked.

"I don't want either way. It's your choice and only yours."

"Then my choice is to go."

Her mother reached up and wiped her cheeks with her thumb. She offered a thin smile.

"Will anything else be different when I go?" Angie asked.

"Yes, but you'll discover those differences on your own. Let's just say that once you've experienced yourself beyond the limitations of the codified world of illusions, life changes dramatically."

Angie nodded, needing no further clarification. If her mother said she would learn herself, then she would.

Her mother held up the quantum drive between her thumb and forefinger. "What's that for?"

"This disk may give you some assistance. You can't take it with you, but you can scan its contents now, before you go back in. Take it."

Angie took the data drive. "Assist me how?"

"The Image Maker portal in the gate room showed you every scene connected to your own life. I'm assuming you navigated it as best you could."

"I didn't have much time, but yes."

"This disk contains the entire history of everything connected to your life while you were alive in the virtual world."

"Everything?"

"Everything in your own timeline. Search it for whatever you like, but I would practice some discrimination. Too much information will only bog you down. Allow some people their privacy." Her mother was showing courage, but Angie could only imagine her emotions. "Consider it a small gift." She forced a smile.

"Thank you." She leaned forward and kissed her mother's cheek. New tears were already forming in her eyes. "You're no more of this world than I am of that one. In the world but not of it, isn't that what you've always said? We will meet again."

"Without question," her mother said. "And now that world awaits."

Angie thought about Convergence and the governor and Randy and Jamie, who was her father, and all the trouble that threatened that world from its own perspective. The data in her hand would show her far more than any of them could possibly know.

"Can I say good-bye to the others?"

Her mother smiled and tenderly tucked her hair behind her ear. Then kissed her forehead.

"Of course. Your father's the one I worry about the most. He'll think the world has come to an end, but an hour with you in the holodeck will go a long way."

"When?"

"As soon as you learn what you need from the drive. You can work here while I make the arrangements."

She squeezed Angie's hand and walked for the door.

"Mother?"

"Yes?" she said, turning back.

"Have you ever wondered if this world's a virtual world too? We would never know it."

Her mother's brow arched.

"No, we wouldn't."

CHAPTER
THIRTY-EIGHT

IN ONE MOMENT, Angie was swallowed by the void of unconsciousness in the Play Dead portal, and in the next she was fully awake, standing in the middle of a room. For a few long seconds she remained still, allowing the disorientation of her passage to dissipate, grasping for thoughts, feeling her heart beating heavily. The fog cleared and details filtered into her awareness.

She'd entered the needle gate and awoken from this virtual world by surrendering to the light. Given the choice, she'd decided to return to this world. Her body was now in a coma in Prime, oblivious to all but this world, as it would remain until she died. Using Play Dead's space-time navigation, she'd chosen to integrate herself here, in Clair Milton's bedroom.

Strange, but she felt no concern whatsoever about her life in Prime and those she'd left behind. This was now her world. Her calling. Her mission. And her father, who was Jamie, was central to that mission now.

She'd been naked when she'd left Prime and she was naked now, so the first order of business was to find some clothes.

Angie stepped to the door, entered the hall, and walked for the living room. She already knew no one would be at home. The data had shown her that as well.

Her mother had said she would experience this world differently now, and, apart from the deep knowing that accompanied her every heartbeat, she wasn't sure how that difference would manifest. But she felt no urgency. No anxiety. No fear, only a deep peace.

She glanced at her feet, walking across the stone floor. She was naked but felt not even a tinge of shame, even though anyone on the street would be able to see her through the large windows. Her investment in her body had been replaced by a simple acknowledgement of it and appreciation for it. Without this body, she wouldn't be able to taste and touch and feel and see and hear. Without it she wouldn't be able to experience either suffering or pleasure. It was such a beautiful gift. How it appeared to others was completely immaterial. Pun intended.

Something banged into the window when she was halfway across the living room and she jumped back, startled. A bird had hit the glass and was flapping away. Okay, so she could still feel startled. That was good, because it meant she wasn't stripped of basic human survival instincts or emotions.

It wasn't fear but self-preservation. She wouldn't put her hand in the fire, not because she *feared* fire, but because she still wanted use of that hand.

How deeply would she feel other emotions? She would find out soon enough, she supposed.

Angie headed for the bedroom, ducking under the yellow tape strung across the door. Susan Milton's hanging had been called a suicide, but Renee Dalton, the chief of police, had ordered a forensic sweep anyway. She wasn't a part of the conspiracy to hack the code and manipulate this world for personal gain. It was one of the many things she'd learned from the disk in Prime because this, too, was a part of her life story here.

So was Jake Barnes's discovery that they lived in a virtual world. And her role as one of his lab rats as a young child along with Jamie and nineteen other orphans, beginning in 2031. Of the twenty-one, only she and Jamie were still alive in this world. Four of the others had been killed, the rest had died inexplicably in their twenties, an outcome of the Red Protocol's effects on their brains when the technology was still in its infancy.

None of it bothered her. Even the deepest, darkest, most horrifying acts had presented themselves to her as what they were: the folly of mankind attempting to know itself in blindness. How could she blame anyone for only doing their best to know what and who they were? Outside the system, there was no difference between a murder and a harsh word. All of it was essentially made of the same folly.

Jamie had found the gate room in his dreams years ago but was stuck there because he couldn't hold on to the gate upon waking. She'd only found it a few weeks ago. All of this had been observed by Barnes, who could step into their minds whenever they were dead heading through a trace he'd encoded in their brains when they were five years old.

She and Jamie were bonded by that trace, which is why they'd found each other in the gate room. She wanted to believe that him being her father in Prime had something to do with it, but that's not how the virtual world worked, her mother said.

Using the Red Protocol, Barnes had been in the gate room many times without progressing. A rich mind such as his was more difficult to surrender even when presented directly with the truth.

Awakening required surrendering to a great unknown, not clinging to certainties of what was 'known' about oneself and the world as taught by history, society, religion and science. Surrendering all concepts of what was true was a narrow way that few found, thus depicted as a needle in the gate room.

Angie stepped into the master bedroom. The rope and body were both gone, but Angie had seen the room as it appeared when the maid discovered Susan's body, three days earlier. Susan, who was really Kristen in Prime, had learned what she'd come to learn. Only the decaying body called Susan remained here, in a morgue or grave somewhere. That body, like all bodies, was virtual, encoded with a self-destructive program called decomposition.

And yet, even knowing this, Angie felt a stab of deep compassion. Susan had suffered far too much in her life, particularly in these last few weeks. They said fear was False Evidence Appearing Real. The whole world was trapped in that false evidence and was experiencing it as real—thus suffering.

Angie was here to point to the truth that would set them free before they destroyed themselves in terrible cataclysm and deep suffering. She wouldn't do so by convincing the world that it was virtual—doing so would fall on deaf ears. Instead, she would point to the truth by offering the path of transformation to those who sought it. This world and Prime would change one heart at a time. And then ten. And then a hundred.

And then by the millions.

She took a deep breath and walked into Susan's closet. They were roughly the same build, though the character of Susan had been slightly taller. It was immediately clear that Susan preferred splashy colors and dresses, whereas Angie preferred jeans and T-shirts, mostly neutral colors or, better, black.

So Angie still had her preferences. But of course, all characters had personalities. She would accept herself as she was.

She pulled a drawer open, was greeted by a carefully folded stack of jeans, and was about to reach in when she first noticed the shimmer. She blinked, hand half extended.

The shimmer was gone.

But as she focused on the jeans, the shimmer returned, as if she herself had asked the jeans to reveal themselves as they truly were, obligating them to comply. Was this what her mother had meant when she said Angie would experience the world differently?

She looked around the large closet and saw it all in shimmer now. It was all information codified and collapsed into an experience of solidity, just like in all virtual experiences. This one called the Practice was just so finely tuned that only death would shed its imaging.

That or waking from this world while in it, as she had.

Angie reached for a white blouse on a hanger. Her fingers passed halfway through the material before the shimmering shirt moved. She could evidently see through the illusion of all matter in the simulation simply by focusing. Interesting. Even more interesting was the fact that, with even a slight shift in focus, the shirt became just a shirt.

In the world but not of it.

She found a pair of jeans and pulled them on. Too long by a couple inches. She could roll them up. The black Texas Tech T-shirt that she pulled off a hanger fit wonderfully. She was good to go. No need for shoes.

Now for the encrypted key that Clair had wisely hidden behind a perfectly fitted but loose tile under the bathroom sink across the hall from her room, far from prying eyes. There was nothing on it that would help Jamie—it had been made before the murders and, in fact, made no mention of Jamie. Angie would have to help Jamie another way.

Neither did the drive prove that this world was virtual. But it did provide other leverage that was of significant value. She would retrieve it as planned and then she would call Randy.

RANDY SAT at the small conference table adjacent to the chief's office, grateful that she'd pulled the blinds and, so far at any rate, sequestered him. Matteo was dead, but whoever had been pulling his strings had other strings to pull. One way or the other, they would silence him.

Three hours had passed and still no word from Angie, at least not that Renee was sharing with him. With nothing to distract him, he'd rehearsed every turn of the last two weeks, hoping he'd missed a connection that might persuade Renee to consider the possibility that Jamie was being framed. But he was coming up empty. There was no recording of Matteo's confession at the cave; the copy of Clair's letter was gone, presumably taken by Matteo when he killed Susan; the footage that cleared Jamie had been taken; the encrypted key was nowhere to be found. Everything else he had was either circumstantial or hearsay.

That left only Angie, and she'd gone into the wolves' den.

The door opened and Renee walked in, phone in hand. She shut the door behind her and faced him, jaw firm.

"She's coming," she said.

"Who's coming?"

"Your girl. Angie Channing."

She'd succeeded? Randy shoved his chair back and stood, ignoring the pain in his side and shoulder. "She's at Convergence?"

"They say they have no record of her visiting today. She claims she was at the Milton residence before going to her own house. She'll be here in ten minutes."

The key. Why else would she go to the Milton house?

"You talked to her? Why didn't you tell me?"

"I *am* telling you. She called for you but they routed the call to me." Renee shifted nervously. What was she withholding?

"For heaven's sake, Renee. Just tell me what's going on."

"Well, for starters, she confessed to killing this Matteo fellow. It clears you, but you need to know that we'll treat her as we would any murder suspect. She's being intercepted now and will be under heavy escort."

"Whose idea was that? Olsen's?"

"Mine, Randy. I don't like this. It's all gotten way out of hand!" She was pacing now. "I don't like that two kids died such a horrible death on my watch. I don't like that another kid with ASD snapped and killed them. I don't like mothers committing suicide. I don't like you going AWOL and I definitely don't like the idea of some conspiracy. Andrew Olsen's going ballistic and I'm getting calls from the governor, which I'm deferring for no good reason, and now Angie Channing's waltzing in with what she claims is new evidence. When did she become law enforcement?"

Relief washed over him. Not only was Angie alive, she'd found something.

"Tell me exactly what she said."

"She asked to meet with the two of us and Andrew Olsen. No one else. Said she'd meet us out front. She also said she's already informed the media of her intentions to come in. There are three news vans out front as we speak. I don't like it, Randy. This isn't how we work."

"I knew it!" It was all he could do to not grin ear to ear.

"You knew what? None of this changes anything in my book."

He shoved his hands into his pockets, feeling unreasonable euphoria. She was alive. She was coming. She was a goddess. He caught himself, surprised by the last thought.

"So what happens now?" he asked.

She sighed. "We meet her out front and take her to the main conference room. But believe me when I say she'll be in a cell as soon as she's done telling her stories. Like I said, this changes nothing."

"And the DA?"

Renee hesitated. "He doesn't like it either, but he'll be there."

CHAPTER
THIRTY-NINE

SIX CRUISERS and at least three drones that Angie could see. The drones flew above and behind, so there could be ten for all she knew. Two cruisers with flashing lights had pulled in front of her on Caesar Chavez, one on either side, and two behind. They'd brought the entire fleet to make sure their guest in crime made it safely. It was amusing and oddly comforting. Little could they know how the information she brought might change their world.

Mother would be proud.

She pulled into the left lane to take Red River north at the next light, forcing one of the cruisers to fall back—it was either that or be run over by her. The officer in the cruiser objected with two short *blurps* from his siren, but she ignored them. What did two digital *blurps* in a virtual world mean to her now anyway?

Four media vans were already parked across from the police department on Eighth Street as she angled her BMW for the wide steps leading to the towering plaza. The last thing on her mind was a parking ticket—she needed to be seen by all. Now several of the cruisers were *blurping* like angry hornets, motioning her to pull forward to one of the parking spaces reserved for criminals who were turning themselves in, or something to that effect.

Humans were so interesting.

She stopped the car in the no-parking zone directly in front of the sweeping steps, opened the door, and stepped into the sunlight.

The moment she felt the sun's hot rays on her cheeks and the warm asphalt under her bare feet, her awareness of the world around her shifted. She focused on the temporal nature of everything she could feel, see, smell, and hear in this moment. The bright sun, the smell of popcorn from the street vendor, the sound of cars and chirping birds squabbling over a nest—it was all a virtual construction called Play Dead in the Prime world.

Beautiful. Stunning. A world within a world.

In this world, four officers were swarming her car, two with weapons drawn. In this world, three cameras were already rolling, capturing every moment. In this world, no fewer than ten officers and department staff stood on the steps, watching the scene unfold.

"Stand against the car!" a well-meaning officer with long blond hair snapped. The woman was just doing her job, and now Angie would do hers. Standing against the car as ordered didn't facilitate that job.

Ignoring the officer, Angie reached her hand into her jeans pocket to retrieve a copy of the no-longer-encrypted key drive that she'd modified.

"Hands where I can see them!" the same officer barked.

"It's okay, Mary." It was the voice of Renee Dalton, who stood on the steps with the others, ordering the officer to stand down.

Angie gave Mary a nod and pulled out the small data key. She walked past two other officers who stood in the street and approached one of the reporters. A petite dark-haired woman who might be in her late twenties.

"What's your name, sweetie?"

"Celine," came the response after a moment.

Angie held the data key between her thumb and forefinger and spoke loudly enough for others to hear.

"I'm giving Celine a copy of the information that I've come to offer the police. This data key can only be unlocked with a code in my possession. If the authorities refuse to hear me out, I will give you that code and you may release the data to the public. If they do hear me out, you can throw away the drive. It will be useless." To Celine: "Is that agreeable?"

The young reporter glanced at a gray-haired gentleman to her right and nodded. "Okay."

"Thank you." She set the key drive in Celine's hand, but the moment her finger contacted Celine's palm, a flood of images crashed into her mind and she gasped.

A crippled daughter named Sarah in a wheelchair with an electromagnetic drive. A golden retriever puppy named Brownie licking little Sarah's scrunched up, giggling face. A man screaming at Celine—her husband, Peter, who was drunk, hurling devastating accusations about the useless pile of flesh that had come from Celine's belly. And more. Many more scenes, coming with such ferocity that Angie forgot where she was or what she was doing.

She jerked her hand away and the images immediately stopped. Celine was looking at her with confusion and Angie managed a thin smile. She wanted to say something, but a lump had lodged itself in her throat. She wasn't sure she could speak, much less offer any words of comfort.

At a loss, Angie turned and walked toward the station's sweeping steps. She made it to the street's yellow center lines before pulling up.

Except for the din of traffic on I-35, everything was quiet now. All eyes were on her, waiting for her to surrender herself into police custody. But how could she turn her back on a woman in such dire straits? Her heart wouldn't let her.

She turned and looked at Celine, who was watching her with wide eyes along with the rest. But behind those eyes hid a deeply wounded young mother who was drowning in lies and accusation, most of them from her own mind, against herself. Angie returned to her and this time put a gentle hand on the woman's sleeved shoulder, grateful that no images came when she wasn't in contact with skin.

She spoke in a soft voice for Celine's ears only.

"Your daughter Sarah isn't just the little girl you see, Celine. I think you know that."

Celine's lower lip was quivering. She was hearing, not just listening.

"She's much more evolved than those who judge her. And so are you. That's why you've both chosen to experience a life that seems so hard to most people. You're both very loving souls, Celine. And you're here to learn an even deeper love. It's why your daughter chose you. You're helping each other discover that deeper love beyond judgment. Don't let her believe the lies that something's wrong with her or that she's not good enough. She's far more than good enough. She's like an angel walking this earth. And so are you."

As if a spring had been uncovered, tears flooded Celine's eyes. She dropped her head into one hand and hitched with a silent sob.

Angie felt Celine's pain and suffering as if they were her own and for a moment she thought it might all be too much. Her mother had said she would have to deal with emotions, but she hadn't expected this. To know the world's suffering inflicted through self-judgment was overwhelming. To also know the pointlessness of all that judgment was far more so.

Thinking she might break down in front of them all, Angie turned back and walked for the steps again. The ravaging compassion wasn't releasing her.

Breathe, Angie. You'll learn how to deal with these new emotions, but right now, just breathe.

She hurried up the steps, determined to gather herself, but her resolve broke when she reached the landing. Randy stood to her right beside the chief, and when their eyes met, he gave her an encouraging nod.

He'd made it, that was good. But she didn't feel any encouragement. Instead, she was suddenly seeing all of his pain as well, not from touch this time, but from her memory of his story. He was still living with a debilitating sorrow over his wife and daughter's terrible fate, not knowing that they had learned what they came to learn in this Practice and moved on. Regardless, they were now living in another world, very much alive and hopefully well.

Randy wasn't. He was trapped in his own pain, blinded to reality as it truly was. She would help him with that.

Angie slowly turned to face the gathering of police cruisers and officers and media and a couple dozen curious onlookers. Now the din from the nearby freeway was completely gone, leaving only silence. They were all still staring at her, clearly struck by the eccentric behavior of the barefooted, dark-haired woman they all knew to be Angie Channing, the unhinged closet Dead Head whose world had been shattered by the murder of her husband three days ago.

Angie could feel their emotions, almost as if they were her own. She had to find a way to settle her emotional mind. Maybe seeing the world in shimmer would calm her.

Immediately, the surfaces of everything she could see changed into a truer representation of what they were: raw energy. Vibration expressed in myriad forms. What had appeared to be solid was now undulating, brimming with hues of light that formed the street, the cars, the officers and media, the towering buildings, the trees—everything.

See, Angie? It's just information collapsed into form.

She let the shimmer go, expecting the reminder to settle her emotions. It didn't.

Seeing Celine still crying into her hand, Angie was struck by a profound realization that she could have come as Celine and lived that life, with a cruel husband and a physically challenged daughter, instead of coming as Angie. In a way Celine was her, in another role. Not just like her, but actually her in another place and time.

In that moment Angie knew that every soul on Earth was her. The police, the reporters, the onlookers now craning for a view. Also Andrew Olsen and Jack Barnes. They were all from the same source code as she was. What she did to the least of them, she was doing to herself and to all.

As if a dam had broken in her soul, an ocean of raw compassion flooded Angie, fueled by a deep knowing that all of their stories were different versions of the same narrative.

There, a newly married man whose wife had drowned on their honeymoon.

Here, a teenager who hated her belly.

There, an older woman smothered by shame for not having shown more love to her now-grown children.

All suffering was fashioned from the same fabric: fear and shame rooted in illusion and lies, beginning with the lie that there was something wrong with them. The world had bound itself to those lies and longed to be free. The lies were their hell.

Her legs felt like lead and her throat burned. She stood still, arrested by the deception that imprisoned this world, allowing the emotions to flow through her. She felt powerless to hold back tears, so she let them slip down her cheeks, but otherwise managed to appear calm.

What others thought of her no longer meant anything. Fear and shame were gone, leaving only this gut-wrenching compassion. She was here to do something, and now that purpose returned to her. She was here for Jamie and Randy. She was here for them all.

Angie swallowed, took a deep breath, turned away from the street, and walked through the double glass doors into the police headquarters.

RANDY STEPPED into the conference room following Renee, who was following Angie. There was no sign of the DA. Angie's entrance had been both striking and surreal.

She carried herself like a totally different woman. Still Angie, but with a new authority that refused to be denied. She could whisper a few words to a reporter on the street and bring her to tears. What else could Angie do? Something profound had happened to her.

Angie had entered the station, eyes fixed ahead, and walked past a dozen officers watching her, straight to the conference room. Here, only two weeks ago, the first evidence against Jamie Hamilton had been presented, much of it by Randy. Fitting, he thought.

Angie stood at the head of the thick cherrywood conference table, staring out the window as if momentarily lost. Randy exchanged a glance with Renee. They had no grid for the unspoken authority Angie was leveraging. No words to describe what about Angie gripped them. It was something felt, not understood, and by the look on Renee's face, she was feeling it as much as he was.

"Where is Andrew Olsen?" Angie asked, turning to face Renee.

Renee glanced through the glass wall between the conference room and the cubicles. "He'll be here."

"It's important that he is. Please call him. And do you mind closing the blinds?"

After only a brief hesitation, Renee tapped her phone and headed for the blinds.

Angie faced Randy, eyes filled with compassion and assurance. Her jeans were rolled up, her Texas Tech T-shirt was a size too large, and she wore no shoes—hardly the image of someone put together. But facing her now, he felt like a novice.

"Then cancel it!" Renee was saying into her phone. "I need you here now, Andrew. Not in ten minutes."

Angie approached Randy, wearing a thin smile. "I did it," she whispered. Now she looked more like a proud schoolgirl than the woman who was directing Austin's police department.

"Did what?" he mouthed.

"I made it out," she whispered.

Out of what? he wanted to ask. She wasn't really suggesting that she'd made it out of this gate room of hers to discover that this reality was virtual, was she? That couldn't be.

Her smile faded and sorrow twisted her face. The shift surprised him. First on the steps and now here. What had happened to make her so emotional?

Angie stepped up to him, lowered her head to his shoulder, and shook with gentle, silent sobs, like a warrior who'd just fought through hell and returned with the prize, exhausted and overcome.

Not knowing what else to do, he awkwardly placed his hand on her shoulder, ignoring Renee, who'd finished her call and was watching them.

"You okay?" Randy finally whispered.

She nodded and pulled back, drawing a deep breath. "I'm more than okay. It's just . . . It's a lot to take in."

"I can imagine." But he couldn't imagine, not really. He had no idea what she'd been through since he'd left her at Joseph Conrad's property.

She pulled a red data key out of her pocket and returned to the head of the table, where she set it down. "We need to do this," she said, facing them both. "Where is Andrew Olsen?"

"He said—"

The door opened and Andrew Olsen's short, hairy frame appeared. His cheeks and forehead were red, peppered with sweat, and his yellow necktie was smudged, only half knotted. The DA looked like he was coming down from a bad drug trip.

Avoiding eye contact with Angie, he closed the door behind him.

"I don't know what you think a Dead Head who's clearly gone off the deep end has to—"

"Shut up, Olsen," Renee snapped. "You're here to hear potential evidence, not offer argument."

Properly scolded, the man finally faced Angie at the head of the table. There was no accusation in her expression, only compassion.

"It's okay, Andrew," she said. "There are only four of us in this room. The last thing I want is for you to be dragged through the mud. You've only done the best you can. Please . . ." She indicated a chair. "Have a seat."

The DA refused to move, still defiant, but confusion tempered him somewhat.

"Or you can stand," Angie said. She began to pace. Neither Renee nor Olsen were seated, so Randy remained standing as well.

"Much of what I'm about to tell you can be corroborated by the data on this drive, which I recovered from under Clair Milton's bathroom sink." She glanced at the red key drive. "I also took the liberty of making a copy of select files on this drive, which are now in the hands of the media. No one else needs to know what I'm about to tell you—you can decide what's appropriate after you've digested it. Fair enough?"

Olsen huffed. "If you think you're going to derail the state's case against Jamie Hamilton, you don't understand the law."

"I have no intention of derailing your case against Jamie," Angie cut in. "I do understand your law and, based on it, I have no evidence that would exonerate him. This is much bigger than Jamie."

Randy pulled out a chair and sat. "More than fair," he said, answering her original question.

Renee sat as well, and finally Olsen, warily.

"Good," Angie said. "Thirty-two days ago, Steve Milton visited Jake Barnes in his office at Convergence to discuss a purchase offer for Mistletoe, Steve Milton's software company. He took his daughter, Clair, with him, and she managed to lift this encrypted key drive off Barnes's desk while their backs were turned. Those thirty seconds of distraction changed the course of history. How much is now up to you."

Olsen cleared his throat. "It's encrypted?"

"It was, but I removed the encryption."

He sat back, challenging. "How?"

"In Play Dead with my mother's help," she said. "But that means nothing to you, so just hear me out. Yes?"

He glanced at Renee and finally gave a short dip of his head.

"Thank you. The data details a comprehensive conspiracy between Jake Barnes and Judith Patterson to control all virtual reality technology for personal gain. That alone is enough to end the governor's bid for the presidency. The drive I gave the media only contains information related to the governor, but this drive outlines why Barnes is so obsessed with controlling virtual technology. It's for your eyes only."

Randy's heart was thumping. She'd actually done it. She'd tapped into some greater network, found the encrypted key, and was going to bring down the governor.

"Barnes is obsessed because he stumbled on what he considers incontrovertible evidence that this world is actually its own virtual reality. That we live in a holographic universe, as speculated by numerous quantum theorists over the last few decades. Everything we see is fundamentally only ones and zeros. In other words, the whole world is dead heading without knowing it. This fact becomes apparent in certain Deep Dives utilizing emerging VR technology. If the world is essentially a program, that program can be hacked. Whoever hacks it will have more power than any human yet to live."

A chill snaked up Randy's spine. But was it true? Neither Olsen nor Renee appeared disturbed. They couldn't comprehend much less accept what they were hearing. Randy wasn't sure he really could either.

"It doesn't matter if Barnes is right, only that he thinks he is. The best way to control advanced VR technology is to install a climate of fear surrounding that technology and then introduce legislation to regulate it at the highest level. Legislation that would favor Convergence. Do you follow?"

"This is nonsense," Olsen muttered.

Renee held a hand out to him. "Hear her out."

"All of this was on the encrypted key that Clair not only managed to open but shared with Timothy Blake, making both of them a liability to Barnes.

Clair Milton and Timothy Blake were murdered for that data which, if leaked, would likely destroy Convergence."

"You're suggesting that Jamie was manipulated?" Renee asked. "He was somehow forced to kill Clair and Timothy?"

"No," Angie said. "Jamie had nothing to do with their murders. Clair and Timothy were killed by a contractor named Matteo Steger. This morning I shot him in self-defense. He could have killed them while they slept, but there was a better play: turn their deaths into a horrific ordeal that would both reinforce the dangers of virtual technology and provide a political windfall for the governor's presidential bid. All she needed was a quick conviction."

Silence fell over the conference room.

Renee glanced at Randy, face drawn. "I know her, for heaven's sake! I just can't see it." But she didn't sound quite so sure.

"It's all on the key drive," Angie said. "Regardless, when they decided to make a spectacle out of Clair's and Timothy's murders, they identified the solution to another problem. Jamie, one of Convergence's test subjects, was showing erratic signs of breaking—another threat of unwanted exposure. He had to go. So he was conveniently selected to take the fall for Clair's and Timothy's deaths."

"He was framed," Randy said.

"This is absurd!" Olsen grunted, pushing himself to his feet. Desperation had broken his composure. "Outrageous! How could a data key that was stolen before the murders have any information about those murders? This is utter nonsense!"

"The drive contains nothing about the murders. But it does contain, among other things, details regarding the operation and structure of Barnes's organization including all those attached to it."

Olsen's trembling fingers suggested he knew his name was on that drive. He slowly sank to his seat as Angie continued.

"There's enough here to put Barnes, Judith Patterson, a handler named Katrina Botwilder, Bill Evans, and yourself in prison for the rest of your lives."

Andrew Olsen turned his bulging eyes to Renee, who was clearly taking Angie's claims seriously. His voice came out gravelly and pathetic. "You can't buy this, Renee. They're framing me, can't you see that? Anyone can manufacture evidence on a drive!"

Renee was looking at Angie, ignoring Olsen.

Angie continued. "The date and time stamps on the data go way back, Andrew. It's quite convincing and includes a full dossier on Matteo Steger, the contractor I killed, as well as those on his payroll. And their assigned tasks."

She let the statement stand for several seconds.

"Please understand my intentions here," she said. "None of this needs to become public. The media can't access the information on the drive I gave them without the quantum code only I possess. There's no need to prosecute anyone. I'm sure you can convince them to cease and desist through other means. Jack Barnes is terminally ill, so please be kind to him. The governor will need to step down and you'll need to resign, Andrew. But this is a time for healing, not punishment. Punishment only perpetuates fear, which is the only real problem in this world. Living by the code of an eye for an eye has made this world blind. Only love can heal anything."

"You're saying that all of this is on that drive," Renee said, still trying to come to grips with a conspiracy that seemed inconceivable to her. "I'm not sure it's enough to convict." She looked at the DA. "Normally I'd defer to the DA."

"There's no way," Olsen rasped. "It's just one drive."

"Two drives," Angie said. "If you don't accept what I've presented today, the one the media has will bring down the governor and those she works with."

Olsen seemed to be searching for an argument that wouldn't come.

"Even if you are right," Renee said, "none of this will affect Jamie's case. He murdered another inmate. You do realize that, don't you?"

"For now, yes. We'll see what happens with his case later, but this isn't about Jamie."

They stared at her, but she had no more to say about the boy.

"Would you like to see with your own eyes what Jack Barnes discovered about this world?" Angie asked.

Renee hesitated. "See how?"

Angie looked at the cherrywood table's corner, reached under it and slowly lifted her hand. Randy watched with stunned fascination as the table's two-inch-thick, solid cherrywood surface curved under her hand as if made of putty. She held the corner there, a foot higher than it should be, for a full three seconds before releasing it to its former shape.

Randy's palms were sweating. She'd been right. Dear God . . .

"Ones and zeros," Angie said, tapping the wood. "I wouldn't tell anyone what you just saw, because no one will believe it. But I don't have time for any of you to doubt me. Hopefully now you don't."

Olsen was staring at the table's corner, shocked and stripped of reason. What could he say? Renee gawked as well, but in wonder, not defeat. What could any reasonable human mind do with what they'd just witnessed?

Randy had never felt so awed and humbled. She'd played her cards with mastery.

"I'm sorry, Andrew," Angie said softly. "If I'd been born and raised as you, with all the accusations of unworthiness that have crushed you for so many years, I would have done the same thing. One day all of this will make sense to you."

Andrew Olsen lowered his forehead to the table and began to sob.

Angie turned to Renee. "If those implicated on this drive haven't stepped down within three days, I'll give the code to the media. Fair enough?"

Renee couldn't seem to find her voice.

"In the meantime, I have to speak to Jamie," Angie said, stepping for the door. "I only need ten minutes."

CHAPTER
FORTY

ANGIE APPROACHED Jamie's cell with Randy, peering in to see the tall boy seated on the single metal cot, dressed in that obnoxious yellow jumpsuit. An hour had passed since she'd given the data drive to Renee Dalton. They would comply—facing public shaming was too much for anyone to bear. Jack Barnes would likely end up behind bars, but she would see him tomorrow and share some good news with him.

He'd been right, though he'd gone about it all wrong. There was still time to surrender to the light before he died, even if they put him in prison.

Jamie's cell was in isolation on the east wing.

"Hi, Jamie."

His blue eyes darted up at the sound of her voice. "Hi, Angie!" He jumped up, took two strides and was at the bars, peering out. "Where did you go?"

She smiled at him, struck by the knowledge that he was her father in Prime. No wonder she'd been so drawn to him.

"I've been busy making things right. How are they treating you?"

"No one bothers me now, and they gave me pancakes with syrup for breakfast this morning. Do you like syrup?"

"I do. But I don't eat it very often because it makes my stomach hurt."

"Really? Do you like peanut butter? I like peanut butter with syrup, but they don't have peanut butter."

"I love peanut butter! And peanuts. I eat them every day."

"Yup. Me too. And Coke. But they don't give me peanuts here."

Angie glanced at Randy, who was watching their exchange with bright eyes.

"Randy wants to tell you what happened today, but he's going to leave the best part for me. Is that okay with you?"

"Randy's the good cop. I like the cops. They keep people safe."

Randy nodded. "We try. But sometimes even cops make mistakes. Do you remember Andrew Olsen, the district attorney?"

"The fat man," Jamie said. "He's upset."

"A little bit, yes. Because today he was exposed for his part in blaming you for Clair's and Timothy's murders. So were Bill Evans, who is the prosecutor, and the governor."

"Because I didn't kill them. But I killed Snake-man. I had to because I need to keep playing the game. Darey told me to keep playing the game."

"Yes, he did. And you'll need to keep playing because they're still going to blame you for killing the snake man."

"Yup. I had to."

He didn't seem to care. He never had. It was amazing that such a brilliant mind, able to see the world in far more complex ways than other highly intelligent humans, was hidden behind the language skills of a six-year-old. It was almost as if spoken language was too limited for him, so he'd never practiced it.

"But maybe you shouldn't put the fat man in this place," Jamie said. "Most people don't like it here."

"That's true," Angie said, stepping up. "But *you* don't mind, do you?"

"It's a game. It's all a game. And I still haven't won."

"What game, Jamie?"

"The game where I get out on my own," he said.

"Out of what?"

He looked bewildered.

She gently pressed. "Out of here or out of the white room?"

Jamie studied her for a few seconds. "That's just the game in my dreams," he said.

She gripped the bar and leaned closer. It was all there, just below the surface.

"The game called Play Dead?" she said.

Jamie didn't respond but his mind was turning.

"Do you remember anything about a man named Jake Barnes, Jamie? Or a Matteo Steger?"

He hesitated. "Maybe."

Again she was struck by how his mind worked. The details of this world weren't important enough for him to retain them. He'd seen too much of greater realities to care much about this one.

"Jake Barnes was the man who took you as an infant and put you in a Deep Dive when you were only three years old," she explained, hoping to jog his memory. "It's why you're so good at games. He called you an unveiled one. When you were six, he gave you to your mother, Corina. Do you remember any of that?"

Another long pause. She would visit Corina as soon as possible.

"Maybe," Jamie finally said.

"Jake Barnes took me when I was little too. I'm like you, Jamie. And I'm in the game in your dreams, aren't I?"

His eyes were wide. "Those . . . Those are my dreams."

"No, they're more than dreams, Jamie. They're real."

"They are?"

"Yes!" She was speaking with some urgency, eager for him to open his mind. "You've been in the white room with two gates and the gears and the Play Dead books many times. I know you've been there because you helped me go through the needle gate. And I think I'm supposed to help you do the same thing."

"I helped you."

"Yes! That's Play Dead, and it's the only game you came to play."

He looked like he'd been slapped out of a dream. Literally. He blinked.

"Play Dead," he said. "The game in the white room. We . . . We solved the butterfly book. So you . . . You made it out?"

"I made it out. So did my mother, she was the first, then me. We're the only ones so far, and I decided to come back. You need to know that you can do it too. All you have to do is give all of yourself to the light. And you don't need a RIG because you *are* a RIG. Everyone is, they just don't know it. But you . . . you're an unveiled one."

A part of him was still doubting.

"Do you want to know what I learned to do when I beat the game?" she asked.

He gave her a nod.

Angie focused on the bar she was gripping and the cell revealed itself in the shimmer. Without looking to see if they were being watched, she passed through the bars made of energy and stood beside Jamie, who'd stepped back, eyes as round as saucers.

"Wow!" he said.

"Angie . . ." Randy was looking at the camera in the corner of the cell. *True*, she thought. They would have to erase that footage.

She reached up and touched Jamie's face. "See? I'm real. But this isn't the whole of reality. Not even close. And you already know that."

As if a veil had been withdrawn from his understanding, he brightened.

"I know how," he said. "I showed *you* how!"

She withdrew her hand. "Yes, you did."

"The room in my dreams is real," he said, eyes full of wonder.

"Yes. But you have to surrender to the light while you're fully aware, not in a dream that's disassociated with this reality. A lucid dream might work, but you have to believe you're surrendering *this* world, not just your dream world. When I was under at Convergence, I was fully aware of what I was doing the whole time."

Jamie paced to his right, then back, mind spinning behind lost blue eyes. When he faced Angie again, he looked calm and certain.

"We were both unveiled ones and our minds were connected in the program, just like in my dreams. But they aren't just dreams. They're real. All of it's real."

"As real as this world," she said.

"Which is only as real as we make it."

She nodded. "Something like that."

Angie turned the cell back to shimmer and slipped back into the hall next to Randy. Jamie sat on his bed, nervously tapping his heel. He eased back on his pillow and stared at the ceiling, lost in thought.

"Tell my mother that I love her," he said.

A strange comment, she thought, but her mind didn't work like Jamie's. It was a lot to take in for anyone, even a boy as gifted as him.

At the end of the hall, a door squealed. She and Randy both turned toward the sound. A guard was leaning in, looking at them curiously. "All good in here?"

"Everything's fine," Randy said.

"You sure? Got a message from watch that something's not right."

The guard on watch had seen her in the cell.

Randy casually stepped in front of her, yielding to his protective instincts. *Sweet*, she thought.

"No problem here," Randy said.

"Okay, just checking. Shift change in two so wrap it up."

"Of course."

The guard pulled back and shut the door, leaving them alone again. Randy gave her a warning glance but she ignored it, turning back to the cell.

Jamie was still lying down, but his eyes were closed and he was breathing heavily.

"Jamie?"

His body began to shake, gripped by a seizure, and only then did Angie realize what he was doing. Why he'd told them to tell his mother that he loved her. He was already in the gate room.

"I'll get the doctor!" Randy said, already turning toward the door.

She grabbed his arm. "They can't help. Just hold on."

"He's having a seizure! We can't just stand by. All of this is on tape!"

"Just hold on," she urged. "Watch him."

He followed her eyes. Jamie was groaning now, trembling like a leaf, chin thrust back and straining.

"No, Angie," Randy objected, starting to pull away again. "He needs . . ."

It happened right there, in front of both of them, cutting Randy short.

One moment they were looking at Jamie, who was shuddering on the bed's gray blanket, and the next they were looking at only the gray blanket on the bed.

Jamie had vanished. Her father had transcended Play Dead.

For several long seconds they both just stared, Angie in wonder, Randy in horror, surely.

"Dear God, what just happened?" Randy breathed.

"The truth just happened," she said, and she took his hand, noting that with a little focus she could shut off the images revealing his life. "It's time for us to leave."

Randy let her lead, his hand still in hers.

"Just act normal," she said. "It's all going to be okay."

"He's really gone?" he managed. "Just . . . gone? How's that possible?"

"He did what I did, that's all. He helped me and so I helped him. He awoke from the game while in it. That's the whole point of the Practice. He's home."

They walked halfway down the hall in silence. One thing was now certain: There would be no case against Jamie Hamilton. Together, she and Jamie had settled it once and for all.

"We'll need to erase the footage," she said.

"I don't know how. It's secure."

"We'll figure something out."

A few more steps.

"Please don't do anything else that needs to be erased," Randy said.

"No, of course not. But you're going to be okay, I promise."

"How can you say that?" he rasped. "Jamie's gone and we were the last two people to see him alive. There's evidence of you entering his cell, for heaven's sake! Everything you told him is on record."

Angie stopped in the middle of the hall and looked up at him, smiling. Then stood on her toes and kissed the corner of his mouth.

"Everything's going to be okay because you're with me, Randy," she whispered in his ear. "And I'm going to show you a whole new world." She settled back to her heels and saw that he was blushing. She winked. "Fair enough?"

Randy hesitated only a second. "Fair enough."

Angie took his hand again and headed for the door.

"Now let's go and see if we can't keep this world from destroying itself."

THE END